**Mose looked up and saw Sarah hurry into the shop, her dress spotted with fat drops of rain.**

Sarah looked young and happy. Mose's heartbeat quickened as he walked toward her. "You picked a fine time to be out. It's about to storm, from the looks of you."

Sarah whirled at the sound of his voice and rushed over to him. "Mose, the cart ride was wonderful. I felt like a child again, the rain hitting me in the face and the golf cart sliding on the pavement."

He pulled his handkerchief from his pocket and gently wiped her face dry, her eyes sky blue and shining at him. He fought down the urge to kiss her; his feelings for her were becoming more obvious to him every day.

"I'm sorry I dampened your handkerchief," she apologized.

"Silly girl. That's why I carry the rag. To help beautiful damsels in distress." He heard himself flirting, like he might have done as a young man of nineteen.

Sarah was turning him into a schoolboy again. And he liked it.

**Cheryl Williford** and her veteran husband, Henry, live in South Texas, where they've raised three children, numerous foster children, alongside a menagerie of rescued cats, dogs and hamsters. Her love for writing began in a literature class and now her characters keep her grabbing for paper and pen. She is a member of her local ACFW and CWA chapters, and is a seamstress, watercolorist and loving grandmother. Her website is cherylwilliford.com.

## Books by Cheryl Williford

### Love Inspired

*The Amish Widow's Secret*

# The Amish
# Widow's Secret

## Cheryl Williford

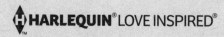

Recycling programs for this product may not exist in your area.

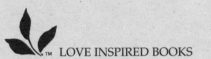

LOVE INSPIRED BOOKS

ISBN-13: 978-0-373-81842-6

The Amish Widow's Secret

www.Harlequin.com

Printed in U.S.A.

Take delight in the Lord,
and He will give you your heart's desires.
Commit everything you do to the Lord.
Trust Him, and He will help you.
He will make your innocence radiate like the dawn,
and the justice of your cause
will shine like the noonday sun.
*—Psalms* 37:4–6

This book is dedicated to the memory
of my grandfather, Fred Carver,
who encouraged me to reach for the stars,
and to my Quaker great-grandmother,
Clarrisa Petch, who inspired me.

## Acknowledgments

To my patient and understanding husband, Will,
who read and critiqued way too many manuscript
chapters and blessed me with honesty. To my
eldest daughter, Barbara, who graciously gifted
me with fees for contests and conferences. To the
ACFW Golden Girls critique group, Liz, Nanci,
Jan, Zillah and Shannon; you are loved.
To Eileen Key, the best line-edit partner in the
business. To Les Stobbe, my wonderful agent
and mentor; to my amazing Love Inspired editor,
Melissa Endlich, who believed in me; and last but
not least, to my Lord and Savior, Jesus Christ,
who has opened many doors, enabling this book
to be written and published.

# Chapter One

It was the most beautiful thing she'd ever seen.

Sarah Nolt couldn't resist the temptation. *Gott* would probably punish her for coveting something so fancy. She allowed the tip of her finger to glide across the surface of the sewing machine gleaming in the store's overhead lights.

She closed her eyes and imagined stitching her dream quilt. Purple sashing would look perfect with the patch of irises she'd create out of scraps of lavender and blue fabrics and hand stitch to the center of the diagonal-block quilt.

"Some things are best not longed for," Marta Nolt whispered close to Sarah's ear.

Sarah jumped as if she'd been stung by a wasp. A flush of guilt washed over her from head to toe. "You startled me." She shot a glance at her lifelong friend and sister-in-law—

the two had grown up together and had even married each other's brothers. Had Marta seen her prideful expression? All her life she'd been taught pride was a sin. She wasn't convinced it was.

Compared to Sarah's five-foot-four frame, Marta appeared as tiny as a twelve-year-old in her dark blue spring dress and finely stitched, stiff white prayer *kapp*. Marta's brows furrowed. "It is better I startled you than your *daed*, Sarah. He's just outside the door waiting for us. He said to hurry, that he has more important things to do than wait on you this morning. Did you do something to irritate him again? One day he'll tell the elders what you've been up to and—"

"And they'll what? Call me in for another scolding and long prayer, and then threaten to tell the Bishop how unruly a widow I am?" Sarah turned for one last look at the gleaming machine and moved away.

"If they find out about you giving Lukas money, you'll be shunned. You know they're looking for someone to blame and wanting to set an example since he ran away with young Ben in tow. Everyone believes they've joined the *Englisch* rescue house. The boys' father is beyond angry. Nerves have become rattled throughout the community. People are asking who else is planning to leave."

"I'm not joining if that's what you're thinking. I wasted my time by looking at a sewing machine I can't ever have. I dream. Nothing more. How can that fine piece of equipment be so full of sin just because it's electric and fancy? It's made to produce the finest of quilts."

Sarah shoved back a lock of hair and tucked it into her *kapp*. "Last week an *Englisch* woman used one of the machines for a sewing demonstration. My heart almost leaped out of my chest, Marta. You should have seen the amazing details it sewed. It would take a year or more for us to make such perfect stitches by hand. *Daed* needs money for a new field horse. If I had this machine, I could make quilts more quickly and sell them to the *Englisch* on market day. I could make enough money to keep my farm and eat more than cooked cabbage and my favorite white duck."

"All you have to do is ask for help, Sarah. You are so stubborn. The community will—"

"Rally round? Tell me I must sell Joseph's farm because a family deserves it more than a helpless widow. *Nee*, I don't want their help."

"Careful. Someone might hear you."

Marta had always tried to accept the community's harsh rules, but today her words of mindless obedience angered Sarah. "I *will not* ask for help and will not be silent. Will *Gott* finally be satisfied if He takes everything dear from me, including my dreams?"

"*Ach,* don't be so bitter. Your anger comes from a place of pain. You need to pray. Ask *Gott* to remove the ache in your heart." Marta took her hand and squeezed hard. "Since Joseph died you've done nothing but stir up the community's wrath. You know what your *daed's* like. He'll only take so much before he lets the Bishop come down hard on you. You can't keep bringing shame on the Yoder name."

"I don't care about my *daed's* pride of name. Is his pride not sin too? I am a Nolt now, not a Yoder. I'm a twenty-five-year-old widow. Not a child. I will make my own decisions. You wait and see."

"*Meine liebe.* The suddenness of Joseph's death brought you to this place of anger and confusion. Don't grieve him so. His funeral is over, the coffin closed. It was *Gott's* will for Joseph to die. We must not ever question, Sarah. Joseph was my older brother, but I'm content to know he's with the old ones and happy in heaven."

Memories of the funeral haunted Sarah's sleep. "I'm glad you are able to find peace in this rigid community, Marta. I really am. But I can't. Not since *Gott* let Joseph die in such a horrible way. To burn to death in a barn fire is too horrible. What kind of *Gott* lets this happen to a man of faith? This cruel *Gott* has *nee* place in my life." Sarah sighed deeply. *Will I ever be happy again and at peace?*

She reached out a trembling hand and grabbed a card of hooks-and-eyes and threw it in the store's small plastic shopping basket that hung off her wrist. She added several large spools of basic blue, purple and black thread and turned back toward Marta, who stood fingering a skein of baby-soft yarn in the lightest shade of blue. "Do you have something you want to tell me?"

*"Nee."* Marta's ready smile vanished. "I'm not pregnant. *Gott* must intend for me to rear others' *kinder* and not my own."

Marta had miscarried three times. Talk among the older women was there would be no *bobbel* for her sister-in-law unless she had an operation. Sarah knew the young couple's farm wasn't doing well. There would be no money for expensive procedures in *Englisch* hospitals for Marta, even if the Bishop would allow it.

Sarah said, "I wish—"

"I know. I wish it, too. A baby for Eric and

me. And Joseph still alive for you. But *Gott* doesn't always give us what we want or make an easy path to walk."

Heavy footsteps announced Sarah's father's approach. Both women grew silent.

"Do you realize the sun is at its zenith and a man grows hungry?" Adolph Yoder's sharp tone cut like a knife. The short-statured man rubbed his rotund stomach and glared at his only daughter.

Sarah straightened the sweat-soaked collar of her father's blue shirt and smiled, trying hard to show her love for the angry man. "I'm sorry, *Daed*. Time got away from us." Sarah gathered the last of the sewing things she needed and tried to match his fast pace down the narrow aisle.

Her father stopped abruptly and turned toward her. His blue eyes flashed. "You must learn to drive your own wagon, daughter. Do your own fetching. Enough time has passed."

*"Ya."* Sarah nodded. He turned away and moved toward the door. She thought back to the times she'd begged him to teach her the basics of directing a horse or mending a wheel, but nothing had ever come of it. He had always been too busy trying to be both *Mamm* and *Daed* to her and her younger brother, Eric. She blamed herself and her mother's sudden

disappearance into the *Englisch* world on her father's angry moods. Once again she wished her *mamm* had taken her with her when she'd left Lancaster County.

Joseph would have been happy to teach her to drive, but *Gott* had taken him too soon. Bitterness swelled in her heart, adding to the pain already there. Tears pooled in her eyes and slid down her cheeks as she thought of him. She brushed them away, not willing to show her pain.

Moments later the familiar woman at the checkout line greeted Sarah as she might an *Englisch* customer. "Hello, Sarah. How are you today, dear?"

"*Gut*, and you?"

"Oh, I'm fine as I can be," she responded. "You're buying an awful lot of thread. You ladies planning one of your quilting bees?"

"*Nee*, just stocking up." Sarah emptied the small basket on the counter and began stacking the spools of thread.

"Well, you let me know if you need someone to help sell your quilts. I'll be glad to place them in the shop window for a small fee. You do beautiful work. You should be sewing professionally."

Distracted by her thoughts, Sarah tried hard to follow the older woman's friendly banter.

"*Danke.* I'll speak to the Bishop's wife and see what she says, but I don't hold much hope. There are rules about selling wares in an *Englisch* shop. You know how strict some are."

"Yeah, I do." She patted Sarah's hand.

Sarah's father walked past and glanced at the two women. He hurried out of the shop, letting the door slam. His bad mood meant problems for Sarah. When riled, he could be very cruel. She had no one to blame but herself for his bad attitude today. She knew he grew tired of her lack of control and rule breaking. People were openly talking about her. She had to learn to keep her mouth closed and distance herself from the *Englisch*.

Sarah hurried out of the store and trailed behind Marta. Fancy *Englisch* cars dotted the parking lot. She made her way to her father's buggy parked under a cluster of old oaks.

He stood talking to a man unfamiliar to Sarah. The man turned toward her as she approached. He wore a traditional blue Amish shirt, his black pants wrinkled and dusty, as if he'd been traveling for days. The black hat on his head barely controlled his nest of dishwater-blond curls. Joseph had been blond and curly-haired, too. Memories flooded in. Her heart ached.

Men from all around the county were coming today. The burned-out barn was to be torn down and cleared away. The man standing next to her father had be one of the workers who'd traveled a long distance to lend a helping hand. She often disapproved of many Amish ways, but not their generosity of heart. Helping others came naturally to all Amish. She honored this trait. It was the reason shc'd helped the neighbor boys get away from their cruel father.

"Sarah," Marta called out and motioned for her to hurry. Sarah picked up her pace.

"Come, Sarah! Time is wasting," her father called out.

*"Ya, Daed."*

The tall, well-built man smiled. She was struck by the startling blueness of his eyes and the friendly curve of his mouth. His light blond beard told her he was married. She gave a quick smile.

Marta stepped forward. "This is Mose Fischer, Joseph's school friend. He came all the way from Florida to help us rebuild the barn."

Mose Fischer took her hand. The crinkles around his eyes expressed years of friendly smiles and a good sense of humor.

Sarah wasn't comfortable with physical contact, but allowed him to take her hand out of respect to Joseph. She returned his smile. "Hello. I'm glad to meet you." She meant what she'd said. She was glad to meet him. She'd only met her husband's sister, Marta. Meeting Joseph's childhood friend made her feel more a part of his past life.

Adolph put his hand on Sarah's shoulder. Touching her was something he rarely did, especially in public. "Sarah loves *kinder*. Perhaps you'd like her to care for your young daughters while you work?"

"If Sarah agrees, I'd like that very much." Mose Fischer seemed to look deep into her soul, looking for all her secrets as he spoke. *Why hadn't his wife come to Lancaster with him?* "I'd be glad to care for the *bobbles*, and I'm sure I'll have help. Marta seldom gets a chance to play with *kinder* and will grab at this opportunity."

Marta nodded with a shy laugh and smiled. "Just try to keep me away."

"How old are the *kinder*?" Sarah grinned, happy for a chance to be busy wiping tiny fingers and toes. She'd be much too preoccupied to fret or watch the last of the barn come down.

"Beatrice is almost five and Mercy will soon be one. But, I warn you. They miss their *mamm* since she passed and can be a real handful." Pain shimmered in his eyes.

"I'm sorry. I didn't know you were a widower. You were very brave to travel alone with such young daughters."

"We came by train from Tampa, but my memories of Joseph made all the effort worth it. I didn't want to miss the chance to help out his widow."

"Where are you staying?"

"Mose and the girls will stay on my farm, and so will you." Adolph gave Sarah a familiar glare.

"That's fine. I can stay in my old room for a few days, and the girls can sleep with me." Sarah nervously straightened the ribbons hanging from her stiff white prayer *kapp*. Since she was in deep mourning, her father knew she wanted to continue to hide herself at her farm, far away from people and gossip. "If that suits you, Mose." She held her breath. She suddenly realized she needed to be around the girls as much as they needed her.

Dressed in a plain black mourning dress and *kapp*, her black shoes polished to a high shine, Mose could see why Joseph had chosen Sarah as his bride. There was something striking about her, her beauty separating her from the average Amish woman. She tried to act friendly, but he'd experienced the pain of loss and knew she suffered from the mention of Joseph. Greta had been the perfect wife to him and mother to his girls. After almost a year, the mention of her name still cut deeply and flooded his mind with memories.

"I hope they're not a handful for you." A genuine smile blossomed on the willowy, red-haired woman's face. She looked a bit more relaxed. The heavy tension between Sarah and her father surprised him. Surely Adolph would be a tower of strength for her. She'd need her father to lean on during difficult times. Instead, Mose felt an air of disapproval between the two. He'd heard Adolph Yoder was a hard man, but Sarah seemed a victim in this terrible tragedy.

"I'll bring the girls around in an hour or so, if that's all right."

"*Ya.* I'm not doing anything but cooking today. The girls can help bake for tomorrow's big meal." Sarah smiled a shy goodbye and followed Marta into the buggy. She pulled in her skirt and slammed the door. Through the window she waved, "I look forward to taking care of the *kinder.*"

"Till then," Mose said, and waved as the buggy pulled onto the main road, his thoughts still on the tension between father and daughter.

Walking came naturally to Mose. He set

out on the two-mile trip to his cousin's farm and prayed his daughters had behaved while he was gone. Dealing with her own grief, he wasn't sure Sarah was up to handling the antics of his eldest daughter. Four was a difficult age. Beatrice was no longer a baby, but her longing for her dead *mamm* still made her difficult to manage.

The hot afternoon sun beat down on his head, his dark garments drawing heat. He welcomed the rare gusts of wind that threatened to blow off his straw hat and ruffle his hair. Lancaster took a beating from the summer heat every year, but today felt even more hot and muggy. He would be glad to get back to Sarasota and its constant breeze and refreshing beaches.

A worn black buggy rolled past, spitting dust and pebbles his way. To his surprise, the buggy stopped and a tall, burley, gray-haired man hopped out.

"Hello, Mose. I heard you were in town."

*I should know the man.* He recognized his face but struggled with the name. "Forgive me, but I don't remember—"

"*Nee.* It was a long time ago. I'm Bishop Ralf Miller. It's been five years or more since I last went to Florida and stayed with your family. I've known your father for many years. When we were boys, we shared the same school. I believe you'd just married your beautiful bride when your father introduced me to you."

"My wife died last year," Mose informed him. "Childbirth took her." Saying the words out loud was like twisting a knife in his heart.

"I'm sorry. I had no idea."

"There's no reason you would know,"

"*Nee*, but it worries me how many of our young people are dying. I assume you're here to help with Joseph Nolt's barn clearing."

"I just met his widow. Poor woman is torn with grief."

"Between the two of us, I'm not so sure Sarah Nolt is a grieving widow. One of the men at the funeral said they heard her say Joseph's death was her fault. The woman's been unpredictable most of her life. Her father and I had a conversation about this a few days ago. He's finding it hard to keep both farms going, and Sarah is stubbornly refusing to return to her childhood home. Joseph's farm needs to be sold. If she doesn't stop this willful behavior, I fear we'll have to shun her for the safety of the community."

Surprised at the openness of the Bishop's conversation and the accusation against Sarah, Mose asked, "What proof do you have against her, other than her one comment made in grief? Has she been counseled by the elders or yourself?"

"We tried, but she won't talk to us. She's always had this rebellious streak. Her father agrees with me. There could be trouble."

"A rebellious streak?"

"You know what I mean. Last week she told one of our Elders to shut up when he offered her a fair price for the farm. This inappropriate behavior can't be ignored."

"You've just described a grieving widow, Bishop. Perhaps she's..."

Bishop Miller interrupted Mose, his brows lowered. "You don't know her, Mose. I do. She's always seemed difficult. Even as a child she was rebellious and broke rules."

"Did something happen to make her this way?" Mose's stomach twisted in anger. He liked to consider himself a good judge of character and he hadn't found Sarah Nolt anything but unhappy, for good reason. Adolph Yoder was another matter. He appeared a hard, critical man. The Bishop's willingness to talk about Sarah's personal business didn't impress him either. These things were none of Mose's concern. He knew, with the community being Old Order Amish, that the bishop kept hard, fast rules. In his community she'd be treated differently. If she had no one to help her through her loss, her actions could be interpreted as acting out of grief. Perhaps the lack of a father's love was the cause of his daughter's actions. "Where is Sarah's mother?"

"Who knows but *Gott*? She left the community when Sarah was a young child. She'd just had a son and some said raising *kinder* didn't suit her. Adolph did everything he could to make Sarah an obedient child, like his son, Eric, but she never would bend to his will."

"I saw little parental love from Adolph. He's an angry man and needs to be spoken to by one of the community elders. Perhaps *Gott* can redirect him and help Sarah at the same time."

"We're glad to have your help with the teardown and barn-building, but I will deal with Sarah Nolt. This community is my concern. If your father were here, he'd agree with me."

Mose drew in a deep breath. He'd let his temper get the better of him. "I meant no disrespect, Bishop, but all this gossip about the widow needs to stop until you have proof. It's your job to make sure that happens. You shouldn't add to it."

"If you weren't an outsider you'd know she's not alone in her misery. She has her sister-in-law, Marta, to talk to and seek counsel. Marta is a godly woman and a good influence. If she can't reach her, there will be harsh consequences the next time Sarah acts out."

"I'll be praying for her, as I'm sure you are." Mose nodded to the bishop, and kept on walking to his cousin's farm.

But he couldn't help wondering, who was the real Sarah?

Beatrice squirmed around on the buckboard seat, her tiny sister asleep on a quilt at her feet. "I want cookies now, *Daed.*"

Mose pulled to the side of the road and spoke softly. "Soon we'll be at Sarah's house and you can have more cookies, but if you wake your sister, you'll be put to bed. Do you understand?"

The tear rolling down her flushed cheek told him she didn't understand and was pushing boundaries yet again.

"*Mamm* would give me cookies. I want *Mamm.*" An angry scowl etched itself across her tear-streaked face.

These were the times Mose hated most, when he had no answers for Beatrice. *How can I help her understand?*

"We've talked about this before, my child. *Mamm* is in heaven with *Gott* and we must accept this, even though it makes us sad." He drew the small child into his arms and hugged her close, his heart breaking as he realized how thin her small body had become. He had to do something to cheer her up. "Let's hurry and go and see the nice ladies I told you about. Sarah said she'd be baking today. Perhaps she'll have warm cookies. Wouldn't cookies and a glass of cold milk brighten your spirits?

"I only want *Mamm*."

Tucked under his arm, Beatrice cried softly, twisting Mose's heart in knots. His mother had talked to him about remarriage, but he had thrown the idea back at her, determined to honor his dead wife until the day he died. But the *kinder* definitely needed a woman's gentle hand when he had to be at work.

His mother's newly mended arm limited her ability to help him since the bad break, and now her talk of going to visit her sisters in Ohio felt like a push from *Gott*. Perhaps he would start considering the thought of a new wife, but she'd have to be special. What woman would want a husband who still loved his late wife? But he couldn't become someone like Adolph Yoder either, and leave his young children to suffer their mother's loss alone. Adolph's bitterness shook Mose to his foundation. Would he become like Adolph to satisfy his own selfish needs and not his daughters'?

Deep in thought, Mose pulled into the graveled drive and directed the horse under a shade tree. Sarah Nolt hurried out the door of the trim white farmhouse, her black mourning dress dancing around her ankles. She approached with a welcoming smile. In the sunlight her *kapp*-covered head made her hair look a bright copper color. A brisk breeze blew and long lengths of fine hair escaped and curled on the sides of her face. The black dress was plain, yet added color to her cheeks. Mose opened the buggy's door.

Beatrice crawled over him and hurried out. A striped kitten playing in the grass had attracted her attention. Mercy chose that moment to make her presence known and let loose a pitiful wail. Mose scooped the baby from the buggy floor.

Beatrice suddenly screamed and ran to her father, her arms wrapping around his leg. "Bad kitty." She held out a finger. A scarlet drop of blood landed on the front of the fresh white apron covering her dress.

Sarah took the baby and tucked the blanket around her bare legs as she slowly began to rock the upset child. Tear-filled blue eyes, edged in dark lashes, gazed up at the stranger. "Hello, little one."

Amazed, as always, that the tiny child could make so much noise, Mose watched as Sarah continued to rock the baby as she walked to the edge of the yard. Mose soothed Beatrice as Sarah moved about the garden with his crying infant.

Moments later Sarah approached with the quieted baby on her shoulder. "The *bobbel* has healthy lungs." She laughed.

Mose ruffled the blond curls on Mercy's head. "That she does. You didn't seem to have any trouble settling her."

"I used an old trick my *grandmammi* used on me. I distracted her with flowers."

Beatrice looked up at Sarah with a glare. "You're not Mercy's *mamm*." She pushed her face into the folds of her father's pant leg.

"I warned you. She's going to be a handful." Mose patted Beatrice's back.

Sarah handed the baby to Mose and dropped to her knees. Cupping a bright green grasshopper from the tall grass, she asked, "Do you like bugs, Beatrice?" She held out her closed hand and waited.

Beatrice turned and leaned against her father's legs, her eyes red-rimmed. "What kind of bug is it?" She stepped forward, her gaze on Sarah's extended hands.

Motioning the child closer, Sarah slightly opened her fingers and whispered, "Come and see." A tiny green head popped out and struggled to be free.

"Oh, *Daed*! Look," Beatrice said, joy sending her feet tapping.

Sarah opened her hand and laughed as the grasshopper leaped away, Beatrice right behind it, her little legs hopping through the grass, copying the fleeing insect.

Mose grinned as he watched his daughter's antics. "You might just have won her heart. How did you know she loves bugs?

"I've always been fascinated with *Gott's* tiny creatures. I had a feeling Beatrice might, too."

Mose's gaze held hers for a long moment until Sarah lost her smile, turned away and headed back into the house.

# Chapter Two

Steam rose from the pot of potatoes boiling on the wood stove. The men would be in for supper soon and Sarah thanked *Gott* there'd only be two extra men tonight and not the twenty-five hungry workers she'd fed last night.

She glanced at the table and smiled as she watched Beatrice use broad strokes of paint to cover the art paper she'd given her. The child had been silent all afternoon, only speaking when spoken to. The pain in her eyes reminded Sarah of her own suffering. They grieved the same way—deep and silent with sudden bursts of fury. The child's need for love seemed so deep, the pain touched Sarah's own wounded heart.

Almost forgotten, Mercy lay content on her mat, a bottle of milk clutched in her hands. Her eyes traveled around, taking in the sights of the busy kitchen floor. The fluffy ginger kitten rushed past and put a smile on the baby's face. Sarah saw dimples press into her cheeks. If she and Joseph had had *kinder*, perhaps they would have looked like Mercy and Beatrice. Blonde-haired with a sparkle of mischief in their blue eyes.

Joseph's face swam before her tear-filled eyes. She missed the sound of his steps as he walked across the wooden porch each evening. His arms wrapped around her waist always had a way of reassuring her. She'd been loved. For that brief period of time, she'd been precious to someone, and she longed for that comfort again. Her arms had been empty but *Gott* placed these *kinder* here and she was grateful for the time she had with them.

"Would you like a glass of milk, Beatrice? I have a secret stash of chocolate chip cookies. I'd be glad to share them with such a talented artist."

*"Nee,"* she said.

"Perhaps—"

"I want my *mamm*," Beatrice yelled, knocking the plastic tub of dirty water across the table and wetting herself and Sarah's legs.

Sarah stood transfixed as the child waited, perhaps expecting some kind of reprimand. There would be no scolding. Not today. Not ever. This child suffered and Sarah knew the pain of that suffering. She often felt like throwing things, expressing her own misery with actions that shocked.

Quiet and calm, Sarah mopped up the mud-colored water, careful not to damage Beatrice's art. "This would look lovely hung on my wall. Perhaps I could have it as a reminder of your visit?"

Beatrice looked down at her smock, at the merging colors against the white fabric, and began to cry deep, wrenching sobs. Unsure what else to do, Sarah prayed for guidance. She knelt on the floor, cleaned up the child before wrapping her arms around her trembling body. "I know you're missing your *mamm*, Beatrice. I miss my husband, too. He went to live in heaven several months ago and I want him back like you want your mother back."

"Did he read stories to you at bedtime?" Beatrice asked, her innocent gaze locked with Sarah's.

Their tears fell together on the mud-brown paint stain on Beatrice's smock. "Joseph didn't read to me, but he told me all about his day and kissed my eyes closed before I fell asleep." The ache became so painful Sarah felt she might die from her grief.

"My *mamm* said I was her big girl. Mercy was just born and cried a lot, but I was big and strong. I help *Grandmammi* take care of Mercy. Do you think *mamm's* proud of me?"

Sarah looked at the wet-faced child and a smile came out of nowhere. Beatrice was the first person who really understood what Sarah was living through, and that created a bond between them. They could grieve together, help one another. *Gott* in his wisdom had linked them for a week, perhaps more. Time enough for Beatrice to feel a mother's love again.

She would never heal from Joseph's death, but this tiny girl would give her purpose and a reason for living. She needed that right now. A reason to get up in the morning, put on her clothes and let the day begin.

The screen door banged open and Mose walked in, catching them in the warm embrace. Beatrice scurried out of Sarah's arms and into her father's cuddle. "Sarah likes me," she said and smiled shyly over at Sarah.

Mose peppered kisses on his daughter's neck and cheeks. "I see you've been painting again. How did this mess happen, Beatrice?"

"I was angry. I knocked down my paint water." Beatrice braced her shoulders, obviously prepared to deal with any punishment her father administered.

"Did you apologize to Sarah for your outburst?"

*"Nee."* Beatrice rested her head on her father's dirty shirt.

"Perhaps an apology and help cleaning the mess off the floor is in order?" Mose looked at Sarah's frazzled hair and flushed cheeks.

"Sarah hugged me like *Mamm* used to. She smells of flowers. For a moment I thought *Mamm* had come back."

Sarah grabbed the cloth from the kitchen sink and busied herself cleaning the damp spot off the floor. She didn't know what Mose might think about the cluttered kitchen. Perhaps he'd feel she wasn't fit to take care of active *kinder*. She scrubbed hard into the wood. *Maybe I'm not fit to care for kinder.* She and the child had cried together. She was the adult. Shouldn't she have kept her own loss to herself?

"I'm sorry I made a mess, Sarah. I won't do it again. I promise."

Sarah looked into the eyes of an old soul just four years old. "It's time some color came into this dark kitchen, Beatrice. Your painting has put a smile on my face. There's no need for apologies." She smiled at the child and avoided

Mose's face. She felt sure he'd have words for her later. She leaned toward Mercy, kissed her blond head as she toddled past, checked her over and then handed her a tiny doll with hair the color of corn silk. "Here you are, sweet one. You lost your baby." Sarah expected a smile from the adorable *bobble*, but the child's serious look remained.

Sarah scrambled to get off the floor. Mose stood over her, his big hand outstretched, offering to help. She hesitated, but took his hand, feeling the warmth of his thick fingers and calloused palm. His strength was surprising. She felt herself pulled up, as if weightless. She refused to look into his eyes. She'd probably find anger there, and she couldn't handle his wrath just now. She'd be more careful to stay in control around the girls.

"You've broken through her hedge of protection." Mose leaned in close and whispered into Sarah's ear. She looked up, amazed to see a grin on his face, the presence of joy.

"I just—"

"*Nee*, you don't understand. You reached her, and for that I am most grateful."

Sarah didn't know what to say. She'd never received compliments such as this before, except from Joseph and her brother, Eric. Joseph had constantly told her how much he loved her and what a fine wife she made. Receiving praise from a stranger made her uncomfortable.

"I have supper to finish before my father returns. He likes his meal on the table at six sharp. If I hurry, I can avoid his complaints."

"I'm sure he'll understand the delay with two *kinder* underfoot."

"You don't know my father. He runs his home like most men run their business. I must hurry."

Sarah prepared the table with Beatrice trailing close behind. She let the child place the cloth napkins in the center of each plate and together they stood back and admired their handiwork.

Beatrice glanced around. "We forgot Mercy's cup."

"I have it in the kitchen, ready for milk." Sarah patted Beatrice's curly head.

"And the special spoon she eats from."

Sarah laughed at the organized child. Beatrice had the intensity of an older sister used to caring for her younger sister. "You'll make a great *mamm* someday," Sarah told her, moving the bowl of hot runner beans closer to her own plate. No sense risking a nasty burn from a child's eager hand.

"Do you think my *daed* will be proud of me?" Beatrice looked excited, her smile hopeful.

Sarah pulled the girl close and patted her back. "I'm sure he'll notice all your special touches."

"My *mamm* said... I'm sorry. My *grossmammi* said I was to forget my *mamm,* but it's hard not to remember."

Sarah's face flushed hot. How dare someone tell this young child to forget her *mamm*? Had her own mother missed her when she'd left the Amish community for the *Englisch*? She had no recollection of how her *mamm* looked. No pictures graced the mantel in her father's house. Plain people didn't allow pictures of their loved ones, and she had only childhood memories to rely on, which often failed her. If she brought up the subject of her mother to her father, there always had been a price to pay, so she'd stopped asking questions a long time ago.

"I believe remembering your mother will bring joy to your life. You hang on to your memories, little one."

A fat tear forced its way from the corner of Beatrice's eye. "Sometimes I can't remember what her voice sounds like. Does that mean I don't love her anymore?"

Sarah lifted the child into her arms and

hugged her, rocking her like a baby. "*Nee*, Beatrice. Our human minds forget easily, but there will be times when you'll hear someone speak and you'll remember the sound of her voice and you'll rejoice in that memory."

Beatrice squeezed Sarah's neck. "I like you, Sarah. You help me remember to smile."

Sarah felt a grin playing on her own lips. Beatrice and Mercy had the same effect on her. They reminded her there was more to life than grief. She would always be grateful for her chance meeting with them, and Mose.

Bathed in the golden glow of the extra candle Beatrice had insisted on lighting before their supper meal, Mose noticed how different Sarah looked. Her hair had been neat and tidy under her stiff *kapp* earlier that morning, but now she looked mussed and fragile, as if her hair pins would fail her at any moment. He didn't have to ask if the *kinder* had been a challenge. She wasn't used to them around the house. He read the difficulty of her day in her pale face, too, and in the way she had avoided him the rest of the afternoon.

As if feeling his eyes on her, Sarah glanced up, a forkful of runner beans halfway to her mouth. Her smile was warm, but reserved. He needed to get her alone, tell her how much he appreciated her dealing with his daughters. He knew they were hard work. She deserved his gratitude. He'd worked hard on the barn teardown, endured the sun, but knew she'd worked harder.

"Beatrice tells me she had a lovely day." He smiled at his daughter's empty plate. It had been months since she'd eaten properly, and watching Beatrice gobble down her meal encouraged his heart.

Sarah and Beatrice exchanged a smile as if they had a secret all their own. "We spent the afternoon in the garden and drank lemonade with chunks of ice," Sarah said. "I learned a great deal about Mercy from your helpful daughter. She knows when her baby sister is hungry and just how to place a cloth on her bottom so it doesn't fall off. She's a wealth of information, and I needed her help." Sarah patted Beatrice's hand.

The child smiled up at her. "I ate everything on my plate. Is there ice cream for dessert?"

Mose found himself smiling like a young fool. Seeing his daughters back to normal seemed a miracle.

Adolph banged his fork down and dusted food crumbs from his beard. "There will be no ice cream in this house tonight. *Kinder* should be seen but not heard at the table. There'll be no reward for noise." He glared at Sarah, as if she'd done something terrible by drawing the child out of her shell.

"My *kinder* are encouraged to speak, Adolph. Beatrice has always been very vocal, and I believe feeling safe to speak with one's own parent an asset, not a detriment. I'm sure we can find another place to stay if their noise bothers you."

"There is no need for you to leave. I'm sure I can tolerate Beatrice's chatter for a few more days." Adolph frowned Sarah's way, his true feelings shown.

Mose fought back anger. He wondered what it must have been like to grow up with this tyrannical father lording over her.

As if to avoid the drama unfolding, Sarah pushed back in her chair and began to gather dishes.

"The meal was *wunderbaar.* You're an amazing cook," Mose said.

Sarah nodded her thanks, her eyes downcast, her hands busy with plates and glasses.

Beatrice grabbed her father's hand and pulled. "Let's go into the garden. I want to find the kitten." She jumped up and down with excitement.

Adolph scowled at the child.

Mose scooped Mercy from her pallet of toys

and left the room in silence, Beatrice skipping behind. Seconds later, the back door banged behind them.

Mose heard Adolph roar. "You see what you did? Can I never trust you to do anything right?" Adolph walked out of the kitchen, leaving Sarah alone with her own thoughts.

Moments later the sound of splashing water and laughter announced a water fight had broken out in the backyard. Sarah longed to join in on the fun, but instead went for a stack of bath towels and placed three on the stool next to the back door and a thick one on the floor. Mose would need them when their play finished.

She peeked out the window, amazed to see Mose Fischer soaked from head to toe, his blond hair plastered to his skull like a pale helmet. Beatrice had him pinned to the ground. Water from the old hose sprayed his face. She'd had no intention of watching their play but was glad she had. Mose's patience with his daughter impressed her. Even young Mercy lay against her father's legs as if to hold him down so Beatrice could have her fun with him.

Their natural joy brought Joseph to mind. He'd been playful and full of jokes at times. It had taken her a while to get used to his ways when they'd first married, and she'd known he'd found her lacking. She'd soon grown used to his spirit and had found herself waiting with anticipation for him to come in from the fields. She missed the joy they'd shared. A tear caught her unaware. She brushed the dampness away and sat in her favorite rocker. Minutes passed. She listened to the *kinder's* laughter and then Mose's firm voice reminding them it was time for bed.

The quilt she was stitching was forgotten as soon as the back door flew open and three wet bodies rushed in. She laughed aloud as she watched Mose try to keep a hand on Beatrice while toweling Mercy dry.

"Would you like some help?"

"I think Mercy is more seal than child." He fought to hold on to her slippery body. Mercy was all smiles, her water-soaked diaper dripping on the kitchen floor.

Sarah rushed over and took the baby. The child trembled with cold and was quickly engulfed in a warm, fluffy towel. Sarah led the way to the indoor bathroom, baby in arms. Mose filled the tub with water already heated on the wood stove. Sarah added cold water, checked the temperature of the water, found it safe and sat Mercy down with a splash. Mercy gurgled in happiness as Sarah poured water over her shoulders and back.

"You're a natural at this." Mose spoke behind her.

Sarah reached around for Beatrice's hand and the child jumped into the water with all the gusto of a happy fish. Water splashed and Sarah's frock became wet from neck to hem. She found herself laughing with the *kinder*. Her murmurs of joy sounded foreign to her own ears. *How long has it been since I giggled like this?*

In the small confines of the bathroom, Sarah became aware of Mose standing over her. "I'm sure I can handle the bath. Why don't you join my father for a chat while I get these *lieblings* ready for bed?"

Beatrice splashed more water. Mercy cried out and reached for Sarah. Grabbing a clean washcloth from the side of the tub, Sarah wiped water from the baby's eyes. "You have to be careful, Beatrice." She held on to the baby's arm and turned to reach for a towel. Mose had left the room silently. She thought back to what she had said and hoped he hadn't felt dismissed.

The girls finally asleep and her father in his room with the door closed, Sarah dried the last of the dishes and put them away. Looking for a cool breeze, she stepped out the back door and sat on the wooden steps. Her long, plain dress covered her legs to her ankles.

Fireflies flickered in the air, their tiny glow appearing and disappearing. She took in a long, relaxing breath and smelled honeysuckle on the breeze. Somewhere an insect began its lovesick song. Sarah lifted her voice in praise to the Lord, the old Amish song reminding her how much *Gott* once had loved her.

*"Dein heilig statthond sie zerstort, dein Atler umbgegraben Darzu auch dein knecht ermadt..."*

No one except Marta knew how much she'd hated *Gott* when Joseph had first died. She'd railed at Him, her loss too great to bear. But then she'd remembered the gas light in the barn and how she'd left it on for the old mother cat giving birth to fuzzy balls of damp fluff. She'd sealed Joseph's fate by leaving that light burning. When she woke suddenly in the night, she'd heard her husband's screams of agony as he tried to get out of the burning barn. Her own hands had been scorched as she'd fought to get to him. She hadn't been able reach him and she'd given up. She'd failed him. He had died a horrible death. Her beloved Joseph had died, they'd said, of smoke inhalation, his body just bones and ashes inside his closed casket.

She stopped singing and put her head down to weep.

"Something wrong, or are you just tired?" Mose spoke from a porch chair behind her.

With only the light coming through the kitchen window, Sarah turned. She strained to see Mose. "I'm sorry. I didn't know you were there." She wiped the tears off her face and moved to stand.

"*Nee*. Don't go, please. I want to talk to you about Beatrice, if that's all right."

Sarah prepared herself for his disapproval. She'd heard it before from other men in the community when she'd broken *Ordnung* willfully. The Bishop especially seemed hard on her. She sat, waited.

Mose cleared his throat and began to talk. "I wanted to tell you how much I appreciate your taking such good care of my girls. They haven't been this happy in a long time, not even with their *grandmammi*."

Sarah touched the cross hanging under the scoop of her dress, the only thing she had left from her mother. If her father knew she had the chain and cross, he would destroy them. "I did nothing special, Mose. I treated the *kinder* like my mother treated me. Your girls are delightful, and I enjoy having them here. They make my life easier." She clamped her mouth shut. She'd said too much. Plain people didn't talk about their problems and she had to keep reminding herself to be silent about the pain.

"Well, I think it's *wunderbaar* you were able to reach Beatrice. I've been very concerned about her, and now I can rest easy. She has someone to talk to who understands loss."

Understands? *Oh, I understand.* The child hurt physically, as if someone had cut off an arm or leg and left her to die of pain. "I'm glad I was able to help." She rose. "Now, I need to prepare for breakfast. Tomorrow is going to be a busy day for both of us. There is food to cook, a barn to haul away."

"Wait, before you go. I have an important question to ask you."

Sarah nodded her head and sat back down.

"I stayed up until late last night, thinking about your situation and mine. I prayed and prayed, and *Gott* kept pushing this thought at me." He took a deep breath. "I wonder, would you consider becoming my *frau*?"

Sarah held up her hand as if to stop his words. "I…"

"*Nee*, wait. Before you speak, let me explain." Mose took another deep breath and began. "I know you still love Joseph and probably always will, just as I still love my Greta. But I have *kinder* who need a mother to guide and love them. Now that Joseph's gone and your *daed* insists the farm is to be sold, you'll need a place to call home, people who care about you, a family. We can join forces and help each other." He saw panic form in her eyes. "Wait. Let me finish, please. It would only be a marriage of convenience, with no strings attached. I would love you as a sister and you would be under my protection. The girls need a loving mother and you've already proven you can be that. What do you say, Sarah Nolt. Will you be my wife?"

Sarah sat silently in the chair, her face turned away. She turned back toward Mose and looked into his eyes. "You'd do this for me? But…you don't know me."

"I'd do this for us," Mose corrected and smiled.

The tips of Sarah's fingers nervously pleated and unpleated a scrap of her skirt. "We hardly know each other. You must realize I'll never love you the way you deserve."

"I know how much Joseph meant to you. He was like a *bruder* to me. You'd have to take second place in my heart, too. Greta will always be my one and only love." Mose watched her nervous fingers work the material, knowing this conversation was causing her more stress. He waited.

She glanced at him. "I'd want the *kinder* to think we married for love. I hope they can grow to respect me as their parent. I know it won't be the same deep love they had for their *mamm*. I'll do everything I can to help them remember her."

"I'm sure they'll grow to love you. In fact, I think they already do." Mose fumbled for words, feeling young and awkward, something he hadn't felt in a very long time. He'd never thought he'd get married again, but *Gott* seemed to be in this and his *kinder* needed Sarah. She needed them. If she said no to his proposal he'd have to persuade her, but he had no idea how he'd manage it. She was proud and headstrong.

"What would people think? They will say I took advantage of your good nature."

Mose smiled. "So, let them talk. They'd be wrong and we'd know it. I want this marriage for both of us, for the *kinder*. We can't let others decide what is best for our lives. I believe this marriage is *Gott's* plan for us."

Sarah's face cleared and she seemed to come to a decision. She smoothed out the fabric of her skirt and tidied her hair, then finally took Mose's outstretched hand with a smile. "You're right. This is our life. I accept your proposal,

Mose Fischer. I will be your *frau* and your *kinder's* mother."

Sarah paused for a moment, then spoke. "Being your wife brings obligations. I expect you to honor my grief until such a time I can become your wife in both name and deed, as a good man deserves." She looked him in the eye, seeking understanding. He deserved a woman's love and she had none to give him right now.

Mose smiled and nodded, gave her a hand up and stepped back. "I wish there was something I could do to help you in your grief."

Sarah didn't know what to say. Few people had offered her a word of sympathy when she'd lost Joseph. They'd felt she'd caused his death. "I'm fine, really. I just need time." She lied because if she said anything else, she would be crying in this stranger's arms.

"Time does help, Sarah. Time and staying busy."

She could feel his gaze on her. She hid every ache and hardened her heart. This was the Amish way. "*Ya*, time and work. Everyone tells me this."

"Take your time, grieve." He murmured the words soft and slow.

Her heart in shreds, she would not talk of grief with him, not with anyone. "I don't want to talk anymore." She moved past him and through the door, ignoring the throbbing veins at her temples. She would never get over this terrible loss deep in her heart. This unbearable pain was her punishment from *Gott*.

Mose wished he'd kept his mouth shut. He'd caused her more pain, reminding her of what she'd lost. Joseph had been a good man, full of life and fun. He'd loved *Gott* with all his heart and had dedicated himself to the Lord early in life. His baptism had been allowed early. Most Amish teens were forced to wait until they were sure of their dedication to *Gott* and their community, after their *rumspringa*, when they're time to experience the Englisch world was over and decisions made, but not Joseph. Everyone had seen his love for *Gott*, his kindness, strength and purity. He felt the painful loss of Joseph. What must Sarah feel? Like Joseph, she seemed sure of herself, able to face any problem with strength…but there was something else. She carried a cloud of misery over her, which told him she suffered a great deal. What else could have happened to make her so miserable?

He heard a window open upstairs and movement, perhaps Sarah preparing for bed. Mose laughed quietly. Was he so desperate for a mother for his *kinder* that he had proposed marriage to a woman so in love with her dead husband she could hardly stand his touch? They both had to dig themselves out of their black holes of loss and begin life anew. Could marriage be the way? He knew he would never love again, yet his *kinder* needed a mother. Was he too selfish to provide one for them? Would marrying again be fair to any woman he found suitable to raise his *kinder*? No woman wanted a lovesick fool, such as he, on their arm. They wanted courtship, the normal affection of their husband, but he had none to give. He was an empty shell. Mose looked out over the tops of tall trees to the stars. *Gott* was somewhere watching, wondering why He'd made a fool like Mose Fischer. Stars twinkled and suddenly a shooting star flashed across the sky, its tail flashing bright before it disappeared into nothingness. It had burned out much like his heart.

# Chapter Three

Sarah's eyes were red-rimmed and puffy. She placed her *kapp* just so and made sure its position was perfect, as if the starched white prayer *kapp* would make up for her tear-ravaged face.

"My mother wore a *kapp* like that, but it looked kind of different." Beatrice clambered onto the dressing table's stool next to Sarah.

"It probably was different, sweetheart. Lots of Amish communities wear different styles of *kapps* and practice different traditions."

"How come girls wear them and not boys?" Beatrice reached out and touched the heavily starched material on Sarah's head.

"Several places in the Bible tell women to cover their heads, so we wear the *kapps* and show *Gott* we listen to His directions." Sarah wished she could pull off the cap, throw it to the ground and stomp on it. Covering her head didn't make her a better person. Love did. And she loved this thin, love-starved child and her sweet baby sister. She felt such a strong need to make things easier for Beatrice and Mercy. "Would you like to help me make pancakes?"

As if on a spring, the child jumped off the stool and danced around the room, making Mercy laugh out loud and clap her hands. "Pancakes! My favoritest thing in the whole wide world."

Sarah pushed a pin into her pulled-back hair and glanced at her appearance in the small hand mirror for a moment longer. She looked terrible and her stomach was upset, probably the result of such an emotional night. She'd lain awake for hours, unable to stop thinking about her promise to wed Mose. She'd listened to the *kinder's* soft snores and movements, thinking about Joseph and their lost life together.

*Gott* had spoken loud and clear to her this morning. The depression and grief she suffered were eating up her life. She'd never have the love of her own *kinder* if she didn't come out of this black mood and live again. But why would Mose want her as a wife, damaged as she was?

"Your eyes are red. Are you going to cry some more?" Beatrice jumped off the bench and danced around, her skirt whirling.

*The child heard me crying last night.* She

forced herself to laugh and join in the child's silly dancing. Hand in hand they whirled about, circling and circling until both were dizzy and fell to the floor, their laughter filling the room.

A loud knock came and her father opened the door wide. "What's all this noise so early in the morning?"

Her joy died a quick death. "Beatrice and I were—"

"I see what you're doing. Foolishness. You're making this child act as foolish as you. It's time for breakfast. Go to the kitchen and be prepared for at least twenty-five men to eat. We have more work to do now that the old barn is to be towed away. We'll need nourishment for the hard day ahead."

Beatrice snuggled close to Sarah, her arms tight around her neck. "This may be your home, but you're out of line, *Daed*. Close the door behind you. We will be down when the *kinder's* needs are met." Sarah looked him hard in the eyes, her tone firm.

Her father's angry glare left her filled with fury. She hated living at his farm, at his mercy. She longed to be in her own home two miles down the dusty road. She would not let him throw his bitterness the *kinder's* way. She'd talk to him in private and make things very clear. She'd be liberated from his control once she and Mose were married. But, right now she was still a widow and had to listen to his demands. But not for long. *Gott* had provided her a way to get away from his control.

"Come darling, let's get Mercy out of her cot and make those pancakes. We have a long day of cooking ahead of us and need some healthy food in our bellies."

"Is that mean man your *daed*?" Beatrice asked.

Sarah helped her off the floor. *"Ya."* She lifted Mercy from her cot and nuzzled her nose in the baby's warm, sweet-smelling neck. She checked her diaper and found she needed changing. Mercy wiggled in her arms, a big grin pressing dimples in her cheeks. She held the warm baby close to her and thanked *Gott* her father's harsh words hadn't seemed to scare the baby.

Watching her sister get a fresh diaper, Beatrice spoke, "Why is he so angry? I don't think he loves you." Confusion clouded Beatrice's face, a frown creasing her brow.

"Of course he loves me," Sarah assured her. But as she finished changing Mercy's diaper, she wondered. *Does he love me?*

The narrow tables lined up on the grass just outside Sarah's kitchen door didn't look long enough for twenty-five men, but she knew from experience they would suffice. She, Marta and three local women laughed and chatted as they covered the handmade tables with bright white sheets and put knives, forks and cloth napkins at just the right intervals.

As the men began gathering, Sarah placed heaping platters of her favorite breakfast dish made of sausage, potatoes, cheese, bread, onions and peppers in the middle of each table and at the ends. Bowls of fresh fruit, cut bite-size, added color to the meal. Heavy white plates, one for each worker, lined the tables. Glasses of cold milk sat next to each plate.

"The table looks very nice," Marta whispered.

"It looks hospital sterile." Sarah loved color. Bold, bright splashes of color. What would happen if she'd used the red table napkins she'd hemmed just after Joseph died? In her grief she'd had to do something outrageous, or scream in her misery. She longed to use the napkins for this occasion. Bright colors were considered a sin to Old Order Amish. *How could Gott see color as a sin?* Some of the limitations she lived under made no sense at all.

"We're plain people, Sarah. *Gott* warned us against adorning ourselves and our lives with bright colors. They attract unwanted attention."

Marta straightened a white napkin and smiled at Sarah.

"I know what the Bishop says, Marta, but I think too many of our community rules are the Bishop's rules and have nothing at all to do with what *Gott* wants. The older he gets, the more unbearable his 'must not's and should not's' get."

"Everything looks good," Marta said in a loud voice, drowning out Sarah's last comment. Bishop Miller's wife walked past and straightened several forks on the table close to Sarah.

Marta rushed back into the kitchen, her hand a stranglehold on Sarah's wrist. "Do you think she heard you?"

"Who?"

"Bishop Miller's wife."

"I don't care if she did."

"Well, you should care. I know she's a sweet old woman and always kind to me, but she tells her husband everything that goes on in the community, and you know it."

Sarah shrugged and looked out the kitchen window, watching Mose approach the porch and settle in a chair too small for his big frame. Her future husband wore a pale blue shirt today, his blond hair damp from sweat and plastered down under his straw work hat. Beatrice left the small *kinder's* table and crawled into her father's lap, her arms sliding around the sweaty neck of his shirt.

"That child loves her *daed*." Marta grabbed a pickle from one of the waiting plates of garnish.

"She does. It's a shame she has *nee* mother to cuddle her."

"I'm worried about you, Sarah. Lately all you do is daydream and mope."

Sarah considered telling Marta her news but decided against it. Marta would never approve of a loveless marriage. "Don't worry about me. I'll be fine. I like having the *kinder* here. They've brightened my spirits. I've never had a chance to really get close to a child before. They can make my day better with just a laugh. They are really into climbing, even Mercy. This morning I caught her throwing her leg over her cot rail. She could have fallen if I hadn't been close enough to catch her. I'm going to see if someone has a bigger bed for her today. She's way too active to manage in that small bed *Daed* found in the attic."

Sarah grabbed two pitchers of cold milk and headed out the back door.

"Is there more food? These men are hungry." Adolph grabbed Sarah by the arm as she passed through the door, his fingers pinching into her flesh.

"*Ya*, of course. I'll bring out more." She placed the pitchers on the table and returned the friendly smile Mose directed her way.

"See that you do," her father barked, as if he were talking to a child. He moved down the table, greeting each worker with a handshake and friendly smile.

Sarah hurried into the kitchen and grabbed a plate of hot pancakes from the oven and rushed back out the kitchen door, a big jar of fresh, warmed maple syrup tucked under her arm. Her father was right about one thing. The men were eating like an army.

The last of the horse-drawn wagons carrying burned wood pulled out of the yard and down the lane, heading for the dump just outside town.

Mose grabbed the end of a twelve-foot board, pulled it over and nailed it into the growing frame with three strong swings of the hammer. A brisk breeze lifted the straw hat he wore, almost blowing it off his head. He smashed it down on his riot of curls and went back to work. The breeze was welcome on the unseasonably hot morning.

"Won't be much longer now," the man working next to Mose muttered. The board the man added would finish the last of the barn's frame, and then the hard work of lifting the frames would begin.

Sweat-soaked and hungry, Mose glanced at the noon meal being served up a few yards away and saw Sarah carrying a plate piled high with potato pancakes. She'd been in and out of the house all morning, her face flushed from the heat of the kitchen. Beatrice trailed behind her, a skip in her steps and the small bowl of some type of chow-chow relish dripping yellow liquid down the front of her apron as she bounced.

He laughed to himself, taking pleasure in seeing Beatrice so content. Sarah had a natural way with *kinder*. She'd make a fine mother.

"Someone needs to deal with that woman."

"Who?" Mose turned his head, surprised at the comment. He looked at the man who'd spoken and frowned. Standing with his hands on his hips, the man's expression dug deep caverns into his face, giving Mose the impression of intense anger.

"The Widow Nolt, naturally. Who else? Everyone knows she killed Joseph with her neglect. Bishop Miller might as well shun her now and get it over with. No one wants her in the community anymore. She causes trouble and doesn't know when to keep her mouth shut."

Mose mopped at the sweat on his forehead. "What do you mean, she killed Joseph? There's no way she's capable of doing something like that. The police said he died of smoke inhalation."

Stretching out his back and twisting, the man worked out the kinks from his tall frame, his eyes still on Sarah. "She did it, all right, *bruder*. She left the light on in the barn, knowing gas lights get hot and cause fires."

"I'm sure she just forgot to turn it off. People forget, you know." Mose knew he was wasting his breath. Some liked to think the worst of people, especially people like Sarah, who were powerless to defend themselves.

"Sarah Nolt is that kind of woman. Her own father says she's always been careless, even as a child."

"I believe *Gott* would have us pray for our sister, not slander her for something that took her husband's life."

"Well, you can stand up for her if you like, but I'm not. She's a bad woman, and I wouldn't be here today if it weren't for my respect for Joseph. He was a good man."

"He'd want you to help Sarah, not slander her." Mose threw down the hammer. His temper would always be a fault he'd have to deal with, and right now he'd best move away or he'd end up punching a man in the mouth.

The food bell rang out. He dusted as much of the sawdust off his clothes as he could. Still angry, he moved toward the long table set up in the grass and took the seat closest to the door. A tall glass of cold water was placed in front of him by a young girl. *"Danke."* He downed the whole glass.

"You're *welkom*," the girl muttered and refilled his glass. Mose watched Sarah as she served the men around him. She acted polite and kind to everyone, but not one man spoke to her. The women seemed friendlier but still somewhat distant. He saw her smile once or twice before he dug into his plate of tender roast beef, stuffed cabbage rolls and Dutch green beans. Sarah knew her way around a kitchen. The food he ate was hardy and spiced to perfection.

A group of men seated around the Bishop began to mutter. A loud argument broke out and Mose could hear Sarah's name being bandied about. Marta hurried past, her face flushed, and the promise of tears glistening in her eyes. Her small-framed shoulders drooped as she made her way into the house. Soon

Sarah was out the door, her eyes locked on Bishop Miller who sat a few seats from Mose.

"You have much to say about me today, Bishop Miller. Would you like to say the words to my face?" Her small hands were fisted, her back straight and strong as she glared at the community leader.

Adolph shoved back his chair and stood.

"Shut your mouth, Sarah Yoder. I will not have you speak to the Bishop like this. You are out of line. You will speak to him with respect."

"My name is Nolt, *Daed*. No longer Yoder. And I will not be told to hush like some young *bensel*. If the Bishop has something to say, he need only open his mouth or call one of his meetings."

Mose rose. *Gott, hold Sarah's tongue.* She had already dug a deep well of trouble with her words. Her actions were unwise, but he would not stand by and watch her be pulled down further by her father's lack of protection. Let the Bishop show proof of her actions and present them in a proper setting if he had issues with her.

Bishop Miller's wife hurried to Sarah and put her arms around her trembling body. "Let us leave all this for today and have cold tea in the kitchen. We're all tired and nerves frayed.

Today a barn goes up. It is a happy day, Sarah. One full of promise. Let us celebrate and not speak words that cannot be taken back."

Mose waited, wondering if Sarah would relent. She turned and stared deep into the eyes of the woman next to her. Moments passed and then she crumbled, tears running down her face as she was escorted away.

Mose watched the door shut behind the women. He longed to know if Sarah was all right but knew she wouldn't want him interfering. "What's going on?" Mose murmured to Eric, Sarah's brother.

"Someone has found proof that Sarah was the one who gave money to Lukas, a young teenager who recently ran away from the community."

"Money? Why would she do that?" They spoke in whispers, his food forgotten.

"I only heard a moment of conversation but it seems *Daed* saw her speaking with the boy's younger brother the day before Lukas took him and left for places unknown."

"That's not solid proof. Sarah must be given a chance to redeem herself."

"She'll get her chance. A meeting has been called, and I plan to talk to Bishop Miller before it comes around. I suspect she'll be shunned, but I have to make an effort to calm the waters. Lord alone knows what would happen to her if she's forced to live amongst the *Englisch*." Eric got up to leave, but turned back to Mose. "Marta's offered to look after the *kinder* at our house until tomorrow. Sarah is too upset to think clearly."

Tired from the long day of cooking and cleaning, Sarah lay across her childhood bed on the second floor of her father's house, her pillow wet from tears. She cried for Joseph, for the life she'd lost with him, and for the loneliness she'd felt every day since he'd died. She needed Joseph and he was gone forever.

Marta held her hand in a firm grip. "You mustn't fret so, Sarah. The children can stay with Eric and me tonight. Most likely you will be given a talking to tomorrow and nothing more."

"And if I'm shunned, what then? You and Eric won't be allowed to talk to me. The whole community will say I'm dead to them. Who will I call family?"

"Why did you give Lukas money? You knew you ran the risk of being found out."

Sarah sat up, tucking her dress under her legs. Marta handed her a clean white handkerchief and watched as Sarah wiped the tears off her face. "I couldn't take it anymore. Every day

I heard the abuse. Every day I heard the boys crying out in pain."

"Did you talk to any of the elders about this?"

"I talked to them but they put me off, said I was a woman and didn't understand the role a father played in a boy's life." Sarah blew her nose and tried to regain control of the tremors that shook her body.

"But surely beating a young boy senseless is not in *Gott's* plan. Do you believe your *daed* would tell on you if he knew it was you who gave the boys money?"

"Of course he would, but he didn't know. I made sure he was gone the day I slipped money to Lukas."

"Then how?"

Sarah smoothed the wrinkles out of her quilt and set the bed back in order. "It doesn't matter now."

"How would you survive among the *Englisch*? You know nothing about them. Your whole life has been Amish. I fear for you, Sarah." Marta brushed away her tears as they continued to fall.

A shiver ran through Sarah as she thought about what Marta said. She wouldn't be strong enough to endure the radical changes that would have faced her. Thank *Gott* for Mose's offer of marriage, for the opportunity to go to

Sarasota and leave all this behind. But would he want to marry her if she was shunned and was she prepared for a loveless marriage? She feared not. *Gott's will. Grab hold of Gott's will.*

# *Chapter Four*

Sarah roamed through the small farmhouse, gathering memories of Joseph and their time together. She had no picture to keep him alive in her mind, only objects she could touch to feel closer to him.

A sleepless night at her father's farm, after her confrontation with the bishop, had left her depressed and bone tired.

Downstairs, she smiled as she picked up a shiny black vase from the kitchen window. When Joseph had bought it that early spring morning, he'd known he'd broken one of the Old Order Amish *Ordnung* laws laid down by Bishop Miller. The vase was a token of Joseph's love. It was to hold the wildflowers they gathered on their long walks in the meadows. The day he'd surprised her with the vase she'd cried for joy. Now it felt cold and empty like her broken heart. The vase was the only real decoration in the farmhouse, as was custom, but their wedding quilt, traditionally made in honor of their wedding by the community's sewing circle, hung on the wall in the great room.

In front of the wide kitchen windows, she fingered the vase's smooth surface, remembering precious moments. Their wedding, days of visiting family and friends, the first time she'd been allowed to see the farmhouse he'd built with other men from the area. He'd laughed at her as she'd squealed with delight. The simple, white two-story house was to be their home for the rest of their lives. He'd gently kissed her and whispered, "I love you."

Moved to tears, her vision blurred. She stumbled to the stairs and climbed them one by one, her head swimming with momentary dizziness. On the landing she caught her breath before walking into their neat, tiny bedroom. Moments later she found the shirt she'd made for Joseph to wear on their wedding day hanging in the closet next to several work shirts and two of her own plain dresses.

Sarah tucked the blue shirt on top of a pile of notes and papers she'd put in the brown valise just after he'd died. He used the heavy case when he'd taken short trips to the Ohio

Valley area communities to discuss the drought. In a few days she'd use it to pack and leave this beloved farmhouse forever.

Her dresses and his old King James Bible, along with the last order for hayseeds written in his bold print, went into the case. The Book of Psalms she'd given him at Christmas slipped into her apron pocket with ease. Her memories of him would be locked away in this heavy case, the key stashed somewhere safe.

Most of her other clothes and belongings would be left. She'd have no need for them now. Mose would take care of her. A fresh wave of anxiety flushed through her. She had no idea if she could go through with this marriage.

She thought back to Joseph and wondered what he'd think of the drama surrounding her. *He'd be disappointed.* He'd followed the tenets of the Old Order church faithfully. The rules of the community were a way of life he'd gladly accepted. Yes, he'd be disappointed in her.

She faced shunning. Bishop Miller preached that those who were shunned or left the faith would go to hell. Joseph was with the Lord. *I'd never see my husband again.*

A wave of dizziness caught her unaware and she grabbed the bed's railings to steady herself. Moments later, disoriented and sick to her stomach, she sat on the edge of the bed and waited for the world to stop spinning. All the stress had frayed her nerves and made her ill.

A loud knock came from downstairs. Sarah froze. She didn't want to talk to anyone, not even Marta, but knew she'd have to see her before she left. There were others in the community she'd miss, too. Her distant family members, her old schoolteacher, the friendly *Englisch* woman at the sewing store…all the people who meant everything to her. They'd wonder what really had happened, why she suddenly had disappeared, but she knew someone would tell them what she'd done. Her head dropped. A wave of nausea rolled her stomach, twisting it in knots.

The knock became louder, more insistent. She moved to the bedroom window. No buggy was parked out front. Perhaps one of the neighborhood *kinder* was playing a joke on her. She checked the front steps and saw the broad frame of a man. Had her father come to give her one last stab to the heart? It would be just like him to come and taunt her about her coming marriage to Mose.

"Sarah? Are you there? Please let me in."

Mose's voice called from her doorstep. He sounded concerned, perhaps even alarmed. Had something happened to one of the *kinder*?

Why would he seek her out? He'd heard it all. He was an elder in his community. Even if he wasn't Old Order Amish and didn't live as strict a life as she did, but he'd be angry she'd given the boys money and would judge her. Still, he was a good man, a kind man. Perhaps he just wanted to talk to her.

The thought of his kindness had her rushing down the stairs and opening the heavy wood door Joseph had made with his own hands. She used the door as a shield, opening it just a crack. *"Ya?"* She could see a slice of him, his hair wind-blown, blue eyes searching her face.

"Hello, Sarah. I thought I might find you here."

She nodded her head in greeting.

"Are you all right?" Mose's hand rested on the doorjamb, as if he expected to be let into the house.

Sarah held the door firm. "I'm fine. What do you want, Mose? I have things to do. I'm very busy."

"I'm worried about you. You've been through so much."

"And none of it is your business," Sarah snapped, instantly wishing she could take back her bitter words. He'd done nothing but be kind to her. She missed the girls and wondered how they were, if Marta was still caring for them.

She pushed strands of hair out of her eyes and searched his expression. She saw no signs of judgment.

"You're right. All this is none of my business, but I am soon to be your husband. I want to help, if I can. Please, can I come in for a moment?"

On trembling legs, she stepped back to open the door all the way. "Come in."

Mose stepped past Sarah into the silent house. Sarah glanced around. Nothing seemed out of place. There was no dust, no evidence anyone even lived here.

He turned back to Sarah. "I tried to find you after everyone left yesterday. Beatrice was asking for you. *Kinder* don't understand why adults do what they do."

"I did what everyone is saying," Sarah blurted out, then offered a seat to Mose, but stood, swaying to and fro.

"Sit with me before you fall, you stubborn woman." Mose took Sarah's elbow, guided her to a wood-framed rocking chair with a padded seat and back rest. She didn't resist, but once down, her fingers went white-knuckled on the chair's arms.

Mose sat on the couch opposite her. "You said there was no misunderstanding. Did you give the boy money so he and his brother could leave the community as the bishop said?"

"*Ya*. I did."

"Why did you help them? They have a father who's very worried about them," Mose said.

"I'm sure he is concerned. He needs their strong backs to run his farm. They're better off away from him." Sarah stared into space, her features ridged, unrelenting.

"You've heard from them?"

She looked at him. "*Ya*, I did. They're staying with their sister, Katherine, in Missouri. She took them in after..." Her voice trailed off.

"After what, Sarah?" Emotions played on her face. Something was not being said. Mose felt sure she'd acted out of kindness. He hadn't known her long but felt sure she wasn't the type to interfere in other people's business, especially to separate a family.

Sarah drew in a ragged breath. "After the boy's father beat Lukas until he could barely move, that's what. His *bruder*, Ben, was getting older and had begun to talk back to his father, too. Lukas knew it was only a matter of time before his *daed* would use the strap on him. Lukas asked me to help them get away. I knew the boy was telling the truth about the risks of more violent beatings. They were in danger.

"Lukas's father is a harsh man and had

taken to drink. He took his anger out on his sons when the crops failed or something went wrong. Lukas had made the mistake of asking to go on *rumspringa* with some of his friends in the next community, and his father had flown into a rage. This beating wasn't the first Lukas had endured, but it was the worst. He was often whipped with a cane. I could hear his cries for mercy blowing across the field that separates our land. Joseph and I had often prayed for the boys, asking *Gott* for a hedge of protection." Sarah swallowed hard and went on. "Joseph wouldn't stand for the whippings and had warned the father, even threatened to talk to Bishop Miller about the situation…but after Joseph died, the beatings began again."

Mose reached across and took one of Sarah's hands and squeezed. Her fingers were cold and stiff. "Does Bishop Miller know all this?"

Sarah jerked her hand back. "I tried to tell him many times, but he told me to keep my nose out of other people's business. He said men were supposed to discipline their *kinder*, but this wasn't discipline, Mose. This was pure abuse." Sarah pushed back her hair and gasped. "Oh, I'm sorry. I didn't realize my *kapp* was missing. It must have fallen off when I…" Her head dropped and she sat perfectly still.

"When you what, Sarah?"

"I almost fainted. I've been ill and forgot to eat this morning."

"You need to be in bed with someone taking care of you."

"*Nee*, that's not possible. The Bishop's called a meeting. I decided I must be there to defend my actions. I have to at least try."

Mose watched her as she spoke. He could see she was terrified of being shunned. Who wouldn't be? As strict as Bishop Miller was, anything was possible, including shunning. "I could speak to the Bishop and the elders and see if—"

"*Nee, danke* for offering, but I'd rather you didn't."

"He may still declare you shunned, even if we marry and you leave the community."

She paled a chalky white. "But...I thought if I left, all that could be avoided."

"*Nee*. I don't think he's feeling generous, but I could be wrong."

"Then shunned it is. I'll have to learn to live with it, though I don't know how."

Mose leaned forward, their gaze connecting. He meant it when he'd promised security, strength. Things she no longer had. "Don't fret, Sarah. *Gott* will make a way."

Sarah checked the position of her *kapp* and dreaded the thought of what was about to take place this evening. Mose sat tall and straight, his hands folded in his lap, the picture of calm. She wished she had his determination. She was too emotional lately. Everything seemed so hard, as though she was climbing a hill, her feet sliding out from under her in slippery mud.

The moments ticked by. The room darkened as dusk surrendered to the shadows of night.

The heavy door to the bishop's chambers opened with a squeak. Sarah jumped.

Mose stood, pulling her up off the chair as he took his first step forward. She hesitated. He turned back to her. "All will be well, Sarah. Leave it to me. I will be your strength."

She knew the bishop. Doubt flooded in. She tried to clear her thoughts and prepare herself for the ugly confrontation.

An old wood table with chairs all around filled the small, stifling room. "Sit here, Sarah, and you there, Mose," Karl Yoder prompted, motioning to two empty chairs positioned at the middle of the table. The position would place them directly across from Bishop Miller. The elder walked with them toward their chairs. A distant cousin, she'd known Karl all her life. He'd been Sarah's favorite church leader growing up. She'd gone to him and his wife when life had gotten to be more than she could bear as a teenager. She wondered what he thought of her now. He looked stern, but flashed a smile, giving her hope.

Hands were extended to Mose as he greeted each man. He introduced himself to those who didn't know him. Sarah counted six men at the table. Sneaking a glance at Bishop Miller, she saw his jaw tighten. Just for a second their eyes met and she quickly looked away, only to notice her father sitting bent over in the corner of the room. She averted her gaze and looked down at the floor. Her hands gripped in a knot on her lap. She waited. Mose cleared his throat, the only nervous sound he'd made since they'd come into the room.

Ernst Miller, the bishop's son, stood. "This meeting is called to discuss the matter of Sarah Nolt."

Off to the side, Sarah's father rose, almost knocking over his seat. He blurted out, "I want to know why Mose Fischer is allowed to sit in on this meeting? He's not a member of our community. What's going on today has nothing to do with him."

"All will be explained in good time," Ernst

assured him and motioned for Adolph to take his seat.

The high color in her father's cheeks told her he was in a fine temper and nothing they said would keep him calm.

"As I was saying," Ernst continued, his tone holding a slight edge. "We are here to discuss the recent actions of Sarah Nolt." His gaze drifted to Sarah.

She looked directly in his eyes. *Don't let him ask me about the beatings.* She had enough problems without stirring up a hornet's nest of accusations against her neighbor, accusations she couldn't prove.

"How well did you know Lukas and Benjamin Hochstetler?"

"Not well," she replied. "I knew they lived at the farm next to ours. They moved in several weeks after Joseph and I married." Bringing up Joseph's name set her heart pounding. She paused for a few seconds and then continued, "I used to take the boys drinks of cool water on hot afternoons when they'd plowed the field closest to our home."

"So you did get to know them well?" Ernst asked.

"Not really. They were always busy about the farm and I seldom left the house, so that didn't leave much time for socializing."

"But you spoke to them from time to time?"

"Yes, I did. I liked the boys. They were lonely, hardworking *kinder* and seldom saw people other than their fa—"

"How did you hear they had run away and ended up in Missouri?" The bishop spoke up, stepping on her last word. Ernst sat down, content to let his father continue.

Sarah pulled her feet under her skirt. *How do I answer this without digging up more dirt?* "I received a letter."

"A letter from Lukas?"

"*Nee.* The letter was from Benjamin."

The Bishop's voice rose. "Not from Lukas?"

"*Nee.*" Sarah shook her head.

Bishop Miller leaned forward on his elbows. "What did the letter say?"

Sarah couldn't help but smile, remembering Benjamin's barely legible scrawl. The note told about the joy he felt with his sister's family. "He said they had arrived in Missouri and that their sister was happy to see them."

"Did you know they were going to Missouri?"

"*Nee.* I didn't." Sarah was glad she could answer with honesty. Lukas had never told her their destination, only that family wanted them.

A man, someone Sarah was unfamiliar with,

leaned over to the Bishop and spoke quietly in his ear. The man spoke at length. Each word seemed to last an eternity. Finally the man sat and Bishop Miller continued.

"Sarah Nolt. Did you give money to Lukas, knowing he planned to use the funds to leave this community?"

Sarah swallowed hard, preparing herself for what was to come. The truth had to come out, whatever the cost. "*Ya*, I did."

Loud conversation broke out amongst the men. Bishop Miller slammed his fist on the wood table to regain control of the room.

"You know what you're admitting to, what the consequences could be?"

Mose stood, surprising Sarah. "The only thing she's admitting to is helping the boys out of a life-threatening situation, nothing more. In all fairness, I think this question should be asked." He turned to her. "Sarah, why did you help the boys?"

The same poker-faced man leaned over and spoke to the Bishop again. A quiet barrage of words went back and forth before the question was asked by the bishop. "Why did you feel it necessary to help the boys, Sarah?"

The loud heartbeats in her ears made it hard for her to hear his question. She looked at Mose and he nodded, encouraging her to tell them her story. "Joseph and I made it a habit to sit out on the porch swing each evening. Right after the Hochstetler family moved into the old farm across the field, we often heard the sound of a child crying and a man yelling in anger. More than once Joseph hurried over to the farm and would come back red-faced with frustration. He wouldn't tell me what happened, but the child's crying always stopped."

"Did you ever ask Lukas about these times?" The man sitting next to the Bishop asked this question.

Sarah pulled on one of the strings to her prayer *kapp*, working out how she could speak without some kind of proof. "He told me his father often whipped him with a strap."

The bishop stood. "We spoke of this before, Sarah. You were told to stay out of this family's business. I spoke to the father myself. He said the older boy was rebellious and had to have these whippings as a form of correction."

Sarah looked up, holding Bishop Miller's gaze. "Did he tell you he beat Lukas so badly the child couldn't walk for a time? Or about the scars on the child's back from being whipped with a buggy whip? Would you have whipped your son in this manner, I wonder? Would you lock him up in a chicken coop for a week with nothing to eat but raw eggs?"

"*Kinder* are prone to lie, Sarah. We all know the problem you had with lying as a teen."

The bishop's voice cut into her like a knife. She'd cried out for help as a child, but no one had taken notice of her father's cruelty.

"I did not lie as a child, and I do not lie now. It's all true. I have no proof, but I have the satisfaction of knowing I helped rescue those boys from an abusive father, someone Joseph kept in line until his death."

Her father was out of his chair and leaning over Sarah in seconds. "Do you accuse me of abuse, too?" Fury cut hard edges into his face.

Mose rose and stood next to Sarah. "This is not the time to—"

"This is the perfect time to bring up this girl's past." Adolph bent low, shaking his finger in Sarah's face. "This is all a lie, isn't it, Sarah? A lie about me and a lie about the reason you sent the boys away."

Sarah took in a deep gulp of air, stood and prepared for the worst. "I did not lie about you. You *are* cruel, Father." She faced him. Her heart hammered.

"I've lived this lie long enough. It is time for all to be made clear," Adolph yelled at the bishop.

Bishop Miller jumped to his feet and walked

toward Adolph. "This is not the time or place, *Herr* Yoder."

"It is the perfect time, Ralf. I will not be silent and have my good name tainted by this girl. She is no longer my responsibility and I want no further contact with her. She brings back painful memories, memories I need to forget."

"Years ago we agreed—"

"You told me what I had to do, and I did it. But I will not be held responsible any longer. I have done my share of giving to this community when I married her mother, that pregnant Amish woman."

Sarah's body shook with cold. Blood drained from her face. "What are you saying, *Daed*?"

"Don't call me *daed* again, Sarah Nolt. I am not your father. Your father was an *Englisch* drunk."

The small room seemed to close in around Sarah. Everyone went silent. Their gazes shifted from Sarah to Adolph. Her father's hands clenched into fists. "I will not be shunned because of you, do you hear me, woman?" His balled fist pounded the table, startling everyone. "I did nothing but try to help a stranger in our midst, an Amish girl who was pregnant and desperate."

An ugly smirk grew on his face, narrowing

his eyes and slashing his mouth. "The thanks I got for all my kindness was a spoiled *kinder* and a lying witch of a wife who finally ran off with the same *Englisch* drunk who got her pregnant."

He leaned in, his hands palm down on the table, facing Sarah. "You are their bastard child. I don't guess you knew that, did you? I raised you as my own, but no more. You've broken too many *Ordnung* rules and deserve to be shunned. I will not have my family's name besmirched by your actions."

Sarah stood, her legs trembling out of control.

Adolph began to pace the room. "Eric is my son, my blood. He makes me proud. But you!" He turned, his bony finger pointing at her. "You bring me nothing but shame. You are not my daughter by blood and the bishop knows it." He moved toward Bishop Miller's chair and stared directly at him. "You know I'm telling the truth. Tell her." He turned back to Sarah. "You must go. Now."

Mose caught Sarah around the waist as she swayed.

"Come. Let me help you to the chair." He propped her limp body against his. She groaned. He looked up, his eyes sparking fire at Adolph Yoder. "You're an evil, cruel old man. You don't deserve a daughter as fine and loving as Sarah. All you know is hatred and cruelty. *You* should be banned from this community, not this tenderhearted girl." He looked down at Sarah's bowed head and wished he could strike the man who'd made her like this. He believed problems could be fixed with prayer and conversation, not violence. But today he yearned for a physical release to his anger. He wanted to physically hurt him until Sarah's pain ended.

Bishop Miller and the community elders stood, their chairs scraping back as they faced Adolph. "There was no need for this, Adolph. I would never have let you come to the meeting if I'd known you would act in this manner," Bishop Miller said. "*Herr* Stoltzfus, go find Eric and tell him to come collect his father. We no longer have need of him at this meeting."

"You can't do that," Adolph blurted out. "I only said what was true." He glared at Sarah. "She's been nothing but trouble, that girl. I'm innocent of any wrongdoing. You all know I am. Everyone here knows who she really is, what she's done. I'll share none of the blame for her actions. Eric and I want nothing to do with her any longer. You must…"

"*Nee*, Adolph. I think you are mistaken. I do *not* have to listen to you." Red-faced, Bishop

Miller spat out his words. "I want you out of this room and gone from my home."

"But…"

"You will leave or be shunned today. Do I make myself clear?" He sat and began to write in a ledger. "I declare there will be no shunning for Sarah Nolt this day, but she must leave the community as soon as possible. What she did was wrong, even if her actions were prompted by her love for these *kinder*. I should have listened to her when she came to me with her story. All of this could have been avoided."

Sarah lifted her head, shocked the bishop would admit fault of any kind. Tears cascaded down her pale face. Her voice shook as she spoke. "I wish no harm to come to my…to Adolph Yoder. Mose and I will leave here as soon as we are married. I hope to be allowed back into the community to see my brother and his wife sometime in the future, if you will allow it."

The bishop laid down his pen. "You can come back from time to time, Sarah, but you'll be watched closely. Your actions were just too foolhardy to be swept away. Mose has informed us of your engagement. I'll arrange for one of the preachers to marry you before you go, but only because of my love and respect for his father and family."

Sarah rose from her chair. *"Danke,"* she murmured, swaying. She avoided looking into the bishop's eyes. Mose grabbed her hand and assisted her across the room and then quietly shut the door behind them.

# Chapter Five

The freshly pressed blue cotton wedding dress hung on a plain wire hanger. Sarah put the still warm iron on the woodstove's burner and shoved the padded wooden clothes press back under the sink.

She took a glass from the kitchen cupboard Joseph had made and filled it with water. Tired beyond words, she pulled out a kitchen chair and sat. Her trembling hands covered her face. Warm tears slipped through her fingers. She would be married just hours from now. She'd prepare the same meal she'd cooked for Joseph on their wedding day and wear the same wedding dress she'd sewn for their special day. It was tradition.

Memories flooded in, choking her throat closed. Joseph had looked so handsome in his black suit and white shirt the afternoon they'd married. That bright morning all those months ago, she'd cooked several dishes for their wedding meal. Her heart light, singing old gospel songs, she'd hurried through the preparation.

The meal prepared, she'd dressed with care and anticipation. She'd slipped her homemade blue wedding dress over her head just moments before he'd rung the doorbell. Joseph had arrived with flowers picked from the field behind her father's farmhouse. Laughter and joy had filled the house as they'd eaten together. Later many people had come and filled the house with more love than she'd ever dreamed possible.

Marta's hand on Sarah's arm jerked her from her memories.

"I'm sorry, Sarah, but it's time. It's almost seven and we have to meet Eric for the wedding." She looked into Sarah's eyes. "You need to wash your face and remove all traces of red from your eyes. I know all this has been hard on you. I don't know how you can marry a man you don't love, but then I've not walked in your shoes. We all survive *Gott's* will the best we can."

Marta helped Sarah prepare, pulling her wedding dress over her head and letting the fabric settle around her hips.

"There, just right." Marta gave an appreciative sigh, adjusted the garment here and there and smiled. "I was worried the dress would be too small for you since you put on some needed weight. Thank *Gott* you did. You'd gotten so thin after—"

"After Joseph died?" Sarah finished for her.

"Well, yes…but you're back to your normal weight now and look *wunderbaar*. I'm so glad this day has finally arrived. I've been concerned for you for so many months."

"I've had to force myself to eat. Joseph would want me strong and living life to the fullest."

"But today is not about Joseph. This is Mose's day and you must put your memories of Joseph away now. He is gone. The grave is—"

"Closed. Yes, I know." She'd heard the phrase a hundred times, knew it was true, but somehow she couldn't put the memories of Joseph away, like he'd never existed. "Yes, I know better than anyone the grave is closed."

Marta sighed. "I don't mean to be cruel, but you must find a way to release Joseph. This marriage to Mose is for the rest of your life. If you don't settle these feelings for Joseph, you'll grieve yourself to death."

Sarah hugged Marta, something frowned on by her Old Order Amish community, but often shared by the two friends. She appreciated how hard it must be for Marta to say all these things about Joseph, her own dead brother. She'd loved him without limit. Somehow she'd found a way to release him to *Gott*. Sarah knew she had to find a way to do the same.

Forcing a smile, she rested her hands on Marta's tiny shoulders. "I'll get through this day and all the days to come. Mose has been so kind to me, so understanding. He deserves a wife who loves him. I will be true to *Gott's* plan and be the best wife I can be." Sarah took a deep breath and pushed it out. "Now, let's get this dress hooked up and go downstairs. We shouldn't keep Mose waiting any longer."

They worked the back hooks of the dress up together, Sarah twisting and turning, trying her best to close them at her waistline. "They just won't close here," she said, and they both laughed. "I guess I've gained more weight than I thought."

"Don't fret," Marta smacked away Sarah's scrambling fingers. "Your apron will hide the gap. No one will notice."

The dark mood lifted; both women smiled as Marta began to work on Sarah's long hair. "Your *kapp* must be perfectly placed. Every old woman at the service will be gauging and measuring."

Sarah looked into the mirror and wished the dark circles under her eyes would go away. "Will people come to the wedding?" Sarah wrung her hands.

"Oh, some will come out of morbid curiosity, some to mutter and make harsh comments, but the rest will be here for you because they love you. You must be prepared for what some might say and ignore them." She beamed at Sarah. "Now we talk only about good things, like how beautiful you look."

"Do you think Mose will approve of my dress? He may be used to finer things." Sarah fiddled with the waistband of her apron. *Please, don't let anyone notice my weight gain, Gott.*

"I think he'll be too busy being nervous to notice the shadows under those beautiful eyes of yours. Now, let's get going before Eric comes up to drag us to the house. It's good the service was allowed to be held at our home," Marta said. "Just remember the important people in your life will be there, and that's what matters."

"I need to pray," Sarah insisted, remembering the promise she'd made to *Gott*. She would put all she was into this new marriage. Mose deserved her loyalty and she had every intention of giving it to him.

They bowed their heads in reverence. Sarah closed her eyes. *Lord*, Gott, *please bless this union. It might be wrong to marry without love, but Mose and I need each other. Pour your favor on the wedding guests and bless the meal afterward. Give us your approval today. Help me get over this draining virus. I need to be strong for the girls as we travel to Florida. Help me to be a good mamm to the kinder and an acceptable wife for Mose Fischer. Amen.*

"You look radiant." Marta stood just behind Sarah and adjusted the back of the prayer *kapp*, making the placement perfect. "I've asked a few of the women to take the baby up to the bedroom if she fusses, and Beatrice has been warned to be quiet, or she'll find herself in bed with her sister."

Lingering for a moment, Sarah breathed deeply. Marta finally put her hands on Sarah's back and pushed her toward the door.

They walked slowly down the stairs and into the great room, where benches were lined up in rows. The sound of the back door shutting told her people were still arriving. She looked around and smiled at the sight of Beatrice sitting at the back. Mercy sat on the lap of one of Sarah's cousins. The little girl chewed on a toy. She took in their freshly washed appearance and plain dresses and smiled. These little girls would soon be her daughters. Her forced smile warmed to a happy grin.

She turned toward Mose. He looked handsome in his borrowed black suit and newly purchased white wedding shirt. She watched with pride as he walked in her direction. He moved with purpose, his demeanor calm, so different from her high-spirited Joseph the day they had wed. She knew so little about Mose Fischer, the man who would become her husband in a matter of minutes. He walked up to her and she suddenly felt shy and as tonguetied as a young, innocent girl. "You look very handsome."

"So do you," Mose said, then quickly corrected himself. "I didn't mean to imply you looked handsome. What I meant is, you look exceptionally beautiful tonight." He laughed, but the sound came out edged with nerves. Perhaps he'd been thinking similar thoughts, that they barely knew each other. She accepted Mose's outstretched arm and let him lead her toward the back of the room.

A handful of people sat scattered around the room, somber-looking men on one side and their wives, most busy with restless schoolage *kinder*, on the other.

Someone cleared his voice and Sarah jumped. Ruben Yoder, her distant cousin, came out of the room off to the left and stood at the front of the room, prepared to sing. In a fine tenor voice, he sang a single verse of an ancient song of praise, one she'd never heard before. The congregation sang seven stanzas of another old song from the Ausband. Sarah joined in, listening to Mose's voice for the first time.

Several songs later, *Herr* Miller, the bishop's son, stood and recited Genesis 2:18 from the King James Bible.

The hour of songs and scripture verses seemed to go on and on. Out of the corner of her eye, she saw Beatrice being led out of the room and through the kitchen door. The child had done well, waiting all this time for something interesting to happen before being sent away.

Bishop Miller came into the room, her brother, Eric, following behind him. Several of the other ordained preachers lined up. As Eric moved to take the song leader's place at the front, Sarah realized her brother would be performing the wedding service and not the Bishop. Eric had been elected as one of the community's new preachers a few weeks ago and she was so pleased she and Mose would be married by him.

Bishop Miller settled in a chair behind Eric. He flashed Sarah a glance. Sarah felt Mose take her hand and squeeze hard, sending a silent message of reassurance. His hand felt warm, the rough calluses on the palm reminding her how hard he'd worked with the men to tear down the old barn and rebuild the new one in just a matter of days. She linked her fingers with his.

Sarah looked at her hand entwined with Mose's tanned fingers. Her pale skin looked so different from his brown skin. They were about to become united in the holy bonds of marriage and she didn't even know his favorite color or what foods he liked to eat. Feeling eyes on her, she glanced up and met his gaze. The iris of his eyes had gone a deep blue with emotion. He was taking this marriage ceremony seriously, and she had to do the same. She respected him beyond measure, but love? A new feeling stirred in her heart. Friendship could grow into love, could it not?

Mose stood and walked to the end of the bench. Sarah rose and stood by his side. Hand-in-hand they walked to the front of the room. Marta met her there and Mose's cousin, Eli Fischer, stood beside him.

Sarah watched her brother's mouth move as he spoke words over them, but had no idea what he said. In her mind she was standing with Joseph, answering the hard questions the pastors and deacons had asked about their loyalty and love for one another. She would answer as if responding to them. She pulled herself from her dream-like state and heard Mose speak.

"I will love Sarah with all my heart and give her my respect and loyalty until the day I die."

Eric turned her way, his face formal. His eyes met hers. "Will you be loyal to Mose and lean only on him for the rest of your life?"

Sarah turned toward Mose and held his eyes. "I will be loyal to you in all ways and let my love for you grow until my dying day."

Sarah brother's hand encompassed theirs. "The mercy of God and His blessings be on you today, and every day hence. Leave us now in the name of the Lord. I declare you now man and wife. What *Gott* has put together, let no man put asunder."

In a traditional wedding service, songs would have been sung now, but their marriage was anything but traditional. Months ago she'd been given the name Sarah Nolt. Now she would be known as Sarah Fischer. The name sounded strange to her, almost foreign.

They left the room and headed out into the dreary day. A strong wind blew and Sarah shivered. She tried to be excited for Mose's sake. He was a generous man, had rescued her.

Thanks to him she could still be connected to her brother, Eric, and sister-in-law, Marta. She was the new bride of Mose Fischer, a fine man in good standing in his community. She'd have two beautiful daughters to care for and love. She turned to Mose and excused herself, a forced smile spread across her face. She should be happy, but she wasn't. Joseph's memory was always there. Memories of what she'd done and how he'd died. "I'll be right back and meet you in the kitchen, just before the meal."

Well-wishers interrupted her walk up the stairs several times, but she finally made it to the room and fell across the bed, her pent-up tears releasing.

Moments later, Marta rushed into the room, sat on the edge of the quilt-covered bed and took Sarah's hand in hers. "You didn't answer the door when I knocked."

Sarah wiped her tears away and forced a smile. "I'm sorry."

"Do you want to be left alone? I can come back in a bit and help you prepare for your trip."

"*Nee*, there's no need for you to leave. It's time I pull myself together and rejoin my guests, eat and say goodbye. Beatrice and the baby should be awakened. They will need to eat before we go."

"That's why I came in. Mercy's just up from her nap. Mose said to tell you he'd be back in a few minutes. He's got a surprise for you and seems very excited."

Sarah sighed. "He's been nothing but wonderful. I don't know what I would have done without him. He deserves so much better than me."

"*Ach*, I will not listen to such foolishness." Marta hugged her. "He is a fine man, I'll give you that. But you're a wonderful woman and will make him a great wife and mother for the girls."

"I pray you're right," Sarah said. "Where are the girls? Did Mose take them with him?"

"Beatrice insisted she be allowed to go. Seems she's been told about his surprise and can't wait to…"

Sarah grinned. Marta never could keep a secret. "She can't wait to what?"

Marta changed the subject abruptly. "I'll miss you when you're in Florida."

"I know, but its best we leave as soon as possible. My fath—" Sarah paused and corrected herself "—*Adolph's* inappropriate behavior played a large part in the Bishop's decision not to shun me. I don't want to risk him changing his mind at the last moment."

Not wanting to think about it anymore, she

changed the subject. "Mose says his community is strict, but not old-fashioned. Gas and electric lights are allowed in the houses there and some carry cell phones for their businesses. I'm extra thrilled because I've heard women can own sewing machines, and you know I want one so bad."

"That's the brightest light I've seen in your eyes in a long time. I'm so excited for you. Who knows? Maybe Eric and I will head south and someday you'll find us on your doorstep."

Sarah laughed. It felt good to feel joy. "It would be wonderful if you did, but Eric will never leave his *daed.*"

Sounds of the screen door slamming shut brought Marta to her feet. "You'll be needed in the great room. I have a feeling Beatrice is holding her breath until you get there.

"You're probably right." Sarah hurried down the stairs, toward the sounds of a giggling child.

"Sarah, come see," Beatrice called out just as Sarah walked past the front door and into the great room. Mose stood in the middle of the room, a huge bouquet of beautiful wildflowers in his hands.

"For my bride," Mose said.

Sarah wilted to the floor in a faint.

# Chapter Six

"She's coming round." Marta sounded so far away.

Wisps of fog swirled and blurred Sarah's vision. Confusion rattled her thoughts, making her stomach clench with fear. *Where was she? What had happened?* She reached out a hand. She was lying on the braided rug she'd made months ago.

Something touched the side of her face. She opened her eyes and a man's face came into focus. Mose. He leaned over her, his brow knitted close together.

"Sarah, are you all right?"

She lifted her head and stared into his sky-blue gaze. Mose made her feel safe again. "Yes, I'm fine." But she wasn't. Dizzy spells had plagued her for days.

"She's been looking pale, Mose. She must

be completely stressed out, and she's not eating regularly." Marta spoke from somewhere behind Mose.

He pushed a lock of hair back from her forehead. "Do you hurt anywhere?"

"*Nee*. I don't think so." Mustering all her strength she leaned on her arm and made an effort to get up, still muddle-brained.

Mose slipped his arm around her waist and eased her into a sitting position. "Don't move. Not until we know you're okay. You might have broken something when you fell."

"I'm fine. I don't feel dizzy. Everything just went a bit hazy for a moment, that's all. My stomach's been upset. It's stress, no doubt." Mose had shocked her, his tall frame standing in the great room, his hands full of wildflowers. For a moment he'd looked so much like Joseph.

Mose took the glass of water Marta handed him and placed it against Sarah's lips. "Drink this. It'll make you feel better."

She sipped and then quickly drank down the whole glass.

"You need to sit for a while until the dizziness passes." Mose put his hand on her shoulder. "When was the last time you had a proper meal?"

"I think it was yesterday, but I can't be sure. So much has been going on."

"You've been through a lot. It's no wonder you fainted."

"I'm fine now, Mose. Really." Determination had her pushing up off the floor with Mose's help. Sarah stood and found her footing.

Mose helped her into a chair. "I think a meal is in order, don't you?"

Sarah nodded and glanced around the room. Wildflowers lay strewn across the wide-plank wood floor. Forgotten, Beatrice stood ankle deep in the pile of stems and blooms, her tiny black shoes peeking out. She seemed frozen in time, her face a mask of horror, eyes wide. Tears streamed down her pale cheeks. Sarah made eye contact and Beatrice flew across the room, into her waiting arms, her eyes still rounded with fear. She leaned in and rested her head on Sarah's shoulder. Beatrice's hand patted her softly. In a rhythmic tattoo, she whispered, "You won't die. You'll be all better. *Gott* has made you my new *mamm*."

Marta hovered close. "Why don't I go get you something to eat from the meal outside? It will only take a minute."

Mose spoke before Sarah could respond. "That sounds like a good idea. Beatrice, why don't you go with Marta and make sure she gets Sarah some of her favorite sour pickles. You know how they help sick stomachs."

Pried out of Sarah's arms and led to the kitchen, the little girl shouted over Marta's shoulder, "*Nee*! Sarah needs me."

Sarah took in a deep breath and found a smile. "I'd love a plate of hot food, but only if you fix it for me." The child grinned as Marta carried her away.

"You looked like you needed a moment to regain your composure." Mose smiled, one tiny dimple showing in his right cheek.

"I did." Sarah nervously rubbed the soft fabric covering the padded chair. "It was the oddest thing, Mose. One minute I was fine, the next I was falling flat on my face. But I feel fine now, like nothing happened."

"You can't skip meals and expect to remain healthy. You have two small *kinder* depending on you now, and we have a long trip ahead of us. The girls can run healthy women into the ground." He laughed, a twinkle in his eye.

"I know. I don't know what I was thinking. It was very foolish of me."

Mose bent on one knee in front of her. "*Nee*, not even the strongest person can experience the tragedies you've gone through and come out unscathed. Together we'll work our way through this."

"But your reputation will be sullied by our quick marriage."

"You're not to fret. I'm your husband now. You're my wife and the mother of my *kinder*. I will always be here for you. Joseph would have wanted it this way. I feel honored to have you as my wife." He smiled so tenderly Sarah almost broke down. Her lip quivered as she took the rough hand he held out to her. She grasped it, their fingers entwined. Time stopped and Sarah's heart beat a bit faster. "Nothing will come between us." Mose promised. "You'll see."

Sarah looked completely over her illness after eating, but he could sense her nervousness. Mose knew Sarah had never been in an automobile, much less on a train. The black machine had to appear imposing and impossibly large to her. She might be frightened and rethinking the wisdom of going to Florida inside such a massive contraption. At least the *kinder* had experienced the train ride up to Lancaster County and seemed calm and ready for travel.

He was glad the tiny wedding party had piled into Eric's old hay wagon and the few well-wishers had been able to wave them off just blocks from the train station.

"How much time do we have, Mose?" Sarah's white-knuckled grasp on her suitcase showed she was frightened.

"We'll be boarding in a few minutes. You

have time to say your goodbyes." He held Beatrice tight by one hand. Mercy was cradled in a warm blanket in his other arm. He watched as Sarah wrapped her arms first around Marta and then Eric. She clung to her brother for a moment, her tears flowing freely. He saw her whisper something to Marta, which made them both laugh.

"*Ya*, we will be coming to see you. Maybe in the fall, I think. When life has settled down after harvest." Marta grabbed Sarah close once more. Eric joined the hug and the three stood as one, whispering words of love to each other.

Mose shifted the baby to his shoulder. "I hate to tell you, but the train will be leaving soon. We should get settled."

Sarah broke away and scooped Mercy out of Mose's arms, allowing Beatrice to grab hold of her skirt. The two men hugged. "*Gott* be with you and keep you. Make my sister happy and bring her peace or I'll come find you," Eric said with a smile.

Mose's big palm slapped Eric on the back. "May *Gott* bring a *bobbel* into your household. May he prosper you and bring you joy."

Marta and Sarah laughed as the two grown men shed tears, their own eyes red and glistening.

Mose set down his case, then added Sarah's

smaller valise, which weighed next to nothing in his hand.

Eric gave one last hug to his sister and then looked straight into her eyes. "We are brother and sister. We will always be connected by blood. If you need me, you know where I am. You are a wonderful sister. I was lucky to have you close by my side."

Sarah's face grew red, fresh tears slipping down her cheeks. "You are my blessed brother."

Beatrice pulled at Sarah's skirt. "Hurry, Sarah. We don't want to miss the train."

Mose saw Sarah smile sweetly at his daughter.

"Yes, *liebling*. Our new life awaits us."


"I'm tired, *Daed*. Hold me," Beatrice whined, reaching her arms out to Mose for comfort.

"Would you hold Mercy while I see to Beatrice?" Mose offered the baby up to Sarah.

"The poor *liebling* is one tired little girl." Sarah took Mercy and cuddled the baby's small, warm body close to her own quick-beating heart and breathed in the sweet smell of her neck. The child stirred and Sarah adjusted her blanket, covering her cold legs. Sarah cooed in the baby's ear, comforting her with a rhythmic backrub until the child slept. She'd been taking care of Mose's *kinder* only a short time but already the weight of the baby in her arms seemed perfectly normal, as if she'd been the child's mother since birth.

Mose shifted an already sleeping Beatrice to his shoulder. "I think we board the train down this way."

Sarah hurried past a young *Englisch* couple and saw them exchange a look. She'd seen that glance before. She was too tired to give it more than a passing thought. Moving about in the *Englisch* world always brought out the worst in her. She hated feeling odd, like she was a freak show put on just for them. Their clothes were odd to her, too. She gave a disapproving glare to the woman's short denim skirt that showed off more of her legs than Sarah deemed respectful. Had Mose averted his eyes as this woman passed, or had he admired the beauty of her youthful body?

With nervous fingers she set her *kapp* on straight and determined to ignore the looks and laughter coming from the *Englisch* couple. She patted Mercy on the back, her walk brisk, her gaze on Mose's strong back just inches away.

Mose slowed, ushering her toward a door on the side of the train. The immense size of the metal monster gave her pause and she stopped for a second, her fear so great she considered running in the opposite direction. Then she stepped up into the train, and her fear gave way to determination. She would make a fresh start with Mose and the *kinder*. No matter what.

They switched trains in Philadelphia taking one heading south. To their delight, both *kinder* fell asleep before lunch. An hour later Mose opened one eye and watched as Beatrice tried to climb over his body without waking him. "Where do you think you're going, young lady?"

"I'm going with Sarah and Mercy," she said in a sleepy voice, her small fists rubbing sleep from her eyes.

The seat next to him was empty and the diaper bag gone. "I have a feeling your sister needed a change of clothes and a fresh diaper. Sarah will be right back, if you wait just a moment."

Beatrice bounced up and down on the empty seat. She frowned at him. "I have to go to the bathroom." She began to grimace, a look of strain on her face. Mose lost no time grabbing her up and hurrying her down to the nearest ladies' room. He knocked once and then knocked again. Beatrice's squirms became wild and insistent.

Mose knocked again on the bathroom door. "Sarah. I know you're busy in there with Mercy, but Beatrice seems to be in a real hurry. Do you think you could…?"

The door slid open just a crack and a clear-eyed Sarah greeted him with a shy smile. "Come in, Beatrice," she said, but only opened the door wide enough for the child to slip through. Mercy smiled at her father, her naked little body squirming in Sarah's arms. "We had a bit of a wet diaper situation and her bottle didn't stay down, but she seems fine now."

"Why don't I wait here for Beatrice? You can send her out to me when she's finished."

It struck Mose how formal they still were with each other. Almost strangers…but then, they *were* strangers…married strangers. Time would take care of the formality between them over the *kinder*, but what about their relationship? Hadn't he noticed signs of genuine regard from Sarah already? They were growing closer and one day might fall in love.

Sarah was a spirited woman, the type of person he could be drawn to in a powerful way, like he had been with Greta. Would Sarah ever get over her guilt, the love she felt for her dead husband? He wanted to care for this woman standing just inches away. She deserved love. Would *Gott* bless their marriage? *Gott's* will be done.

# *Chapter Seven*

Sarah stood behind Mose as he approached the dining car and pulled open the heavy door. *Englisch* filled the plush car. Their lively chatter and robust laughter engulfed the narrow hall where she waited. Her experience with mealtime had always been one of quiet conversation and hadn't prepared her for such loud volume or casual interaction.

Glancing around, all the booths looked full. There was only one empty booth located at the back of the car. The thought of walking past more staring, inquisitive eyes didn't appeal to Sarah, but she had two hungry *kinder* to feed. Mercy wailed for her bottle and almost wiggled off Sarah's hip. She resigned herself and endured the curious glances. Head down, she moved forward.

Mercy squirmed hard and Sarah almost

dropped her. She had to get used to the small child's strength. She clasped her hands behind the little girl's back and held on. She'd get the hang of carrying an energetic baby. It would take just a short time.

Mose led the way down the narrow corridor between the tables. Sarah watched as, like Beatrice, he greeted each person who turned his way. His demeanor was calm and at ease. Sarah envied him. She wished she could accept the stares as easily, but he had more exposure to the *Englisch*. Perhaps time in a less strict community would teach her to be less formal, too.

Beatrice claimed the bench seat nearest the window and pressed her nose against the huge glass pane. Mose scooted in beside her. Sarah slid into the bench seat across from him, placing Mercy on her lap.

"What would you like to eat, Beatrice?" Mose moved aside the crayons lying on a colorful sheet of paper and glanced through the small children's menu placed on the table. "They have burgers, hot dogs and pancakes."

"Pancakes!" The child's voice rang loudly through the dining car. Several people close by laughed at her excited response.

"Pancakes, it is. And you, Mercy? What does *Daed's* little girl want?" The look of love sparkled in his blue eyes as he gazed at his younger daughter and spoke louder.

Mercy continued to play with the rag doll in her hands, her head down, her blond curls short and shiny. Had she not heard her *daed's* question? Sarah touched the child's shoulder and watched as she turned her head and glanced up, her eyes questioning. "Would you like pancakes, too?" Sarah asked with a grin.

Mercy smiled at her and went back to playing with her doll. Sarah looked at Mose. His forehead creased in a troubled expression.

"Does she talk at all, Mose?" Sarah waited for him to say something positive about her limited vocabulary and attention span.

He laid the menu down and sighed. "*Nee*, she doesn't talk, but my mother says that's nothing to worry about. Her words will come. Some *bobbel* are just late bloomers, and Mercy seems to be one of them."

Their conversation was interrupted by a tall, lean, uniformed waiter carrying a tray of short glasses filled with ice water. He looked at them with obvious curiosity and lifted his pad, ready to take their order. "What can I get you folks?"

"My *frau* and I just sat down, but I think we're ready to order." The word *frau* slipped off Mose's tongue with ease, as if he'd been calling her his wife for years. A knot formed in Sarah's throat. *Frau*...she liked the sound of it.

Sarah ordered dry toast, hoping to squelch the remaining effects of the virus she'd been dealing with. She sipped from the glass of cold water in front of her.

Mose ordered fried chicken and mashed potatoes, and confessed with a little boy's grin, "I'd eat it every day of my life if I could. No sense changing habits now." He smiled, his deep dimple showed, making him look younger than she knew him to be. For the first time she realized how handsome he was. Heat flushed her face and her heart fluttered.

The sudden sound of a loaded tray of food hitting the floor startled them. Beatrice began to cry. Mose collected her in his arms and patted the child's back. "It's okay. Someone just dropped some plates. All is well, my rose."

Sarah looked at Mercy and was amazed to find the child fast asleep, her breathing soft and regular. Her finger caressed the lovely child's velvety cheek and watched as she stirred. Fear clenched Sarah's stomach. Mercy should have been awakened by all the noise.

She glanced over at Mose as he shoveled one of Mercy's crackers into his mouth. She started to say something about Mercy's lack of reaction, but decided she'd best bring up her concerns when Beatrice wasn't around to hear.

Sarah realized there had been one other time Mercy had failed to react to loud noises on the train. How many times had the child's lack of reaction gone unnoticed? *Gott, don't let this child be deaf.* Could it be possible the child had hearing problems? How should she approach her concerns with Mose without sounding like an inexperienced mother?

"You look very serious." Mose wiped his mouth with the bright red cloth napkin.

"I'm new at being a mother and worry over everything. We'll talk about it when the *kinder* are asleep."

Hour after hour the train rolled on. Beatrice fought her nap with the stubbornness and energy only a four-year-old could maintain. Mose walked the child to the end of the corridor and spoke to her firmly, but the talk did nothing to dispel the sour mood, or the loud crying that erupted from her.

"Any suggestions," Mose asked after a half hour of the child's wailing. A deep frown revealed how upset he was. Being a single parent had to have been hard on him. He had been very fortunate to have his mother's help.

"Perhaps she's too old for naps now," Sarah suggested. She rubbed Beatrice's back and got a bad tempered kick in the leg from the child for her efforts.

"Beatrice Fischer. You will be kind to your *mamm*. There is no need for violence." Mose's tone was quiet, but firm with frustration. Several people turned to stare at Beatrice.

"I will *not* go to sleep. I'm not tired and I want my real *mamm* to pat my back, but she's with *Gott*. *Grandmammi* Ulla says I'm not to ask for her, but I want her." Fresh tears began to pour down her already mottled face. "I wish I was with her. I hate you," Beatrice shouted, then twisted around and buried her face in her small pillow, sobbing in earnest.

Mose began to rise but Sarah stopped him. "*Nee*, please don't scold her again. What she says is true. I'm not her real mother. She's confused by her feelings. She needs time to adjust. She's just tired and cranky from the long train ride. She'll be asleep any moment now and everything will be okay."

Beatrice curled herself into a small ball on the train's bench seat, snuggled close to her sister and together the two girls hugged. Mose watched Sarah's expression and saw love sparkle in her eyes as she soothed his eldest daughter. *Kinder* could be so hurtful without realizing the gravity of their cruel words.

Beatrice finally ran out of steam and grew quiet. He reached over and took Sarah's small, soft hand in his and smiled, wishing this emotionally frail woman knew what a gift she was to him. A mother for his *kinder*, someone who'd love them no matter what. To him she was lovely and priceless. He squeezed her fingers and smiled. "I'm sorry. I know her words must have hurt."

"She'll come around. You'll see." Sarah squeezed his hand. "There are times I'd like to stamp my foot and cry myself," she confessed.

"You must be tired." Mose hadn't missed Sarah's yawn or the way she pulled her hand away and tucked it under the fullness of her skirt. He had to remember she was still a widow grieving for her dead husband. Sarah had only been mourning Joseph for six months. Not nearly long enough to welcome him into her heart. What a fool he was.

"I didn't know you worked in the school back in Lancaster." He lightened the mood with his chatter and watched her facial expression relax.

"Yes, I did, but only for a short while. We had an abundance of trainable girls, and I took my turn when it came. Naturally I failed miserably as a teacher. I just wasn't the right material for such a job. I turned to quilt-making instead. I love to sew."

"My wife is—" He stopped himself, and his smile disappeared.

"Please, go on. I want you to feel free to talk about your wife." Sarah's smile looked genuine.

"*Danke*. I appreciate your understanding. Sometimes her name just slips out. It's almost as if she's still alive in Florida and waiting for me to come home."

"I understand. I often wake and think Joseph is out in the fields…until I remember he's dead."

"His death was so sudden. There was no warning, no illness to give you time to prepare." Mose lifted his hat and ran his fingers through his curls.

"And so final. I still find it hard to believe he's dead, even though I know he is. There was no body to see. Joseph was always careful with the gas lights. I was the one he said would burn the house down some day with my carelessness." One lone tear slid down her cheek.

He leaned toward her. "You're a good woman, Sarah Fischer. Without you I'd be a lonely man heading back to an empty home. I don't believe for a moment you caused Joseph's death."

* * *

Moments later, the aroma of coffee moved closer to their table. A wave of nausea washed over Sarah. She fought hard to hold down her meal but knew she had to make a run to the bathroom or throw up on one of the sleeping *kinder*. "I'll be right back." She sailed past Mose and quickly maneuvered around arriving diners.

The door to the bathroom was unlocked. She burst in, her hand to her mouth, frantically looking for an open toilet door. She got as far as the row of shiny sinks and lost all hope.

A female voice said, "Oh, you poor girl. Let me get a cold compress for your neck. That always helped me when I was pregnant."

Sarah looked into the mirror and watched as a stout *Englisch* woman of about sixty wet down the fluffy white washcloth she'd jerked from her makeup bag. "I'm fine, really. I'm not pregnant. I'm fine."

"Nonsense. You're not fine at all. Let me at least put the cloth on your neck. It's a trick my dear ol' mama taught me as a child." The older woman's gaze locked with Sarah's in the mirror. She approached and gently laid the cold cloth across Sarah's heated neck. Relief was instantaneous and much needed. A few moments of deep breathing and Sarah began to feel better.

"How far along are you?" the woman asked as she washed her hands.

Sarah froze. *She thinks I'm pregnant?* What foolishness. There was no way she could be pregnant. Joseph died almost six months ago. She would have known before this if she was pregnant. *Wouldn't she?*

The woman sat down on a short bench against the wall and continued to smile at Sarah. "I assume this baby is a wanted child."

For the first time, Sarah allowed herself to think about what it would mean to be carrying Joseph's child. She'd have a part of him she could treasure forever. Joy shot through her and she began to count her skipped periods, the ones she'd thought stress had caused her to miss. It had been over five months since her last one. She lifted her head and smiled back at the woman through the mirror. "If I am pregnant, he or she would be a gift from *Gott.*"

"I have three gifts from God and one is driving me nuts right now, but he's still my little boy at thirty-nine."

Sarah moved to a clean sink, and then wiped her pale face.

How would she explain to Mose she might have to see a midwife? Her mind had been so preoccupied with Joseph's loss, the missed cycles hadn't worried her. Dealing with her father's demands about selling the farm after Joseph's death had kept her out of sorts and in a flux of grief.

What kind of reaction would she get from Mose when she told him about the possibility of a *bobbel*? She knew he was a good man, but could she ask him to raise another man's child? A pregnancy might be more than he bargained for.

The *Englisch* woman smiled at Sarah before they left the bathroom. "Good luck with that new baby."

"Danke," Sarah murmured and followed her out the door.

Sarah slid into the bench next to a still sleeping Mercy and sipped her water. "I'm sorry I took so long."

The *Englisch* woman walked over to Mose and Sarah. "You have lovely children, ma'am." The woman continued to walk down the narrow aisle. "I'm sure this next child will be just as darling as the other two."

"Stomach problems again?" Mose asked. "You're as white as a sheet."

Sarah felt in a state of shock. She nodded, not trusting herself to speak. *Could I be pregnant?*

# *Chapter Eight*

Mose glanced up from the checker board, his gaze resting on Sarah's face. "We're almost in Tampa. You should hurry. You might not have time to make that last move you're so busy contemplating." He grinned. She scowled back but then broke out into a wide smile, her fingers poised. Alone on the board full of black checkers, his last red king sat ready to be served up.

Her teasing expression made her face appear young and spirited. She wore an impish grin of victory. "I have time for this." She moved her black checker toward his lone red king and snatched it off the board.

"Beginner's luck," Mose taunted, laughing at the cross expression stealing her smile.

Sarah's huff confirmed his suspicions. He had a competitive wife.

"We'll see if its beginner's luck next time

we play." She straightened the ribbons on her *kapp*, then busied herself with wiping drool from Mercy's neck.

He loved that he'd married a feisty woman, and looked forward to their next checker game. He would only throw a game once. He was competitive, too.

The train's arrival in Tampa was announced over the intercom. The man's voice carried a heavy Southern accent. "Please remain seated while the train comes to a complete stop."

"We're finally home," Beatrice declared with a deep sigh.

Moments later Sarah held on to Beatrice and Mercy as the train lurched to a stop and people stood and gathered their belongings.

After grabbing the bag of small toys, she scooped up Mercy, and Mose inched his way off the train with Beatrice hanging off his back, the child's thin arms locked around his sunburned neck. Her head bobbed as his long legs ate up the distance to the outer doors. "Let's go, my little dumpling." He laughed as he stepped off the train, turning to take Sarah's hand as she stepped into the sweltering after-noon heat. *"Danke,"* she said.

Burdened with *kinder* and the carry-on bag, they made their way across the parking lot to-ward a small bus stop. Mose pulled out his cell phone from his pants, checked that it still had power and punched in numbers. "I'm calling my brother to let him know we've arrived. He should be here already," he told Sarah.

"Your community allows the use of phones for everyday use?" Sarah watched him, amazement on her face as he spoke into the quickly dying phone, then ended his conversation.

Mose smiled. "Our phones are mostly for work. We get a lot of business calls from out of state. Customers have to be able to communicate with us. Without their furniture orders we'd quickly go out of business in this difficult economy."

"I'm just not used to having one, that's all. We always had to use the phone box across the road for emergencies."

"My brother, Kurt, said they're at the back of the parking lot under a tree."

He watched relief spread across Sarah's face as she glanced over at the big buses parked in rows on the glistening tar-covered parking lot. Had she thought they would be their mode of transportation to Sarasota? She was probably unprepared for a bus ride.

As they waited, loving family reunions erupted all around them. Smiling faces dotted the small bus walkway. Mingled among them were Amish and Mennonites alike, most dressed in plain clothes and sensible shoes. Seeing so many Amish in one place, Mose wondered if they reminded Sarah of the community and the people she'd left behind. He pushed away those thoughts and glanced around. He hoped she liked what she saw of Tampa. Palm trees grew everywhere and shops of every kind lined the wide streets. They'd arrived before the gray gloom of night could steal the day's last glorious rays of sunshine. The tall, swaying palm trees gave the town a tropical feel. He hoped she'd find Sarasota just as beautiful as Tampa.

Mose swung Beatrice onto his shoulders and caught Sarah's attention with the wave of his hand. "I don't want you to be concerned about meeting Kurt. I spoke with him early this morning. He knows all about our marriage and is very happy for us. He knew Joseph, too. We all grew up together in Lancaster, as boys. When we heard about Joseph's coming marriage, we both decided to go back up and help build the farmhouse. We wanted only the best for Joseph and his new bride."

"*Danke* for all your work. So much was going on during that time. I failed miserably at giving a proper thanks to all the workers who came to do the hard work. You and Kurt must have thought me terrible."

"*Nee.* I saw you at a distance one day and thought you lovely and Joseph a lucky man."

Sarah blushed at his compliment. She clutched Mercy to her chest and looked away.

Mose leaned down and grabbed Sarah's free hand, leading her away from the buses. Mose rubbed her wrist with his thumb and she smiled, accepting his touch.

Walking along with Sarah, a sudden breeze cooled his neck.

"What did you tell your *bruder* about our circumstances? Does he know I was going to be shunned? That you were there for me when I needed you most?"

"I told him I found you to be a wonderful woman who makes me happy. That's all he needs to know."

Sarah sighed deeply. Mose knew she probably dreaded meeting his family, but hoped for the best. *Will they accept her after all the rumors floating between Lancaster and here?* He longed for a start fresh for her in Pinecraft, the tiny Amish community he lived in just outside of Sarasota. *Gott* had provided a haven for her. There were a lot of things she didn't know about his family, but he knew them to be generous with their love.

Just feet away, a shiny black van with the sign Fischer's Transport came into view. Sarah's brows lifted. She tugged at Mose's hand, her questioning gaze seeking his. "Who owns the van?"

Beatrice broke free of her father's grip and ran toward the front passenger door, her small fists pounding on the metal as she yelled, "Unlock the door, *Aenti* Linda. We're finally home."

Mose waved at someone inside and placed his hand lightly on Sarah's back, directing her closer to the back passenger door. "My *bruder* does."

"I'm surprised he doesn't drive a horse-drawn wagon." Sarah knew her words came out sounding judgmental. She hadn't meant to be rigid. The idea of riding in the back of this huge vehicle, instead of an Amish wagon, left her breathless with anticipation.

"Kurt usually brings the mini bus, but tonight you get a special treat and get to ride in his new touring van."

Sarah wasn't so sure riding in the back of a van was a special treat, but she would tolerate anything to get a chance to settle the *kinder* down and get some rest. They walked up to the driver's door and she held her breath. *Gott, let them like me.*

*"Hoe gaat het, bruder?"* Mose greeted his lanky younger brother with a bear hug and sev-

eral warm-hearted back slaps. He grinned at his sibling's attempt at growing a beard since his recent marriage, the beard unkempt and scraggly. Reddish-blond hairs jutted in all directions. "I see you're having some problems here." Mose jerked the straggly beard and laughed. "I hope your marriage is going better than this mess."

"Not everyone can jut out a forest of hair in weeks, *bruder*." Kurt laughed.

Enjoying his brother's discomfort, Mose grinned over at his sister-in-law, Linda. Beatrice had already managed to connect herself to the thin woman, her blond head snuggled against her chest.

Mose brushed aside a momentary pang of concern for Linda. Pregnant with her first child, she didn't look a day over seventeen, even though he knew her to be close to Sarah's age. She oozed healthy confidence and looked forward to the birth of her first child. Not everyone had complications. *But Greta had. Gott, let all will go well for this baby.*

"You're looking very rosy-cheeked and happy," Mose teased. "Pregnancy seems to suit you. It's given you that motherly glow everyone talks about."

He watched as Linda glanced over at Sarah and a smile lit her face. Not prepared to explain anything about Sarah and their marriage, he pretended to pat Linda's tiny, protruding tummy.

Kurt seemed happy now that he had married his childhood sweetheart. Mose grinned. He would pray for an easy birth for Linda and leave their fate in *Gott's* capable hands.

Standing behind him, Sarah tried to hide herself. He reached around and urged his new wife forward to introduce her. "This is Sarah, my *frau*."

Sarah had never been a shy person, but today she felt dimwitted and backward. She had dreaded meeting Mose's family and worried they might reject her. Only *Gott* knew what Kurt must think of her, marrying his *bruder* so soon after Joseph's death. Amish custom in her Old Order community required a two-year waiting period to remarry and, even then, people would talk about the short interval. She moved forward and did her best to smile at him in a friendly manner.

Kurt extended his hand. Sarah took it and he squeezed her fingers in a firm grip. She was surprised at the *Englisch* gesture coming from an Amish man. Back in Lancaster, handshaking was often avoided. She had to keep reminding herself she didn't live under harsh rules anymore. This new community would allow her freedoms she'd always longed for. *Everything will be okay, please Gott.*

Kurt looked nothing like Mose with the exception of his piercing blue eyes. He had a slight but muscular build, with a thick mass of sandy red hair. His skin color, which should have been pale and freckled, looked tan and glowed from the warm days in Florida's sunshine.

Sarah finally allowed her gaze to move to her new sister-in-law and her knees almost buckled with relief. Linda Troyer stood at Kurt's side. She was an old friend Sarah had known since childhood. They'd gone to school together, and years later, had taught the younger *kinder* during the same semesters. Linda smiled at her, draining all the stress and fear from Sarah's body.

"Linda Troyer! I can't believe my eyes. I knew you'd moved to Florida, but I didn't know you knew Mose's family."

"Kurt and I got married last fall, just a few months after my family moved down here. My last name's Fischer now, like yours." The two women hugged tightly, their reunion as warm as the brothers had been. Their happy tears mingling as they kissed each other's cheeks and laughed.

"I forgot. You did tell me you'd met a man named Fischer during *rumspringa* a couple of years ago. I guess I was too wrapped up in my own courting and coming marriage to Joseph to remember everything. Forgive me."

Linda grabbed Sarah's hand. "I don't know how you forgot. I must have mentioned Kurt's name a million times. I bored you with details for weeks. Remember, you even threw a going-away party when my family decided to leave for Florida. Your dad got so mad at me for dancing like a heathen in your front yard. Don't you remember him running me off and calling me an ugly name?" Linda laughed as she drew Sarah close for another hug, her fingers pinching Mercy's chubby cheeks before she leaned away. "Those were the good ole days. I've missed you."

Sarah grinned. "I probably missed you more. I am so thrilled that you're living in Florida."

"Not just Florida. We live in Sarasota, at Pinecraft. We're going to have the best time picking out a new home for you that's close to ours. You won't mind, will you, Mose?"

Both women turned toward the two silent men standing next to the van.

Strong emotions flitted across Mose's face, his brow furrowed, but his words came out friendly and light. "Wherever you want to live is fine with me. As long as it's near the school-house." His smile seemed genuine, but there was still something in his expression, something she couldn't define that troubled her.

# Chapter Nine

"You're being awfully quiet for a guy who's got a lot of explaining to do." Kurt lifted the girls' bag of toys and threw it over his shoulder.

Not sure what to say, Mose slowed his pace. He shifted the suitcase he was carrying from one hand to the other and repositioned the bulging dirty clothes bag slipping out from under his arm. Mose cleared his throat. "I really don't know where to start."

"Start at the beginning. What made you propose to Sarah, and why does she look so ill?"

"We really don't have the time to dig into all this right now. The van's just a few more rows over and the women will be wondering what happened to us. We're supposed to be picking up the remaining luggage from the train, remember? Not having a friendly chit-chat like two old women."

Kurt stopped in his tracks and gave Mose a piercing look that spoke volumes. He seemed determined to get the facts, one way or another.

"Do it now, or do it later, but tell me you will."

"All right. Sarah was in a deep depression over Joseph's passing. She needed help. We got to know each other while she cared for the girls. I offered to marry her to get her out of a bind."

"A bind? Marriage is an awful lot of help, Mose. I know you're a kind man, but people don't up and marry a widow of less than six months just because she's in a bind. Not even when they were best friends with the widow's dead husband. There has to be more to this story than you're telling me."

"I didn't marry her just to help her out. I need help, too. She had to leave Lancaster and the girls were desperate for a mother. They fell in love with her while I helped rebuild the burned-out barn. Sarah's a very loving woman and so good with the *kinder*. Her situation came up suddenly and we married out of convenience, nothing more. We have a clear understanding. Now, can you stop making more of this than there is, and let's get going? We can talk later. These bags are heavy and it's getting late."

Mose took off, his leather soles smacking against the parking lot pavement. He had enough on his mind without trying to satisfy his younger brother that he hadn't completely lost his mind. He knew he hadn't lost contact with reality and needed time to think, to talk to Sarah. This would all work out. He just prayed to *Gott* the rest of the family wasn't going to be this inquisitive.

Sarah looked inside the big van, comparing it to the small Amish wagons she was so used to. This vehicle was amazing, plush and definitely not plain. Three rows of soft leather seats lined the back, enough room for at least eight people. The space amazed her beyond words. She stepped in, the carpet under her feet like walking on marshmallows. Weak as a kitten, she longed for a nap. A sigh of relief escaped her as she bent forward and lifted Mercy's body into a child's car seat. A few minutes of fiddling had the baby secure in the strange contraption. Jerking on each strap, she made sure everything snapped into the right slots and flopped down next to Mercy for a moment of rest.

Linda slid Beatrice into the child seat at the

front of the van with experienced ease, then gave her a box of animal cookies to quiet her.

Linda patted the seat next to her and motioned Sarah deeper into the van. Both women slid into the third row. Linda grinned. "It's really wonderful to see you, Sarah. I've been wondering how you were doing. I started to write when we first moved away, but figured your *daed* would just throw my letters away."

They laughed. Sarah enjoyed the moment of relaxation. "You know, he probably would have thrown them away." Sarah grinned and hugged her friend. "You have to no idea how wonderful it was to see you standing there next to Kurt. Recognizing your smiling face was such a surprise and a blessing." Sarah took Linda's hand and squeezed. "I've missed our friendship so much."

Linda laid her hand on her protruding stomach and rubbed lovingly. "Did you notice I'm pregnant? I told Mose to tell you when he got to Lancaster, but knowing him, he probably didn't."

"Sarah patted her friend's hand and squeezed it with joy. "I'm so happy for you and Kurt. Having a *bobbel* is such a blessing from *Gott*. You must be so excited."

"I am, but it's Kurt who's behaving like a

fool. He's thrilled over the prospect of being a father."

Sarah listened as Linda laughed and continued to ramble on. But in the back of her mind, the words of the woman on the train came back to haunt her. *Could I be pregnant, too?* Was it possible all the nausea and lethargy she'd been experiencing were from an unexpected pregnancy? How could she possibly be pregnant and not know it? *Wouldn't I have suspected something by now?*

"Just listen to me. I'm rattling on about my life and I haven't asked you if you're doing okay." Linda's expression became somber. "I was so sorry to hear about Joseph's death. I can't imagine what you've been going through."

Sarah felt a warm tear slide down her face. "It was all so sudden. Joseph and I were so happy. Life was perfect for the first time in my life…and then he was gone and everyone kept saying his death was *Gott's* will. I was told not to talk about him, to forget him. They expected me to act as if he never existed." Sarah wanted to share how she'd blamed herself for his death. Linda deserved to understand why she'd married Mose so soon after Joseph's death. A quick remarriage was completely out of line with their teachings. *She'll be wondering, thinking I've made a big mistake.*

What would Mose's people think when they heard she had been threatened with being unchurched for helping the neighbor boys leave their abusive father? Her heart ached with regret, but not for helping the boys. She hoped her old friend would understand that her motives had been pure, but what about the other family members? Beads of sweat dampened her forehead.

"You're so pale. Have you been eating well and drinking enough water?" Linda handed Sarah a lacy handkerchief and watched her as she mopped her face.

"I'm fine, really." Sarah reassured her. "I've just been sick to my stomach lately. Probably just a bug."

"When did these stomach problems start?"

"A while back. Nothing big, just off-and-on nausea and I'm tired all the time. But that could be from all the stress and chasing after the girls." Sarah leaned over to cover Mercy's bare legs with a lightweight blanket. She smiled as the tiny girl puckered up, as if she was nursing on a bottle.

Linda's hands pressed into her growing waistline. "Have you seen anyone about the stomach problems?"

Sarah watched for Mose and Kurt. "*Nee*, I thought about it, but I've been so busy that I put it off. I'm sure I'll be fine in a day or two." Sarah fiddled with the dangling ribbon on her *kapp* as she turned back to Linda. "You'll get a good laugh from this. A lady on the train saw me throw up and assumed I was pregnant. Can you believe it?" Sarah held her breath as she waited for Linda to laugh, to reassure her she had nothing to worry about.

"Are you?"

Sarah hadn't expected her serious question. Linda wasn't laughing. "I don't see how. It's been six months since Joseph died."

"Pregnancy can sneak up on you. One morning I smelled coffee brewing and threw up in front of Kurt's *mamm*. She knew right off I was pregnant."

Sarah flashed back to her problems with the smell of food and began to tremble. "I've been having to eat crackers to calm my stomach and..."

"What, Sarah?"

"My breasts are tender. They have been for weeks. I thought it was from my period being late...it's been months. I've been so wrapped up in Joseph's death. I thought it was just the stress keeping it away."

"I think we'd better get a test."

"What do you mean, a test?" Sarah asked.

"The *Englisch* have pregnancy tests. They cost a few dollars and within minutes you know if you're pregnant or not. I took one, just to be sure. It was positive."

"Mose might not approve of such tests."

"Are you kidding? He's the one who picked one up for me. You aren't in Lancaster anymore, Sarah."

Sarah began to cry. She was so confused and torn. She'd know for sure if she was pregnant and then how would she feel? Had *Gott* blessed her with a baby from Joseph? How would Mose react? He hadn't bargained on raising another man's child in the agreement they shared.

"I didn't mean to bring up Joseph and make you cry." Linda leaned forward and smoothed a tear from Sarah's cheek. "We'll get a pregnancy test in a bit and you'll take it. No more guessing and worrying. You hear?"

Always a take-charge kind of person, Linda leaned back into the soft seat of the van. Her gaze cut back to Sarah. "How did you and Mose end up married, anyway? I know you, Sarah. There's no way you'd marry again so soon after Joseph's death. Not unless something was seriously wrong. What happened?

How could you have fallen in love with Mose so soon?"

The sound of the men approaching stopped Sarah's response, but she knew there'd be time for explanations later and prayed Linda would understand.

Linda greeted the men loading suitcases into the back of the van as if they'd been talking about the weather. "Listen to them huffing and puffing, Sarah. You'd think they'd been carrying luggage for a family of six."

"These bags are heavy. Sarah must have packed everything she owns in here," Kurt teased.

Mose smiled through the window at Sarah and waved, his expression friendly and calm. She put on a brave face, smiling and pretending everything was fine. If he did see her tears he'd think it was just her nervousness about her first van ride, not to mention her concerns about meeting his family. She willed her stomach to calm down.

"Let's hit the road before it gets dark. I want Sarah to be able to see some of Tampa's sights before we head down to Sarasota." Kurt slipped into the driver's seat and waited for Mose to slide in and shut his door.

Mose looked back at Sarah. She grinned, silently reassuring him she was fine. *But I'm not fine.* Her mind raced like a runaway train. Kurt started the big van's motor and Sarah sucked in her breath.

"Remember, this is Sarah's first automobile ride," Mose reminded Kurt. "You don't want to scare her to death with some of your wild driving."

"As if I would," Kurt teased and gunned the powerful motor seconds before the van roared off down the road.

Sarah tucked her shaking hands under her legs and closed her eyes. It was going to be a long ride to Sarasota.

Florida was more beautiful than Sarah had imagined. Palm trees lined every street and the sky looked bluer than any sky she'd ever seen. Highway 275 quickly turned into HI 19 and the impressive Sunshine Skyway Bridge came into view, amazing Sarah with its massive size and length that stretched out over the bay. She was fascinated and terrified at the same time.

*I can do this.* She'd been through so many impossibly hard things the past few months. She looked back at Linda. Her friend seemed perfectly calm, as did everyone in the van. Digging her toes into the soles of her plain black shoes, she closed her eyes and prayed.

*Give me strength to get through this trip across what looks like a death bridge.*

Kurt spoke, "What's wrong, Sarah?" His tone was playful but without mercy. She opened her eyes and met his gaze in the van's mirror. "You're not scared of heights, are you? It's either the bridge or walk."

Mose turned toward Kurt and sliced him a cutting look. Anger built inside Sarah, a typical example of her shifting moods of late. She would not have her husband pitying her over something as silly as a fear of heights. "Would you like me to sit in the back with you while we cross?" Mose offered.

Sarah looked back to the bridge and glared at Mose. He probably had no idea he'd just insulted her. "*Danke*, but I'm fine." Sarah pulled at the strings of her prayer *kapp*. She squared her shoulders in determination. "I'm sure thousands of people go across this bridge every day. I'm fine."

The awkward moment evaporated when Beatrice woke from a sound sleep and chimed, "I'm hungry. Aren't we there yet?"

## Chapter Ten

Before leaving Lapp's restaurant, located a few miles from the edge of Sarasota and the tiny town of Pinecraft, Sarah watched as Mose paid their bill and shifted Beatrice in his arms as he slipped the change into his pocket.

Sarah's hands shook as she placed Mercy's empty formula bottle on top of the restaurant counter. She used a clean napkin to wipe the milk ring from Mercy's lips and smiled when Mose glanced her way.

"I want cookies," Beatrice demanded. Determined to grab the plate of plastic-wrapped chocolate chip cookies on the counter, she began to squirm in her father's arms, her arm stretching out.

"You ate enough food for two." Mose patted his daughter's stomach. "No cookies for you this time, young one." Her golden ringlets danced as she shook her head in disagreement. They headed out the door, following after Kurt and Linda.

Dusk had fallen and Sarah marveled at the glorious sunset. She drew in a long breath, taking in the smell of the sea. She kissed Mercy on the crown of her head and followed close behind Mose.

"Why don't Sarah and I go over to the pharmacy across the street? I need to pick up a few things before we go home." Linda told the lie with a big grin.

Kurt smiled down at his petite wife, oblivious to the prearranged plan. "Sure. You ladies take your time. Mose and I will strap the kids in and enjoy the last of the sunset."

Sarah was surprised at how normal Linda's voice had sounded as she'd lied and how easily she'd manipulated her husband.

Mose looked Sarah's way and dug into his pant pocket. "You might need some money." She held out her hand and he slipped two twenty-dollar bills onto her palm. "Enjoy." He smiled.

Sarah pulled on her prayer *kapp* ribbon. "I will. *Danke*." She waited until he turned toward the van before she picked up her long skirt and ran, finally catching up to Linda just as she opened the store's glass door.

"You could have waited for me," Sarah scolded, and then became speechless as she took in the big, bright store with shelves full of things she'd never laid eyes on before. *What do the Englisch need with all these things?*

"Over here." Linda grabbed Sarah's wrist. "I see makeup. The tests should be somewhere close to that section."

"Where are the tests?" Sarah glanced around. "I don't see them." These mood swings concerned her. She hadn't meant to bark at Linda.

"Don't snap, *liebling.* You're stressed out. It won't take a moment to find them, and then we'll know for sure if you're with child." Linda's head twisted back and forth as she looked up and down the aisles.

Sarah tapped her on the shoulder. "Shh. Someone might overhear you."

"And who would hear?" Linda snapped back. "Kurt and Mose are in the car." She led Sarah in a different direction, then pointed to a brightly lit ceiling sign. "The pharmacist can tell us where the tests are located. Come on. Time's wasting."

Linda rushed off and Sarah struggled to keep up. A large-boned woman with kind eyes and a friendly smile spoke to Linda in a quiet voice from behind the shiny counter. Linda handed the woman money and Sarah heard Linda say, *"Danke."*

The lady smiled. "Good luck. Hope you get the answer you want."

Sarah backed up as if the package Linda carried would jump out and bite her like a snake.

"Come on. This way." Linda grabbed Sarah's wrist as she flew past.

A shiver rippled through Sarah as she rushed forward, her feet heavy.

Linda pulled the box out of the flimsy bag and extended it toward Sarah. "Read the back carefully and then pray before you…ah…you know. The lady said this test is a good one and only takes about thirty seconds to show results."

"But…"

"You need to know, Sarah. This is no time to be stubborn. Take the test, find out if you are carrying Joseph's baby or not. You have to get on with your life. Mose deserves more than a nervous woman for a wife."

Linda's simple words reached her. The package in her hands felt light as a feather. This test kit would tell her all she needed to know. She had to take it. Heading toward the door marked Women, Sarah turned back. "I know you're right. I'll be out in a minute."

Moments later she held the plastic device out

in front of her, waiting for something to happen. Sarah picked up the box off the edge of the sink and reread the instructions just to be sure she'd done everything right. Time seemed to stand still. The music playing overhead grew silent. A line formed. She was pregnant. She didn't realize she was crying until tears began to hit the box in her hand.

With a shove to the door she exited the bathroom and smiled at Linda, their secret a strong bond between the two women. She gushed, "I'm pregnant."

"How far along do you think you are?" Linda called out as they'd darted across the street.

"I have to be at least six months. How can it be? Why didn't I know, Linda? Am I simple-minded?"

Stopping, she hugged Sarah. "*Nee*. It's your first pregnancy, silly. You were in a state of shock after Joseph died. It's no wonder you didn't notice the changes in your body. You'll have to go see the *Englisch* doctor for a sonogram." Linda turned toward the parked van. "You didn't take care of yourself or see a doctor. Something could be wrong and you wouldn't know it.

Sarah digested Linda's words. She would have to see a proper doctor. She owed it to the baby and to Joseph. "I will go as soon as I tell Mose."

"Don't take too long, Sarah."

"I promise I won't."

Moments later Sarah and Linda entered the van and settled down for the short drive to Mose's mother's house. Nervous that Linda might blurt out something, Sarah pulled at her prayer *kapp* ribbons. A sign on the side of the highway declared Sarasota was just three miles ahead.

Mose turned on an overhead light and glanced back at her and then the girls. "Everything good back there?" His tone was calm but his face appeared tense, his brow furrowed. Was he having second thoughts? Did he regret marrying her? Was he concerned how his family would react to her now that they were almost there?

"Everyone's good," Linda chimed in, grinning.

The light went out and Sarah breathed in. She had to stop holding her breath.

"I'm hungry," Beatrice spoke in the darkness, drawing Sarah's attention.

"I'll find you a snack," Sarah said, rummaging through the diaper bag. Her fingers hit the pregnancy test tucked deep at the bottom of the bag and she froze. Had Mose seen the box when he'd grabbed Mercy's bottle moments before they'd driven off?

She found the plastic container of cheese crackers and handed several to Beatrice. "These ought to tide you over until we get to your *grandmammi* Theda's house, sweetheart." She closed her eyes and prayed, determined in her heart to be a good wife and mother.

She'd dozed off, and then someone said, "Sarah. It's time to wake up."

Sarah blinked and looked directly into kind blue eyes. It was Mose. Reality rushed in and she struggled to wake up completely. "I'm sorry. I must have dozed off." She blinked and looked around. It was growing dark outside, the small van light shining overhead. Her prayer *kapp* lay in her hand. With care she searched for her pins and put the wrinkled covering back on her head.

"It's been a long and tiring trip. I'm not surprised you nodded off."

Her body felt sore from sitting still for so long. She struggled to step out of the van. Mose offered his hand and she grasped it, noticing the roughness of his warm palms. "Where are we?" She looked into the creeping darkness shrouding the last rays of sunlight. Rows of wood-framed white houses lined the short street, the van parked in a long gravel driveway. The flat yard, filled with sand, grass and palm trees, was illuminated by a tall black gas lantern positioned at the front of the box-shaped white house trimmed with black storm shutters.

"This is my mother and father's home. We'll be staying with them for a few days. Just until we can move into a home of our own," he re-assured her.

"Yes. You did tell me that on the train." She shook out her skirt and fussed with her *kapp*, making sure it was pinned in the right places.

Mose held her arm for support until she started moving toward the door. Thick grass underfoot made walking difficult. She almost fell. Mose grabbed her around the waist, sta-bilized her and then took his arm away from her midsection. "You okay now?"

It had been a long time since she'd been held so close. His hand felt natural. It was as if he belonged with her. She pushed the thought away. Mose was in love with his dead wife. They had an arrangement. Nothing more. She stepped on the wide porch step. The wood creaked underfoot. A line of white rockers with colorful cushions welcomed her. A bright elec-tric bulb attached to the door frame washed the big porch in artificial daylight.

The front door flew open and Beatrice came

racing out. A smaller, dark-haired girl followed close behind.

"Where are you going, young lady?" Mose asked and grabbed his daughter by the sleeve.

"To *Grandmammi* Ulla's. She has candy for me." A layer of thick chocolate candy smeared a dark circle around Beatrice's mouth.

"I think asking permission to go out is in order, don't you?" Mose used the palm of his hand to turn and lead Beatrice back into the house. Her little friend followed meekly behind.

Beatrice's outburst of tears came instantly. Mose moved through a small group of welcoming people and headed to the back of the house. A dining-room table burdened with food blocked his path. Plain men and women sat at the table together, something Sarah had never seen before. Old Order Amish folk ate separately, the men always first while the women were busy feeding the *kinder*.

Beatrice tried to run off, but Mose caught her by the collar of her dress. "I think some time in the back bedroom is the answer to all this commotion."

An older woman, her gray hair wrapped in a tight bun and covered with a perfectly positioned prayer *kapp*, lifted her portly body to her feet. Her blue eyes flashed fire. "You've upset her now. It will take me hours to calm her down. Why don't you let me take care of this and you find yourself a spot at the table?"

Sarah stood just inside the great room's door watching the scene play out across the room. "I could…" she began, only to be cut off by Mose.

"*Danke*, Sarah, but I think I can manage this young rebel without anyone's help."

The woman turned in Sarah's direction and glared at her with a hard stare that twisted her features. "Who is this woman and why is she here, Mose?"

"This is none of your concern, Ulla. As Greta's mother, I'm sure you only want what's best for Beatrice and meant no harm, but babying the *kinder* only makes her moods worse."

Mose turned toward Sarah, Beatrice still in tow. He motioned for Sarah to join him and then put his arm around her waist as they walked toward the dining-room table at the back of the room. "*Mamm*, *Daed*, let me introduce you to someone very special. This is Sarah, my new *frau*. We met in Lancaster and married there. I hope you will make her feel *willkummed* in your *haus*."

Sarah didn't know what to do or say. She stood stone still next to Mose, watching the tiny woman who birthed Mose smile at her in bemusement from across the table. *How could such a small woman have given birth to someone as large as Mose?* His *mamm* looked to be in her late sixties. Even dressed in Amish clothes, she looked more *Englisch* than plain because of her wild shock of red hair. Thick locks pushed at her prayer *kapp* from every angle and left it tilted in disarray.

His father, an older version of Mose, wore his blunt cut, blondish-gray hair to his ears. His beard reached his shirt front. Impressive gray streaks blended in with wiry red and blond strands, making him look distinguished.

She waited for their reaction to Mose's declaration. *Let this go well.* Linda came over and put her arm around Sarah's shoulders in a show of solidarity.

Mose's mother looked at her husband in confusion, as if someone had just said the moon was made of green cheese. His father, clear-eyed and alert, was the first to come to grips with Mose's words. "*Willkumm*! Congratulations, my son and new daughter. This is *gut* news. It's time you found a woman, Mose. Come, Sarah. Sit with us, and eat. You have to be tired from your long journey."

The look on Mose's father's face told her he knew who she was. He'd grown up with Bishop Miller. Mose had told her they were still friends. He must have heard everything by now. News traveled fast in their world. He restrained himself as he spoke words of welcome he might not feel. "I'm sure you will make my son very happy. *Bitte*, sit. Its humble food we offer, but I'm sure you're used to eating this plain way."

Several people rose from the table and took their plates to the front of the house, making room for them at the long table. Sarah and Linda chose a spot next to each other. Sarah's stomach roiled, the meal's aroma so strong she thought she might be ill. "*Danke* for your warm *willkumm*." She struggled to smile. "I'm sure my arrival has come as quite a surprise to you all."

A loud voice rang out in the great room. "I will not be hushed. Mose had no right. No right. Greta is barely cold in the grave and he marries this woman. I will not have it, do you hear." The front door slammed shut. Silence screamed through the house.

Sarah looked around for Greta's mother, the silver-haired woman who'd made such a fuss just moments before. She and the beautiful young woman standing next to her had disappeared from the gathering.

Linda reached for a bowl of buttery potatoes placed in front of Sarah, and whispered in her ear. "That was Greta's mother. She's upset. Time will heal her pain and anger."

Sarah's stomach churned. She took the bowl of potatoes and quickly passed them to the man on her right. The smell of them was more than she could manage. Reaching out, she grabbed a hot roll and stuffed it in her mouth and chewed fast. *Please, Gott. Don't let me get sick. Please.* She glanced up and saw Mose's mother looking at her, her brow knitted with a questioning glance. Mose had sisters and brothers. The older woman had been pregnant many times. Did she know already, just by the look on Sarah's face, that she was pregnant?

When the meal was over and Theda and her two teenage granddaughters had cleared the dishes away, the men made themselves comfortable on a well-stuffed couch in the great room. Linda led the way to the back bathroom.

Beatrice, excited by the promise of bubbles in her bathwater, undressed herself with lightning speed. Sarah undressed Mercy and slipped the toddler into the warm, sudsy water next to her older sister. "The bubbles tickle me," Beatrice insisted, splashing water toward her little sister, who cried the moment the water touched her warm body.

"That wasn't very nice," Sarah scolded and felt disappointed when the girl didn't seem the least bit ashamed of her actions. She had splashed Mercy in the face intentionally. Sarah knew the child needed discipline, but wasn't sure what to do. She handed Mercy over to Linda and took a seat nearer Beatrice. In her most authoritative voice, she said. "I think it best you wash and get out, Beatrice."

Beatrice ignored her directions and dived under the water, coming up as slick as a seal. Sarah took the washcloth Linda handed her and began to apply soap to the soft rag. Hitting all the important spots, she cleaned Beatrice as the child wiggled and squirmed to get away. With a fluffy white towel she'd pulled from the rail, she wrapped it around Beatrice and pulled the resisting child from the tub. As soon as Beatrice's feet hit the bathroom rug she tried to get away from Sarah's grasp and run. Sarah held her by the arm.

"Perhaps tomorrow, after you've thought about how you scared Mercy, you can have a longer bath. But for tonight, it's bedtime for you."

Sobbing, Beatrice slapped at Sarah's hands but finally put up with being dried as a shiver hit her.

"Sounds like someone needs an early night." Mose stood in the bathroom door, his hand braced against the wood framework. He smiled at Sarah, but his brows lowered as he glanced over at Beatrice. "We've talked about this before, young daughter. Your sister does not like water splashed in her face."

Beatrice shrugged but seemed to know better than to talk back to her father. "I'm sorry, *Daed.* I was just having fun."

"I don't think Mercy was having fun. Do you?"

*"Nee."*

"Tell your sister you're sorry." Mose waited.

"I'm sorry, Mercy." Beatrice's frown told Sarah this spoiled little girl would need a lot of love and training in order to set her on a straight path.

Mose glanced at Sarah. "I guess we've let her get away with too much. It was hard to know when to discipline and when to overlook her behavior."

Sarah thought of Greta and how much this child must miss her mother. Any child would act out after the loss of her mother. She thought back to her own behavior after her mother had left, and sighed. "Time and lots of love will work all this out."

"I hope you're right." Mose smiled at Sarah.

Mose was a sweet and understanding man. Sarah only hoped she could someday give him what he deserved. A wife's love.

# Chapter Eleven

Mose drained the last drops of his second mug of coffee and reached for the pot.

"Too much of that will put your nerves on edge."

Mose poured a half cup and flashed his mother a welcoming smile. *"Guder mariye, Mamm."*

She scuffed toward the deep farm sink. A black apron already draped her light pink day dress. Her swollen feet were stuffed into the same fluffy blue house shoes she wore every morning, the bright shade of blue a secret passion of hers. After grabbing a white cup from the open shelf overhead, she pulled out a wooden chair and joined him at the small kitchen table littered with egg-smeared breakfast dishes.

Sunlight streamed in through the small window at the sink, filling the once dim room with the bright yellow glow of early morning. For as long as he could remember, his mother had risen with the sun and gone to bed with the chickens. "I know I drink too much coffee. I have a lot to do today and not a lot of time to do it in. I need the energy." Mose poured her a cup of the dark brew. He murmured a laugh when she scooped out three heaping teaspoons of sugar and made a terrible racket stirring the coffee, erasing the evidence of her sweet tooth.

Mose patted her wrinkled hand and met her gaze. She'd done her best to pin down her prayer *kapp* but a froth of ginger curls, brought on by high humidity, had left her disheveled. He noticed deeper lines and wrinkles on her face and made a mental note to spend more time with her now that he was home. She was getting older and he wanted her to know how much she meant to him. "Everyone still sleeping?"

"All but your *daed*. He woke up with the roosters. He had an early job over at the big house he bought last week."

"I didn't know he was interested in enlarging the community." Mose downed the last of his coffee and added his heavy mug to the pile of dishes in front of him.

"He's been talking about expanding for

months and is excited about this last *haus* purchase now that you've remarried. You'll be needing a new place to live. He's decided to fix it up real nice for you and Sarah."

Mose watched his mother draw circles on the wooden table, a sign she wanted to talk. She probably needed to ask a few questions. Questions he had no interest in answering. "He doesn't have to do that, *Mamm*. The *kinder* have loved living here the last year, but Sarah and I can start out our marriage at my *haus* for a while. I'm sure the girls will feel more at ease in familiar surroundings."

She looked at him, her brows furrowing. "Do you really think your new wife will want to live with all of Greta's things around her, reminding her you had a beloved wife who died and left everything behind for her to dust?"

Mose heard his mother's common sense. "I hadn't thought—"

"*Ach*, a man wouldn't, would he? But a woman would, and I can tell you, I'd have a problem with it. Let your *daed* do what he can to make you and Sarah comfortable in this new place. He wants to help, to feel useful in his old age. You can pay us rent until you find a different place if this house doesn't suit Sarah. Or is your pride the issue?" Her ginger eyebrow went up in an arch. She knew how to push his buttons.

"*Nee*, it's not pride. I just didn't think how living around Greta's things would make Sarah feel. She deserves her own home, things that make her happy."

"She does." His mother busied her fingers tidying her *kapp*. "I'm not sure what's going on between you and Sarah, but I know you. I trust your wisdom. She's only been a widow for six months. I can't see how she'd be over Joseph's death so soon, not the way I hear those two were in love. You showed no interest in getting a new *frau* before you left. All this leaves a *mamm* to wonder what's going on. There's been rumors floating around and people talking. Some say Sarah was to be shunned before you married her. I was wondering if it's true."

"Ignore the rumors. You know how people are. They have too much empty time on their hands. Do you really think I'd have married Joseph's widow if there hadn't been a good reason? Sarah and I need each other, so we got married. It's as simple as that. Joseph would have done anything for me, and I'm just making sure his widow is well cared for. You know better than I that love can grow from friendship. You and *Daed* married after knowing each other just two weeks."

"Now, let's not go throwing stones in my direction," his mother said with a frown. She snatched up his dishes and started to stand.

"*Mamm*, my girls needed a *mamm*. Sarah needed a husband. If she was good enough for Joseph, she's good enough for me. We struck a deal. She makes me happy and I think she's happy, too. Time will tell if we can make a strong marriage out of this friendship. I trust *Gott* to direct us, and as long as the girls are happy and well cared for...that's all I need."

Placing her son's dishes in the sink, she turned on the faucet and ran water. Sloshing the dishes around, she turned toward him, a playful glint in her blue eyes. "You know I never meddle. Do what's best. I didn't mean to sound critical of your choices."

Mose smiled at his petite *mamm*, but then got serious. "I do have something I need to talk to you about, and I don't want you to start to worry." He watched her cheerful smile disappear.

"You sound so serious. Is it Sarah?" She sat back down, her damp hands flat on the table.

Mose shrugged. "No, Sarah's fine, but she did notice Mercy has difficulty hearing. We're taking her to the pediatrician. I called their office a minute ago. We have an appointment this afternoon." He patted her hand. "I don't want you to worry. Sarah said this could be nothing more than built-up ear wax, but we need to be sure. Please don't mention any of this to anyone."

"If you mean to Ulla, of course I won't. She's already upset with you for bringing home a wife. What do you think I am, a trouble-making gossip?"

Mose laughed out loud. Gossip was the Amish woman's television. "Of course I don't. It's just better to know what we're dealing with before we mention to family that Mercy might be deaf."

"Oh, dear. You think it could be that bad? But if she is, we must know this is *Gott's* will for her life." She reached out for his hand, her fingers digging into his skin.

Mose unplugged his charging cell phone from the electrical outlet and turned back to his mother. "As soon as we find out what's up, I'll call you from the doctor's office. I'm leaving my phone on the table so you won't worry any longer than you have to."

His mother's face paled. She took the phone and slid it into her apron pocket.

Mose had no memory of ever being in a doctor's office. Greta always took the girls to their medical appointments. He wasn't sure what he'd expected, but it certainly wasn't this big, modern office, or the crowd of people peppered around the room. Comfortable-looking chairs lined walls painted a pleasant tan color. Pictures of *Englisch* children's favorite cartoon characters were everywhere.

Glancing about, he was surprised to see several plain people clustered together in the corner of the room, just on the edge of *Englisch* mothers, their children in tow or playing nearby with simple toys.

He motioned for Sarah to sit in one of the chairs nearest the door and watched as she made herself comfortable.

He walked to the opened window at the left of the room and waited for the young woman typing on a computer to look up.

"May I help you?" She spoke loudly when she finally acknowledged him. No doubt trying to be heard over the crying babies and chattering mothers.

"My name is Mose Fischer, and this is Mercy Fischer. We have an appointment with Doctor Hillsborough at ten o'clock." He kissed his daughter on the top of her *kapp* and returned the woman's half smile.

All business, the young woman continued to type, her fingers dancing across the keyboard. She glanced at him. "Doctor's running a bit late. Just have a seat, and I'll let you know when you're next."

*"Danke."* He sat next to Sarah, who seemed mesmerized by all the colorful art around her. "Your first time in a doctor's office, too?"

She smiled, a dimple he'd never noticed before making her look young and very attractive. He watched as she began to rummage through her big bag and brought out a faceless doll for Mercy. Knowing her background and Adolph's rigid ways, he doubted she'd ever set foot in a doctor's office, much less a pediatrician's office, no matter how sick she'd been.

"Yes, my first time. You?"

"I'm sure I must have gone to the doctor at one time or another when I was young. I just don't remember, so it's like the first time."

Mercy reached for the bottle in his hand and began to suckle. She seemed so calm and healthy. How could anything be wrong with her? "Do you think we've made a mistake?" Mose asked. "She looks fine."

Sarah leaned back in her chair and pondered his question. "Right or wrong, we have to know. She deserves to be checked. If it's not her hearing slowing down her speech, we have to find out what is wrong. She should be saying words by now, making sounds. She's too quiet."

Mose saw her concern and felt foolish for asking his question. Sarah was a good mother, kind and attentive. He and the girls were blessed to have her. *Gott* had filled an empty spot in his heart. Every day he grew more grateful to have Sarah in his life. "I know you're right. I guess I'm just nervous."

She looked at him. Worry etched her face with lines. "I'm concerned, too. Let's try to stay calm until the doctor tells us something concrete. *Gott* has a plan for her life, and I'm praying it doesn't involve deafness."

"Mercy Fischer."

Mose grabbed Sarah's hand and together they walked behind the woman holding Mercy's chart.

Down to just a cloth diaper, Mercy squirmed in her father's arms, her face red from crying throughout the extensive medical examination given by the pediatrician.

Standing next to Mose, Sarah brushed back the sweaty fair hair from the child's forehead and glanced into her husband's face. To a stranger his expression may have appeared calm, but she noticed the slight tick of nerves twitching his bottom lip. She knew he was as nervous as she felt. Would the *Englisch* doctor's diagnosis be grim?

"I have a good idea what's going on." Dr. Hillsborough finally spoke. She looked at Sarah and Mose and smiled. She grabbed her prescription pad off her desk and began to write. "I'm pretty sure Mercy has had several serious ear infections, which is very common in children her age. It looks like fluid's now trapped behind her eardrums, keeping her from hearing little more than muffled sounds. This much fluid could cause uncomfortable pressure. Has she run a temperature recently, or seemed unusually cranky?"

Mose hung his head. "She seemed hot and cried a lot on the train a few weeks ago, while on our way to Lancaster. I thought I'd just dressed her too warm and didn't pay much attention to her crankiness. She's cried a lot since her mother died and she's been teething recently."

"You shouldn't feel guilty, Mr. Fischer. Ear infections can easily crop up and get out of hand fast, even under the best of conditions. Babies are often cranky, and we assume it's their teeth breaking through or a sour stomach. Let's just make sure she takes a full ten days of the antibiotic I'm prescribing, and then we'll have her in for a myringotomy. I'll insert drainage tubes, so this buildup of fluids doesn't happen again. The procedure is simple and then the tubes can alleviate any pressure pain she's experiencing." She tossed her pad on her crowded desk and turned to take Sarah's hand. "Stop looking so concerned, Mrs. Fischer. Children are very resilient. They bounce back faster than we adults do."

"You're positive surgery is necessary?" Mose's arms tightening around Mercy's thin body.

"I do this procedure almost every day. It's not a serious operation, I promise you. She'll only be in the hospital for a few hours at most and then go home. Simple infections have been known to become very serious if ignored over a period of time. It's good that you noticed the problem so fast, Mrs. Fischer, and brought her in. Children have gone deaf from ear infections left untreated."

Sarah leaned in. "Is it possible the medication can work out her problems and the surgery not be needed?"

"Sadly, no. The tubes in Mercy's ears are very tiny, and she's probably going to have problems until they grow a bit larger. I suggest we start her on the medication today and go from there. We'll schedule the operation while you're in the office…for two weeks from now. I'll recheck her the day we do the surgery. Does that plan work for both of you?"

Mose and Sarah nodded their head in unison. Sarah spoke up. "She will be able to hear clearly again?"

"Oh, yes. She'll be catching up with her sister's chatter in no time. I know this has been a trying time for you and your husband, but now you can relax. You're doing your very best for her."

Sarah was relieved when they walked out of the doctor's office, into the warm breeze. She glanced over at Mose, saw the grin on his face and knew he was as thrilled with the doctor's diagnosis as she was. There was only the surgery to get through and Mercy's hearing would be restored. She lifted her face toward the morning sun and enjoyed its warmth. *Thank you, Lord. You are ever faithful.*

That evening Mose ate his meal, but didn't taste the food. His mind stayed on Mercy and the upcoming surgery in a few weeks. Sarah had given the baby her first spoonful of antibiotic and he prayed *Gott* would protect the child sitting next to him.

Mose leaned over, cutting Beatrice's chicken, and reminded his daughter to use her napkin. He smiled at Mercy. The child banged her spoon at him, her grin growing into a drooling river of squished peas.

"Today we took Mercy to see the doctor," Mose said, picking a quiet moment at the table to speak.

Otto's fork full of cottage fries froze halfway to his mouth.

Theda leaned forward. "You told me on the phone she'd be fine, but what else did you learn?"

Mose looked into his mother's eyes. "Mercy has an infection in her middle ear. She'll need to have tubes inserted to help drain the fluid."

Otto finished his bite of potatoes. "Has this infection you speak of...has it damaged her hearing?"

Mose pushed his peas around the plate. "Yes, her hearing was affected, but the doctor feels the surgery will fix the problem."

"Is the doctor sure?" Theda's gaze was glued to Mercy.

"We will ask for *Gott's* will. He loves her more than we do." Mose looked over at his *mamm* and then to Sarah and forced a smile.

"Yes," Otto agreed. "When is this surgery to happen?"

"Soon. Two weeks," Mose said, looking at his father.

"*Gott* has a plan for Mercy. We must not question why this happened." Otto continued to eat. The conversation had ended as far as his *daed* was concerned, but Mose's brows pinched with concern. He'd believed in *Gott's* will for Greta, and she had died in his arms.

Would *Gott* protect Mercy? He wasn't so sure. Mose looked at his food on his plate, his appetite gone. His thoughts swirled. Could he live with another loss?

Sarah reached across the table and grasped his hand, her eyes conveying her love for his youngest child. "She will be fine, Mose. We have to believe *Gott* knows what He's doing."

# *Chapter Twelve*

The shiny black car Mose had borrowed from his brother to run errands that morning seemed quiet without Beatrice's constant stream of questions and comments coming from the backseat. They'd dropped the girls off at their *Grandmammi* Ulla's house, and then gone for a ride through Sarasota, giving Sarah some much-needed rest and relaxation.

The sway of the automobile soothed her, as Mose drove through the streets lined in plain white houses and tidy lawns. She fought the urge to close her eyes and sleep. Florida, with its sunny beaches and tall palm trees, was so different from the rolling Lancaster farmland she was used to.

This morning she'd been glad to discover the town of Pinecraft was bigger than she'd first thought a week before. Small, brightly painted storefronts, with unique names, offered homemade goods and hot Amish meals to the constant flow of tourists invading the town in staggering numbers during the winter months. Pushing aside the damp hair that escaped her *kapp*, Sarah welcomed the cool breeze blowing in through the car window. It had rained in the early morning hours, just long enough to make the hot Florida air feel drenched with humidity.

"*Daed* said the *haus* will be ready later today. I want you to see it before I tell him we'll take it." Traffic was brisk but Mose flashed a quick smile Sarah's way.

A small scar next to Mose's mouth came into view. She'd never noticed it before, but then, there were a lot of things about Mose she didn't know. Things she needed to know if she was going to be a good wife to him.

"That's *gut*," she said. "The girls no longer have a place to call home. They're desperate for order in their lives. Things have been so hectic this past week and Beatrice is having a hard time."

"If you mean she's behaving badly, I agree." Mose drove slowly down the street just blocks from his parents' home. Every house in the neighborhood of central Pinecraft looked exactly the same. Square, white and set back from the road. Mose turned into one of the long driveways and slowed to a stop at the edge of the wide, wooden porch painted a glossy white. He jerked the keys out of the car's ignition and turned back to her.

"You sound like my *mamm*. Always making excuses for Beatrice. The time has come to get that young lady under control. I won't have her treating Mercy badly, and the way she talks to you is completely out of line." Mose reached over and touched Sarah's hand, spreading a warm tingling sensation he'd come to enjoy. "I'm glad she has you, Sarah. You're a kind woman and wonderful *mamm*."

"She doesn't see me as her *mamm* yet. I'm just someone who takes time away from you. Give her grace until she's adjusted."

Otto Fischer walked out of the house and waved, beckoning them to get out of the car. Cream-colored paint dotted the navy overalls that covered his shirt and pants. His gray hair stood in spikes, as if he'd been running his fingers through the thick mop.

"Looks like *daed's* ready to get this *haus* inspection over with."

"I've noticed your *daed's* not a man to waste time." Sarah gazed around the front yard as she stepped out onto sparse, crispy grass that begged for a soaking from the cracked hose on the ground.

"You two took long enough." Otto's smile took the bite out of his words.

"*Guder mariye* to you, too, *Daed*." Mose stepped aside and insisted Sarah go into the house first. "We had to take the *kinder* over to Ulla's, and she had much to say to me before I left."

"How many times did she mention she hasn't seen the girls in a while? She called last night and you'd have thought it had been a year since their last visit to her *haus*. *Guder mariye*, Sarah. Did you sleep well?"

"I did, *danke*." Sarah glanced around the large open room they'd stepped into, taking in the dark wood floors and creamy walls. She hurried over to the gleaming kitchen in the corner, drawn like a bug to a light. She touched the island's stone counter with her fingertips and marveled at the swirl of colors within the large slab of smooth granite. Making bread here would be a joy.

She took a slow turn and tried to take everything in. She'd never seen a house as big as this. Linda had told her these large, newly built homes existed on the fringe of the small Amish community of Pinecraft, but to live in one herself? Sarah was used to small, closed-in rooms. This large area glowed with early morning sunshine. She'd never seen such fancy fixtures or appliances. How would she learn to cook on this gleaming stove with five burners? The house had to use electricity. She looked up and saw the light fixture and knew these were not oil lights. Perhaps a gas generator fueled the electricity? She turned to face Mose. This was an *Englisch* house he'd brought her to. What was he thinking?

"I'll leave you two to have a look round. I'll be back inside later. I've still got to fix that sliding patio door. The thing keeps sticking." Otto shifted the paint bucket and plastic sheeting he held in his hands. He scrubbed one paint-spattered hand down his overalls before opening the front door and letting it bang behind him.

Mose turned to Sarah. "So, is the *haus gut* enough, or do you want to look at a few more? *Daed* can rent this one to someone else. We won't hurt his feelings."

The grin on his face told her he liked the house. Would he understand if she didn't want to live here? She wanted to please him, not be picky and difficult, but would she ever feel at home in this modern palace? "There seems to be plenty of room."

"I hear a but on the end of that sentence."

Mose moved closer and took her right hand. His thumb rubbed her palm in a swirl of rough skin against soft. His gaze flirted with hers until she looked away, a shy smile on her lips, the room suddenly uncomfortably warm. She pulled her hand away and turned toward the window above the deep sink. Somehow Mose had gotten under her skin, made her feel things she hadn't felt since Joseph was alive. The emotions swirling in her stomach scared her. Clearing her voice, she spoke, hoping she wouldn't sound as shaky as her legs felt. "*Nee…nee.* I like the house. It's just more modern than I'm used to, that's all. And so large."

"We can look at other houses."

She turned back to Mose and silently chastised herself. Mose's father had gone to a lot of trouble to make this house nice for them. The least she could do was make a fair assessment before coming to a decision. "Please." She forced a smile and prayed *Gott* would speak to her about what to say and do. Often she handled things wrong and she so desperately wanted to get this right. "Let's look through the rest of the house and see if we can make a home here. I'm just surprised by the extras. I'm not used to such grand living. Pinecraft is so different from Lancaster. I hope you understand."

His grin was back, his gaze warm. He took

her by the arm and playfully propelled her forward. "Let's go take a look."

Sarah smiled and let him guide her down a long hall lined with closed doors. She enjoyed his lighthearted manner and thanked *Gott* she'd found him. Joseph had been easygoing and had often made her laugh, too. Her heart ached as soon as she thought of Joseph. She touched her stomach with the flat of her hand and felt the bump, their child growing deep inside. She had to tell Mose about the baby. There was no use putting it off. The truth had to come out.

"Look at this bedroom. It's perfect for the girls."

Sarah realized she still stood in the hallway, her hand on her stomach, reeling with new, raw emotions. She was going to be the mother. The thought was so wonderful she had to fight not to cry.

"I'm coming," Sarah called and entered the soft pink room. She whirled around, her long skirt fluttering about her ankles. The room had big windows and a closet large enough to hold all their clothes and then some. "What a terrible waste of space." Shelves filled one side and two clothes bars filled the other. "Do the *Englisch* really have this many clothes?"

"I can't speak from experience but since this

house was once owned by *Englisch*, I have a feeling they do." He walked a few feet and opened a pair of double doors at the end of the hallway.

Sarah gasped as she took in the sheer size of the light tan room. Large windows and a sliding glass door allowed light to flood inside.

"It's not that big." Mose's laughter mingled with his words.

"Maybe not to you, but to me it's the size of a barn." Sarah tried to imagine a bed and dresser swallowed up in the expansive room. "What will we fill the room with?"

"The new king-size bed I finished just before I left for Lancaster. It's been waiting in the barn for someone to buy." Mose grinned and disappeared through a door at the back of the room.

She'd never seen a king-size bed, but couldn't wait to see it. Several pieces of furniture in his *mamm's* house showed his fine workmanship and she grew excited.

She walked into the master closet and shook her head in disgust. Again, what a waste of space. She owned a handful of dresses and two pairs of shoes. She had no clue how many clothes Mose owned, but they'd never fill this large walk-in closet.

"The bathroom's nice." Mose's voice echoed, bouncing off the walls.

Sarah moved toward the door he'd disappeared through and paused. Two sinks, a toilet and bathtub gleamed in the bright overhead lighting. Stepping in farther, Sarah saw her own reflection in the massive mirror over the sinks. She had no idea her hair was so bright red, or that she'd put on so much weight. What made Mose look at her as though she was a plate of iced cookies? She turned on her heel and scurried back to the kitchen.

"You don't like it, do you?" Mose's disappointment was palpable.

"I do like it. It's just not what I'm used to," she murmured.

"We don't have to take it, Sarah. Like I said, *Daed* can easily rent it out to someone else." He stood just inside the kitchen, his shoulder resting against a smooth wall.

"You like it, don't you?" Sarah knew his answer before he spoke. She was able to read his expressions.

"I can see the *kinder* running and playing without bumping into walls." He grinned, adding, "We'd have lots of room for a couple more *bobbels* here."

Sarah's tongue glued to the top of her mouth. She forced herself to look up. His smile was infectious and she returned a trembling, shy grin. They were alone. Nothing held her back from telling him her secret. She trusted him. Wanted him to know. Longed for him to be happy for them. Sarah took in a breath. "I need to talk to you about something wonderful, and I want you to hear me out before you speak."

Mose frowned at her, his concern adding wrinkles to his forehead. "Did I upset you with the suggestion there could be more children growing up in this home?" He reached out to her.

Sarah grasped his hand in hers and smiled, strong feeling for this vibrant man building in her heart. "No, not at all. It's just the opposite. I'm having a *bobbel*, Mose. I wanted to share the news with you."

Mose pulled her into his arms and crushed her to his chest as he murmured, "I already know."

Sarah leaned away. Mose's smile of joy left her breathless. "You already knew?"

"Of course I knew, silly. I'm the father of two. I know when a woman is carrying a child. I've known since I met you."

"But why didn't you say something? Why would you marry me if you knew I was pregnant?" Sarah's mind reeled, memories flashing like a slide show. She'd never known anyone as generous a Mose Fischer. He'd known all along and had never said a word, never questioned her.

"I first married you because I loved Joseph like a *bruder*. We grew up together, shared our hopes and dreams. I found his wife in need of me, and I found her fascinating. I needed a mother for my *kinder*. There was never a question of what should be done. It made perfect sense to do the right thing. Who else would love Joseph's child as much as me? I'll make a good father for him or her. I promise you."

He pulled her closer as tears began to flow down her face. Tenderly he held her in his arms, patting her as she clung to the front of his shirt. Grief flowed out of her, and in its place came relief and gratitude. Weak with emotion, she leaned against his chest and took in gulping sobs of air laced with joy.

Joseph was gone, but Mose was here now.

"Have you seen a midwife yet?" His warm breath stirred her hair as he spoke softly in her ear.

"Not yet," Sarah admitted, her head still pressed against his chest. She liked the feel of his arms around her, the way he tenderly kissed her cheek. "I just recently found out. But Linda says I must go to the *Englisch* doctor for a sonogram, to make sure the *bobbel* is okay."

"We'll get an appointment for you." Mose rubbed her back, making her warm and breathless in the cool, air-conditioned house.

Sarah was thrilled and relieved that she wasn't alone anymore. But did she truly deserve this happiness? She wasn't so sure.

A few hours later, Mose and Otto lifted out the heavy sliding glass door and together leaned it against the patio wall.

"I just need to take these old runners out and put in some new ones." Otto glanced Mose's way. He grunted as he squatted, his old knees cracking like popcorn. It took only a moment to remove the old tracks, stuff the plastic packaging into his overall pocket and slip the new tracks in place. "I'm glad you two decided to take this place." Otto checked the rollers and grinned in satisfaction. "I have a good feeling about this *haus*. It may be a bit fancy, but it will make a great home for the *kinder* to grow in."

"Sarah's finally okay with the *haus*. At first she was concerned what people might say, it being so different than the tract homes close by."

Otto's brows arched. "How are you two

doing? Rumor has it the girl's got a temper. She use it on you yet?"

Mose frowned in frustration. He dreaded the talk he knew he had to have with his father.

Together the two men replaced the door in its railing. Mose stretched out his back. "That door was heavy. Let's rest." He pointed to the wooden steps that led down into the shaded yard and sat on the first step. His father sat one step down.

Mose prayed to *Gott* as he looked at his scuffed steel-toed boots and tried to gather the right words to say. "I don't know what temper you're referring to, *Daed*. Sarah's never flared up at me, but that's not saying she won't, or that she doesn't have a temper. Most women do, including *Mamm*." He and his father shared a secret grin. "Sarah and I are getting along fine and the *kinder* seem happy, which makes me happy. I've got nothing to grumble about, except certain family members who keep poking their nose where it doesn't belong. Especially Ulla. You know what she's like. You're her bishop. Maybe you could help keep her in line and out of my personal life."

"I have talked with her, Mose…but you must talk to her, too." Otto swatted at a mosquito. "Ulla thinks you've replaced Greta too soon. She's hurting. *Gott* made women tenderhearted. She needs time to heal. It's the other rumors causing all the family to chatter. Ever since you brought Sarah home there's been speculation flying back and forth between Pinecraft and Lancaster County. Mostly about her behavior back home. Even your *mamm's* guilty of adding to the drama. She thinks Sarah's pregnant."

Mose rubbed his hand across his damp forehead. "Sarah *is* pregnant."

"Then why in the world would you…" Otto's sandy brows furrowed in astonishment as he looked up at his son.

"Marry her? Is that what you're asking? Why would I marry Sarah and raise Joseph's baby as my own?"

"How can it be Joseph's *kinder*, Mose? Do the math. He's been dead for six months. She's feeding you a lie and you're believing her. Ralf Miller warned me Sarah would bring trouble to our community. I'm beginning to believe him." Otto stood up, his face flushed with anger.

"Lower your voice, *Daed*. Sarah's just inside the *haus*. She might hear your foolishness."

Otto sat back down on the step with a thump. "Then tell me. How do you know for sure this baby is Joseph's?"

"Because I trust Sarah. I've never caught her in a lie. She's an honorable woman. She didn't suspect she might be pregnant before Joseph died, and later blamed her weakness and bad stomach on grief, but I knew better. She's had a test and it was positive."

"*Gott* bless her. Poor woman." Otto wiped sweat from his upper lip. "Joseph died in such a tragic way. I can see how she could have missed the signs."

"Life's caught up with her. The *bobbel* will be due in a few months, maybe less. Sarah will have an appointment for a sonogram in a couple of days. When we tell the family, they'd better be kind to her, *Daed*. I won't have her upset over their unwarranted suspicions. She's been through enough."

Otto's shoulders visibly slumped. "Pregnant. Who would have guessed? I'll talk to the family and church elders. They'll be good to her and the *kinder* or they'll answer to me. What a blessing this child would have been to Joseph's *mamm* and *daed*." Otto met Mose's gaze. "I'm sorry I didn't trust you. I should have known there would be more to her story."

Mose put his hand on his father's bony shoulder. "Sarah and I are going to break the news about the baby at Mercy's birthday gathering tomorrow night. Maybe once everyone knows the facts, they'll shut their mouths."

"Don't count on it, especially when it comes to Ulla." Otto smirked. "She likes to talk."

Sarah slid open the glass door and stepped out onto the wooden deck behind them. "The door opens so easy now. You two did a fine job."

"That we did." Otto stood and wiped his brow.

Mose patted the wooden step his father had just vacated. "Come, join me. You haven't seen the back yard yet."

Sarah hurried over, gathered up her full skirt and eased down on the wooden plank. She scooted close to Mose as Otto stepped past her with a smile.

"It's lovely out here. Just look at that palm tree." She pointed to a tall, well-trimmed tree in the corner of the fenced yard. "It has to be twenty-feet tall. The *kinder* are going to enjoy playing in the shade in the afternoon." Sarah's eyes were bright with excitement.

"I can see the two of them digging in that flower bed. Beatrice loves to eat dirt. We'll have to watch her closely." Mose laughed and grabbed her hand, his thumb rubbing the top of her knuckles, his heart full of joy. Sarah had become his friend, and now other emotions flooded his mind. He longed to pull her close, touch her hair, where a soft curl danced in the wind.

Sarah laughed with him. "This is going to make a wonderful home for us, Mose. You, me and the *kinder*."

Mose glanced at his father and smiled. Everything seemed to be falling into place. He hadn't felt this worry-free since before Greta had died, and the feeling was wonderful. Thunder rumbled overhead, the fast approaching cluster of dark clouds threatening a storm soon to come.

# Chapter Thirteen

Linda honked from outside, the golf cart motor revving as the front door opened. Sarah gave her impatient friend a wave. She grabbed her satchel and turned to Mose's mother.

The old rocking chair groaned with Theda's every movement. Her fingers knew when to pull and tug on the thick yarn as she crocheted a pink blanket for Beatrice.

"I won't be long. Linda and I are just going to Mose's shop to pick out some furniture for the new *haus*." Sarah rubbed her hand across her slightly protruding stomach, the baby's movements growing stronger as each day passed. "The girls should sleep for at least another hour."

"Don't worry about those two. Do your shopping and have a nice time. And tell that girl I said not to drive so fast in that fancy cart." Theda sounded firm but softened her words with a generous smile.

Pausing at the opened door, Sarah straightened her *kapp* and reinforced several pins to make sure the lightweight prayer covering was firmly held down. The brisk Florida winds often caught her unaware.

"Is there anything I can get you while I'm out? We're going to the market for a few things for the party tonight."

"*Nee.* Everyone's bringing a dish. There'll be enough food. Go. Enjoy yourself. You spend too much time in the house worrying about those girls."

Sarah hurried out the door, her blue dress flying behind her as she ran across the grass to the light blue golf cart. She plopped on the passenger seat. The new cart's seat cushions were made of the softest leather. She allowed her fingers to knead into the soft hide before buckling her seat belt, and then fiddled with the dangling white leather canopy that embellished the fancy cart. "Another *Englisch* contraption, Linda? Does no one use a buggy in Pinecraft?"

"Not really. There's one parked at the restaurant on the edge of town, but it's just for show. Kurt took the van this morning, so it was the old tandem bicycle or this. What would you have grabbed?"

Her question was accompanied by a mischievous grin. Linda's dress, the palest pink, matched her flushed cheeks to perfection. Sarah noticed her white *kapp* sat sideways on a twisted bun of dark hair positioned at the back of her head. Her sister-in-law looked surprisingly spry for a very pregnant woman due to have her first baby soon.

"*Ya*, I think the golf cart." Sarah had no idea what kind of driver Linda might be. A shiver of excitement tingled down her spine. She'd longed for change and now she had it. "I shouldn't be enjoying all these new experiences so much. *Gott's* going to get angry at my growing *Englisch* ways."

With her petite hands on the steering wheel, Linda looked at Sarah and made a silly monkey face. "Don't be ridiculous. You're no longer Old Order Amish or under your father's thumb. *Gott* just wants us to love Him. He doesn't worry Himself with how we get to and fro. Besides, the cart only goes 25 miles an hour and that's only if the wind's blowing at your back." Linda hit the gas pedal, glanced behind them and backed out of the drive. The street was quiet, not a car in sight, which wasn't unusual that early in the morning. "I won't be able to drive much longer. I'm going to enjoy my time behind this wheel while I can." The cart sped down the tree-lined street, going full out. Loose strands of Sarah's long hair whipped her in the face. She leaned back, grabbed the metal frame of the canopy and held on with a death grip.

The old barn smelled of freshly cut wood, stain and the heavy cologne of Mose's last *Englisch* customer.

He wiped a tack cloth over the dusty spindle he'd just cut, admiring the shape and feel of the wood in his hand as much as hc had as a boy, when the dream of owning his own furniture business began to form and then consume him.

His father had expected him to become a farmer, like him and his father before him. But Mose had stood his ground, only working on the family farm during harvest, when everyone was expected to pitch in before the weather changed and ruined the crops with frost back in Lancaster County.

The family exodus to Florida had been his dream's saving grace. He'd bought the old barn with his own hard-earned savings, and soon orders for oak furniture were coming in faster than he could fill them. He'd been forced to hire help, and even with the economy's downturn, he'd found himself dedicating more and more time to furniture-making.

Mose dusted off his pants and ran his fingers through his sweaty hair. He never wore a hat while he worked, but he reached for it now. His growling stomach reminded him he had a roast beef sandwich waiting for him in the cooler up front. Placing the straw hat on the back of his head, he made a move for his office, his mouth watering.

"Another order for that bishop bench came in," Samuel Yoder called over to Mose as he weaved through the sales floor littered with furniture waiting for pickup or delivery.

"*Gut.* You can work late tonight making the seat since you're so good at it."

Short, blond and full of energy, the young new hire gave his boss a grin. His apprenticeship was going well, and he'd soon be working in the back next to Mose. Another man would have to be hired. Someone who would learn like Samuel, by trial and error. They would soon need another hand to fill orders. Mose had learned from the beginning, you got more work out of a happy employee.

"I'm eating early," Mose called over his shoulder. "Sarah made roast beef last night and the leftovers are calling to me. I'll be in the office if you need me."

Samuel sent an envious smile Mose's way and playfully flipped the dust cloth at him as he dusted the table tops around the showroom. "Someday I'll find myself a wife and have a fine sandwich waiting for me, too."

Mose laughed and went into his office just off the main door, his thoughts on Sarah, until Greta's face pushed its way into his mind. His smile faded. He'd begun to miss Greta in a different way since he'd married Sarah. Thoughts of his dead wife came less and less often. He tried to remember how her voice sounded, but Sarah's voice filled the void in his mind. Was it possible to love two women at once?

The bell over the sales door rang out. A strong gust of wind blew in, disheveling papers on his desk. Mose looked up and saw Linda hurry in with Sarah close behind, both women's dresses spotted with fat drops of rain. They busied themselves righting their *kapps*. Sarah waved at Samuel and greeted him. "How are you this fine morning?"

Samuel blushed a fire-engine red as he always did when he saw Sarah. He smiled and dipped his head. "*Guder mariye*, Mrs. Fischer."

Sarah looked young and happy, her pregnancy beginning to show under her loose-fitting dress. Joseph would never see the glow of pregnancy on her face or watch her body blossom with child. Mose pushed away the grief he felt for his friend and forced a smile of welcome on his face. His heartbeat quickened as he walked toward Sarah. "You ladies picked a fine time to be out. It's about to storm from the looks of it."

Sarah whirled at the sound of his voice and rushed over to him. "Mose, the cart ride was wonderful. I felt like a child again, the rain hitting me in the face and the golf cart sliding on the pavement."

He stood and pulled his handkerchief from his pocket and gently wiped her face dry as her eyes shined at him. He fought the urge to kiss her, his feelings for her becoming more obvious to him every day.

"I'm sorry I dampened your handkerchief."

"Silly girl. That's why I carry the rag. To help beautiful damsels in distress." He heard the flirting in the tone of his voice, like he might have done at nineteen when he'd first met Greta. He cleared his throat and sat back on his leather chair, his thoughts scrambled with joy and sorrow. Greta was his past. Sarah his future. He got up and walked around the old wooden desk that had been his *grossdaadi's* pride and joy. "You've come to pick out furniture?"

Linda stumbled into the room, using the

hem of her skirt to wipe away the last of the rain drops from her face. "We have. I hope now's a good time."

"It is. Business has been slow all morning, but Samuel tells me he sold another bench earlier."

Samuel grinned, still busy dusting furniture. "I put all the pieces you mentioned in the corner."

Mose took Sarah's elbow, leading her through a maze of dining-room tables and chairs.

Linda followed and then stopped to touch a rocking chair with a padded seat. "We'll both need one of these soon, Sarah."

Mose watched a happy expression soften Sarah's face. Her hand went to her protruding stomach. "We will, but for today its dining-room furniture that brings me." A warm glow coursed through his body. He'd felt the same draw to Greta while she had been pregnant. The urge to protect and provide. To love.

The king-size bed he'd told her about came into view and he slowed. "That's the bed I mentioned. Do you think it's going to fit the room okay?"

Sarah glanced toward the bed and then turned to Linda. The women exchanged looks he couldn't read. Neither of them spoke for a moment. Linda finally said, "It's lovely. Did you make the frame?"

"I did. Just finished the project this morning with a mattress set. I'm having it sent over to the house this afternoon if it meets with your approval, *mein frau*."

Sarah's skin grew pink. "I love it. It will make a fine bed for us. *Danke*."

Mose nodded. "*Gut*, I'm glad you like it." In Lancaster he'd felt sure this arranged marriage would work as just a convenience. But now? His heart had become engaged. These new feelings for Sarah made him uncomfortable, as though he was being unfaithful to his dead wife, but he was growing to care for Sarah. Very much.

"There's two sets of dining-room furniture to choose from over there." Mose gestured toward two large wood tables and matching chairs at the back of the showroom. His voice sounded perfectly normal, but he didn't feel normal. He felt like a fool torn between two women. One vibrantly alive. The other...dead.

Sarah and Linda moved toward the tables and examined the matching chairs, their voices low as they chatted and compared styles and colors. Sarah let her hand slide across the smooth surface of the light oak top. "I like this one." The oblong table with simple lines also appealed to him.

Mose motioned to Samuel. "Make sure that dining-room set goes on the truck, too."

"Will do."

"I have to get back to work, Sarah. I can hear my phone ringing." Mose hurried away, leaving the two women to look around the big store on their own. As he grabbed the phone, he threw his hat on his desk and plopped down in his chair, his thoughts on Sarah and the pending birth of the *bobbel*, rather than the customer talking in his ear.

The rain shower passed. Linda chatted as she drove the cart, her thoughts about the furniture they'd seen bubbling out. Sarah couldn't shake the feeling something had been wrong when they'd met up with Mose. He'd seemed quiet and distracted before they left. "Do you think Mose was acting himself?"

"What?"

"Mose. Did he seem tense to you. Withdrawn?"

"*Nee*, just busy. Why?" Linda frowned over at Sarah as she drove down the main road to Pinecraft.

"I just thought he wasn't himself."

"Maybe something's up at work. Or he's

just behaving like a man. Kurt's always acting strange. Men, they're different. Kind of weird and romantic at the strangest times."

Had she imagined his mood? He might have just been hungry or tired. "Do you think we could stop by a clothing store? Beatrice needs a few pairs of socks and that sweater she wears is terrible. I'll make her one for winter, but for now a store-bought one will have to do."

"I have a better idea. Why don't we go pack up the rest of her clothes and take them to the new house. We've got plenty of time before we have to be back." Linda did a quick turn down an unfamiliar street and pulled into the driveway of a simple white house.

Sarah realized this had to be the home Greta and Mose had shared. "I think I'll wait in the cart."

"Don't be silly. Mose won't mind you coming in. He's had the place locked up for almost a year. It's time Beatrice has all her things, and someone's got to bring the clothes over to the new *haus* anyway. It might as well be us."

Sarah slid out of the cart. "Do you have keys?"

"Sure. I used to babysit Beatrice when she was little, before the temper and your bad influence on her." Linda grinned. "She's become a little terror since Mercy was born."

"She got a new sister and lost her *mamm*. That's a lot for a four-year-old." Sarah understood the child's loss, but was being firm and consistent with her rules and affection.

Linda stuck the key in the lock. It turned with ease. The front door swung open to a dark house. "It smells dusty in here. Probably from being closed up for so long. Mose needs to think about selling this place or at least renting it out."

Sarah stepped in and looked around, her eyes slowly adjusting to the darkness. She bumped into an overstuffed chair and rubbed her shin. "No electricity?" She tried a switch and was surprised when the overhead light came on and a warm, inviting room was exposed.

Toys lay on the hardwood floors by a comfortable-looking overstuffed couch. Two glasses sat next to each other on the coffee table. The only time Mose had spoken of Greta at length, he'd said her labor had come on suddenly and had lasted for days. She'd hemorrhaged just hours after Mercy's birth and had passed away quietly. She remembered how sad Mose had sounded when he'd told her there had been nothing the doctors could do.

A shiver scurried down her back. No one had disturbed the house in a long time. The dust layer was thick. This had to be the way the house had looked a year ago when they'd left in a hurry for the hospital, their hearts joyful, and the *bobbel* finally coming. She backed up toward the door, feeling like an intruder. This had been Mose and Greta's home. She needed to leave.

"What are you doing here?"

Sarah whirled around, wishing the floor would open and swallow her. Mose stood at the doorway, his face pinched, a mask of pain. "I… We were…"

"Get out!" Mose's tone was harsh, almost whip-like.

Sarah brushed past him in a run, her legs jelly under her, her hand protectively holding her stomach.

*What have I done?*

# Chapter Fourteen

"Please be still, Mercy," Sarah pleaded. "It's almost time for your party and you're not dressed." Bending farther over the bed, Sarah raked her fingers through her disheveled hair and poked wayward strands under her *kapp* and out of her eyes.

She made a grab for one of Mercy's chubby little legs. Wiggling like a worm, Mercy proved too fast and flipped over, her dimpled knees digging into the quilted bedcover. She quickly got away from Sarah, one shoe on, one shoe off. Mercy twisted into a sitting position and smiled a toothy grin.

"*Ach*, for a second pair of hands." Sarah groaned and reached for Mercy again.

Out of thin air, Mose's hand appeared and grabbed Mercy by the foot. He pulled her kicking and giggling toward Sarah. "She's in rare form today." He held the baby's foot while Sarah quickly tugged on the shoe.

"*Danke.*" Sarah slipped the soft cotton dress she'd made for Mercy over the baby's silky head. Two snaps up the back of the dress took forever to fasten. "Let me put your apron on and you'll be ready to meet the world one year older."

Mercy smiled at her and pulled her hand out of her mouth. "Ma...ma...ma," Mercy cooed and grabbed for Sarah's skirt with wet fingers.

"That's right," Sarah encouraged and slipped her white prayer *kapp* on her small head. "You practice your words. After tomorrow's surgery you'll be talking as well as your sister, I promise." She quickly tied the two white ribbons under the child's drool-soaked neck and lifted the baby into her arms.

Mose sat down on the edge of the bed and bent to remove his work shoes. "Put Mercy in her cot for a moment, please. We need to talk."

They hadn't spoken since Mose had ordered her out of his home that morning. Sarah tensed. His demeanor had alarmed her. She raked at her hair, trying to gather up the loose strands. All afternoon she'd replayed what had happened and had regretted her actions. She'd inadvertently crossed an invisible line. What he had to say couldn't be good. Sarah sat Mercy in her bed with one of her favorite cloth books and turned back.

Bent at the waist, Mose placed his elbows on his thighs and sighed deeply. Sarah looked down at his clenched, white-knuckled hands. "I'm sorry for the way I acted. What I said earlier was out of line. Please forgive me." Mose looked up, his eyes rimmed red, his face contorted with pain.

"You mustn't ask for my forgiveness. I should never have gone to your *haus* without permission. I knew it was wrong the moment I stepped through the door. I ask for *your* forgiveness, Mose. I never meant to hurt you." Sarah sat beside him, reaching to take his hand. Her insides trembled.

Mose turned to her. "You didn't hurt me." He patted her hand and kissed her knuckles. "You didn't hurt me at all. I hurt myself. Greta is dead. Life should go on, but I thought... I don't know what I thought." He dropped her hand and pushed his fist into the soft mattress. "I thought if I could keep the house the way it was the day she...perhaps Greta would come home again. I was crazy with pain. Out of my mind and not thinking clearly. That's no excuse for my behavior. I know she's never coming home. I have to face facts and get on with my life. The house needs to be emptied. Someone else will make it a home and bring it back to life with *kinder* running through the halls."

Sarah squeezed his hand in hers and sighed. She knew the depths of his pain and understood completely. She'd left Joseph's clothes at the foot of their bed for months, waiting for him, yet knowing he'd never wear them again. If someone had disturbed them she would have lashed out, too. Sarah wiped a tear from her cheek and blinked. They had this loss in common.

Mose's eyes darkened. Deep lines cut into his forehead. "I'm selling the house. I hadn't been back to our home since the day she died, and yesterday I sought clarity and closure. I needed to feel her presence one last time. I struggle with the fear that I might forget her, the way she smiled, the sound of her voice."

His revelation shook her. Mercy chose that moment to cry and broke the bond of trust building between them. Sarah moved to the cot and picked up the squirming baby. "You'll never forget her as long as you have your *kinder*, Mose. Greta lives on in them."

Mose reached for Mercy. Sarah placed the child in his arms. She watched as he snuggled his face in her neck and whispered, "I have you, *liebling*."

Sarah slipped out the door and hurried to

the kitchen to help Theda finish the birthday meal. Father and daughter needed a moment together, and she needed time to remind herself she would have a baby soon. Her heart ached so deep in her chest it was almost painful. She worked on a fresh green salad, tearing lettuce leaves and slicing onions and tomatoes. Her child would never know the love of its *daed*, but it would have Mose, wonderful Mose, and for that she was grateful.

Explaining birthdays to a four-year-old became a battle royal minutes later. "Where is my cake?" Beatrice stamped her tiny foot against the kitchen tile. "Why does Mercy get a cake and not me?"

"It's her first birthday. A time to rejoice with her. You'll get a cake soon. Your birthday is just a few weeks away. That will be your special day."

"Mercy never had a special day before." Beatrice poked her finger toward the cake for a taste.

Sarah brushed her hand away just before the child's finger reached the edge of the swirled buttercream frosting. "You could end up on the naughty step if you keep acting like this, Beatrice. Mercy is the birthday girl today. Next time you'll be the birthday princess."

"I don't want Mercy to have a birthday.

*Mamm* went to heaven because of Mercy. I heard my *groossmammi* say so. I want my *mamm*. Not Mercy." Tears poured down the child's face. Beyond control, Beatrice stormed into the bedroom and slapped her sister.

Sarah rushed into the room as Mercy cried out, and saw the deep red handprint on her face. Without a word, Mose scooped Beatrice away. The unhappy child kicked and screamed for her *mamm* as they hurried out of the bedroom. Sarah's heart pounded in her ears as she lifted Mercy off the quilt on the floor and embraced her. She headed for the rocking chair and cuddled her. "It's all right, *liebling*. Your sister is just unhappy. She loves you. She's just missing your *mamm* and doesn't know who to blame." Sarah wept for Mose's motherless *kinder*, for Mose's loss and for her own baby to come.

When she returned to the kitchen, Theda moved around the wood island in the middle of the room, leaving the food she had been preparing. She wiped her hands on her apron, her forehead creased. "Don't upset yourself, Sarah. Mose will deal with Beatrice. He's good with her when she gets like this."

"I just feel so sad for the *kinder* and Mose. Life can be so cruel." Sarah brushed back the damp blond curls from Mercy's forehead and pushed out a deep sigh.

"Death always hits the *kinder* hardest, Sarah. Beatrice doesn't understand yet. She's too young, and it doesn't help that Ulla's bitterness is rubbing off on her. *Ach*, only *Gott* knows what that old woman has said to her. I blame her for this outburst, not Beatrice. It's time Otto had another long talk with Ulla. Maybe the threat of the ban will bring about change."

Sarah was glad for her caring mother-in-law. By marrying Mose, she'd gained Theda, Otto and the rest of the Fischers as her family. She was truly blessed.

Two long tables with benches on either side provided enough room for everyone to sit together in the dining room. Men at one table, women and *kinder* at the other.

The afternoon drama seemed all but forgotten. Mercy ate her food and grinned when Sarah placed a slice of birthday cake on her tray.

Beatrice sat with her father, away from the other *kinder*. His arm pulled her back when she tried to get down from the bench.

"You're deep in thought," Linda murmured close to Sarah's ear.

Sarah wished she had a private moment to talk to her friend. "I'm sorry. It's been a difficult afternoon."

Linda leaned closer. "I'll bet. Did Mose give you a hard time about going to the house? I thought he was going to bust a blood vessel when he kicked us out."

"He was very apologetic about the whole incident. He's still grieving."

Linda looked around, making sure no one was listening. "It's been a year, Sarah. You're more forgiving than I would be. I'd have Kurt's head on a platter if he'd spoken to me like that."

Sarah fed Mercy another bite of cake. "He's been through a lot. I think he just reached his breaking point and lost control."

"You're too kind. He doesn't deserve you, but I'm glad he's got you." Linda shrugged. "I guess I'm just mean-spirited. Why don't we go make sure everyone's got cake and get this mess cleared away? My feet are swollen, and I need to get home."

Sarah nodded and wiped Mercy down before putting her on her unsteady feet. The baby toddled away and headed for the toy box in the corner.

Generous slices of cake were cut, and Sarah began to hand them out to the ladies who'd been busy serving and were still eating. Ulla sat at the head of the table. She looked away as Sarah approached and sat a plate of cake in front of her. With a shove, Ulla pushed the plate away and got up from the bench.

Linda pulled Sarah into the kitchen. "Don't let that old woman get to you again. She's full of bitterness. She'll never forgive you for marrying Mose."

Sarah ran hot water into the sink and added homemade soap. She slid a stack of dirty dinner plates into the swirl of soapy bubbles.

Linda kept up with Sarah, each piece placed on the island behind them until the last dirty dish was finished. "I'll go get the silverware. Linda paused as she turned toward the door. *"Was tut Sie hier?"*

Sarah turned, her apron damp against her round stomach, wondering who Linda was talking to.

Ulla stood just inside the kitchen door, her burning gaze on Sarah. "I can't have what I need, Linda. You know that. *Gott* has taken my Greta away from me, and Mose has replaced her with *this* woman," she spat out in fury, her bony finger pointing in Sarah's direction. "I will never accept her as the *mamm* of my *enkelkinder. Nee.* I know the wrong she's done. She brings trouble. She will not be accepted in *die familye* as long as I breathe." Ulla hurried out of the room, her loud weeping permeating the house just before the front door slammed behind her.

Sarah took off her *kapp* and laid it on a wave of wrinkled fabric at her knees. She looked into the sky, through the palm tree next to the wooden steps and pushed a deep sigh through dry lips. Peeking out from palm tree fronds, the moon glowed golden and then disappeared.

Behind her the house grew dark, only a slice of light cut across the porch from the nightlight in the front bathroom. Winds carrying the scent of jasmine picked up and blew hard, mussing the knot of hair at the back of her head. Somewhere nearby a frog croaked, disturbing the blessed silence calming her troubled soul.

The words in her *bruder's* recent letter came back to her. *We've had a few chilly days and I thought of you in sunny Florida.* A million miles away, Lancaster County shivered in the cold.

The screen door groaned and footfalls announced an intruder. Sarah turned and silently grumbled as she made out the shape of a man.

"Can I join you?" Otto murmured.

Sarah heard the creak of the white rocker as

he sat behind her. She wanted to shout at him to go away, to leave her to her thoughts. Instead she said, *"Ya."* She'd had enough drama for one day.

Silence, interrupted by the steady squeaking of the rocking chair, fled.

The old German clock in the house chimed twice. She should be in bed sleeping. Moving day would come early and she needed her rest. The boards grew hard under her, and she resettled herself. She lay her hand on her stomach and enjoyed the *bobbel's* strong movements. The *kinder* lurched, restless, too.

"When Theda and I married, her *grossmammi* disapproved of me."

Sarah jumped at the sudden sound of his voice. She didn't know if he expected a response. She had none to give.

"She caused as much trouble as we'd let her." Otto stopped rocking. "My *daed's* advice made all the difference back then and still rings true today. 'Live your life to please *Gott* and no one else.' I still practice this advice and find it profitable today. I shared it with Mose and now you."

Sarah bowed her head. *"Danke."*

"There's nothing to thank me for, Sarah. We all need advice from time to time. I know Ulla is causing you grief, but she's just an angry old woman. The rest of the community is happy you're here. I see the difference in Mose, and so do they. He's opening up. Ready to go on with life since he found you. Sarah Fischer, you are an answer to prayer."

"But I thought…"

Otto began to rock again. "Then you thought wrong."

Sarah slipped on her shoes and stood. "I'd best go to bed."

"*Ya*, you best had. The sun will be up in a few hours and moving day is fast approaching."

Sarah looked at the moon one last time. A cluster of billowing clouds hid the golden globe. "Good night," she whispered. She opened the door and stepped into the house.

"Sleep well."

Sarah sighed. "I will."

# Chapter Fifteen

Dressed in an old, soft dress she'd often slept in, with a medium-sized box tucked between her legs, Sarah concentrated on the task at hand. She folded a plain slip of Beatrice's and tucked it down the side of the bulging container before fighting a roll of sticky tape to finally seal the box.

Mose walked into the bedroom, his light blond hair darkened and mussed by the shower he'd just taken. A towel draped around his neck and his pajama top was damp from the water dripping from his hair.

"Can I help you finish packing? It's late." Mose rubbed his head dry and threw the towel in the dirty clothes basket, still damp.

Sarah watched the wet towel flop on dry clothes. Joseph had always hung his towel on the shower pole and let it dry. The idea of wet clothes in her laundry basket annoyed her beyond reason. Perhaps she should say something, but she seemed to be nagging him a lot for little things that didn't really matter. Linda told her she did the same to Kurt. That they were just having pregnancy mood swings and had nothing to worry about. Sarah hoped her friend was right. She couldn't remember being so prim and proper with Joseph. She looked Mose's way. "*Danke*, but this is the last box. I think we're ready for the move tomorrow."

Mose padded over to Mercy's cot. "She looks so restful. Like nothing's wrong."

"*Ya.*"

"Linda's coming for both girls early in the morning, but I guess you already know that." Mose turned toward her, his hand raking through his wet beard.

The action reminded her of Joseph. Pain stabbed her heart but she pushed the memory away. "Linda said to have them ready at seven. Beatrice likes to sleep in. I have a feeling she'll be a handful unless she gets an early nap." Sarah took of sip of water from her glass, poked a vitamin pill into her mouth and swallowed. "Her offer to watch the *kinder* was a blessing. Try to imagine them underfoot during the move."

"A nightmare." Mose smiled. "I'm sorry for

what Ulla said. She must be dealt with. *Daed* plans to see her tomorrow with several of her favorite deacons in tow. Her harsh attitude has to stop."

"She said what she saw as truth, Mose. We did marry fast. She's old and having a hard time dealing with her daughter's death. Plus, she's heard the rumors."

"You're more generous than I am," Mose said. "That woman doesn't deserve your kindness."

"I seem to take trouble wherever I go."

Mose looked over to Sarah, who was still sitting on the edge of the bed. "I was drawn to you from the moment I met you. Do you know that? Your kindness to my *kinder* convinced me you were the right woman for this family before your problems with your father began. Did I love you?" His eyes grew dark. "*Nee*, but I was fond of you. Now I treasure you. Things will get better, *frau*. You'll sce. Sleep well." He got into bed and snapped off the lamp.

Sarah placed her hand on her stomach and felt her child kick. *Please be right. Let this marriage work. Help Mose to love me.*

Gray skies and a light drizzle didn't slow their moving day, or the flow of boxes, small pieces of furniture and lamps into the house.

Sarah opened the front door to let in workers loaded down with all manner of things. She handed them bottles of water and pointed out places to place unmarked boxes. Mose made it very clear at breakfast that she was to do no lifting or moving of furniture. None. Rebellious since the day she was born, Sarah shoved over boxes with her foot and kept the path clear. When no one was watching, she added an extra push when the front door fought the new refrigerator for space. She was pregnant, not sick.

Theda hurried up on the porch, her mitt-covered hands holding a covered bowl that smelled wonderful. "I see they found a job for you, too. I was put on lunch duty."

Sarah opened the screen door to let the short woman pass. "*Ach*. Whatever that is smells wonderful."

"*Danke*, Sarah. Look, it's really starting to rain now. We could have done without the showers but *Gott* knows what He's doing. His way is best."

"*Ya*," Sarah agreed and sniffed the bowl. "*Wunderbaar.*"

"I made Mose's favorite dish. I hope you like chicken and dumplings."

Sarah's mouth watered. "*Ya*, very much."

His arms full of folded quilts and blankets,

Mose stumbled through the opened door and grinned at Sarah, rain dripping off his nose and beard. "We're almost finished. Just one more load of toys and Beatrice's wagon."

"You all have worked so hard." Sarah opened the door again, letting Otto in carrying Mercy's bed slats and headboard. "The cot will have to be wiped down before it can be set up. Mose better do it before tomorrow or you'll have two kids in bed with you," he chortled, dabbing at the rain on his face. "Kurt said the *kinder* are coming home tomorrow morning, early. They slept well, but Beatrice is running Linda ragged."

"*Ya*, we know. She called Mose this morning and complained about Beatrice's energy level." Sarah shared Otto's laugh and then got serious. "Don't forget, Mercy has her surgery in the morning. Please pray *Gott's* will for her life, Otto. Ulla graciously offered to care for Beatrice until the procedure is over." Sarah couldn't help but wonder how the conversation had gone between Ulla and Otto the night before, but didn't dare ask.

Otto and Mose dropped their burdens and hurried to the kitchen, the aroma of chicken and dumplings drawing them back. Sarah followed, the tower of boxes and furniture scattered around bothering her sense of rhythm and order.

Theda set the table with deep paper plates and napkins. Sarah helped her add plastic knives and forks, and then sat down next to Mose. A river of thick chicken broth, chunks of white meat and fluffy dumplings swallowed up their plates as Theda ladled out the steaming food.

"The meal looks *wunderbaar*, as usual." Otto dug in.

Sarah smiled, growing more and more comfortable with the Fischer family. In Lancaster only silence and hurtful looks had accompanied their meals. Thoughts of her father brought nothing but pain. Sarah pushed the memory away and began to eat.

Mose pulled out the plastic trash bag and tied a knot in it. "*Danke* for lunch, *Mamm*. I appreciate you taking some of the strain off Sarah."

Has she seen the doctor yet?"

"*Nee*, but she has an appointment."

"You go with her, Mose. She will want you there."

"I have…"

"*Ach*, you men are all alike. You have no idea what you'd do there. I know men take no interest in such things, but she will need you that day, son. Trust me."

Mose stopped throwing away paper napkins. "*Ya*. I think you could be right. Linda can't go with her. She has her own doctor's appointment. I'll offer to go and see what Sarah says."

"You're a good husband. Just like your *daed*." Theda threw an empty box his way. "You best hurry up or you'll be living in this mess for days."

"Do you think Sarah likes the *haus*? I mean, *really* likes it?" Mose set the stack of boxes down and pulled out a chair.

"I'm sure her past keeps her from enjoying a lot of life's pleasures, but she'll get over that in time. Be patient with her. Once the baby comes, all will be well between you and her."

"I'm praying you're right." Mose hugged his mother, wanting this kind of parental love and connection for his *kinder* with Sarah.

Handed over to the pediatric nurse, Mercy smiled as she was carried away. Mose wanted to call her back. He didn't completely trust doctors, and allowing one of them to cut into his daughter's eardrums shook him to the core.

"I think this is the waiting room." Sarah took a seat close to a big picture window and patted the comfortable-looking chair next to her.

Mose shook his head and began walking up and down the narrow path between chairs, too restless to do anything but pray and pace. *Gott, keep my daughter in your hands. Bring her through this surgery with healing and restoration.*

Sarah sat completely still, eyes closed, head, hands clenched in a prayerful pose.

"She'll be fine. It's not a complicated surgery. Just tubes inserted. We have nothing to worry about." Mose didn't completely believe the words he spoke. But he wanted to reassure Sarah, keep her from stressing.

Sarah opened her eyes. "You're not worried at all?" Her eyebrow arched, waiting for his reply.

Mose hung his head. He hadn't fooled her. Of course she knew he was worried. "*Ya*, I'm worried, but I always am when doctors are around."

"I hate hospitals. I have no reason to. I just do." Sarah shrugged her shoulders and picked up a magazine. She read the title splashed across the front, threw the limp book back on the table and murmured, "Hunting books! Who wants to see dead animals in a hospital waiting room?"

Mose smiled and walked over to the vending

machine. He turned Sarah's way. "Would you like some chocolate?"

"It's not good for the baby, but *danke*."

He'd become infatuated with her. He longed to see her when he was at work, took joy in the sound of her voice and the way she moved. Mose grabbed the bag of chocolate peanuts from the dispensing tray and tore open the bag. He wished Sarah would pick a fight with him or debate the merits of growing hay versus barley. Anything to keep his mind off Mercy and what was going on.

"Beatrice was in a good mood today." He settled in the chair next to her and reached for the hunting book.

"*Ya*, she was. Did Ulla say anything about your dad's conversation with her?"

"*Nee*. She acted quiet, but very polite when I dropped Beatrice off. Something she hasn't been in a long time."

Mose put down the book and slipped the candy bag into his pocket. He tried to find a place for his hands, failed, and then gripped the chair arms in frustration. Moments later he looked at his pocket watch and sighed. Only twenty minutes had passed, but it felt like hours.

Sarah laughed, then snorted.

"What's so funny?" Mose knew what she was laughing at and he didn't like it one bit.

"You, you silly goose. Relax. Pray, but don't work yourself into a nervous fit." She smoothed her skirt and adjusted her prayer *kapp*.

Sarah didn't look any too calm to Mose, with her lopsided *kapp* and worry lines as deep as corn rows across her forehead. "Oh, and you're so calm? *Nee*, I think you're just as concerned as I am and poking fun to distract me."

Sarah turned toward Mose, the smile gone. "*Ya*, I was teasing but you need to remember *Gott* loves our Mercy, and all will be well. We have to believe."

Mose smiled, his lips dry. "I'm so glad you're here with me. You bless me, *mein frau*."

He felt strong emotions for Sarah. His heart raced when he thought of Sarah, saw her or smelled the fragrance of her soap. Could he be falling in love with this kind, thoughtful woman so quickly?

Two hours later Mose lifted Mercy from her car seat and handed the sleeping baby into Sarah's waiting arms. Small squares of cotton gauze covered Mercy's ears, but her cheeks weren't flushed and she'd smiled at them when she'd woken up in recovery earlier. A sense of calm came over Mose. Mercy was home, all was well with the *bobbel* and they were almost settled into their new home.

"You hungry?" Mose opened the refrigerator door and poked his head in. The leftover baked chicken looked good to him. Maybe a sandwich and warm potato salad would satisfy his hunger pangs.

"I am." Sarah washed her hands, pulled out a loaf of homemade bread and sliced off four perfectly carved servings. "Chicken or roast?"

"Chicken." Mose grabbed the plate of chicken and bowl of potato salad out of the refrigerator.

Working together, they prepared the meal and sat down to eat, both hesitating for prayer. Mose bowed his head and Sarah followed suit as they prayed silently.

Mose took a giant bite from his sandwich and Sarah watched as thick slices of chicken toppled down his clean shirt, covering the front with creamy smears of mayonnaise. She handed him a napkin and watched as he cleaned up the shirt and placed the chicken back on the bread slices.

"Do you want me to make you another sandwich?"

"I'll eat this one. If you knew some of the

things I've eaten in my life, you probably wouldn't have married me."

Laughing together released some of the tension built up from the morning.

"You have plans for this afternoon?" Mose stuck the last of the sandwich in his mouth and popped in a pickle slice for good measure. "The doctor said Mercy would probably sleep the day away, and Beatrice isn't home for hours."

Sarah pondered the idea of free time without Beatrice underfoot. She grinned. "I think I'll put some order to my sewing room. I've been wanting to do that for days."

Mose returned her grin, a smear of mayonnaise on his face making him look more like a five-year-old child than a twenty-five-year-old adult. She grabbed a napkin and wiped his mouth like she might one of the girls. "I can't take you anywhere," she scolded and seemed to enjoy watching him flush. She gathered up the dishes, a smile on her face.

"I think I'll call *Daed* and let them know how the surgery went while you're busy."

"Make sure you call Ulla, too. She's bound to be concerned and won't rest easy until she hears Mercy is all right."

Mose left the room, reaching for the cell

phone in his pocket, grinning from ear to ear as he headed for the bedroom where Mercy lay sleeping.

# Chapter Sixteen

Boxes littered the small beige room with north-facing windows. Sarah had dreamed of a room such as this all her life. Somewhere to sew until her eyes grew tired and blurry.

She stood in the middle of a pile of boxes and turned slowly. She pictured a big cutting table in the corner, and a fixture on the wall to hold all her spools of thread. Not that she had that many right now, but she would. Soon.

She stepped, and stumbled over an oblong box, the weight of it almost knocking her over. She tried to lift it but the box fought back. She struggled to open it and groaned when she found heavy brads clamping the box shut. *What can this be?*

She read the label printed on the container and recognized the name of a professional sewing machine manufacturer, the brand so expensive she'd never dreamed of owning one. *Do I dare hope?* Her hands became claws. She tore at the cardboard box, ripping away bits and pieces of cardboard.

Frustration sent her scurrying around looking for a screwdriver, box cutter…anything. She finally found a suitable tool in the least likely place. On the floor.

"Argh." She grabbed the large screwdriver and forced it under the heavily clamped cardboard flap. Five or six pokes and the flap gave way, sending Sarah flying forward so violently she had to grab the heavy box to steady herself.

With sore, trembling fingers she tore the last of the box away and reached in, removing the clear plastic zip bag with a medium-sized book inside and some kind of small tool kit. Peering back into the box, a white sewing machine waited for her release. Like giving birth, she pushed and pulled, willing the sewing machine to come out. The idea of using the sharp tool on the box again gave her pause. She might scratch the fine machine, and she loathed the idea. Her heart pounding with excitement, she took a long, deep breath and pulled hard. The heavy sewing machine skidded across the floor and landed inches from the doorway and Mose's booted feet.

Sarah glanced past his rain-dampened boots,

wrinkled pants and shirt, to his smiling face. His generosity overwhelmed her. Tugged at her heartstrings. She didn't deserve such kindness.

"Need some help?" Mose squatted down in front of Sarah and her precious sewing machine.

"Looks like I do."

The next morning, the doctor's office was empty except for Mose and Sarah. He paced the length of the office, his hands stuffed deep into his pockets.

Sarah, determined to look calm, leafed through a modern *Englisch* magazine. She gazed at the faces of beautiful women and handsome men and wondered what their lives were really like. Were they as happy as their smiles implied? *Am I happy?* Her life certainly had taken a sudden turn for the better. She felt more content now that Mercy was on the mend and doing so well, and Mose seemed more and more attentive to her. *But do I dare love him?*

"Eight o'clock, right?" Mose looked at his pocket watch, a frown wrinkling his face.

"What? *Ya*, the appointment is for eight o'clock." Sarah held back a smile, afraid she'd offend him. Mose was one of the most impatient men she'd ever met, but she wouldn't rub his nose in it. Let him have his impatience. *Gott* knew she had enough flaws of her own.

"You filled out all the papers?" He flopped down next to her and pulled his long legs under the chair as far as they would go. He glanced at the woman sitting behind a short partition.

"She'll call us soon." Sarah smoothed out her collar and straightened her *kapp*. She caught Mose glancing over her shoulder and smiled to herself when he made a noise deep in his throat, almost like a cat hacking up hair balls.

"What?"

"Nothing." Mose stood and began to move about the room. The watch came out again. He snapped it shut, mumbling under his breath about punctuality and professionalism.

"Sarah Fischer?"

Mose turned on his heel. Sarah stood to her feet. Neither moved.

"Mr. and Mrs. Fischer?" Tall and lean, and dressed in white slacks and a pullover top covered in colorful zoo animals, the technician motioned them back and waited at the door as they passed into the back office. "Find a seat, Dad. Mom, please get on the table." The woman smiled at both of them.

Sarah looked at the metal table covered in paper in the middle of the room and fought the urge to run. A gown lay folded on the paper.

*Would she have to get undressed in front of Mose?*

Preparing the machine, the technician scurried around, moving things on and off. "I'll let you change into the gown. Just leave the door open a crack when you're ready."

Sarah looked at Mose and then the exiting nurse. "I…"

Mose turned his back to her and faced the wall. He murmured, "I'll keep my back turned."

Sarah complied, her dress flying off and then her slip. They lay in a crumpled pile on the chair next to the table as she pulled on the gown, leaving the thin cotton open at the front but pulled tightly closed against her body. With difficulty, she sat on the edge of the table and covered her legs as much as the short gown would allow. She wiggled her toes, not sure what to do next. "All right," she murmured. "Open the door."

Mose did as he was directed and sat in the chair at the back of the room.

"Is this your first sonogram, Mrs. Fischer?" The technician hurried in and shut off the bright overhead light. The room was bathed in a gray glow. She sat down in a swivel chair and turned knobs and flicked levers on the strange machine next to the table.

Fascinated with what the technician was doing, Sarah almost forgot to answer. "*Ya.* My first."

The woman pushed buttons, opened a drawer and took out a tube of some kind of cream. "If you'll lie back, we'll get started." She smiled reassuringly at Sarah and then glanced over at Mose. "You'll need to get closer, Dad, if you want to see the baby." She opened the gown just enough to see Sarah's stomach.

Sarah jumped when cold liquid hit her skin.

"Sorry, I should have warmed that with my hands." She began to rub an extension of the machine on Sarah's stomach. With her finger she pointed to a screen. "You'll both want to be looking here."

Sarah saw strange wavy images and movement. A sound filled the room, its rhythmic beat fast and steady.

"That's your baby's heartbeat."

"Oh…" Emotions she'd never felt overwhelmed her. The beat sounded strong, but fast. "Is it normal for the heart to beat so fast?"

"Sure. New moms always ask me that." She moved the apparatus around Sarah's stomach again and more images appeared. She pointed to the screen. "There's a hand and that's the baby's spine."

Sarah blinked, not sure what she was looking at, but determined to see her child's image.

"Look, Sarah. There's the face." Mose's words came from the end of the table.

The woman pointed and suddenly the image became clear. A face, with closed eyes, a tiny button nose and bowed mouth became clear. Then the face disappeared and Sarah felt deflated. She wanted to see it again but there was more to see. Slender legs squirmed and kicked, floating in and out of view, a tiny foot with five distinct toes flexed.

"Do you two want to know the sex of your child?"

*"Nee,"* Sarah said. She longed to know, but knowing would take away some of the thrill of birth, and she'd have none of that.

"Better turn your heads away then."

Sarah looked away, longing to look back.

"Okay, let's see if we can find the head again and take some measurements. Then we'll be through."

Sarah looked back at the screen and saw what looked like a head full of curly hair. The screen went blank, and Sarah drew in a deep breath, holding back tears of disappointment. She wanted to see more, much more.

"Looks like everything's fine." The technician wiped the jelly off Sarah's stomach with a paper towel. "Your about 30 weeks pregnant, even though the baby is a bit small. I'd put your due datc around six weeks from now, give or take a day or two, but the doctor may change that a little when you see her. You have an appointment with her, right?"

*"Ya."* Mose cleared his throat.

"Good. You did really well for a first-timer, Mom. You can both rest easy. Your baby appears healthy."

*"Danke,"* Sarah murmured, pulling the gown closed as she watched the woman leave. Mose gave her a hand up and she sat still for a moment, letting everything she had seen and heard sink in.

*"Danke* for letting mc be here." Mose's emotion deepened his voice and moved her to tcars.

Sarah held the gown closed with one hand and wiped a tcar away with the other. *"Nee,* Mose. I should be thanking you for coming with me. This *Englisch* way of checking the baby had me afraid, but now I wish they could do it all over again."

A silly smile played on Mose's lips. *"Ya.* I wish that, too." His look was different. Almost as though he was in a daze.

They had shared the wondrous moment together, but then Mose faced the wall once more. "Time to get dressed, I guess."

*"Ya."* Sarah dressed quickly and touched Mose's arm. "Okay. I'm ready."

Mose took her by the elbow and led her through the hall. They passed the technician and stopped as she called out to them.

"I almost forgot to give you these." She handed over a white office envelope and scurried away.

"What is this?" Sarah pulled out stiff pieces of paper. She looked down, right into the face of her child. "Mose. It's pictures of the *bobbel.*"

Mose gave Sarah a hand up into the old furniture delivery truck. He waited until she'd buckled her seat belt and tucked her skirt under her legs before he shut the door. A quick maneuver around two golf carts vying for his vacated parking spot, and the truck merged onto Bahia Vista Street. The slow-moving traffic wove through the quaint town of Sarasota, sweltering in the late spring humidity.

Quiet and still, Sarah held on to the envelope of pictures, her fingers white-knuckled. "Hungry?" Mose asked as he shifted gears. The engine strained, making an unfamiliar noise. He shifted into third and sped up.

Sarah tucked the pictures in her white apron pocket and patted the spot. "Not really."

"I'll bet the baby could use some eggs and

bacon with a side of cheese grits." He grinned at her, trying to keep the mood light. "He or she could use some meat on those tiny bones."

"You're right. I need to eat more. I just don't have much of an appetite lately."

Mose felt guilty. He'd used the baby as a reason for her to eat. Sarah looked thoughtful. Was she thinking it was her fault the baby was a bit undersized? He kept his voice easy and calm, knowing she was stressed. "How about Yoder's? We ate there when we first got into town. They always have great food and you can get another look at the only buggy you'll see around here for miles. Kind of a reminder of what you're missing."

Sarah smiled at his last remark. "I don't miss those hard seats, Mose Fischer. Not one bit."

Mose pulled into Yoder's parking lot five minutes later and parked between a seldom-seen shiny black BMW and a couple of beat-up tricycles so common-place in Pinecraft and Sarasota. After opening Sarah's door, he offered her his hand and smiled when she took it and squeezed his fingers tight. Her pregnancy was obvious to anyone who looked her way now. She glowed in a way Greta never had, her hair shining in the bright sun, her complexion rosy and smooth. He felt a sharp pang of guilt at the thought. It was wrong to think such things. He marched up the driveway, Sarah at his side, his mood suddenly soured.

Sarah forced down toast and scrambled eggs, not even looking at the glass of orange juice she would normally down in one long gulp. The juice gave her heartburn now, and she avoided it like a poison. Linda often teased her the baby would have lots of hair because of her stomach issues. The scan of the baby proved her sister-in-law's theory correct.

"You're deep in thought. Something troubling you?" Mose scooped up a spoon full of grits and shoved it in his mouth as if he was eating orange ambrosia, her favorite desert.

"We need to talk, Mose." Sarah nibbled on her last slice of dry toast and washed it down with a sip of cold milk. "Seeing the baby on the scan made this pregnancy so real to me." She pushed back her glass and looked into his eyes. "I've finally awakened from my stupor. I have just over a month before the baby comes, and I haven't made diapers, much less gowns and bibs. Plus, we haven't mentioned the baby to Beatrice. She has to be told. There's no telling what kind of reaction we'll get from her."

"You're a worrier. Worriers get wrinkles. Didn't anyone ever warn you about that?"

Hormone levels sending her mood into overdrive, Sarah flung her triangle of toast on her plate and glared at him. "I'm trying to have a serious talk with you about important issues and you want to joke around. Seriously! Sometimes you are one of the most infuriating men I've ever had the misfortune to meet."

Mose looked across at her, his sparkling eyes holding her gaze as he sipped coffee from a big white mug. He sat the mug back on the table. "In time you'll realize nothing is going to change, no matter how much you fret. The baby will be born. It will have clothes to wear, even if we have to buy them from an *Englisch* store. And the girls will love the baby because that's what *kinder* do. They love *bobbels*."

With one quick swipe Sarah wiped her mouth, threw the red cloth on her plate and stood. "I'm going to the bathroom, and while I'm gone I'd appreciate it if you'd pay the bill. I'd like to go home now."

"Sure. I can do that, or I can wait for you in the truck and take you to the fabric store for supplies. It sounds like you're going to need piles of material for all those diapers and outfits." Mose grinned as he walked to the front of the café.

# Chapter Seventeen

The sunny, late-spring morning started off rough. Beatrice crawled out of bed grumpy and demanded she be allowed to wear her new church dress. Sarah's calm insistence finally prevailed and peace was restored. The sounds of two active *kinder* laughing and tearing through their playroom rang through the house and put a content smile on Sarah's face.

She flopped in an oversize chair in the great room for a moment of rest and put up her swollen feet on the matching ottoman. The breakfast dishes were washed and put away, and the last load of baby clothes gently agitated in the washer. A month of Florida living had calmed Sarah's troubled spirit. Life was calmer, more serene.

A shrill scream rang from the back of the house. Sarah sprang up and ran, her heart lodged in her throat. "What's happened?" At the door of the playroom she relaxed and chuckled as she took in the situation.

Beatrice lay sprawled on the carpeted floor on her stomach, her healthy little sister's chubby legs straddled across the middle of her back, a hand full of her curly hair wadded up in Mercy's tugging, pudgy fingers. Mercy jerked with all her might. Beatrice wiggled and tried to dump her sister off her back. Her legs pummeled the floor as she wailed, "Make her stop. Get her off me."

Sarah had known the day would come, when Mercy could hold her own and pay back her older sister for all the times she'd been pushed or forced to play with toys she didn't want.

"Mercy. You mustn't hurt your big sister." Sarah lifted the younger child off Beatrice's back and pulled the silky strands of golden hair from her fingers. "Beatrice won't want to play with you if you hurt her. You have to be kind to your big sister."

*"Nee,"* Mercy shouted, using her new voice, her words still not crystal clear, but getting better every day. She grabbed her doll from Beatrice's hands and smiled. "Mine."

"Did you take her doll and give her yours?" With difficulty, her protruding stomach getting in her way, Sarah bent over Beatrice and gently combed her fingers through the child's snarled hair. Strands of pure gold went into the trash container, the remnants of the sister's fight over the doll.

"Yes, but she likes my doll. I wanted to play with her doll, but she yelled at me and pulled my hair."

"We've talked about you taking your little sister's toys before, right?"

Beatrice glared at Mercy playing across the room. "Yes, but…"

"You have to allow Mercy to have toys of her own, too. You like having your own special babies, don't you?"

*"Ya."*

Sarah handed Beatrice her favorite doll and smiled as it was swallowed up in the older child's warm embrace. "You love your doll and sometimes you like to be the only one to play with it. Mercy loves her doll, too, and she doesn't want anyone else to play with it. Do you understand?"

Head down, Beatrice nodded.

*"Gut.* In a minute I'll talk with Mercy about not pulling your hair anymore."

Beatrice began to gather up the plastic dishes scattered at her feet. "I'll make pretend juice for Mercy and me. We can have a party."

Offered an opportunity to talk with Beatrice

without her being too distracted, Sarah helped the child place tiny cups and saucers on the round table Mose had made for them just weeks before. He had agreed she'd be the best person to break the news to the *kinder* about the *bobbel*. She had waited and prayed for a time just like this. "How would you feel if you and Mercy got a real *bobbel* to play with?"

"Do we have to keep Mercy?" Beatrice pretended to pour tea into a tiny cup.

"Of course, silly girl. We would never send your sister away." Sarah pulled over a sturdy wooden stool and sat, waiting for more questions.

"If you have a baby, will you go to live with Jesus like my *mamm* did?" Tiny blond brows furrowed as she placed pretend cake on several little plates and handed one to Sarah.

"*Nee*. What happened to your *mamm* doesn't happen very often. Something went wrong and your *mamm* got very sick." Sarah was not sure what she should say about Greta dying. How much the child should be told. She prayed for wisdom and allowed *Gott's* love for this child to direct her. "A new baby is always a blessing, Beatrice. Like you and Mercy were when you were born."

"Mercy's mean. I don't like her sometimes." Beatrice knocked the dishes on the floor. The troubled child's shows of temper came less frequently now, but still had to be handled with care.

Sarah dropped to her knees in front of Beatrice and held her gaze. "Throwing down dishes doesn't solve anything. It only gets you in more trouble. Maybe together we can think of better ways to express your anger with Mercy, like telling her how it makes you feel when she makes you angry. You're her big sister."

"But I don't like being her big sister today." Beatrice looked at Sarah defiantly. Her lip puckered and tears rolled down her flushed cheeks.

"I know you don't like her right now, but remember when you two were on the swings yesterday? You had so much fun together. You laughed a lot, and it was fun to have a little sister then, right?"

Beatrice looked up through tear-soaked lashes, her eyes sparkling. "*Ya*, it was fun."

"Well, Mercy needs you to help her grow into a nice young lady. She's going to be a big sister, too, when the baby comes. Someone older, like you, has to help Mercy be a good big sister. Do you think that someone could be you?"

Sarah watched the play of emotions flit

across the child's face. She finally smiled a dimpled grin. "I could teach Mercy to be nice to the baby when it comes. I'm the oldest, and she listens to me…sometimes."

"That's right. You're the big sister." Sarah took Beatrice's hand and placed it on her protruding stomach. The baby had been active all morning, and it seemed the perfect time to introduce the unborn child to Beatrice. "Did you feel the baby kick?"

Like it was planned, the baby kicked hard under Beatrice's hand, putting a glowing smile on the child's face and a sparkle in her blue eyes. "*Ya*, I felt him kick."

"I bet you did. You know, we have to think of a good name for the new baby. What do you think we should call her if she's a girl?"

Beatrice looked up, smiling, but serious. "It's a boy. I know it is. We have to call him Levi."

Shaken, Sarah tried to stay calm. Levi had been Joseph's *daed's* name, a name she had already considered for a boy. "Why Levi, Beatrice?"

"Because Jesus told me my brother would be named Levi and that he'd grow up to be a good man, like his *daed*."

Sarah pulled the little girl close and hugged her, tears swimming in her eyes. "Then Levi it will be, liebling."

* * *

After church the next day, Linda carried a tray of salt and pepper shakers over to the extra deep counter at the back of the church kitchen and put it down with a bang.

"That Sharon Lapp makes me so mad."

Used to Linda's rants, Sarah smiled her way. "What did she say?"

Linda slid onto a kitchen stool and braced her feet under the slats, her protruding stomach bullet shaped.

"It's not what she said. It's how she treats me. She acts like I should just sit in a chair and wait for the pains to start just because I'm overdue. It's not some kind of sin being two weeks late. The baby's just lazy like his *daed*." She laughed at the remark as if it was the funniest thing she'd ever heard. "And now she just told me I can't help with clean up. Who is she to tell me anything? I'm not bedridden, for goodness—" She broke off her words and let two women pass before she restarted her private rant with Sarah. "Besides, I feel great and have so much energy."

"I think she's right. You look ready to pop at any moment. Maybe Kurt should take you home and let you put your feet up. Church lasted a long time today with all the new preachers showing off. You're bound to be tired. I know I'm ready to get off my feet."

Linda's scalding glare wrinkled her forehead and put a twist to her lip as she spoke. "Your feet might be hurting you, but I feel fine and I'm not…" Eyes wide, Linda's expression turned from anger to opened mouth horror. "*Ach*! *Gott* help me, Sarah. I think my water just broke."

Sarah put down the pan she'd been drying and hurried over to Linda. "Are you sure?" Liquid dripped off Linda's shoe and onto the floor.

"*Ya*, I'm sure. I'm not prone to wetting myself on kitchen stools. What am I going to do? I'm soaked and everyone will know what's happening. Oh, mercy, even that know-it-all, Sharon Lapp."

Sarah thought for a moment, her legs trembling. "I'll go get Kurt and Mose. One of them can bring the truck around, and the other can carry you out the kitchen's back door. No one will see you. I'll make sure."

"Hurry. I feel like a fool sitting here in a puddle."

Sarah found Mose first, the last of his celery soup forgotten as soon as she whispered the frantic situation in his ear. He motioned for Kurt to come over and within seconds both men were at a full run, Mose headed out the front of the church to pull the truck around back. Kurt fumbled his way to the kitchen, knocking over a chair as he hurried. Minutes later, Linda waved a frantic goodbye to Sarah as Mose peeled out of the church parking lot and burned rubber down the farm road.

Thoughts of her own birth raced through her mind. She'd been warned the pain could be overwhelming. Plus, there were the added responsibilities to consider. Was she ready to be the mother of a tiny *bobbel*? Joseph's *bobbel*. What if the *kinder* resented it?

Would she be able to cope with three children and still be a good wife to Mose?

# Chapter Eighteen

The soft mallet tapped the last spindle into place, and then Mose twisted the chair to an upright position. The back fit snugly into the seat, all four legs flared in perfect alignment. He stood back and looked at the completed project, his hands testing for weak joints. His trained eye searched for flaws, anything that might require a minor adjustment, and saw none.

Otto Fischer breezed into the back workroom, his pants and shirt covered in mud splatter. "*Wie gehts*, Mose?"

"*Gut*. I can see you've been working hard." Mose smiled at his father. "Will you ever retire?" He put away tools and then downed a bottle of water as he listened to his father's ramblings.

"Not while there's still breath in my body.

I'd rather slop pigs and dig trenches all day than spend all my time with Theda when those gossiping women are in my *haus*. They pretend to make quilts every week, but really they gather to talk." He used his hand to imitate a duck quacking. "You should see them leaning over that big quilt frame, their mouths working as hard as their thimbles." Otto grabbed an old wooden chair and sat, his legs sprawled out in front of him.

"*Mamm* would keep you busy doing little jobs around the *haus*. You'd never have time to be bored." Mose sat in the new chair, wiggling in the seat, still testing. "You get her off to her sister's in time?"

"*Ya*. But she took too many suitcases, as usual, and the train was late."

"Maybe she plans to be gone a while."

"*Ach*, she says three, but I can count on four or five days of peace." Otto smirked, his lip curling into a happy arch. "You know how your mother is. Once she gets to Ohio and sees her sister, she'll stick like glue for a while."

"Come eat with us if you find yourself hungry. Sarah's a *gut* cook."

"That she is. Still, I might go to Lapp's every night. I can eat all the things your *mamm* won't let me have. They make good apple strudel." He grinned like a naughty child.

The big room darkened. Mose flipped on the overhead light and jerked back the curtain. Gray clouds billowed overhead. A sudden gust of wind blew a trash can lid across the parking lot. The plastic orb slammed into the fence. "Looks like a storm's brewing. You heard a weather forecast today?"

Otto came and stood next to Mose. "*Nee*, but it got nasty out there fast. Maybe there's something blowing in we don't know about."

Fat splats of rain hit the window. Mose dropped the curtain and turned on a small, dusty radio on the shelf next to him, his finger twisting the knob until he found the weather station.

Both men listened silently. The voice reported a mild tropical depression just off the west coast of Florida. Heavy rain and moderate winds were headed inland, moving toward the Tampa Bay area. Mose breathed a sigh of relief when the man reported the weather bureau didn't expect the depression to grow into a hurricane this late in the season. He flipped off the radio and grabbed his cup. "You want some stale coffee?"

"*Nee*. I should get back to the house and make sure all the windows are shut. I just came by to pick up that footrest you made your *mamm*."

"Sure. It's up front."

The two men walked to the front of the store. "*Guder mariye*, Austin. How are you?" Otto greeted the young salesman now that he wasn't busy with a customer.

"*Gut*, Mr. Fischer. It's been busy, but the rain's run off all our customers."

Otto looked out at the sheets of rain blowing and pulled his hat down around his ears. "This one's going to be a soaker. I think I'll pick up that footrest another time, Mose. Just don't sell it out from under me. Oh, *ya*. I almost forgot. Linda had a seven-pound baby girl last night."

Mose breathed a sigh of relief and grinned. "All went well?"

"*Ya*, no bumps in the road."

"Kurt has to be thrilled." Mose said.

"He is, but he wanted a boy, but don't tell Sarah that bit of information. You know how women are. She'll tell Linda and it could get ugly at Kurt's house." Otto smiled playfully and gave his son a generous smack on the back, then waved to Austin as he headed out the door. "Keep dry," he called over his shoulder and faced the onslaught.

His bike was parked next to the door. Otto kept to the sidewalk. His clothes were soaked to his skin before he rode away.

"*Mei bruder* puts on roofs. I know he got

sent home today," Austin murmured, watching Otto struggle to peddle down the wet street.

"*Ach*, you might as well go, too. I won't dock your pay. No one's coming out in this weather. I'll watch for stragglers for a while. You go before you can't ride your bike home."

Books and toys were strewn all over the playroom. With both girls napping, Sarah dropped to the carpeted floor and began to clear up while she could. Dolls went into the tiny cot Mose had made before she had become his wife. Greta must have been so pleased when he'd walked it through the door. *Kinder's* books were stacked on the low bookshelf, something else he'd built early on. All around her were reminders of Mose and Greta's family. Sarah's family now. She wished she'd met the woman. Everyone had only good things to say about her.

The back door slammed shut and Sarah shuddered. The sudden noise scared her. She hated storms. She had Adolph to blame for that. She remembered the day he'd put her outside for not doing a chore while one had raged overhead. Only a child, she had begged to come in, but her cries had fallen on deaf ears. She'd hidden in the chicken coop, holding her favorite hen to her breast as she'd sobbed and lightning had flashed overhead. She'd screamed every time thunder crashed around her. Pushing the memories away, the tear trailing down her cheek, she grabbed the last toy and put the fat teddy bear on Beatrice's rocker.

Sarah closed the window over the kitchen sink and wiped down the kitchen counters, even though she'd already cleaned them an hour ago. She needed something to do.

The doorbell rang and her hand stilled. It rang again. *Who is out in a downpour like this?* A peek out the front window showed a man in a police officer's uniform wiping rain off his glasses. He stood with another man, this one in a suit and plastic raincoat. He leaned a wet umbrella against the doorframe and waited. Both men looked very official.

Leaving the security latch on, Sarah opened the door a crack. *"Ya?"*

The police officer leaned in to be heard over the heavy rain, his face inches from the door. "Are you Sarah Nolt Fischer?"

She began to tremble. Her legs threatened to collapse from under her. *"Ya*, that's me. Can I help you?" She opened the door a bit more and looked at the badge the man thrust at her. "I'm Officer Luis Cantu from the city of Sarasota. This is Frank Parsons, our liaison officer." Rain dripped off his nose as his head nodded at Sarah through the cracked door. "Can we come in?"

Sarah pulled on her prayer *kapp* ribbon. "*Ya*, come in out of the rain." She unlocked the door and stepped back.

Both men glanced around as they stepped in and wiped their wet feet on the door mat. "I need to talk to you about your late husband, Joseph Nolt. Can we sit down?"

"This way." Sarah showed them to the great room and motioned toward the couch. She sat in a matching chair across the room, and placed her trembling hands in her lap.

The man in the dark navy suit pulled off his raincoat and sat on the edge of the couch. He took a small black notebook out of his breast pocket and flipped through several pages.

Sarah's heart beat so loudly she couldn't hear the rain anymore. She forced her mind to focus, pushing every thought aside until he spoke.

"Are you aware the death of your husband was not an accident?"

Sarah forced herself to breath in. "*Nee*. They told me he died of…the smoke." She held back a sob with her hand.

"Mrs. Fischer, is there anyone I can call for you? Your new husband, a friend?"

Her fingers nervously pulled at the ribbon on

her *kapp*. "Why? Am I in trouble?" A cramp began in the lower part of her back and traveled to her stomach, tearing at her insides. Linda told her to think of the pain as prelabor, her bones moving over to prepare for the baby's birth. The pain was normal. Nothing to worry about.

"No, but since you're pregnant, I thought you might like someone with you. This conversation could be upsetting." His brown eyes looked her up and down, assessing.

Sarah glanced at the clock on the wall. "Mose will be here soon. He usually eats lunch at home."

The man sat back. "Good. We can wait for him."

"*Nee*, tell me what you have to say. This is my business. I was married to Joseph. I have a right to know everything about his death."

He glanced back at his notebook and gave the police officer a quick glance. "Okay." The man cleared his throat. "Your husband did die from smoke inhalation, but he also had blunt force trauma to his head."

"No one told me." Sarah shuddered. "Is this why you came? To tell me this?"

"Not just that. I just thought you'd want to know all the details. That's why I wanted your new husband with you."

Her hand pressed against the pain in her back. "Go on. Tell me the rest."

"The reports from the Lancaster County sheriff's office shows a Benjamin Hochstetler Sr. confessed to the killing of your husband several days ago. I believe you knew the man. Am I right?"

"*Ya*. He was our neighbor, but what do you mean he confessed to killing Joseph? I thought..." Sarah looked away, ashamed to look him in the eyes. Was it true? Had Benjamin Hochstetler killed Joseph?

"Some new facts have surfaced and the community's bishop, Ralf Miller, asked that we contact you now that we've put all the pieces of the puzzle together. He said you'd be interested in what we've learned."

Sarah's mind reeled. Her throat seemed to constrict as she asked, "What is this additional news? I want to know everything."

"Hochstetler was arrested for drunk and disorderly conduct. During questioning he began to talk about his children, how much he hated Joseph Nolt for interfering in his personal business." The police officer flipped the page he'd been referring to and continued. "We put his ramblings down to the drink and he bailed himself out the next morning, still rambling about the loss of his two sons, Lukas and Benjamin Jr." He looked up. "You knew the boys?"

Sarah sighed. "I knew them. They are *gut* boys." Wind-driven rain lashed the windows. Lightning struck somewhere close and thunder rumbled, shaking the house and Sarah. Overhead lights flickered. She longed for a glass of water but didn't think her legs would hold her if she tried to walk to the kitchen.

"When the forensics team got through with the barn, they had noted there was no sign of your cow, Mrs. Fischer. You did say a cow had been in the barn the night your husband died?"

"*Ya.* I thought Lovey died in the fire, too. Are you saying you've found her after all these months?" *Stop asking questions. Shut up. Listen.*

"They did. She was grazing in a nearby field owned by Hochstetler."

"I see." A terrible trembling began to shake her entire body. She fought for control.

Another page turned. The man cleared his voice. "Two days ago the body of Benjamin Hochstetler was found hanging by a rope. He'd killed himself some time during the night. He'd mailed a letter to his lawyer confessing to killing your husband in a struggle. He said he'd come to steal the cow and your husband had caught him. He wrote that during the struggle, he pushed Joseph Nolt, and his head hit a concrete block. Sure that he was dead, Hochstetler set a fire in the barn, hoping to hide any evidence that might connect him to the crime. He ran back to his farm, hid the cow in the barn and went to bed, burning the clothes he'd worn the next day."

"But I heard Joseph's cry for help. I tried to get him out, but the fire…my hands, they were burned. After a moment he stopped screaming and I must have fainted. Someone called the fire department and they found me lying in the dirt just outside the barn. They discovered Joseph's remains later that morning. How can Benjamin Hochstetler's story be true if Joseph called out to me?" Sarah searched the man's eyes for clarity.

"We believe your husband didn't die from the fall. He must have been knocked out and woke, unable to make his way out of the barn. The fire was too hot from the accelerant used and spread fast. It stopped him like it stopped you."

Sarah nodded, tears streaming down her face. "If only… Did he suffer, you think?"

"No, the smoke probably got him before the fire did. I'm sorry for your loss, Mrs. Fischer. You have my condolences. I hope knowing the truth will help you put away this nightmare so you can go on with your new life."

Sarah needed to have time to think about what she'd just learned. She stood to her feet and then fell back against the chair, the sound of rain and her name being called swirled in the black fog enveloping her.

# Chapter Nineteen

❧

Mose unfolded his napkin, wiped food off Mercy's mouth and sat her on the quilt next to Beatrice. "You share those toys. If I see you taking anything from your little sister's hands, it's early to bed for you."

"Sarah told me I'm a big sister now. I have to be good."

"Yes, you do. Now play with your doll and I'll read you a book in a moment." He looked over at the couch, his gaze on Sarah. She leafed through a magazine on child rearing. She seemed okay now, looked normal enough. No pale skin, or grimace. Nothing to indicate something was physically wrong. *So why am I still so worried?*

Coming home and finding an ambulance in his drive had shaken him. He had thought one of the *kinder* had been hurt, but it was

Sarah the two medics were leaning over when he rushed in the door. They explained she'd passed out for a few seconds but checked out fine. Nothing to warrant a trip to the hospital.

She'd been alert when he'd asked her how she felt. While the medic took her blood pressure again she'd reassured him everything was fine. "I heard about the Hochstetler man killing Joseph and later himself. I think I hyperventilated. That's all. Nothing more to worry about."

Now he watched her and prayed. "Can I get you anything? Maybe a cold drink?"

"*Nee*, I'm good. You sure you don't want me to clear the dinner table, Mose? I'm perfectly fine. Really. You're treating me like I'm sick, and I'm not."

"You sit there and relax. I'm good at clearing up, and Beatrice can help me throw away the paper plates, right?"

"But I'm playing."

"It's bath and bed for you. That mouth of yours is getting you into a lot of trouble lately." Mose scowled at his oldest child, his temper already fired up by the policeman he'd almost thrown out of the house. He wiped down the table and counters. "Those police officers should have made sure you had someone with you before they broke the news about Joseph and what happened to Hochstetler. They could see you're pregnant. No wonder you fainted at their feet."

"You're cleaning the color off that countertop."

A grin tipped his lips and he took a final slow swipe. "I'm in a hurry to get the kids to bed. Mercy's tired." On cue, Mercy yawned, her mouth opening wide. He grinned. "See, I told you."

"I can bathe both of them while you finish."

"You're eight months pregnant, Sarah, and stressed out. You've had a shock, need to rest." He loved her spirited personality, but sometimes he wished she was less argumentative... *like Greta?*

Something hit the house with a thump. He turned on the back porch light and groaned. The deck was soaked, the wooden lounge chair he'd made for Sarah blown up against the house. Sarah's newly seeded flower pots were full of rain and overflowing in muddy streams. "Noah, where's that Ark? Looks like we might need it tonight." Mose turned off the outside light and turned to an empty room. Sarah and the girls were nowhere to be seen. *Stubborn woman.* He headed down the hallway.

Warm water gushed into the tub. Sarah tipped in a capful of pink liquid soap and swished her hand back and forth, enjoying the feel of frothy bubbles creeping up her arm. The heady fragrance of strawberries rose with the steam.

Two fluffy towels sat on a stool next to her, along with a soft plastic frog with bulging eyes. Water in her face scared Mercy, and the frog was a great distraction when it came time to rinse the girl's hair.

"Can I sit up front this time?" Beatrice stripped down, her clothes thrown in an untidy pile on the floor instead of in the laundry basket. Sarah gave her nod and the five-year-old jumped in, splashing water on the tile floor with her tidal wave. Soaked, Mercy screamed and wiggled out of Sarah's arms. She slipped on the wet floor and almost joined her older sister in the foamy water with her dress and diaper still on.

"I usually take their clothes off before bathing them." Mose leaned against the bathroom door, his hands in his pockets. "You need some help?"

"*Nee.* I'm fine." Sarah unsnapped Mercy's dress and threw the cotton frock in the basket. Carefully she unpinned her dry diaper and lifted the lightweight child into the bubbles. *There'll be two babies in diapers soon.* A knife-sharp pain pierced her back and Sarah paused before she straightened, waiting for the contraction to pass.

"What's wrong?" Mose stepped forward.

"Just one of those pains Linda warned me about. I get them once in a while. There's nothing to worry about."

"You should have waited for me to do this. I wanted you to rest. You know you're tired."

"*Ya*. But this is my job and I'm fine."

"You're stubborn. You know that?"

Mercy's squirmed and Sarah let go of her arm. "*Ya*. I've always been."

Mose laughed. "What smells so good?"

Sarah shifted to a more comfortable position, her hand reaching for her back when another pain slammed her. She took in a deep breath, held it and then slowly pushed the air out.

Beatrice piped up. "It's me that smells good. My bubble-bath soap makes me smell good enough to eat. Sarah told me." She twisted around to grin at him and almost knocked her sister over with her sudden movement. "I need my bathtub toys," she sang out in a high-pitched tone.

"Use your indoor voice, please." Sarah steadied Mercy. With gentle pressure she began to scrub Mercy's neck and back with a washcloth. She wished she wasn't so tired. "No toys tonight. I'm tired and want an early night. You can have an extra-long bath tomorrow night with lots of toys. I promise."

Beatrice glared at Sarah and silently began to wash herself. Encouraged by the child's co-operation, Sarah decided against washing their hair and grabbed the towels. She dangled one in the air. "Who's ready to get out first?"

Mercy grabbed the edge of the white towel. "Mine."

Mose watched Sarah handle the child with ease, the big towel swallowing up Mercy as Sarah patted her dry. "I have good news for you."

Preoccupied, Sarah murmured, "*Ya*, what is it?"

"*Mamm* called today. Linda and the baby had their doctor's appointment and both checked out fine. The baby weights nine pounds already and is starting to look like Kurt, or so *Mamm* says."

Sarah looked over at Mose and smiled. "I'm so happy for them. It went well for her? No problems with her labor?"

Mose smiled back. "*Daed* said there were no bumps in the road."

Sarah went back to drying Mercy. "Didn't Kurt want a son?"

Mose grinned at her, ignoring her question.

"I think I'll go check the water levels in the yard again. Be right back."

Under the streetlight, windblown rain pelted down at an angle. *When will this rain stop?* Mose dropped the blind slat and put his empty glass in the sink. He padded barefoot through the dining room, flipped on the light in the hallway and pushed open the girls' partially closed door. Both slept soundly, Beatrice sprawled out on her stomach, her head in the middle of her pillow. Mercy lay curled on her side. He covered the baby's bare legs with the light blanket bunched at her feet and touched one blond corkscrew curl before he wandered down the hall to his own bed. It had been a long, stress-filled day. He looked forward to some sleep and a hot meal in the morning.

Sarah had left the bedside lamp on. She lay sleeping in a fetal position at the edge of the mattress, her hand partially covering her face, her long hair in a thick plait on her pillow.

He sat on the edge of the bed across from her, listening to the rain. All he could hear was the downpour and the steady beat of his own heart. Sarah moved. His hand searched for the lamp switch and twisted it back on. He looked across the bed. She lay on her back, her body rigid, as taut as a bow. "Sarah? Are you awake?"

"*Ya*. The thunder woke me."

"I love thunderstorms. *Daed* and I used to stand on the porch and watch the sky light up. *Mamm* always fussed at the door until we came back in." He waited for a laugh, some kind of reaction, but got none. "Am I keeping you awake?" He wanted to make sure she was okay after her difficult day.

"I can't sleep with the storm overhead."

Mose liked the way the soft artificial light made her skin seem to glow. "I'm sorry I was late for lunch today. I had to drive home slow. The streets were flooded past the sidewalks. I wish I had been here with you when the officers brought the news about Joseph's killer."

Sarah looked at him, her eyes intense and bright. "I had to hear what they had to say. Hearing it was hard, but knowing the truth makes a difference."

"Months ago you blamed yourself for Joseph's death. Do you have peace now?"

Her bottom lip quivered. "For so long I've believed I caused the fire. That he died because of my carelessness. I've punished myself because of it. When I heard the truth, I was relieved and horribly angry. I wished his killer dead, Mose. I wished Benjamin Hochstetler would die, and then I learned he had. He'd killed himself." A sob escaped her. Her shoulders started heaving in great, gulping sobs.

Mose scooped her in his arms. She burrowed close, her tears dampening his shoulder. "Don't cry, Sarah." He rubbed her back, the baby kicking at the pressure of his body so close. "*Gott* understands why you were angry. He made us all fallible, with good and bad thoughts. You didn't cause the man's death. He killed himself, probably because his shame was more than he could live with."

"I thought for so long that Joseph had died because of something I didn't do. All those months I grieved, and this man knew the truth and said nothing."

"Be angry, but forgive. For yourself and the baby," Mose murmured softly. "Hatred does horrible things to a person's mind. It burns a hole in your soul. Don't let him steal your peace."

Sarah took in a shuddering breath, her body beginning to relax. Minutes ticked by and as she spoke she pulled away. "*Danke*, Mose. I needed to talk. You are so kind to me, mean so much to me."

The loss of her embrace overwhelmed him as she laid back down on the bed. His eyes watered with unshed tears. She needed comfort but still didn't trust him to understand.

"I think I can sleep now. *Gut* night." She turned onto her side, away from him.

Mose watched the rise and fall of her back become regular and deep. He stood up and got ready for bed.

Something was wrong. Sarah woke with a start. Pain tore at her, her stomach growing hard. Had she wet the bed? Her gown clung to her body, cold and damp. Pain ripped through her back and circled around to the lower part of her stomach. She sucked in a breath, waiting for the heavy cramps to ease. She flipped on the lamp and lifted the light sheet across her legs. Pink fluid circled the sheet and soaked her gown. *Did my water break?* Another pain hit, this one more intense, forcing her to moan. She took in a breath and pushed it out. *Is this labor? I'm not due for days.* Panic grabbed at her throat, made it hard to swallow. She called out to Mose, but her voice was a whisper. She inched across the bed, waiting for each pain to pass. Finally, she could touch his shoulder. She shoved with all her might. Mose murmured something low, unintelligible. She shoved again, over and over until he stirred and turned her way, his eyes opening.

"You all right?"

"I think my labor started." She cradled her stomach as it tightened, prepared for the next round of pulsing pain.

Mose shot out of bed, grabbed his work pants from the closet and pulled them over his pajama bottoms. "I'll be right back." He grabbed his cell phone and dialed his father's number. On the fourth ring he picked up.

"Otto Fischer here."

Mose opened the blinds in the kitchen and looked outside. The storm had calmed, but hours of heavy rain had completely flooded the street. Water lapped at the sidewalk in his yard. "*Daed*, its Sarah. She's in labor. Our roads are too flooded to drive. I can't get her to the midwife. Do you think you and *mamm* could walk over here? I need help fast."

"Mose. Remember, your *mamm's* not here. She left for her sister's yesterday."

"*Ach*. I forgot. I've got the girls asleep and no way to get Sarah help. What can I do?"

"Did you call the hospital, or fire department? Maybe a fire truck can make it through the water."

"I'll call, but I don't think there's time for them to get here. Her water's already broke and I don't have a clue what to do next."

Otto cleared his voice. "I've got a suggestion but you're probably not going to like it."

"I'm desperate. Tell me."

"I can get Ulla."

Mose looked at his cell phone, wondering if his father had lost his mind. "Are you serious? Ulla'd never come, and I don't think Sarah would let her anywhere near her, or the baby."

"Ulla was a midwife for over twenty years. I think you better reconsider your situation before you throw stones."

Mose looked toward the only light on in the house and sucked in his breath. "Okay, ask her if she'll come, and, *Daed*, please be careful. It's bad out there."

"I'll do my best. You call the fire department, quick."

Mose stood looking at his phone. He tore the fire department calendar out of the kitchen drawer and started pushing numbers as he ran to the back of the house. *Gott, don't let her die. I love her. Please don't let her die.*

Sarah watched from a chair as Ulla and her daughter, Molly, worked as one. It was if they knew what the other wanted before being asked. The bed was stripped, remade and a plastic sheet tucked under the bedding. Silently the soiled gown was pulled over Sarah's head and a fresh gown replaced it. She was helped back into bed without a single word being spoken. A fresh wave of pain hit and Sarah lay still, enduring what must happen to deliver her baby.

"Are you in pain?" Ulla placed her hand on Sarah's stomach, allowing a professional smile to crease her lips up at the ends.

"*Ya*, I was." Sarah watched as the older woman began to press her wrinkled hands into her softening stomach.

Ulla looked up, her expression changed, her forehead creased. "Molly."

The young woman stood, abandoning the chair she'd sat in. *"Ya?"*

Ulla's fingers continued to probe, her features pinched. "The baby has twisted. We must turn it before it reaches the birth canal. Put your hands here and push gently when I tell you."

*"Ya."* Molly followed her mother's instructions, pushing, and then waiting as Sarah's stomach hardened with a contraction.

"Breathe slow and easy. This will hurt but we must do what we can to make this baby come head first," Ulla told Sarah.

Sarah nodded, terrified but understanding. The woman's blue-eyed gaze held Sarah's as they pushed and then waited for her contractions to pass.

Excruciating pain tore at Sarah's insides. She stifled a scream. Tremors hit her. She bit on the blanket, her teeth chattering. She wanted Joseph in that moment and then Mose's face filled her mind.

"There." Ulla straightened, waiting at the foot of the bed with Molly by her side.

Pains came at regular intervals, stealing Sara's breath, and then increased until there was only pain. The urge to push overwhelmed her. "I need to push." Sarah waited for Ulla's nod.

"Another moment, Sarah. I have to check the cord's placement first." Ulla finally grunted, "*Ya.* Now."

With all her might Sarah pushed, her face heating, sweat pouring off her.

"Again," Ulla instructed.

A wave of hot misery hit her and she pushed again. She felt movement and looked down. Ulla lifted her silent baby in the air and swung it by its blue feet. Sarah's heart pounded in her throat. *What is she doing?* A lusty cry filled the room and the baby began to squirm, his arms and legs flailing in the air, his skin turning a bright, healthy pink.

"A healthy-looking son with ten fingers and

toes, thanks to his brave *mamm*." The smile was back but wider. Ulla laid the baby on Sarah's stomach. She cut the cord and accepted the baby blanket held out by Molly. Seconds later she handed off the swaddled baby.

Her gaze on the child's face, Molly lay him on his mother's chest and smiled at Sarah as she stepped back. "He is so beautiful."

Sarah looked at her wailing son, his blond curls, and began to weep.

Mose tiptoed into the dim room, trying hard not to make a sound. Sarah lay in the bed, probably asleep after her ordeal, a tiny bundle in the crook of her arm.

"Mose?" Sarah turned his way, a smile gentle on her lips.

He walked to the bed and sat on the edge. *"Ya."* Sarah looked tired but good to his eyes. Her bright hair fanned out against the pillow, lose from its braid and damp at the crown.

She put out her hand and he took it, eager to touch her. The baby stirred, making a mewing sound and she was alert, checking him with her glance.

"Beatrice tells me she's named him Levi. Any chance she's telling the truth?"

"We girls heard from *Gott*. He will be Levi Nolt Fischer."

"And Levi's mother? How is she?" Mose squeezed her hand, longing to take her in his arms and kiss her cheek but afraid to move her.

"Levi's mother is fine." The bags under his eyes told her what kind of night he'd had.

"It was a fast birth." Mose had been through two lengthy births with Greta and was amazed how quickly Levi had been born.

"*Ya*. Levi wasted no time. He's small but healthy. Ulla said his tiny size helped speed things up." Sarah kept her voice low.

"Did she treat you well, she and Molly?" He moved closer, touching the baby's wispy blond hair.

Sarah nodded. "She and Molly were *wunderbaar*, Mose. They showed me every courtesy and were kind and professional. Not a word from the past. It was as if none of the ugliness happened."

"*Gut*, I guess *Daed* threatening her with being unchurched worked, plus, she's really not a bad person. Just missing her daughter. I owe her a debt of gratitude for getting you and the *bobbel* through this."

"It can't have been easy for her." Sarah looked over at Levi and one side of the baby's lip lifted, almost into a smile. "You see, he likes her, so we must try harder for his sake."

"She wouldn't let me come in." Mose looked

like Beatrice when she sulked, his mouth twisted in a grimace. "I wanted to be with you, but she kept me out."

"She's old-fashioned. In her day men drank coffee and slapped each other's backs while we women did all the hard work."

"*Ya*, well. I don't like to be ordered about in my own home. If I want to see you, then I should be allowed. You are my *frau*."

"We'll talk to her about that before the next *bobbel* comes, okay?" Sarah's smile spoke words she was afraid to say aloud. "If you want a child with me?" Sarah held her breath, her heart pounded in her chest. Their arrangement had been a simple one. No required affection, no love expected. Perhaps he didn't feel the way she did now. Maybe he didn't return her love?

Mose grinned down at Sarah and then his new son, love shining bright in his eyes as he gently pressed his lips to hers. "I've always thought six *kinder* would be enough to take care of me in my old age. What do you think, *frau*?"

Sarah looked into her husband's eyes and saw love there in the sparkle of his gaze and more.

So much more.

"*Ya*, I think six is a perfect number."

# *Epilogue*

Sarah's fingers entwined with Mose's free hand. A smiling Mercy giggled, her feet dangling out of the canvas carrier looped around her *daed's* shoulders. Her blond curls bounced with each step he took down to the sun-bleached beach, the late-summer sun hanging low in the sky. Beatrice's tiny hand was engulfed in her father's other hand, her complaints of wet sand squishing between her toes ignored.

Levi lay nestled against Sarah, the chubby boy's shoulder sling protecting him from the setting sun and gentle, late-day breezes. "I've never seen the sky so blue," Sarah said, grinning over at Mose.

"I see beautiful sky blue every time I look into your eyes, *mein frau*," Mose murmured. She knew he didn't approve of public displays of affection, but today he seemed unable to resist and kissed her gently on the cheek.

"Hey, did you kiss my *daed*?" Beatrice squinted one eye as she regarded first her father and then Sarah suspiciously.

"*Nee, liebling*. He kissed me. What do you think of that?"

"I think it's funny, that's what I think. I need a kiss, too." Beatrice puckered up and noisily kissed her *daed* on his arm. "Yuck! Your hair tickles." She scrubbed at her mouth with the back of her hand and started to spit until she caught Sarah's warning glance.

"His beard tickles, too." Sarah turned to Mose and smiled.

Amusement sparkled in Beatrice's eyes as she smiled at her new *mamm*. "If you don't like him kissing you, tell him to stop. That's what I'd do if Danny Lapp tried to kiss me."

Mose woke from his quiet bliss, his tone the typical Amish father's bark. "You're too young to worry about boys, Beatrice Fischer. If that Lapp boy comes near you I better hear about it. You hear?"

"Yes. But, you kissed *Mamm*," Beatrice whined. Joy rushed through Sarah. *She finally called me mamm.*

Sarah gave Mose her best "I love you" smile and grinned as his eyes sparkled back at her.

"Yes, I kissed your *mamm's* cheek, but we're married and it's allowed." He squeezed Sarah's hand. "When you get married, you can kiss your husband, too, but not a minute before."

"Okay." Beatrice began to skip, obviously less impressed with the subject of their conversation than Mose. Her feet kicked up sand. She yanked at her father's grasp, pulling him toward the incoming wave. "Can I go walk in the water? Please!"

Mose turned toward Sarah. He waited for her sign of approval. Sarah nodded and Mose released Beatrice to the churning surf with a firm warning. "Stay close to us. No rushing into the deep water like the last time."

Sarah spread out the full-size quilt she'd carried across her arm and sat down, her gaze on Beatrice. "Did you hear her call me *mamm*, Mose? I thought my heart would burst."

"She asked my permission last night while you were busy with Levi's bath. I told her she could make up her own mind, and I guess she did. I'm happy for you, Sarah. I know it means a lot." He pulled her close for a quick hug and then pulled Mercy's carrier off his back and placed the squirming child down beside him. Sarah kissed her on her blond head and handed the restless little one a bucket of sea shells to play with.

Mose's hands were gentle as he pushed a strand of hair blowing in Sarah's eyes. *"Danke,"* she said as she laid Levi in the shade created by Mose's broad back and changed the *bobbel's* wet diaper while watching Beatrice's silly antics in the inch-deep water.

"I thought it would never happen." Sarah laughed with surprise as Beatrice chased a flock of squawking seagulls up a small bank of sand. "She's come a long way since Levi's birth. I think seeing our love grow has given her a measure of peace, something she'd lost."

Quiet for a moment, Mose laughed, his gaze on Sarah as she frantically dug sand out of Mercy's mouth. She groaned. "You can't turn your back on Mercy for a second. This little *liebling* will eat anything, just like her sister."

Beatrice ran over and rushed round them, her little legs not still for a moment, her sing-song voice raised to the heavens, declaring, "I love *Mamm* and *Daed*, Mercy, Levi, my *grandmammi* Ulla, *Poppy* Otto, *Grandmammi* Theda, *Aenti* Molly and the sand and trees. Did I forget anyone, *Mamm*?"

Sarah leaned against Mose, his arm around her shoulder. "No. I think you remembered everyone." *We're a real family at last*, she thought. Contentment put a smile on her face

as she elbowed Mose and added, "Except…
maybe Danny Lapp."

An elderly *Englisch* couple strolled past,
both casually dressed, the wrinkled old man's
arm linked with his gray-haired beauty in cut-
off jeans and a summer blouse. "Beautiful
family you have there," he said.

Mose nodded his thanks, pulling his straw
hat off as a smile spread across his face. "*Gott*
has richly blessed me with *mein frau* and
*kinder.*"

"I don't know what I'd do without mine,"
the old man said and waved as they continued
down the shoreline.

Beatrice stopped her running long enough
to ask, "Who was that?"

Sarah answered, "No one we know, *bobbel.*
Just a passing couple who knows true joy when
they see it."

\* \* \* \* \*

Dear Reader,

I became a writer because it was on my bucket list of things to do. Little did I know God would take this notion and turn it into His work, for His purpose. He opened and closed doors and set the path, making the way clear.

I began writing *The Amish Widow's Secret* as a testament to my aunt Omie, a strong and beautiful woman who'd loved and lost her husband, Bill, unexpectedly to cancer. In the prime of his life, he had everything to live for. I watched my aunt live through years of loneliness and pain, never to marry again, but to become the strong woman I knew and loved. As a child I wanted to grow into a resourceful and loving woman just like her.

Sensing God had a family planned for my heroine, Sarah, I introduced Mose and his tiny girls, Beatrice and Mercy, a hero and loving family for Sarah to cherish. Visit the tiny Amish town of Pinecraft, Florida, and enjoy the lives of Sarah and Mose as they discover their new love ordained by God.

I hope you enjoyed Sarah and Mose's story of redemption and renewal as much as I enjoyed writing it. I'd love to hear from you.

You can find me at cherylwilliford.com or at cheryl.williford@att.net.

May God richly bless you and bring you peace,

*Cheryl Williford*

# LARGER-PRINT BOOKS!

## GET 2 FREE LARGER-PRINT NOVELS
## PLUS 2 FREE MYSTERY GIFTS

*Love Inspired*®
# SUSPENSE
### RIVETING INSPIRATIONAL ROMANCE

## *Larger-print novels are now available...*

# WHERE DO YOU GO
# AFTER MADISON COUNTY?

# CEDAR BEND.

Readers all across America responded with a passionate intensity to Robert James Waller's first novel, *The Bridges of Madison County*. From Connecticut to California, people told their friends about it, who in turn told their friends, until the spontaneous enthusiasm of men and women for this luminous book made it a *New York Times* bestseller for more than two years—and transformed its author from a business school professor into a larger-than-life legend.

Now Waller tells another haunting, intelligent story about the kind of love between a man and a woman that changes everything. We are still in America's heartland, this time in a small college town at an ordinary faculty cocktail party, where an extraordinary meeting takes place between rebellious professor Michael Tillman, a man old enough to know what he wants, and Jellie Braden, another professor's wife. Jellie and Michael don't expect the attraction they feel at first sight. But they have waited a lifetime to experience it. And, as the power of their emotions leads them as far away as India and as close to home as a quiet Iowa pond, they will discover the immeasurable joy of loving . . . and face a poignant, irrevocable choice.

❁

"Discover the gentle magic of Robert James Waller. He takes us to places where life is full of possibilities and love is a great deal more than a four-letter word." **—Book-of-the-Month Club News**

*more . . .*

"Waller has a perfect, unerring gift."
—*Des Moines Sunday Register*

❀

"MORE, MORE, MORE. That's what you get with Robert James Waller's new book *Slow Waltz in Cedar Bend*. More story, more layers, more character, more enjoyment . . . Take your time and enjoy the music of *Slow Waltz in Cedar Bend*."
—*Grand Rapids Press*

❀

"QUITE WONDERFUL . . . a haunting, intelligent, poignant story about a once-in-a-lifetime love, the cataclysmic kind that changes you forever."
—*Tulsa World*

❀

"The '50s quality of Michael and Jellie's growing intimacy reminds us, as did 'Bridges,' of a nostalgic *Saturday Evening Post* story that invites dreams of true love."
—*San Francisco Chronicle*

❀

"TO DO LIST: Pick up Robert Waller's new book, *Slow Waltz in Cedar Bend*."
—*Mc Call's*

❀

"A GUARANTEED HIT."
—*Miami Herald*

"If you liked 'Madison County,' you'll surely like 'Cedar Bend'. . . . The point remains that we are harder people than we want to be. How many readers feel they have not had the love of their life? How many would have Jellie Braden's or Michael Tillman's love if they could?"
                                    **—San Jose Mercury News**

❀

"[Waller] is playing into the not-so-secret fantasy of women across the land: to be adored unconditionally, passionately, uniquely, and forever. . . . PLEASE, MR. WALLER, DON'T STOP YET—KEEP THESE GUYS COMING!"                **—New Woman**

❀

"[A] MOVING LOVE STORY . . . it allows us entry to a place of warmth and wonder. . . . Waller's strength is that his writing rings true, even as a lyrical, almost magical romance is blooming. . . . Waller's story succeeds because it taps universal feelings. It allows us to believe in a wondrous, all-consuming love. And that's no small feat."                **—Orange County Register**

❀

"What *Slow Waltz in Cedar Bend* makes clear is that Robert Waller is not an accident but a crafty and clever writer who has touched a nerve of wistful romantic longing in his audience and is not about to take his hand away."                **—Fort Wayne Journal Gazette**

*more . . .*

"Some wonderful descriptions of India and funny, but distinctly barbed jabs at academia. You can tell Waller knows both places well. . . . If you adored *Bridges* . . . you'll adore *Waltz*."
**—Greensboro News & Record (NC)**

✿

"Thoroughly engaging. . . . His plotting is much stronger than in his earlier novel and he's first-rate at creating suspense." **—Chicago Tribune**

✿

"It bears the same charm and insights of *Bridges* but is deeper and more passionate. . . . It is a love story with a million-reader appeal."
**—Meriden Record-Journal (CT)**

✿

"A gentle read, which means the reader can snuggle down in the chair with the book, a blanket, a pillow and a cup of tea. . . . Sometimes all we want to do is read a story, and Waller provides a perfect opportunity to do that." **—Beaumont Enterprise (TX)**

✿

"Waller's writing again has the magical charm which drew so many readers to his first novel."
**—Abilene Reporter-News**

✿

"He keeps you turning the pages."**—Seattle Times**

"A good, believable, quick read. The authenticity of Waller's India makes for a fascinating background, especially in contrast to academic small-town Iowa."

—*Lexington Herald-Leader* (KY)

❀

"Don't miss it!"

—*The Reader's Review*

❀

"He is a talented storyteller who writes from the heart and puts intense emotions into words that resonate with readers—this one, too."

—*Arizona Republic*

❀

"A poignant tale of bittersweet love . . . Waller's message continues to be that where there is love, there is hope. And that we would all like to believe."

—*Newport News Daily Press*

❀

"If you like love stories, buy this book!"

—*Jackson Sun* (Mississippi)

❀

"Well written and fast moving . . . vigorous and compelling . . . [Waller] has echoed the feelings of millions of Americans."

—*Times* (London)

ALSO BY ROBERT JAMES WALLER

*The Bridges of Madison County**
*Old Songs in a New Cafe**
*Images**
*One Good Road Is Enough*
*Just Beyond the Firelight*

**\* Published by
WARNER BOOKS**

# SLOW WALTZ IN CEDAR BEND

# ROBERT JAMES WALLER

WARNER BOOKS

A Time Warner Company

WARNER BOOKS EDITION

Copyright © 1993 by Robert James Waller
All rights reserved.

Cover design and illustration by Honi Werner
Book design by Giorgetta Bell McRee

Warner Books, Inc.
1271 Avenue of the Americas
New York, N.Y. 10020

Ⓦ A Time Warner Company

Printed in the United States of America

Originally published in hardcover by Warner Books.

First Printed in Paperback: December, 1994

10 9 8 7 6 5 4 3 2

*For high plumage and southern winds.*

# SLOW WALTZ
## IN
## CEDAR BEND

# One

*T*he *Trivandrum Mail* was on time. It came out of the jungle and pounded into Villupuram Junction at 3:18 on a sweltry afternoon in south India. When the whistle first sounded far and deep in the countryside, people began pressing toward the edge of the station platform. What could not walk was carried or helped along—bedrolls and market baskets, babies and old people.

Michael Tillman got to his feet from where he'd been leaning against a sooty brick wall and slung a tan knapsack over his left shoulder. A hundred people were trying to get off the train. Twice that many were simultaneously trying to get on, like two rivers flowing in opposite directions. You pushed or were left behind. A pregnant woman staggered in the crush, and Michael took her arm, got her up the steps, and swung himself into the second-class car as the train moved out.

Wheels turning, engine pulling hard, running at forty miles an hour through the edge of Villupuram. No place to sit, hardly a place to stand. Hanging on to the overhead luggage rack with one hand as the train curved out of brown hills and into green rice country, Michael slid the picture of Jellie Braden from his breast pocket, looked at it, reminding himself again of why he was doing this.

Bizarre. Strange. All of that. This curious rainbow of man and knapsack out of Iowa and into the belly of India in search of a woman. Jellie Braden . . . Jellie . . . belonging to another. But Michael Tillman wanted her. Wanted her more than his next breath, wanted her enough to travel the world looking for her. He kept thinking this whole affair was like songs you used to hear on late night radio.

How does it all begin? Who knows. And why? Same answer. The old Darwinian shuffle. Something primal, something way back and far down. Something whispering deep in the bones or genes, "That one." So it happened: a kitchen door in Iowa opened and likewise did Michael Tillman when Jellie walked through it in her fortieth year.

The dean's autumn reception for new faculty

in 1980, that's when it was. Just back from India after his second Fulbright there and still jet-lagged, Michael slouched against the dean's refrigerator, tugging on his second beer of the afternoon. He looked past faces looking at him or what they took to be him and answered tedious questions about India, suffering the white noise of academic chatter in the spaces around him.

An accountant's wife had taken over the India interrogation. Michael gave her 38.7 percent of his attention, planning escape routes and taking a long-slow swallow of beer while she spoke.

"Didn't the poverty just bother you horribly?"

"What poverty?" He was thinking about Joseph Conrad now, being halfway through *Heart of Darkness* on his third reading of it.

"In India. It must be awful."

"No. I was in the south, and the people looked pretty well fed to me. You've been watching those television shows that concentrate on good Catholic sisters hobbling around in the guts of Calcutta." She jumped a little when he said "guts," as if it were a word she hadn't heard before or maybe didn't like to think about.

"Did you see any cobras?"

"Yes, the snake charmer in the marketplace had one in a basket. The snake's mouth was sewn shut to keep it from doing any damage."

"How did it eat?"

3

"It didn't. It eventually dies. Then the snake man goes out and finds another one and sews its mouth shut, too. That's the way it works."

"My God, that's cruel, even though I abhor snakes."

"Yeah, working conditions have gone downhill all over. On the other hand, it's pretty much like the university. We just use heavier thread, that's all."

The accountant's wife blinked at him in the way some people do when they encounter lunacy and went on. "Did you see any of those naked men with white paint or whatever on their bodies? Isn't that strange?"

"No, I didn't see any. They're mostly up north, I guess. Benares, or Varanasi as they call it now, places like that. Whether it's strange or not, I can't say, depends on your worldview and career plans, I suppose."

"Jellie Braden's been to India, you know." The senior man in comparative economics leapfrogged the accountant's wife and had Michael's attention.

"Who?"

"Jim Braden's wife. He's the new guy in econometrics we hired away from Indiana." Michael heard a car door shutting in the driveway. The senior man turned and looked out the window. "Oh, here they come now. They're a delightful couple."

Braden? Braden . . . Braden . . . Braden? Ah, yes, Jim Braden. He'd interviewed him six months ago before going to India. Never met his wife. She'd been out with a realtor looking at housing during their recruiting visit. Michael felt like writing "Standard issue, greater than or equal to earnest and boring" on the evaluation form. But he didn't and wrote instead, "Jim Braden is a perfect fit," which amounted to the same thing.

James Lee Braden III came into the dean's kitchen, smiling, shaking hands, being introduced. Jellie Braden smiled, too, in her pale blue suit with a fitted jacket that came to just over her hips and a skirt reaching to midcalf, medium-heeled black boots below the hem. Subtle Jellie Braden.

But not subtle enough. It was all there. The cool patrician face coming only from an upper-shelf gene pool, the night-black hair and good skin. A body the old French called *rondeur*, polite writers would call superb, and flesh magazines would lose control over. Gray eyes coming at you like an arrow in flight and a confidence with men indicating she knew what they could and could not do. Where she had learned those easy truths wasn't clear at first, but you didn't have to be around Jimmy Braden very long to know it wasn't from him.

The faculty and assorted others with short attention spans laid down India and took up repertoire number two, another set of standard questions. This time with the Bradens, leaving Michael slouched there against the fridge by himself, watching Jellie.

"How do you like Cedar Bend?"

"Are you all moved in now?"

"What courses are you teaching, Jim?"

"Jellie—what an *interesting* name."

The dean's wife came over. "Hello, Michael."

"Hi, Carolyn, what's up?" He and Carolyn had always got along well even though the ol' deanaroo secretly wished Michael would pack it up and go somewhere else, anywhere. He occupied a high salary line, mainly because he'd been at the university fifteen years, and Arthur Wilcox would have preferred something a little less expensive and a lot more manageable sitting in Michael's office.

But Carolyn generally looked him up at these affairs, and they'd talk a bit. The decline of romance was one of their favorite subjects. A few years earlier she'd gotten acceptably drunk at the Christmas bash and said, "Michael, you've got balls. The rest of 'em are eunuchs." He'd put his arms around her and whispered in her ear, "Merry Christmas, Carolyn." Over her shoulder Michael had seen the chairperson of accounting watching them. The Chair was holding a glass of nonalcoholic punch and had a green star pinned to his lapel with "Hi! I'm Larry—Happy Holidays" printed on it in red felt-tip. Michael had grinned at him.

For a while he'd called Carolyn "Deanette." She'd liked it well enough to have a T-shirt made up with that handle printed on the front and had worn it to the fall picnic where the faculty was supposed to play volleyball and get to know one another better. Arthur-the-dean had taken offense and wouldn't let her wear the shirt after that.

When she'd told Michael about the T-shirt ban, he'd said "Screw 'im."

Carolyn had laughed. "Fat chance. Arthur's Victorian to the core, all bundled up." When he'd heard that, Michael's faith in things working out all right had died another small death. Carolyn was fifty-three but still had fire in her belly, quite a lot of it, he suspected. And he thought it was a damn shame, not to mention the waste of a good woman. How the hell does it happen, he wondered, these mistakes in the matching?

He and Carolyn talked a few minutes. Michael was looking past her, looking at the back of Jellie Braden's head and wondering if her hair was as thick as it seemed to be, wondering how it would feel to grab a big handful of it and bend her over the dean's kitchen table right then and there. He somehow had a feeling she might laugh and bend willingly if he tried it.

Carolyn Wilcox followed the point of Michael's eyes and said, "Have you met Jellie Braden yet?"

"No, I haven't."

The deanette reached over and tugged on Jellie's sleeve, rescuing her from the fumes of vapidity in which she was swirling. Deans' wives are allowed to do that when they feel like it, and they do it regularly, leaving a small semicircle of people holding glasses in their hands and looking stupid as the object of their focus is torn away. It's a shot they ought to put in the yearbook.

Jellie Braden turned around. "Jellie, I'd like you to meet Michael Tillman. If there's anything incorrigible about this faculty, it's Michael. In fact, he's probably sole owner of that property."

Jellie held out her hand, and he took it. "What makes you incorrigible, Dr. Tillman?"

"Just Michael, if it's okay with you. I don't like titles." He grinned a little when he said it. She smiled at the casual way he discarded something it took him nine years in various medieval institutions to acquire. "Aside from that, I happen to believe I'm highly corrigible, it's only Carolyn and the rest who think otherwise."

Carolyn patted his arm and drifted away. Jellie Braden looked at him. "I recall Jimmy mentioning you when we were here for his interviews. Somebody on the faculty told him you were eccentric or something like that."

"Jaded, maybe. A lot of people mistake that for eccentricity."

"If I remember correctly, he came back from

the interviews and said you're a regular idea factory. He brought it up again the other day and said he was looking forward to working with you. That doesn't sound very jaded to me."

Michael felt a little tight in the chest and needed breathing space. "Word is you've spent time in India."

"Yes, I have." As she spoke, he watched the gray eyes shift up and to the right, to another place, the way people do when they go on time-share, go somewhere else for a while. The way he did, often.

India. The idea of it always brought smells and glinting images rushing back to her for an instant, always the same smells and images—jasmine on Bengali night winds, dark hands across her breasts and along the curve of her back, the scent of a man as he pulled himself up and into her. And his words in those soft and transient moments,

        . . . did I ever play this song before?
        Not in any lifetime I remember.
        . . . will I ever play this song again?
        Not in any lifetime yet to come.

"I just got in from there," Michael said.
"First trip?" She came back from wherever

she'd been and turned to set her glass on the kitchen table.

"Second. I was there in 1976, also."

"You must like it." She smiled and tilted her head. "I noticed the cigarette bulge in your shirt pocket. Is smoking allowed here?"

"Forget it. We can go outside and stomp 'em out on the dean's driveway, though. That pisses him off, so I usually do it at least once when I'm over here."

Someone with less a sense of herself than Jellie Braden would have sideslipped away from the invitation. Bad form and all that, particularly for the wife of a new faculty member. But Jellie tilted her head toward the door and said, "Let's do it." The kitchen was almost empty, since the dean was holding forth in his parlor, and attendance was required unless you had a note from your doctor.

They sat on the dean's back steps, where she bummed a cigarette from him. He asked, "When were you in India, and for how long?"

"Some time back. I spent three years there."

She was being casually imprecise, and he wondered about that. "What part?"

"Southeast, mostly. Pondicherry."

"I've heard of it, never been there. Old French city, isn't it?"

"Yes." She blew smoke out across the dean's azaleas and didn't say anything else.

"Like it?" he asked. "Dumb question. Must have if you stayed three years."

"It was up and down. Overall, pretty good. I went to do some work for my master's thesis in anthropology and kind of got caught up in India in general. Never finished the paper."

"That happens. India pretty much splits people into two categories, you love it or you can't stand it. I'm in the former group."

They were sitting only about a foot apart, and she looked over at him. "So am I."

"How'd you meet, you and Jim?"

"After I came back from India I wanted to hang around Bloomington even though I wasn't in school. I wangled a job as secretary in the economics department. Jimmy was a junior professor, just out of graduate school with his bright, shiny degree. He always was polite to me and wore expensive suits, wrote articles on esoteric topics I didn't understand but which I dutifully typed. I was pretty much lost and wandering back then. When he asked me to marry him, I couldn't think of any good reason not to, so I said yes."

Michael listened to what she said and how she said it. She married Jim Braden because she couldn't think of reasons not to. That was a strange way of putting it. Close to her like this, gray eyes steady on his, he upgraded his earlier idea about putting her on the dean's kitchen table. The new plan involved stripping her naked, taking off his own clothes, and flying in that shimmering state of affairs all the way to the Seychelles, first class. Upon arrival it would be a headlong and forever plunge into lubricious nirvana. He was quite certain Jellie Braden would look better than wonderful under a jungle waterfall with a red hibiscus in her hair.

"How long ago was that, when you got married?" As soon as he asked, a voice in his head groaned, "You dumb ass, Tillman, why'd you say that? It's more than you need to know and too damned forward—you just met the woman." He stood up and stomped out his cigarette on the dean's driveway. Anyplace else he field-stripped them and stuck the butts in his pocket, but not in the dean's driveway. Michael was like an old dog there, staking out his territory, making sure he left a little something behind for Arthur to sniff.

She walked over to her car and put hers out in the ashtray. "Jimmy'll complain like crazy when he sees that. He won't let me smoke at home when he's there. I'll get a lecture on our way out of here, and he'll spray the car with air freshener two minutes after we hit the driveway." She looked at him and chewed lightly on her lower lip. "Jimmy and I have been married ten years. I suppose we better go inside."

He started pulling off his tie. "You go ahead. I'm going back to my apartment and snuggle down with Joseph Conrad."

"Nice meeting you," Jellie Braden said.

"Same here. See you around."

She smiled. "Sure."

And Michael thought of a waterfall in the Seychelles that would be just perfect. Fifteen months later he rode the *Trivandrum Mail* into south India, toward places he'd never been, looking for her.

# *Two*

*H*igh summer 1953, a far place called
Dakota and the wind hot and mak-
ing your greasy clothes stick to your body. Michael
Tillman was fifteen then, leaning under the hood
of Elmore Nixon's car, banker Nixon of First National in Custer. T-shirt riding up his back and toes
barely touching the cement, he listened to the big
V-8's erratic turn, adjusted the carburetor, listened
again as the engine smoothed out and settled down.

"Mikey, get tha' sonabitchin' Olds finished.
We got three more to go yet." His father was
staggering around, whiskey flask buried deep in
the back pocket of gray-striped coveralls.

Outside at the pumps his mother was filling

15

the tank of a grain truck and wiping her forehead with the back of her arm. July 27, 4 P.M. at Tillman's Texaco, a world of heavy smells and flaking paint in fading greens and peeling whites. Roar of traffic on Route 16 out in front; tourists with suitcases lashed to car tops, on their way to see the faces of Rushmore.

Straightening up, Michael removed the protective cloth from the Olds' fender and slammed the hood. He backed the car out of the service bay and parked it off to one side, stood there for a moment, wiping his hands on a cloth. A Lakota Sioux in run-down cowboy boots, short and sweating into his pockmarks, waited by the roadside for someone or something or some other time better than the one in which he lived.

Michael went to the pop cooler and pulled a Coke from where it lay buried in ice and water. He held the bottle against one cheek, then the other. Stuck it up inside his shirt and laid it against his chest, shuddered once as cold met hot. No rain for weeks, dust devils moving down the roadsides.

"Damnit, Mikey . . ."

His father's voice slurred and reverberated from inside the station. He put the unopened Coke back in the cooler.

Michael slid into another car and pulled it into the service bay. His mother's handwriting was on the work order, "lube & oil." The Chevy lifted on the rack with a whirring sigh, and he unscrewed

16

the oil plug on lawyer Dengen's Bel-Air. While the used oil drained into a bucket he looked out at Route 16. One good road is enough, that's what he was thinking.

He walked over to the Vincent Black Shadow parked in the rear of the station, touched the handlebars. His father had taken in the big English motorcycle as payment for a repair bill and said it was Michael's to keep if he'd fix it up and learn how to maintain it. He did and owned it, spiritually and physically, from that moment on. One good road—the Shadow could take him down that road if he learned all there was to know about valves and turning wheels and routes out of here. Michael was already practicing at night, running the Shadow at high speeds through the Black Hills even though he wasn't legally old enough to drive.

On winter nights when the Shadow waited for spring to come again, there was the jumpshot arching through the lights of small-town gymnasiums. People took notice of Ellis Tillman's boy, said he might be good enough to play college ball. When he scored fifty-three points against Deadwood his senior year, they were sure of it.

At pajama parties the high school girls giggled and talked about boys. They said Michael Tillman had sad brown eyes, lonely eyes, and grease on his hands that wouldn't come off. They said he was shy but had cute muscles and looked good in his basketball uniform. They said he had a nice smile when he showed it, but he'd probably end up running his father's gas station and never would get the grease off his hands. Sometimes he'd take one of them to a movie in Rapid City, but mostly he kept to himself. He worked at the station and fished the trout in summer, practiced his jumpshot in the city park until it became a thing of magic. The Shadow, the jumpshot, algebra and Euclid's geometry—they were all of the same elegant cloth, universes contained within themselves, and he was good at them. He wasn't quite so good with girls or rooms full of people or English classes where poetry was discussed until it didn't exist.

Rooms full of people he didn't care about. Poetry could be dealt with sometime. But he wondered about girls who would become women. Somewhere out in these places of the world was a woman with whom he would make love for the first time in his life. And what would that be like? To be with a woman? Not sure. Not sure, but wondering. Would she be pleased with him, and how would a boy-man know what to do? Not sure yet. A little shaky thinking of it and reading the copy of *What Boys and Girls Should Know About Each Other* his mother had discreetly placed on his bookshelf. Neither she nor his father ever mentioned the book. As with everything else, he figured he was on his own. Nobody was handing out anything to anyone as far as he could tell, except small paperback books that were never mentioned and seemed pretty unromantic in any case.

18

The jumpshot took Michael down roads where the Shadow couldn't go. On a December night in 1960, Ellis Tillman leaned close to his Zenith portable and adjusted the tuning, trying to pull in KFAB in Omaha, Nebraska. The announcer's voice came and went: "For . . . information . . . local Farm Bureau agent." Long way, weak signal. Twenty below zero in Custer at 9:14, wind chill minus forty-eight. More static. He swore at the radio, and Ruth Tillman looked up from across the kitchen table. "Ellis, it's only a basketball game, not the end of the world. Have they said anything more about Michael's knee?"

"No. He'll be okay. He's a tough kid." Ellis Tillman took a sip of Old Grand-Dad and bent close to the radio. He was proud of his boy.

The stars shifted or sunspots went away, and the announcer's voice came back in double time:

The Big Red machine's rollin' now, on top of the Wichita State Shockers, eighty-three–seventy-eight, with just under four minutes to go. Tillman brings the ball upcourt for the Shockers, still limping on the bad knee that took him out of action in the first half. Over to LaRoux, back to Tillman, half-court press by the Big Red. Tillman fakes left, drives right, double screen for him by LaRoux and Kentucky Williams. . . .

19

"Go get 'em, Mikey!" Ellis Tillman stamped his feet on yellow linoleum and pounded the chrome-legged table so hard the radio bounced. Ruth Tillman looked at her knitting and shook her head slowly back and forth, wondering about men and what drove them onward to such insanity.

Four hundred miles away in Lincoln, smell of sweat and popcorn and the crowd screaming and the coach signaling for what he called the Tillman Special and you're moving right and slamming your left elbow into the face of the bastard who's grabbing for your jersey and you're cutting hard for the double screen LaRoux and Kentucky are setting up and a camera flash bursts from the side-line and your right knee is swollen to half-again its normal size from blood in the tissues . . . and you've done this a million times before . . . more than that . . . and the power in your legs and shoulders and the grace and balletlike movement and you're high into the air, left hand cradling the ball over your head and right hand pushing it in a long and gentle arc toward an orange rim with silver metal showing where the orange paint has rubbed off from the friction of a zillion basketballs . . . and the ball clears the rim and slices the net just the way it used to in the backyard of your South Dakota home and the crowd screams louder and you land on a knee that crumples into nothing and you go to the floor with Kentucky Williams stumbling over you on his way back down the court . . .

and you lie there
and you know it's over
and you're relieved it is.
And four hundred miles northwest
your mother bows her head.

Two days later Ellis Tillman got his copy of the *Wichita Eagle* in the mail. He'd subscribed to it while Michael was playing ball and would drop the subscription now. On the sports page was the headline

SHOCKERS FALL TO NEBRASKA, 91–89

Tillman Hits 24,
Suffers Career-Ending Injury

He thought about cutting out the article and posting it in the gas station with the other clippings about Mikey. But Ruth Tillman wouldn't hear of any such thing.

Michael's grades barely slipped him into graduate school, but once he was accepted, it was straight, hard work. Brutal work—six years of it, including his dissertation. In Berkeley he grew a beard and fell in love for the first time. Her name was Nadia, she wore black stockings and long skirts and came from Philadelphia where her father was a union organizer. They lived together for two years in the sixties when Berkeley was becoming the center of all that counted, so they believed.

Nadia joined the Peace Corps and thought Michael should do the same. "Give something back, Michael," she said.

He'd been offered a fellowship for doctoral study and wanted to take it. "I'll give something back another way," he told her.

Michael shaved off his beard. Nadia packed and left. Disappointed, but not angry, and on to other things. "It's probably better this way," she told him. "You're an only child, and from what you've said about your life, and from what it's like living with you, I'm beginning to think only children are raised to be alone. At least you were." She softened, looked at him. "It's been good, Michael."

He smiled. "It *has* been good. I mean that, Nadia. You've taught me a lot about a lot of things. Stay in touch." He kissed her good-bye, watched two years of his life roll away on a Greyhound, and walked to the Department of Economics, where he handed in his letter accepting the fellowship. He went back to his apartment and could still smell the scent of Nadia, looked at her posters of Lenin and Einstein and Twain on the wall. He missed her already, but she was right: he liked being alone and had been trained for it. Only children understand it ultimately will come to that, and they live a life practicing for the moments when it happens.

# *Three*

*T*he *Trivandrum Mail* slowed down, halted, arms passing fruit and tea through the windows in exchange for rupees. Mosquitoes passing through the windows in exchange for blood. Sweat running down the curl of his spine, down his chest and face, Michael Tillman stared again at the picture of Jellie Braden. People in the fields working rice, bullocks hauling loads of wood down country roads, birds flying alongside the train for a short distance and then veering off. Whistle far up ahead as the engine plowed past another village.

A face looked over his shoulder. The man smiled and pointed at the photo of Jellie. "Very pretty. Nice lady?"

Michael said she was very nice. The dam crumbled, everyone within a radius of ten feet immediately wanted to see the photo. They handled it carefully, passing it from one to the other and nodding, looking up at Michael and smiling.

"Your lady?" one of them asked.

He'd never thought of her that way and paused before answering. Then he grinned—"Maybe, I'm not sure"—while the train rolled on through the late afternoon and into a purple evening.

Two hours into the ride a seat opened up. He started for it, then noticed the pregnant woman off to one side, the one he'd helped onto the train. He pointed to the seat. She nodded in thanks and sat down. Soon after he felt a tug on his sleeve. Two Indian men had jammed against each other, leaving a corner of their seat for Michael. He tossed his knapsack in the overhead rack and crouched on the space they'd created.

Talk began, mostly sign language, but progress was made. The men were farmers going home from market. They asked simple questions and discovered Michael's profession. Immediately he was honored in the way Indians honor teachers—respect, awe, gratitude. "The highest calling," one man said in heavily accented English, and the others agreed, smiling and nodding. Maybe he's right, Michael thought. It's easy to lose perspective and become cynical when you're close to a profession or a person for decades. You start focusing on the ugly parts, forgetting the overall beauty of what's up close to you.

He'd begun graduate study with soaring thoughts of becoming a scholar and a teacher, indeed the highest calling as far as he could tell. In his early twenties he'd imagined bright students he would lead through the intricacies of advanced economic theory, maybe a Nobel Prize out there if the scholarship was diligent. But in some way he'd never been able to define, graduate school and his early years as a professor had taken the dreams away from him. Something to do with the emphasis on method, with plodding data collection and analysis. Something to do with social scientists trying to operate like physicists, as if the roiling complexities of social reality could be handled in the same way as the study of nature. And something to do with students who cared only for job preparation, who demanded what they called "relevance" and had no real interest in the abstractions he found so lovely, so much like a clear, cold mountain stream running through his brain. "Good theory is the most practical thing you can study," he told them. They didn't believe him.

He gave a little speech at a College of Business and Economics faculty meeting. "We are interested, it seems, not in creating, but only in maintaining—maintaining our comfortable, enviable life-style. If the taxpayers ever discover what's really going on around here, they'll march on us.

We're like the goddamned students and the students are like us dumb bastards: it's come down to cooperate and graduate."

Two heads out of 137 nodded in agreement, 135 wished the dean would get on with the meeting and talk about next year's salary prospects. Michael didn't make any more speeches after that.

So the dreams eroded. And Michael Tillman began to turn inward, to follow only what made sense to him. He was trying to get back the old feelings, the awe he'd once experienced in contemplating the great sweep of time and space, wondering about the peculiar evolutionary magic that had put him and not someone else here at this particular time in a universe still expanding.

People saw him as distant, and he was. People saw him as arrogant, but he wasn't, quite the opposite. He simply decided to go off by himself, go his own way. People mistake shyness and reclusiveness—both of those—for arrogance. It's a convenient label slapped on by those who see only the surface of things and nothing more. He understood as much and let them believe what they chose to believe.

As a teacher he was different, but effective. Good students liked him, the middling ones were afraid of him. The poorer students avoided his classes. He wasn't a kindly Mr. Chips, and never would be, yet he respected grit and determination, spending long hours with those who had trouble in his classes. And he reserved a special disdain for the talented ones who lazed through their student years.

"Do what he asks and you're okay, dead meat otherwise," the graduate students said. "He walks around barefoot in the classroom sometimes, but he knows what he's talking about."

The undergraduates wrote good things and bad things on his evaluations:

"Tests are too hard. Needs to understand young kids and parental pressure better."
"He's a little scary but gives me a lot of help outside the classroom. This is a *hard* course."
"His ideas have caused me to reevaluate my life."
"Seems arrogant at times, self-centered. Nobody can be as smart as he seems."
"I liked his aproach [*sic*]."
"Needs a haircut and sometimes takes the Lord's name in vain."
"Good in class but never seems to be around except for his office hours. I'm working at Kmart to pay off my Camaro and my schedule doesn't fit with his."
"Knows his stuff but lives in another world."
"Great teacher. One of the two best I've had."

Michael had come out of graduate school on the run. The twenty-six articles on his résumé got him tenure in 1970 and a full professorship in 1978, a week before his fortieth birthday. After that he raised his head and began looking around, trying to get the magic back. People still called and asked what he was doing on this or that subject. "Nothing," he'd tell them. "On to other things."

"Like what?" they'd ask.

He kept it vague, enigmatic, matching the drift of his own mind. "I'm fooling around with Jeremy Bentham's early work on the pleasure-pain calculus and its applications to problems of contemporary democracy."

That stopped them. There'd be a moment of silence down the long lines of Mother Bell. Then: "I see. Too bad you didn't keep working on the earlier material; I thought you were on to something with that."

It went along that way, a life of slightly unsettled contentment, all right in general but cut through with an aloneness he simultaneously treasured and disliked. He had his work and the Shadow. He had a woman or two he saw occasionally. And then came Jellie Braden. And then came the *Trivandrum Mail* running southward into traditional India, where the old ways endured.

The train pulled into Madurai at ten o'clock. Michael asked about a place to stay, and the conductor directed him to a small hotel just up the street from the station. "Very clean, very pleasant," he said. Michael trusted him.

When he went through the front door the action level cranked up. Most of the small Indian hotels are designed for people traveling in basic Indian ways, white faces being rare at their registration desks. The desk clerk was obviously pleased with Michael's choice of hotels, and three bellboys were assigned to take him to his room, even though he carried only a knapsack.

One of them ran ahead and slid six feet on the floor tile, stopping exactly at Michael's room and opening the door. Another spoke a little English and said the hotel restaurant was closed, but he would be happy to run down the street and get something.

Michael knew he could count on an omelet. He asked the bellboy to fetch one, along with some bread and tea and cheese or yogurt. Twenty-five minutes later the boy returned with tea, bread, yogurt, chutney, and a three-egg omelet. Just where the eggs came from was useless information at that point. Besides, it's an inquiry Michael never made in India, regardless of the circumstances.

After food, sleep. One of the boys knocked on Michael's door at first light, as requested. Michael cold-showered, had cereal and goat's milk along with toast and tea in the restaurant, then started looking for a car to take him on to a place called

Thekkady in the western mountains. The hotel manager was happy to assist, and a white Premier, one of the small, ubiquitous, Indian-made sedans, pulled up in front of the hotel thirty minutes later.

"He has an all-India license," the manager said.

Michael wasn't sure about the significance of that but took it to be a good omen. The driver used a whisk broom to clean off the backseat, and they headed out on the trail of Jellie Braden.

The day after Michael first met Jellie at the dean's reception, somebody somewhere yanked an autumnal lever and the aging rocket ship called college lifted off. He had a Tuesday–Thursday teaching schedule but went in even though it was Monday and frittered around. He read mail that had come in his absence, posted his office hours, straightened out the schedules of a few students who couldn't get the classes they wanted. Word along the student grapevine was, "Tillman knows how to get around the bureaucracy, go see him if you need help."

He was still thinking about Jellie Braden. He hadn't reacted that strongly to a woman for a long time. Maybe never. No, not maybe . . . never. The physical attraction was there, and maybe something else, too. He'd spent a restless night thinking about primal things versus rectitude, with no conclusion having been reached.

He opened up on Tuesday with his standard lecture, "Complexity and the Boundaries of Human Policymaking," dazzling the seniors with a little fancy stuff out of combinatorial mathematics. A typical first class session, letting them know this was going to be serious business. Most of the faculty merely handed out syllabi and directions to the restrooms. But he'd walk in, look at the students, and say, "We begin with complex systems, an examination of our own limited intellects in a contest with unlimited possibilities."

After that he'd turn to the blackboard and grin to himself as he heard them digging out notebooks and pens they hadn't anticipated using the first day. Michael Tillman, classroom serial killer.

On Thursday he was keeping the office hours posted on his door:

> *Tillman*
> *2:00–4:00 Tues. & Thurs.*
> *By Appointment Otherwise*

Early in the semester traffic was light. The students were still drinking beer and hadn't really gotten into the books yet. Things usually picked up about three weeks farther on, right before the first examination. He was leaning back, feet on his desk, office door propped open with a book praising Reaganomics written by one of the faculty's supply-side economists. It was understood he chose his doorstops carefully and rotated them periodically, a kind of floor-level editorial on the times around him. Quiet rap of knuckles on the open door, and he looked up into gray eyes: Jellie Braden, in tight jeans, red sweater with a white shirt collar peeking out of it, well-traveled hiking boots. Black hair tucked up under a round, short-billed wool cap.

He hadn't fully appreciated her long legs on Sunday. The skirt and boots she'd worn to the dean's party had disguised her lower parts, though he would have guessed as much if he'd thought about it. An old green book bag was slung over her right shoulder.

"Hello, Michael Tillman. I was on my way to Jimmy's office and saw your door open."

He swung his feet off the desk, tossed the computer magazine over his shoulder, and said, "Hello yourself, Jellie Braden. Nice of you to stop by. Come in, sit down, the smoking lamp is lit in here."

"Okay. I have a few minutes before Jimmy's out of class." She gave the impression she didn't have anything better to do with a little downtime, but he didn't really think she meant it that way.

"Jellie, you look like what the admissions crowd calls a mature student, knapsack and all."

"I am exactly that. Well, a student, anyway. My maturity's an open question."

He was about to comment on what he saw as her rather obvious maturity but decided not to. "What are you taking?"

"A course in cultural traditions of the North American Plains Indians—Native Americans, as we know them now. Another one in archaeological field methods. I haven't been able to find a job yet, and I'll be damned if I'm going to lie around the house all day and watch the soaps. What are you teaching this semester?"

"A senior-level course in decision making and a graduate course in quantitative methods. Hot stuff, you ought to sign up for them."

"I thought you were an economist?"

"I still am, sort of. Got interested in more applied topics a few years ago. Age does that to you."

"It all sounds pretty grubby to me. Something to do with making money and screwing consumers, I'll bet."

Michael laughed. "Money, maybe. Screwing consumers, no."

"How do you separate the two? It always looks like the same thing to me."

"Good point. But I'd rather not think about it. I'm like the old A-bomb scientists; I just produce the knowledge, what the public chooses to do with it is not my responsibility. That's rubbish, of course, but it gets me by if I dare to reflect too much on what I'm doing."

"Well, at least you're honest about it. Don't you wear a suit and tie when you're teaching?"

"No, I used to when I first started. Damn chalk dust gets all over the good material. Besides, this climate's just too deucedly cold in the winter to dress very fancy. Somehow I never felt right wearing long johns underneath pinstripes. As the tailors say, the cloth doesn't hang properly. Jeans and sweaters work out okay. That also bothers the dean, but then just about everything I do bothers the dean, whether I'm trying to bother him or not." Michael tapped a pencil on the desk and grinned at her. "I once designed a uniform for the dean, but he didn't take to the idea."

Jellie grinned back. "Just what would a dean's uniform look like?"

"A jumpsuit plus face paint done in what I called 'manager's camouflage,' mottled tones of brown and gray to blend in with filing cabinets and other office equipment. I told him, 'Arthur, you'd be able to skulk around and do all kinds of secret things, check up on us to make sure we're not dancing through the first-floor lobby with garlands in our hair.' "

Jellie's grin twisted into a little crooked smile. "Exactly what did the dean say about your idea?"

"He didn't say anything. Just shook his head and walked away. That was after I went on to tell him how the uniform could be coupled with what I called the 'administrator's go-squat,' a modified duck walk that would keep him down at desktop level. I demonstrated the go-squat for him in the hall outside his office and guaranteed him he'd have the ultimate in close supervision if he'd adopt the uniform and the walk. Guess he didn't grasp the concept. Carolyn liked the idea, however."

Small talk, nothing talk. It went on from there. Jellie began dropping by his office once a week or so, and she and Michael whacked their way toward each other through the old thicket of ignorance separating strangers. Sometimes he had a partial erection just talking to her and was glad he wore his jeans snug, which kind of held events under control. He'd given up on organized religion years ago, but it's handy when you need it, and he said over and over to himself, "O Absolute, give me Jellie Braden; somehow You must do as much for a simple man." The words became a mantra that never left his mind.

At the fall picnic on a Sunday, Michael sat on one end of a teeter-totter in a park along the river, languidly watching the accounting department take on the marketing department as part of an exciting volleyball tournament organized by the dean and his secretary. His secretary liked Michael even less than the dean did, calling him impertinent. Michael thought about impertinence and factored in cigarette smoking, which the dean complained about. The result popped out: *Be gladdened in your heart you have tenure*. He was glad, and the sun was late-September pleasant.

The economists were anxiously waiting in the

wings for their second crack at the marketeers, part of a double-elimination scheme designed by a sports fanatic in the operations research area. The genius had used some fairly high-powered mathematics to make up the pairings based on the departmental won-loss records from the last three picnics and had run off a four-color diagram on one of the Apples.

The dean shot up into the far reaches of delirium when he saw the printout and insisted everyone look at "Don's good work," as he called it (an extra two hundred for Don at salary time, Michael guessed). Michael thought it was using a sledgehammer to drive a tack and said so when the dean asked his opinion of Don's brilliance. What he said was, "I think Don-Don applied high thinking to low living."

Jesus, the faculty was out of shape. Flabby bodies whacking a volleyball into the trees, stumbling around, falling down, the dean tooting on his whistle. He looked to see if the hospital emergency unit was standing by.

"Wanna teeter, Tillman-Michael?" Jellie was coming across the grass toward him, smiling. He'd seen her earlier from a distance. Anytime he was in the same physical area as Jellie his radar kicked in, and he was aware of her location at all times. She and Jim had arrived an hour earlier. Michael had come alone on the Black Shadow, goosing it a little as he passed the dean's car on his way into the park and waving to Carolyn when he went by. No *Deanette* T-shirt this year, and he felt bad for her. That's why he had a bookstore make him up a T-shirt reading *Possible Dean* and was wearing it.

"No, I have the totter end. You'll have to teeter. That's the easy part, anyway, and it's what I do during the week." He stood up a bit, lowering the other end of the seesaw. He outweighed her by about sixty pounds and scooted up the board to balance things out, then tossed her a beer out of the little six-pack cooler by his feet.

"How does Jim feel about his wife sharing an unsanded plank with another man?"

"Mostly he doesn't pay any attention to that sort of thing, but he can be jealous in a petulant way sometimes. And for no good reason, I might add. But he likes you and knows we're friends, so that's different. Anyway, he's totally focused on pounding the marketing department to smithereens in the next round of wretchedness over there."

She was luminous in the soft, slanting light of an autumn afternoon. Her breasts rose and fell pleasantly beneath her cotton blouse as they teetered and tottered. Her jeans stretched tight across her hips and thighs where she straddled the board. Did the Absolute build in this much torment as a last delicious bit of private entertainment for Him or Her or Whatever? Michael Tillman wondered.

"No volleyball, Michael? You look like you're in good shape, and judging by the pathetic little war going on over there at the net, you'd be a dominant force."

He glanced toward the net and saw James Lee Braden III in his horn-rims, sweatshirt, and floppy khakis doing side-straddle hops as he warmed up for a second run at the marketeers. Braden III went into the dirt when he tripped over Dr. Patricia Sanchez's foot. Then he realized he hadn't answered Jellie's question and she was watching him watch her. He took a hit of beer and said, "Nope. I did my four miles on the road this morning at dawn. That's enough for one day. Besides, I might fall into Kipperman-the-accountant's stomach and not find my way out by class time Tuesday."

Jellie Braden laughed, and they went up and down on a September afternoon in Iowa.

# *Four*

In the countryside west of Madurai the morning was sweet and clear, in the way India feels before the heat and dust come up. Especially sweet and clear, because if it all worked out, Jellie was four hours ahead in the high country of the Western Ghats. Maybe tomorrow wouldn't be as sweet and clear. Maybe he had no business doing this, following her. The old doubts again, bothering him for this whole trip. Forget it, push on. Jellie had her problems, whatever they were, and Michael had his —forty-three, sinking toward a time when it would be too late for this kind of thunder in his brain and body. If it came to war, it could be sorted out in the hills of India, as good a place as any. She could send him away, and he'd be no worse off than he was sitting back in Cedar Bend listening to gossip about Jimmy Braden's wife running off on some existential quest.

At Thanksgiving their first year in Cedar Bend, the Bradens invited Michael for dinner. They'd only been in town for three months, but Jimmy was set on having what he called "a major *do*." Jellie protested, saying they didn't know many people and somehow Thanksgiving had always seemed a special time for family and close friends. Her parents were coming from Syracuse, that was probably enough. But Jimmy made up a list, looked at it, and said if two-thirds of them came, it would be a respectable showing.

Jimmy's list was predictable, safe. He said, "I thought about inviting Michael Tillman, but I doubt if he'd come. He doesn't seem the type for Thanksgiving dinner. Then again, Michael's single and so is your friend, Ann Frazier, from sociology. They're both kind of different, maybe we can do a little matchmaking over turkey."

Jellie thought about it. She imagined Michael sitting at their dining room table. Strange and different Michael Tillman, big-shouldered and brown-eyed with brown hair longer than the approved length for a business school faculty member. A little something out of the ordinary. Sunburned in the face, almost a workingman's face, as if he'd be comfortable cashing his paycheck in a bar across the street from where he might have worked as a machinist. And his long, smooth fingers with the faintest imprint of grease even hard scrubbing couldn't remove.

A month before, she and Jimmy had been coming home from a local theater production. The night streets were wet from October rain, and suddenly there was Michael beside them when they stopped for a light. He sat on the Shadow, revving its engine. She remembered the car radio was playing a song by Neil Diamond, "Cracklin' Rosie," while Jimmy was telling her to find the public radio station devoting an entire evening to Beethoven. It stuck in her mind, the song playing at that moment. From that time on, she could be anywhere and hear "Cracklin' Rosie," and instantly she was back on the streets of Cedar Bend, looking at Michael on the Shadow.

Jimmy had leaned out the window of the Buick and said, "Hi, Michael."

Michael—yellow bandanna tied around his head, leather jacket, boots, and jeans—turned and waved to the Bradens, then looked straight ahead. When the light changed he gunned the Shadow and was gone, straddling that smooth black machine of his and disappearing into the countryside.

Jimmy said, "I think it's a bit chilly and wet to be riding a motorcycle, don't you?"

But Jellie didn't hear him. She was watching

41

the Shadow's taillight moving away from her. And she wanted to be riding with Michael Tillman, to be going out there where she had once traveled and was now afraid to go again. She wanted to climb on that black machine and feel the beat of its engine between her legs and the roar of wind in her ears.

Admit it, she'd always had a taste for a peculiar kind of man, the sort that seems ill designed for the world in which they live (Jimmy is a whole other story—those were her break-even years). Michael Tillman was like that, she sensed, as if a great fist had reached back and plunked a hard-drinking, hard-cussing, nineteenth-century keel-boatman into the 1980s, given him an intelligence out beyond where the rest of us live, and said, "Now, behave yourself," all the while being doubtful that he would. And he didn't.

Her taste in men probably had something to do with the genes arching forward from her great-great-grandmother, Elsa, who had been a radical feminist when it was considered improper if not immoral for a woman to think about such things, let alone speak and parade in the streets on behalf of them. Elsa Markham had left her husband, taken up with an equally radical socialist, and gone on the road as a warrior for women's rights and free love. The Markham family didn't talk much about Great-Great-Grandmother Elsa.

Jellie kept that side of herself hidden for a long time. Not totally suppressed, hidden, tucked way back where it couldn't get hold of her and disrupt the well-designed life her parents had drafted in clear terms for their two daughters. Jellie's older sister, Barbara, had shouldered arms and marched straight into that well-designed life. She got her degree in elementary education, married a success-ful insurance broker, and stayed in Syracuse. The Markhams were pleased with Barbara's choices, and the world was good.

In their late girlhoods, Barbara read *Little Women* and loved it. Jellie told her it was cloying. Jellie read *Madame Bovary* and loved it. Barbara told her it was trash. Then she ratted on Jellie and told Mother Markham that Jellie wanted to be Emma Bovary. Mother grabbed Jellie's copy of Flaubert and read it in one sitting, concentrating on the passages Jellie had underlined. A lecture on virtue followed, but Jellie got out of it by saying she didn't want to be like Emma at all and that you could look at *Madame Bovary* as a kind of primer on how *not* to live. What she really wanted to say was Emma handled it all wrong by being loose with money. A true romantic would have concen-trated on the sex and let it go at that.

Given that Elsa Markham's restless ways had somehow fluttered down to her, it was nearly inev-itable Jellie's life would turn out as it did. Her India experiences early on gave her some pause, however, and Jimmy came along. She was in a space where she needed to paddle flat water for a while, fatigued from the emotional roll and toss high adventure brings with it. Jimmy looked stable, and he was. Jimmy looked comfortable, and he was. Jellie needed peace and quiet. When he proposed she said yes for reasons she wasn't sure of, but they had something to do with stability and comfort and peace and quiet.

Jellie fought hard against the tug of Elsa's genes for years; still, they wouldn't leave her alone. Inside the good faculty wife with a degree in anthropology was a keelboatman's woman who wanted to put her bare breasts against Michael Tillman's face and feel his mouth come onto them.

When Jimmy showed her his list of invitees for Thanksgiving, she hesitated. Her first inclination was to go for comfort and stability. But Elsa Markham took hold of her arm, and Jellie scratched "M. Tillman" at the bottom. "I think that's a good idea. Ask Michael and see what he says." She decided at that moment to wear her red dress with the long puffy sleeves if he accepted their invitation.

Michael Tillman didn't celebrate holidays—any of them—but Thanksgiving at the Bradens was a chance to be around Jellie, and he couldn't pass it up. Jim had said there would be a few other people, but he and Jellie especially hoped Michael would come, and oh, by the way, bring a friend if you want.

He came in from his morning run, got his dog

and cat fed and squared away, then read for a while. Around one o'clock he stood before his bedroom closet and pulled out a gray tweed jacket and a blue, button-down-collar shirt. Most of his ties had fallen onto the closet floor a thousand or so years ago and looked like it, the silk ones wrinkled and dusty. But a dark red wool number, decorated with *Save the Turtles* rampant on a field of the swimming reptiles, looked like a candidate for resuscitation with the help of a good brushing. He pulled out a pair of wrinkled charcoal slacks and held them up. Malachi, the border collie who was named after Michael's favorite professor in graduate school, put his head on his paws and made small, whining sounds. "No dice, huh, Malachi?"

Michael turned, showed the slacks to Casserole-the-cat, and asked, "Whaddya think, Cass?" She blinked, yawned, and headed for the living room. With that kind of poll results on the slacks, he shoved hangers around, located a pair of presentable jeans, and finished off this exercise in hesitant elegance with gray socks and the old reliable cordovan loafers.

He picked up the bottle of red he'd bought for the occasion and walked the six blocks to the two-story brick the Bradens had purchased. Three cars were parked outside, the Bradens' Buick was in the driveway. Jim answered the bell, impeccable—perfect as it gets—in a dark blue pinstripe, white collar—barred starched shirt with a yellow-and-black polka-dotted tie. At the bottom end were black, lightweight wingtips—banker's shoes. Crisp white hanky in his breast pocket. Michael had already guessed Jimmy Braden came from old money, and today he looked it.

"Hi, Michael. Jellie and I are pleased you could come. I think you probably know everyone here except for Jellie's parents, who flew in from Syracuse. Say, that's quite a tie!"

Michael hated entrance scenes. His blue-collar upbringing surged forward when he was paraded into a room full of people, and he'd get sort of stupid and uncomfortable almost to the point of appearing bellicose, which he really wasn't. His growing years didn't provide him with much experience in entrances, that's all.

A motley little outfit awaited him in the small living room: sociologist (female, unpartnered, acquaintance of Jellie's), accountant and wife ("Did you see any cobras?"), the overweight operations research guy with an equally heavy wife and crushing handshake (double-elimination volleyball genius). Patricia Sanchez was in the middle of the sofa, seated next to a guy she dated from the student services office. An older man he took to be Jellie's father sat on Pat's other side. It was stuffy warm, with a perfect fire crackling away and everybody looking at him standing in the doorway to the living room. He took a deep breath and wished he could light up, but there wasn't a chance in hell of that.

Jimmy took him by the elbow. "I think everybody here knows Michael Tillman from my department." The voices reached toward Michael in ragged unison. He gave them all a little wave and handed the bottle of wine to Jimmy.

"Jellie and her mother are in the kitchen. Oh, how clumsy of me, I nearly forgot you haven't met Jellie's father, Mr. Markham."

Mr. Markham was somewhere over sixty, with bright eyes and a firm hand. He grinned. Michael grinned back and judged Leonard Markham to be all right, as long as you didn't cross him.

Through an open door and down the hall he could see Jellie in the kitchen. She looked up, waved, and called, "Hi, Michael, come meet my mother."

He went back to the kitchen while the living room went back to whatever conversations he'd interrupted. Jellie wiped her hands on a white apron that had *HI!* and four tom turkeys with big, floppy red combs printed on it. She kissed him on the cheek, whispering, "I'm so glad you came," then turned him to the gray-haired woman who was doing something or other with giblet dressing. The kiss and the whisper surprised him, but he chalked it up to holiday spirit.

"Mother, this is our friend, Michael Tillman."

Jellie got her looks from her mother. Eleanor Markham was a knock-'em-dead lady about the same age as her husband and with the same gray eyes as Jellie's. "I'm glad to meet you, Michael.

We're so pleased Jellie and Jim have made such nice friends in the short time they've been here."

She turned to Jellie. "Michael's the one who rides a motorcycle, right?" Jellie nodded. "Where do you ride it, Michael? Very far?"

"Oh, here and there. Around town, up to the Great Lakes sometimes, Colorado if I'm really feeling sporty. It's an old buzzard, and you have to carry a full tool kit if you're going any distance at all."

"Don't you live in an apartment, Michael? Where do you keep the motorcycle during the winter?" Jellie was stirring gravy, looking over her shoulder at him.

"In my living room."

Jellie laughed. Eleanor Markham smiled and asked, "Why on earth do you keep it there?"

"Because it's too big for the john."

Both of them were laughing now. Michael was grinning, appreciating a nice groove as much as any jazz musician. "Besides, I can work on it there during cold weather, and if the walls start closing in on me, I sit on it and go 'vroom, vroom.' When I'm not using it, my cat likes to sleep on the seat. I live on the first floor of an old place, been living there for ten years. It's hard to find people in a college town who pay their rent on time, and I do, so the landlord puts up with me."

"Mother, of course Michael would keep his motorcycle in the living room. It all fits, and it's perfect . . . unlike this damn gravy that won't thicken up."

He could see they were busy, so he excused himself and ambled back to the living room, trying to adopt a veneer of sociability, which was just about impossible for Michael Tillman to carry off. The furnishings were typical and a little better than that—good postmodern prints, agreeable pottery pieces, an abstract bronze sculpture about eighteen inches high, and a black-and-white print of Edward Weston's famous portrait of a cabbage, which cost somebody real bucks. A few new chairs, a few old ones. A Mozart quintet came from a system in the den.

He looked back once at Jellie, who was still fretting over the gravy, and tried to articulate in his mind what he'd seen on her face. A blend, maybe, of contentment and weariness, of being happy where she was and yet wishing she was somewhere else. The sense that she was running a long race she believed she was supposed to run but would rather not have been running at all.

"Come over here, Michael." Pat Sanchez reached out for his hand. He'd always liked Pat. She'd fought her way out of the Los Angeles barrios, got her doctorate at Texas, and joined the faculty about ten years before. They'd done a couple of papers together and ended up naked and laughing and drinking margaritas on her bed when they'd finished the first one late on a Friday night.

After that they'd gone out a few times, then let go of it by mutual, but unspoken, consent. The mathematics of transportation networks evidently were not enough on which to sustain a loving relationship.

She introduced him to her friend, who had recently become vice-president of student services, but the friend already knew Michael from their days on the Student Conduct Committee. He had a therapeutic way about him, characteristic of those who devote their lives to dealing with the pleasures of dormitory havoc and other garbage the university continued to tolerate. He shook Michael's hand and said, "I remember you. You're the one who was in favor of expelling anybody who so much as thought about writing on the walls. What was it you said? . . . I used to quote you as an example of the kind of approach that just doesn't work with today's students."

Michael sighed inside himself, then thought about sticking the sweet fellow's head up his ass or in the fireplace, depending on whether he decided the coagulated brain ought to be quick-frozen or hard-boiled, but let it go and leaned toward him, whispering, "I remember almost exactly what I said. It went something like this: 'We're running a university, not a success center or an asylum for those with pounding glands. Cheats are cheats, destructive teenage drunks are just that, and we ought to throw the injurious little bastards all the way back to their mother's tit and let 'em suck on it or boot their asses right down the street to the cops and press charges.' That's what I said. I also said I couldn't stand all the transactional bullshit you people seem to believe in. That was after someone from counseling services called me a fascist."

Sweet Fellow, the veep, turned red while Pat lay back against the sofa cushions, trying to suppress her laughter and failing, and that cooled him down. Michael was glad she was there. He'd shot his mouth off at a little member of the central administration who didn't know what it was like in the gullies of the world, and it could have ruined Thanksgiving at the Bradens, which was the last thing he wanted to happen.

"Oh, Michael, will you never be tamed?" Pat was still laughing, holding her stomach.

At that moment Jimmy Braden came out of the kitchen, daintily ringing a small silver bell. "Ladies and gentlemen, dinner is served."

The crowd straggled off toward the dining room. Michael brought up the rear, wondering what the seating arrangements were and whether they'd be such that he could look at Jellie now and then, preferably often. After all, that's what he'd come for, not to deal with smart-ass little brats from the administration building.

Place cards were on the table, but he decided to let everyone else find their seats and then sort through the residual. The seat assignments gave the appearance of having come out of a random-number generator. But he knew Jellie too well to doubt there was an overall plan designed to get certain people away from their wives and dates and husbands and next to certain other people. Sort of a turkey-centered mixer. Michael watched people seat themselves, the chairs dwindling down to a precious few. Jellie caught his eye and pointed to the second place down from the head of the table, near the kitchen. He walked over and looked at the name card, which had *Possible Dean* printed on it in Jellie's handwriting. The card at the place next to his read *Jellie*.

James Lee Braden III carved, Jellie's mother poured, Jellie ran back and forth to the kitchen, and everyone else talked nonsense. Michael sat there watching Jellie move, feeling, for the first time, something beyond hibiscus and a waterfall in the Seychelles, thinking that maybe the old Darwinian shuffle had some steps to it he hadn't known about before. The physical attraction he felt for her was somehow being melded with deeper and quieter feelings of a higher order, a turn of events he hadn't counted on. And he became a little sad then in a way he couldn't grasp. Sad for her, for him, for Jimmy, and for where this might all lead or probably wouldn't. The voice of the Absolute sounded less certain, the mantra was beginning to waver. Some things were better left alone, he thought. He, and perhaps Jellie, if he was reading her correctly, were mucking around in a dangerous place where they had no business going, a place that was not as harmless as it first appeared. And, for a moment, he wanted to run, to ride the Shadow somewhere, anywhere. Anywhere that had a warm sun and simple ways.

The great turkey dance went on for nearly two hours. Wine and more wine, food and more food. Eleanor Markham told a funny story about Jellie's growing years, and everybody laughed, especially Jellie.

The female sociologist on his right rattled on about her life and times, touching his arm occasionally when she made what she considered a significant point. That left him feeling cramped and a little aggravated, since he was bound by the circumstances to be polite and couldn't look at Jellie out of the corner of his eye while he was talking with this expert on women's contributions to early American frontier life.

Somebody mentioned the afternoon football game between Dallas and Seattle. The sports fanatic from operations research moved into the opening and began citing yardage gained by various running backs, along with other related junk serving only to clutter up people's minds and keep them from thinking about anything that really matters. Jellie's mother was filling her in on what her old high school friends were doing now.

Jimmy was carving—he never ceased carving,

it was his life-way. Jellie's father was talking to the vice-president of student services about fishing for brook trout in Connecticut. And the sociologist on Michael's right was asking him if he ever attended the lecture-concert series, saying she always seemed to go alone and didn't like going alone. He said he didn't go because, as far as he could tell, it was always the same person on the bill—a "scintillating new" (usually pubescent) Korean violinist who flawlessly executed memorized scores. The sociologist was all right, though, lonely in the way most of us were or are, and Michael continued to feign interest in lectures, concerts, and frontier women, once or twice feeling Jellie's hip against his shoulder when she got up to make a food run to the kitchen.

The operations researcher was still talking about the game coming on in less than forty-five minutes and said he hoped nobody would mind if he watched it. Several others said (not directly, of course) they also wanted to see young black men from the coasts have at one another on the plains of Texas, so that was settled. The sociologist straightened her glasses and said quietly to Michael, "All this attention given to athletics is just another capitalist plot to keep the masses occupied, don't you think?"

He really didn't want to think about it. He didn't want to think about anything except the next touch of Jellie's hip against his shoulder. But he nodded and said, "You're probably right. On the other hand, it beats having the proletariat out there stealing hubcaps or sniffing bicycle seats." She turned her attention to the accountant's wife a moment later.

During a pause while the jock expert was wetting his throat and summoning up more good *Sports Illustrated* wisdom to tell everyone, Jim Braden said, "Michael, you used to be an athlete, didn't you? That's what somebody told me."

Jellie followed up. "Michael, is that true? You've been holding out on us."

Trapped. He hoped the subject would pass, but it didn't. Jellie's father pushed it along. "What did you play, Michael?" The operations researcher, who wouldn't know how to pull on a jockstrap if it was required of him, had a hunk of turkey halfway into his mouth and was obviously in a state of complete surprise, since Michael seldom mentioned his athletic history.

Everyone was looking at him, particularly the sociologist, as if she'd suddenly discovered the real reason why he didn't attend the lecture-concert series and why he seemed a little barbarous overall. There was nowhere to go. He would have continued to look for a way out, but Jellie said, "Tell us about it, Michael." She seemed genuinely interested, and he couldn't refuse Jellie.

He took a drink of wine and began. "The short version is this: I grew up in a small town in South Dakota—"

The accountant's wife interrupted him. "Where was that?"

"Custer . . . just outside of Rapid City in the Black Hills."

"It's pretty out there, isn't it?" With a mind like chaff in a high wind, she was now into travel-ogues.

The sociologist came out of her corner with a hard leftist jab: "It's where we stole the Native Americans' land in the nineteenth century."

"Yes, it's very pretty," Michael said, looking at the accountant's wife. "Though unfortunately my parents' small house sat on land stolen from the Lakota Sioux." He waited a moment for additional questions about the Black Hills. There were none.

"By the time I got to eighth grade I was totally bored with school and small-town life in general. So I started shooting baskets in the city park. Then my father helped me put up a basket in the back-yard of our house. He took a real interest in the whole affair and installed a yard light so I could practice in the evenings. I seemed to have a knack for the jumpshot and got pretty good at it. My high school coach had graduated from Wichita State and sent them films of two or three of my better games. They offered me a scholarship, which was about the only way I was going to get to college. I played there for three and a half years until I banged up my knee pretty bad. That's it." He took another drink of wine and waited for the assemblage to move on to matters of greater importance, but they wouldn't let it go.

"What position did you play, Michael?"

"Guard."

"What are you, about six three?"

"Six two, in my socks."

"Were you an All–American or anything?"

"I made the All–Missouri Valley Conference Team my junior year."

Jellie put her hand on his and squeezed it. "Michael, you were a star, then!"

He couldn't tell if she was being genuine or mildly sarcastic. He hoped it was the latter and decided it was, with just a little bit of the former mixed in. "I never thought of it that way. I was just earning room and board, books and tuition."

"I'll bet your parents were very proud of you. Ever think about turning pro?" The operations researcher had found a real live veteran of wars that mean nothing, right at the Thanksgiving table.

"My dad pasted pictures of me from the *Wichita Eagle* all over Tillman's Texaco. My mother was more concerned about my grades. She always thought athletics was a pretty dumb way for people to spend their time."

The operations researcher had batted only one for two and was troubled by that. He plainly wondered how any mother could not love her son enough to applaud his exploits in short pants under the lights of several hundred gymnasiums during his formative years and felt sorry for Michael, believing he'd been deprived of maternal affection.

"As for becoming a professional, I had no interest, plus my first step wasn't quick enough for the big leagues. The phone from the pros never rang, and I wouldn't have answered it if it had."

"Don't you miss playing, Michael?" Jellie's mother was looking at him.

"No, I don't, Mrs. Markham. I truly don't. In fact, I couldn't wait for it to be over so I could get on with my life. Somewhere around my sophomore year in college I discovered I didn't like playing basketball and never really had. I just liked fooling around with the art and physics of the long-range jumpshot. It was a boy's tool for a boy's game, and I haven't touched a basketball in twenty years."

Jellie said, "That's an interesting point of view . . . the art and physics of the long-range jumpshot is all that really mattered. Michael, you ought to do an article on that sometime."

If Jellie had put her hand back on his at that moment, he'd have written an essay about now-fading jumpshots on the linen tablecloth with a turkey bone. But she didn't and changed the conversation by listing the selection of desserts available. Michael went for sour cream raisin pie. Jellie had made it from her grandmother's recipe, and it was a knockout.

Over coffee and brandy, someone asked Jellie

about her name and where it came from. Her parents laughed, and Jellie pointed at both of them. It fell to her mother to tell the story.

"When Jellie was about seven years old, she went through a plump stage. Her father started calling her his 'little bowl of Jelly.' The neighborhood children picked it up and teased her by calling her Jelly-Belly and Jellyroll and Jellybean and just about everything else you could imagine. She used to come in from playing with tears streaming down her face. As soon as that began happening, Leonard quit calling her Jelly and felt bad he'd ever started the whole business. But the kids wouldn't drop it."

Jellie came on line. "Mom bailed me out, though. She convinced me that my nickname was spelled with an *i-e* on the end instead of a *y* and that it was really a French name pronounced with a soft *J*—JahLAY—even though we kept the American pronunciation. I liked that idea and began to take pride in my new name. It stuck with me, and I've used it ever since."

"Then what's your real name?"

For God's sake, Michael thought, looking at the accountant who had been dumb enough to ask the question. Leave it alone. If she wanted you to know, she'd already have mentioned it.

"I never tell." Jellie laughed. "Jimmy, everyone needs more brandy. I'll get some more coffee." That gave the fans time to pull on their jockstraps, backward, of course, and get the television cooking: "Third-and-six on the Dallas five. Heeerrre's the pitch-out. . . ."

The sociologist had papers to grade, Pat Sanchez and her date decided on a walk. Jellie and her mother were cleaning up in the kitchen. Michael went outside for a smoke, and when he returned the rest of them, except Jellie and her parents, were watching the game. Michael sat at the dining room table with Leonard Markham and asked about fishing for brook trout, saying he used to do a little trout fishing in the Black Hills. Mr. Markham knew how to talk about what interested him, giving Michael the right amount of information without getting boring. He'd have made a good teacher instead of the paper box manufacturer he was, Michael thought. He liked Leonard Markham.

Later, Jellie and her mother joined them at the table, Jellie sitting across from Michael. This is what he'd come for, the chance simply to look at Jellie Markham Braden on a cold autumn day in 1980. He was careful, though, because once or twice her mother caught him staring at Jellie in a way not related to the conversation. And mothers know about the secret thoughts of men, particularly when those thoughts concern the daughters of the mothers.

Struggling for something to talk about, Michael brought up India and watched Eleanor Markham's face go dark—just a little, but still there—

when he mentioned it. Jellie quickly turned the conversation in a different direction. That was the second time he'd picked up something strange about her India days. Something that made her reluctant to go into it other than acknowledging she'd been to India and stayed for three years.

Michael could only tolerate being in Jellie's general vicinity for relatively short periods of time back then. His feelings toward her were just too overpowering, escalating in intensity minute by minute, and he was half-afraid he'd blurt out something obvious and stupid, some unseemly remark tipping off her husband or somebody else, including Jellie, about the way he felt. He wanted to be able to see her, be around her as often as he could, without feeling any more surreptitious than he already did. So about six o'clock he excused himself under the pretense of going home to feed his animals.

Jellie wrapped her arms around herself and shivered on the front steps when she said good-bye to him. "Thank you for coming, Michael. I know these affairs aren't your style, but I wanted my parents to meet you. You're a different sort than they normally come into contact with. . . . I didn't say that quite right. I didn't mean to imply you're a curiosity piece, just that you're different. My dad said to me a few minutes ago, 'I like that Michael Tillman; he's got some fiber to him.' I knew he'd like you."

Michael understood what she meant. "I like him, too, Jellie. Thank you for inviting me, I had a nice time." He couldn't help looking hard at her once more before leaving. He just couldn't help it, wanting to put his arms around her and say, "Don't go back in the house. Come home with me, I'll kiss your mouth and your breasts and what surely is your soft, round belly and tear you to pieces and put you back together again. Afterwards we'll go down the road, far away, doesn't matter where."

Jellie set her gray eyes on Michael's for maybe five seconds, her face almost serious. A different look than she'd ever given him before, as if she were half seeing into his thoughts. She said nothing, just looked at him, then dropped her eyes and smiled a little before opening the door and going back inside.

A year later he was west of Madurai and pushing hard into southwest India looking for her. The driver spoke only a few words of English, so it was a quiet ride except for the ceaseless roar of wind through the open windows. Fifty miles out the driver stopped, went over to a roadside shrine, and left some coins. "Bad spirits," he said, getting in. "Evil." He shifted gears, looking back at the shrine.

In Virudunagar the driver had breakfast and the car had a flat tire. Apparently the donation at the shrine had been insufficient. The spare was shot, so it took a major expedition through the streets until a garage was located. After the obligatory haggling over price, the tire was hauled to the shop and cold-patched. That'll be good for another sixty miles, Michael thought. Their stop in Virudunagar had taken nearly two hours.

Michael leaned back on the red vinyl car seat and looked at villages and farm country going by. Near Rajapalaiyam the driver slowed and halted on a bridge over a wide, shallow river. A woman ahead of them was driving a flock of geese across the bridge. On the sandbars below, other women, their skirts hiked up, were doing laundry, waving clothing over their heads and slapping it hard against rocks.

The geese were almost across, moving slowly. Too slowly for the driver. He honked. The woman pushing the geese along turned, giving them a nasty look. Only rich folks rode in cars, and she was having none of it. The beat of life in village India is in adagio time. Only rich folks from somewhere else are in a hurry.

A woman came toward them across the bridge. She wore a torn red sari of the cheapest cloth, toe rings on her brown feet, and carried a load of sticks on her head. One arm was raised to balance the load, the other swung beside her, bracelets jingling. She was stunning. Beautiful by any standards anywhere. The way Bardot looked in her salad days. She glanced through the car window at Michael, and he smiled, couldn't help smiling. He thought she might smile back. She looked as if she might for a moment, but then turned her head and stared straight down the road as she moved past the car.

He leaned forward and saw the Western Ghats rising up far ahead. Somewhere in those mountains was Jellie, near a place called Thekkady, or at least she was supposed to be there. And what she was doing there he didn't know and still wasn't sure he wanted to find out.

An hour more and they were into the foothills, climbing slowly and carefully around hairpin curves, waiting for huge, roaring Indian tour buses demanding the road and giving no quarter. Cooler now. Three thousand feet, maybe, pine trees right outside the car windows. Michael didn't know Jellie had walked this same road in terror fifteen years earlier. She had called herself by another name then.

# *Five*

ollowing her first Thanksgiving in Cedar Bend, Jellie didn't stop at Michael's office for nearly two weeks. Her pattern had been to come by for coffee and a smoke at least once a week, and he decided he'd really screwed it up, that Jellie and maybe other people were beginning to see how he felt and she'd decided to quash anything and everything of that sort right at the front end.

When Jimmy Braden called and asked if they could talk for a few minutes, he was sure Jellie had said something to him. He sat there waiting for the blows, waiting for Jimmy to say Jellie was uncomfortable with the way he looked at her and that she wouldn't be stopping by anymore, let alone sending invitations to subsequent Thanksgiving dinners.

But Jimmy didn't want that. In some ways the news was worse. He was going to teach in London for the spring semester, and Jellie was going with him. He'd applied for a visiting professorship the previous year and cut a deal with Arthur on his way in, allowing him to do the London job if it came through. His application had been lost in the British bureaucracy. But finally it had worked out at the last minute. Now Jimmy was looking for faculty members who would shift their teaching loads around to cover his absence.

Michael had a tight gut just thinking about Jellie being out of his sight for that long, thinking about her black hair blowing in winds coming off the North Sea, about her laughing and going to the theater and never thinking of him, though there was no particular reason she should. Selfish stuff, he knew that, but he recovered and said he'd pick up Jimmy's intro-level course in econometrics or find a graduate student who could do it. Jimmy promised to reciprocate some time, and Michael had no doubt he would.

"Thanks a lot, Michael. That fixes everything up. We're leaving in ten days, right after the semester is over, be back in August. We're going to travel during the summer."

Jellie in Scotland, Jellie along the hedgerows,

Jellie in Paris . . . Jellie where he couldn't see her. An hour later she rapped on Michael's door. "Hi, motorcycle man. How's the war?"

"The war is being won, Jellie. I'm whipping the students up the hills of December, and victory is mine, or will be in less than two weeks." She stood in the doorway instead of coming in and flopping down on a chair the way she usually did.

"Sorry I haven't been by to say hello. I've been getting ready for my final exams, and Jim said he told you about the London trip. God, what a mess, finding a house sitter on short notice, getting bills paid and things set up at the bank. I've been running for days with no letup. What are you going to do over the holidays? Any big plans?"

"No, not much at all. It's too damn cold to crank up the bike and ride it someplace. I'll probably try to finish the paper I'm doing on comparing complex structures so I can present it at the fall meetings. Get my trimonthly haircut, spend a few days with my mother out in Custer over Christmas. Other than that, watch the snow fall, I guess, and listen to the Miles Davis tapes I ordered while I spruce up my lectures for the class I'll be covering for Jim. My notes in that area are a little yellowed. It'll go by pretty fast, it always does." He wanted to say he'd be thinking about her every other minute, but he didn't.

"Sounds pretty low key. No special Christmas wishes?"

He looked at the ceiling for a moment, struggling, trying to pull himself up and out of a self-indulgent funk. Michael had wishes all right, but nothing he could talk about. He recovered and leaned back in his chair, fingers locked behind his head, forcing a little grin. "Well, sometime I'd like a leather belt with *Orville* tooled on the back. Used to be a guy in Custer had one, and I thought it was pretty neat when I was a kid."

Jellie grinned back. "Only you, Michael, of all the people I know, would say something like that. God, it's almost surreal."

"Well, life is surreal, Jellie. Except for Orville. He didn't dwell on those things, just drove his grain truck and whistled a lot."

"I think Orville had it all worked out. I'd like to hear more about him, but I've got to run. I'll try to stop in before we leave. Take care, Michael, and say hello to Orville if you see him. Ask if he'll write a self-help book for the rest of the world."

He watched her jeans as she left and walked down the hall, then got to his feet and went to the door so he could watch her a little while longer. She looked back once, as if she knew he'd be standing there and fluttered her hand in a final wave as she turned the corner, heading for the office of solid, steady James Braden.

Michael ran into her the following week in a small shopping area near the campus. They had coffee at Beano's, sitting in a back booth in midafternoon. Her exams were over and preparations for London were well along, so she was a little calmer and seemed in no hurry this time. She was wearing one of her standard winter outfits: jeans, long-sleeved undershirt beneath a flannel shirt, down vest.

He leaned against the wall, one foot on the seat of the booth, and glanced at all the old posters of campus events plastered on the walls. The undergraduates—those who were finished with exams and some who weren't—were drinking beer. Two men, gay activists from the philosophy department, were playing chess at a table next to them.

Jellie asked if he had any suggestions for London restaurants. He told her, except for a day here and there on his way through, his experience with London was mostly limited to making connections at Heathrow and he didn't know the city well. Michael's tastes ran to societies less well organized than those in the West, and most of his traveling had been in southeast Asia. He didn't mention the women in Bangkok with their long hair and compliant ways. He glanced at his watch and said he had to give his last final examination in twenty-two minutes, starting to make departure motions.

"Michael, I'll miss our talks over coffee, and I'll miss *you*, truly I will."

He looked at her for a long while. For the first

time he really didn't care what she or anyone else thought about him looking at her in a certain way.

She took a deep breath and started to say something, then paused for a moment before continuing, as if she were trying to decide whether or not to speak at all. "I don't want to get deeply into this now, but . . ." She hesitated.

His hands were shaking for reasons he wasn't sure of, and he held them under the table where she couldn't see them. He could feel a small tic in a cheek muscle, just below his left eye. In the spaces of a man's life there are moments when things shift into some other gear. He sensed that was happening now.

"What are you talking about, Jellie? What don't you want to get into?"

"What I'm trying to say . . . is that . . . that I'm not going to just miss you. I'm going to *miss* you. I know more than you may think I know about how you feel about some things . . . how I feel . . . Oh, good God, I'm making a muddle of this. . . ."

He got his hands quieted down and reached for one of hers. She put it out to meet him halfway. He laid his other hand on the little bundle forming on the table. "C'mon, Jellie, say what you've got to say. I want to hear it, whatever it is."

"Michael, it all sounds a little presumptuous, what I'm trying to get across. If I'm wrong, please forget I ever said it. Promise?"

"I promise."

She added her other hand to the stack on the table and stared at them, cleared her throat. "Behind all the laughter and light talk we share with each other, there's something else going on, isn't there?"

He stayed quiet, looked at her. She had the stage, and he wasn't about to climb up on it right at the moment. He wanted her to finish what she had to say, to let it run wherever it was going. Good or bad, it was time for that. A waitress going into the kitchen dropped a stack of dishes, and every head in Beano's, except two, turned to see the disaster. He could see the second hand on his watch going by. Fifteen minutes until his examination on the other side of campus.

"Damnit . . . isn't there? There's something else going on between us, isn't there?" She squeezed his hands in both of hers and rapped them lightly on the table.

He nodded.

"It's been there since we first met at the dean's reception in late August, hasn't it?"

He nodded again and talked straight: "You walked through the door and something started to hum inside me. The hum has now escalated into a symphonic scream I can't turn off."

"Oh, Michael . . . Michael." She looked away from him, at the wall, then at the ceiling. Twelve minutes to exam time. He didn't move. The last

71

fly of a summer past, surviving on the largesse of Beano's, landed on his coffee cup and walked an endless path around the rim.

"My mother saw it at Thanksgiving, something about the way you were looking at me, and I guess the way I looked back. No, that's not being honest enough—I was looking back at you the way you were looking at me. When we were doing dishes in the kitchen, she mentioned it to me and said, 'Be careful, Jellie, be *very* careful.'"

Two forty-seven. Beano's was clearing out as about half the crowd hustled off to the three o'clock exams. "Michael, maybe this will all settle down while I'm gone. It just has to, doesn't it?"

He said nothing, shrugging his shoulders, smiling at her.

She stood, pulling on her parka and mumbling, "I feel like a schoolgirl." She looked down at him. "I'm glad I said what I said, Michael. And I'm glad you said what you said and for the way you've handled it the past few months. You like to think you're a little rough around the edges, but you're actually pretty smooth. You're a damn fine man, Michael Tillman, attractive and kind and everything else—isn't there a woman out there somewhere for you? I mean someone other than . . ." She left off the *me*—couldn't bring herself to say it, though he wished she had said it—and let her voice circle down to nothing.

"I understand what you mean. Who knows?

All I know now is how I feel about you." He picked up his coat and started sliding out of the booth, disoriented, thinking the distance to next August could only be measured in light-years.

She bent over and kissed him on the cheek. "Ride easy. I'll send you a card." And she was gone then, working her way through the tables and out the front door of Beano's.

He left two bucks on the table and began an easy run through the campus, feet on the sidewalk, mind and heart somewhere else. Across the creek, along the duck pond, and only one minute late into a room where he would ask of students what they knew.

## Six

The Bradens lifted off for England on December 20, the day Michael finished grading final exams. Depression over Jellie's leaving was momentarily lightened by several strong performances in both the decision-making and quantitative methods courses. He expected good work from the graduate students, but the undergraduates overcame their senior blues and rose to the task, surprising and pleasing him.

The old Shadow crouched in the living room, waiting for the turn of wrenches and better weather. Michael stacked exam papers on its seat and cranked up the computer, which shared the desk with greasy tools and unwashed coffee cups.

A few taps on the keys and the GradeCalc program came up. In went the scores, GradeCalc churned away for thirty seconds, and out came final distributions, normal curves, standard deviations, and all that other good stuff, most of which he ignored in his grading.

Two hours later, the final grade sheets with one whole cover page of instructions that would make a computer blink—instructions he didn't read and hadn't read for all fifteen years of teaching and apparently didn't need to read since nobody ever complained—were filled in and signed. He had twenty minutes to drop off the grades before the registrar shut down at four-thirty. Coat on, over to the campus, turn in the grades.

Done. Free, for a month. Fifteen years of doing this, another twenty to go unless the dean could prove professional incompetence, which he couldn't, or charged Michael with moral turpitude, which he wouldn't, because the entire university except for the accounting department would be out on its ear if those standards were enforced. Stay away from the coeds in your classes—that was the main rule for survival, put down with no punches pulled by the former dean, an old guy who had hired Michael fresh out of graduate school. Way before sexual harassment started flashing in the front of everyone's mind, the old dean had a famous lecture he gave to young faculty members, the males, that is. The essence of it went something like this:

Gentlemen, I know you're all adults, but let me remind you about a few matters. A lot of these young women are traditional midwestern girls, and they expect to take you home to meet Mother and Father on the weekend following bedroom activity, with wedding announcements to be mailed soon after. Forget about the air of sophistication they seem to exude. The coeds are big trouble, I mean *big* trouble. The undergraduate males are a bunch of donkeys, mostly, and you're going to look sleek and worldly to the coeds, and they're going to look pretty good to you. Some of them will sit in the front row in short skirts with paradise twinkling at you. You'll have plenty of opportunities for good times between the sheets—it's a goddamn cafeteria out there—but forget it, at least until they're no longer in any of your classes, and I would strongly recommend you stay away from them altogether. I have problems enough without sobbing young women sitting in my office and claiming you discriminated against them in your grading because of some kind of confusion involving preconjugal folderol. In other words, cause me that kind of grief and I'll kick your butts down the academic mountain and see you never work in this business again.

It was a lecture on how to avoid trouble, not develop sensitivity toward females. Michael was sure the latter issue never crossed the old dean's mind, given the faculty was 99 percent male.

Having said that much, the dean told them the famous story that had been part of the university saga for twenty-five years. Seems one of the Russian teachers was in his office when a coed came in to see him. He motioned for her to sit down and said he'd be with her in a moment, all the while intently finishing some piece of work he had on his desk. When he looked up, she was standing there in the buff with the office door shut. The issues were a little complicated, but the nub of it was this: Give me a passing grade or I'll scream.

You want cool under pressure? You want big *cojónes*? The professor of Russian had them both, in spades. He could have been a neurosurgeon or a space commando. He got up, threw open the door, and walked forthwith into the hall, where he pointed in at the young woman and shouted in heavily accented English, "Get out of my office. Now!" Passersby were treated to a reasonably decent glimpse of a reasonably good, young female body (that's part of the saga, anyway, though Michael noticed that as the story was carried forward and repeated, her physical attributes approached Amazonian proportions, her body filling out and improving with age, as it were).

He'd always wondered just what lesson should

be drawn from the tale, since it never had been clear whether or not the young woman and the Russian had anything going on the side. But, having told it, the dean shooed the junior faculty out of his office and left them with the following two guidelines for not letting their moral turpitude drift: Keep your pants zipped and your office door open.

About two-thirds of those receiving the lecture followed the dean's advice. The other one-third cut a swath like a combine through the waving fields of coed grain and apparently suffered little for it, partly because those peering out from glass houses have no interest in chucking accusatory rocks at others. Michael left the coeds alone, simply because he didn't find them attractive. Too young, too naive, and what the hell do you say to them in the morning? "Who do you have for Western civ?" C'mon.

So the grades were in, and Michael was unfettered until January 17, when he'd do it all over again. Down the halls of the administration building he went, admiring the waxed oak floors, inhaling the vapors of incompetent power radiating from the walls and oozing from under darkened doors like smoke from a burning village where truth and beauty had once been found. The temporary lightness he'd felt after finishing a good set of exams was dissipating as he thought about Jellie Braden. He was getting angry at her for going to

England, for just bloody taking off and leaving him there to mourn her absence.

Irrational? Of course it was irrational. He had no right to anything other than what he already had when it came to her, which was nothing. She's sitting in Kennedy now, he thought, waiting for TWA to take her lovely body and equally lovely soul onto nine months of new experiences and different people. Maybe she was right, maybe her absence would do it, get him cooled off and refocused on something other than her.

Then he started to waffle: "Come back, come back, Jellie Braden. I need to look at you one more time, just one. I want to continue the conversation we started. I want to hear more of how you feel about me and for us to get the air cleared." But the mail doesn't come on Sundays, and James Lee Braden III had taken his wife on to foreign pleasures, leaving Michael Tillman foundering in his wake.

As he passed by the provost's office, a janitor had the door propped open while emptying wastebaskets. Michael glanced inside. Clarice Berenson, the provost's secretary, stared at a computer screen. The office was empty except for her.

They went back a ways, Clarice and Michael. She'd come home to Cedar Bend from New York when her gynecologist husband dumped her for a psychiatric nurse. After the bad scene with her former husband she had a negative attitude toward men overall. But she and Michael got together occasionally, and they flew pretty close to the sun when they were rolling.

Clarice was into serious opera and worked part-time on an M.A. in Spanish, and that along with her job kept her busy. But now and then she liked to shake it real hard. That's where Michael came in, and their schedules seemed to work in perfect sync when it came to getting crazy.

Clarice looked up, grinning. "Well, it's the campus rebel with no apparent cause. How you doin', Michael?"

"Not bad. Just turned in my grades and resting on my oars. How about you, Clarice?"

"Since the provost–sir flew off to Los Angeles about two hours ago, things have picked up quite a bit. I'm just shutting down. Want to have a beer?"

"Better than that, how about beer and dinner?"

"Now you're talking, Michael. We could even take it up another level and go jump around at Beano's tonight. Bobby's Blues Band is playing there, starting at nine. It'll be end-of-the-semester nuts, but that suits me just fine."

"You're on. But first I need to clean up a bit. Say, about seven? Go down to Rossetti's for pasta, then over to Beano's for the fun?"

"Perfect. I'll pick you up, I think it's my turn to drive."

"Okay, see you in a little while."

Michael started drinking beer when he got home. Sat on the Shadow with a Beck's dark in his hand and John Coltrane on the tape deck. Malachi stood up and put his paws on Michael's leg. He rubbed Malachi's ears while the music played, thinking about Jellie Braden flying through the darkness away from him. But those kinds of thoughts weren't fair to Clarice, he decided, and two more beers got him away from his loneliness and into the evening . . . kind of.

Clarice was not Jellie Braden when it came to looks. On the other hand, that was also a little unfair, since to Michael's way of thinking nobody compared with Jellie along that dimension. But Clarice had that same indefinable quality we lump under "class," and she was more than just presentable. And, just as important, she was not on her way to London.

Clarice knocked on his door at ten to seven while he was pulling on a white cotton turtleneck that worked pretty well with faded jeans. She came in and got a beer from the fridge. He padded around barefoot, looking for a clean pair of boot socks. When he carried his boots out to the living room, Clarice was perched on the Shadow, wearing a maize-colored sweater and forest green corduroys tapering down just above her dainty tassel loafers.

"Lookin' good, Clarice, real good." He said it and he meant it, with three bottles of beer propelling the warmth of the compliment even further than he might have taken it otherwise.

"Thank you, Professor Tillman. How's the winter repair job on the bike coming along? I see you have the chain off and hanging over the back of a chair."

"Aw, the old guy is in need of constant attention these days. Parts are getting just about impossible to find, but the mail-order catalogs keep him going. If I have to, I'll start running off my own parts at a machine shop somewhere. He and I are together for life."

"Well, I'm glad somebody is." The divorce still hurt, Clarice never tried to pretend otherwise around him. "Any big trips planned for the summer?" She tilted back her dark blond head, took a drink of beer, and gave him a lickerish grin. They both knew what was coming down before the night was over.

"Thought I might ride up along Lake Superior. I haven't been there for a while. It's kind of pretty and not too crowded if you stay away from the big holidays. Wanna go with me?" He wasn't sure why he made the offer. He usually preferred traveling alone, but he was feeling deserted and left behind, and Clarice was looking especially good that night. He liked Clarice a lot.

She knew his travel habits and looked surprised, a little quizzical smile on her face. "Maybe . . . when are you going?"

Robert James Waller

"I can go just about anytime, since I don't teach summer school anymore. If you're interested, we can work it out to your schedule. Ready to rumble?"

The spaghetti was good. They took their time over dinner, drinking a bottle of wine and talking before plunging into the maelstrom that was Beano's around nine-thirty. Bobby had the Blues Band cooking: "Put on your high-heeled sneakers, Mama, and your wiglet on your head/Put on your high-heeled . . ." Drummer, lead guitar, bass, Bobby singing and playing harmonica. And, of course, Molly Never (that's what she claims her parents named her) absolutely screaming on electric violin, legs apart, black heels and black stockings, black miniskirt, purple blouse. She looked like a funky Peter Pan who had been around the darker side of life. The band hit 115 decibels and headed up from there.

Bobby'd had this same band for twelve years, and they operated with a hard, disciplined precision. He shouted over the microphone, "Here's a song made famous by three black girls from Memphis, now to be sung by three white boys from small towns in the Midwest. That's why you pay Beano's exorbitant cover charge, to hear that kind of shit, right?" The crowd roared.

Clarice and Michael stood off to the side, waiting for a table to open up, which could take hours. She was screaming at him, him at her, as they tried

84

to talk over the searing lead guitar of one Doppler Donovan, who wore a cowboy hat on his head and military-issue, jungle-style combat boots on his feet. Bobby had gone into a honky version of a Chuck Berry skip as he slid into his harp solo, amplifier cord looking as if it were coming out of his mouth where he held a small microphone against the harmonica.

Michael looked over at the booth where he and Jellie had sat a week ago. It was occupied now by two couples engaged in a pairwise beer-chugging contest. Her words floated through the smoke and the noise of Beano's: "There's something else going on between us, isn't there, Michael?"

Clarice slipped her arm around his waist and hugged him, bouncing up and down to the beat. She wanted to dance, and she'd eventually get him out there. But Michael wasn't comfortable on dance floors, never had been, so he was waiting for the second round of beer drinking to override the spaghetti and give him courage.

A student staggered up, towing a platinum blonde wearing greased-on jeans and a black leather jacket. Ghastly beer breath washed Michael's cheeks as the student shouted over the music, "Great class, Dr. Tillman, absolutely great. How'd I do?"

Michael didn't post grades, particularly in Beano's. But what the hell, beer breath had done all right, and it was party time. He held up one of

Beano's custom napkins and pointed to the *B* on it, grinning.

The student threw both arms over his head in joy and spun back onto the dance floor, where he went into a ponylike boogaloo, pawing the air. Five minutes later he sent the waitress over with two draws for Michael and Clarice. It was semester's end, and they were all burying the dead and praising the living, so the atmosphere was celebrative, sort of like a New Orleans funeral at ten thousand watts. Doppler Donovan led the band into something called the "Drake Neighborhood Slide," and Clarice pulled Michael out on the dance floor.

The evening closed as he knew it would—warm, libidinous, and thoroughly satisfying. He and Clarice were good in bed together, and before it was over she was kneeling on the bed, palms and breasts and face pasted against the wall, with him behind her licking the perspiration off her shoulders and doing several other things that pleased her greatly, as she constantly and fervently emphasized while all of this was under way: "Yes, Michael . . . god*damnit*, yes, yes, *yes!*"

# Seven

ellie from a distance. The ambiguity of those months she was in England was hard on him. His running shoes slushed along the streets of Cedar Bend, and ice clung to his hair where it stuck out beneath his blue stocking cap. The faculty and students were suspended in a climatic purgatory somewhere between the lights of Christmas and the warming of the earth in April. Gray muck draped like a shroud over Bingley Hall, ceiling lights bright and cold. Wind from the Canadian prairies smacked the building's north side and howled through the corridors when an outside door was opened. Unlike wine, or the coed of legend who removed her duds in a Russian professor's office, a midwestern winter does not improve with age.

Thinking almost constantly about Jellie, Michael pushed the students hard and even held an extra three-hour class on a Sunday afternoon, promising them time off for good behavior later in the semester. He knew he'd begin to lose them and himself when the warm came again, so they were getting the hard stuff out of the way early. They hammered onward. By February's close he was thinking of calling for mass, campuswide psychotherapy to counter the late winter blahs. But they hung on, as ancient sailors in pounding seas clung to the mainmast and with the same faith in better times to come.

Then over the bare trees fluttered the first sign of hope in the form of colorful travel brochures pinned to hallway bulletin boards. The words and pictures promised sun and sand, tonic and tans, and, somewhat more slyly, fast times amid the palms of Florida or the south Texas coast. The classroom buzz as they waited for the bell ran to snow conditions in Colorado and who was driving which twelve people to South Padre Island in an old Dodge van.

By that time Michael had frightened the lower 20 percent of the class into filing drop slips. Those remaining were a group of battle-scarred veterans, deserving of a short rest before he bullwhacked them up the slopes of learning toward victory, and maybe graduation. The inevitable questions came: "Professor Tillman, is it all right if I miss your Thursday class before spring break? A bunch of us are going to Daytona Beach, and we want to leave Wednesday night."

He looked at the nice young woman who asked the question—it was a different one every spring, but they all ran together after a while—and said, "Why do you think I dragged you in here for an extra three hours on a Sunday afternoon? Yes, you may leave early, but get the notes for my dazzling lecture on matrix transposition from someone, because I'm not going to repeat it after you get back." He grinned at her. "Now get out of my hair and leave me alone. I have serious work to do in saving a world having no interest in being saved."

Friday came, beginning of spring break. Gusty March winds late in the month, minivans and station wagons filled with impatient spouses lined up outside the building, motors running, waiting for classes to end. The library was nearly empty, except for graduate students catching up on their work and junior professors slogging their way toward a tenure decision. By the time Michael got out of Bingley at five, the campus was quiet.

At home he leaned back in his chair and stared at a Polaroid picture of Jellie pinned to a piece of corkboard above his desk. She looked out at him, standing by a stone wall in Ireland, in her hiking clothes, hair tucked under her round tweed hat with the little bill, leather bag over her left shoulder. She'd mailed him a card saying hello and not much else in late January. The photo came a month later, accompanied by a neutral-sounding note in her small, neat handwriting:

*2/21*

*Hi, Michael.*

*We took a long weekend and came over to Ireland to scout things out for a more extended trip this summer. I hope your spring is going well. Crave our coffee talks and miss you.*

*Jellie*

He noticed she didn't underline "miss" in the way she had said it in Beano's just before she left. Maybe that was looking too hard for what didn't exist. Jellie wasn't coy, and what she said about getting cooled down might be working—for her, at least. For Michael, it wasn't, and the picture only made matters worse. He sat there and stared at it for hours, thinking and wanting. He just didn't see how he could go on living his life without Jellie Braden next to him all the time. Five months to go, and she'd be back. He couldn't wait for her to return and never wanted to see her again, all at the same time. He kept trying to conjure up ways to defend his psyche against the assaults she made on it without even trying, but he failed and sat there waiting for August.

And it came eventually, August has a way of doing that. The summer had passed in kind of a quiet haze. One of those periodic budget crises took hold of the university, the provost's office went into a frenzy, and Clarice had to delay her vacation until autumn. For some reason Michael didn't feel like going up to Lake Superior and instead took the Shadow on a long run into the pretty back roads of the Smokies, enjoying the steady hum between his legs of a machine he'd rebuilt twenty times since his father had given it to him.

He jogged through the streets of Cedar Bend at first light before the heat settled in, staying in shape, beating back the years, though it was getting harder to do. Slowly he could feel his legs going, and on rainy days the old knee injury flashed little twinges of pain as a reminder of his boyhood follies. Sometimes he went by the Bradens' two-story brick. Quite often he did that. Running, then stopping for a moment, looking at the front steps where he and Jellie had stood the previous Thanksgiving, remembering the subtle, unspoken signals they'd both sent that night without being sure the other was receiving them.

In June he wrote a piece on the role of tax incentives in attacking large-scale social problems.

*The Atlantic* surprised him by taking it, sending a check for $1,200. He knocked out a heavy-duty, academic version of the article for the *Journal of Social Issues*, and that one had wings, too, with the following spring projected as the publication date. Michael knew his department head would dismiss the first as catering to popular taste and the second as not having sufficient stature in the field of economics, though it was an okay journal in its own niche. But he didn't much care anymore what members of the administration thought about his work, so none of that bothered him.

By mid-August he was wired tight. East of him a 747 would be loading at Heathrow one of these days, Jellie settling onto her seat with a book, Jimmy Braden running around the cabin looking for a pillow and blanket. She'd once said Jimmy was a master at sleeping on airplanes but absolutely panicked and couldn't sleep at all without his pillow and blanket. So rounding up his bedroom gear was always his first chore after boarding. Michael could picture Jellie in her demure, wire-rimmed reading glasses, glancing at a book, then out the window as the big plane lifted off and brought her back toward Cedar Bend.

Classes started in less than a week, and Michael was in his office fussing around, hoping he might see Jimmy Braden, which would be his signal Jellie had returned. The phone rang.

"Hello, Michael, how are you?" Her voice was warm, soft, the diction clear and crisp as always, except when she was sitting in Beano's talking to a man about secret things she felt and thought he might also feel.

"Jellie—are you back or what?" He noticed his voice shook just a little, and he didn't like it. American males have their standards, after all.

"Yes, we got in late last night. Jimmy's still sleeping, but I'm all fouled up timewise, so I've been up since four o'clock wandering around. Did you get the picture I sent?"

"I did indeed. Thank you. You looked well and happy." He didn't say anything about hanging it on his wall. This was an intricate dance along the halls of ambiguity, and Michael was feeling his way, not wanting to open up things too rapidly.

"Yes, I am feeling well. I ran into one of my old friends from India on the tube in London. She got me back into yoga, and it does wonders for my body *and* my mind."

Oh, Jellie, Jellie, he was thinking, don't say anything about your body. Give a poor man space to breathe, space to be less wicked than you already have made him in his impure thoughts.

"Michael, any chance we might meet somewhere? I'd like to talk, but I don't want to come to your office since I suspect Jimmy will be up at the university as soon as he comes to."

"Sure, anyplace. You name it."

"How about the bar at the Ramada out by the shopping center?"

"Fine. When?"

"What time is it now?"

He looked at his watch. "Twenty to eleven."

Silence on the other end for a few seconds. "Would eleven push you too hard? I'd like to be gone when Jimmy wakes up so I don't have to think up some reason for going out."

"No, that's fine. I have the Shadow tied down outside the building. Eleven, then?"

"Yes . . . Michael?"

"I'm here." Too cool, being way too cool.

"I'm looking forward to seeing you."

"Me too, Jellie. See you in twenty minutes."

It was only a ten-minute ride out to the Ramada, so he went down to the mailboxes, collected a pile of book advertisements and a very pleasant invitation from *The Atlantic* editor to send some more pieces. That got him thinking for a moment: maybe he could hack it as a free-lance writer. Not enough in that to keep him going, probably, but he could take early retirement, annuitize his retirement fund, and maybe pick up ten or fifteen grand a year just by fiddling around with his word processor.

There was also a letter from the University of California Department of Economics inviting all of its Ph.D. alumni to a reception at the winter meetings in Las Vegas. The usual, Michael got it every year. But he never went, even though he was grateful for the degree and sent them money when they asked for it.

He pulled the Shadow out into traffic getting heavier as the students returned for the fall semester and rolled down Thirty-second Street, bumping into Route 81 about ten blocks farther on. The highway ran a winding route through one of the nicer sections of Cedar Bend, and he leaned the Shadow into the curves, noticing a slight valve tick needing attention.

Jellie was already seated when he got there. It was dark in the lounge, and he couldn't see her at first, partly because she was back in one of the corner booths off to his right.

"Michael, over here."

Jellie. After all these months, there she was and calling out to him. Black hair gathered high, big-hooped silver earrings, light yellow summer dress with sandals. Walking toward her, feeling clumsy, estranged from her. She held out her hand, Michael took it and slid in beside her. She kissed him on the cheek, then, butterfly-quick, leaned back and looked at him. He was gone again, over the hill just seeing her, hands sweating and heart valves ticking like the Black Shadow.

"You're all suntanned, Michael. You look great, just wonderful, and no preschool haircut yet."

"Nah, I've been putting it off. I hate going to barbers, something to do with loss of manhood, maybe. More likely because, when I was about four years old, the only barber in Custer threatened to cut off my ears if I didn't sit still while he was working on me."

She laughed. "Really? Did that really happen?"

"Yes, it did. My childhood was one long charge through the brambles of anxiety after that. You look wonderful, too, Jellie. I've thought about you a lot."

She looked down, then up at Michael, then down again. The bartender came around the bar and over to where they sat, lighted a small candle on the tabletop, and asked what she could get for them. Jellie ordered a club soda with lime. Michael asked for a St. Pauli Girl, which the bartender didn't have, so he settled on a Miller's.

While they waited for their drinks, Jellie asked him about his spring and summer. He told her about the two articles, and her eyes widened when he mentioned *The Atlantic*. "Hey, that's the big time. Congratulations."

The bartender came back. Jellie insisted on paying the check, so he let her.

Michael held up his beer, and she touched her glass to his. "What shall we drink to, Michael?"

"How about survival. If not that, retirement."

"Michael, you're just the same." Her chastisement was gentle. "How about we drink to a nice summer day and your success in writing."

"And to your safe return," he said.

"How's the Shadow running?"

"Good, overall. It's a perpetual battle, but good. I took it down into Tennessee this summer, but didn't stay long. The Smokies are a nightmare; they're thinking of limiting the number of tourists that can visit there. Then I rode it out to Custer and stayed a week with my mother."

"How is she?"

"Old, and getting more fragile every day. I'm afraid we're not more than two years away from a nursing home or something along those lines."

Jellie didn't say anything for a while. He drank his beer, she drank her club soda and lime. He took out his cigarettes and offered her one. She refused. "I've stopped smoking. Something about yoga that leads to that, not sure what it is."

He nodded and flipped open the Zippo, lit his, and leaned back against the padded booth. She slid over farther so she could turn and look straight at him.

Michael was tired of the dancing. "Where are we, Jellie, the two of us? It's been a long nine months for me." After he said it he wished he'd moved into this a little slower. Typical male fashion—no foreplay.

She didn't say anything for a moment. He'd forgotten just how gray her eyes were until she kept them on his for at least ten seconds.

"I've done a lot of thinking, Michael." Those were bad-news words, he could tell. Something in the words themselves, something in the way she said them. What they felt for each other didn't require thinking. It required acting, not thinking. The happiness from seeing her again started draining down and out of him.

She paused, then went on. "I had the words all ready to say, but it's much harder than I thought it would be. I'd convinced myself the way I felt about you was a kind of girlish infatuation with a different sort of man than I'd ever encountered before, or at least not for a long time. But with you here looking at me with those good brown eyes, your hair drifting over your shirt collar and all, it's more difficult . . . a lot more difficult."

"Say it, Jellie. I already know what's coming."

"I suppose you do, and I'm going to say what I have to say before I get to the point I can't say it. We've got to cut this clean before real trouble starts." He was prepared for it, but that didn't stop the harpoon from entering his chest and going out the other side. "Jimmy asked me several times in the days before we left for England if there was anything wrong with me. He said I was acting a little strange. It was you, Michael—no, *us*. I was thinking about us, fantasizing about things I don't even want to mention."

"That's all right, Jellie, I've had the same kind of images in my mind since the day I first saw you. Mine would just blow you away if I started talking about them."

"Women have those thoughts, too. Let me go

on. In ways you'll never know, and I don't want to talk about, I owe Jimmy a lot. Look, we both know Jimmy. He's a little goofy in certain ways, but he's very kind to me.

"Jimmy was crushed when the best schools wouldn't accept him for his doctorate. His grades were good, but only because he worked so hard. God, his parents just hammered and hammered at him about the whole idea of success. But Jimmy does not have a truly fine intellect. He knows that and has come to terms with it, though it bothers him because of the world in which he's chosen to earn a living, a world where he's constantly reminded of his limitations just by being around people like you, Michael."

"Oh, hell, Jellie . . ." He started to do a foot shuffle into something resembling modesty, a little dance called the South Dakota backstep. But she'd have none of it and interrupted him.

"Michael Tillman, don't play the country boy with me, please. It's not becoming, and I know better. You scare Jimmy. He knows he's not in your league. He could write all his life and never get an article accepted by the journals in which you've published. I don't mean to imply you don't work hard, I know you do, in spite of the casual way you seem to operate. And Jimmy likes you. He likes you a lot, and he's appreciative of the good ideas you give him. If he ever makes full professor, you'll be responsible for it in good part."

"Jimmy's all right, Jellie. He's a lot different than me, but I respect him for the way he keeps his head down and the numbers crunching. I couldn't do that."

He lit another Merit and took a drink of his beer. This was turning into something a little unpleasant, and he didn't want that to happen with Jellie. She was floating off, getting loyalty and Jimmy's shortcomings and her own emotions all tangled up. Chewing on him in small ways as a means of protecting herself from her own feelings.

"Jellie, let me try and say what I think you're telling me. You feel good things for Jimmy, among them at least a kind of love, I'm sure. You're a loving person. And you feel a gratefulness toward him for something I don't know about and won't ask about. Though I have a feeling India works into it somehow—I figure you'd tell me if you wanted me to know, even though it wouldn't affect how I feel about you no matter what it is. And you want to make sure our feelings for each other don't go any further than just that—feelings. Have I got it right?"

She nodded, tears in her eyes.

He had momentum and kept rolling. "Here's the bottom line, Jellie Markham Braden: I'm in love with you, truly and powerfully in love. I guess I knew it when you walked in the dean's kitchen a year ago in your blue suit and black boots, knew it when we sat on the back steps that day. Christ, teeter-totters in the park. Do you have any idea of how much I've wanted you, all of you, everything that makes you up, tangible and otherwise? The whole works, that's what I want. As much as I can get in the years I have left, and I'm no youngster anymore. Do you understand that, Jellie, how deeply I feel?"

"Michael . . . don't." She reached in her purse, took out a handkerchief, and put it against her eyes for a moment. The bartender was not insensitive; she had a feel for what was going on and turned up the television to cover their conversation. Michael nodded at her in thanks, and she gave him a little wave.

He put his hand on Jellie's neck, the first time he'd ever touched her in that way. Her skin felt exactly as he'd known it would, and the sensation ran up his arm, went down somewhere inside of him, and made a low, sad sound for all the times he'd never feel it again. "It's okay, Jellie. We'll make it work. We'll put some bandages on the cuts and promise not to look under them ever again. I'm not sure I can stay in the same town with you, but I'll try. Really, I'll try, Jellie. Maybe we can eventually work it out so we can have coffee at Beano's now and then. Maybe it'll spiral down and we can do that."

She stuffed her hanky back in her purse and reached out for his left hand, holding it tight in both of hers. "You're right, Michael, in everything you said. Damnit, I know why people get frustrated with you sometimes and are secretly afraid of you. Your mind is like a rifle bullet when you decide to let it run full tilt, and that's scary. Carolyn, the dean's wife, said that about you the first day I met you. She said, 'Michael Tillman frightens the hell out of Arthur, and Arthur retaliates in mean little ways.' The dean was going to turn you down for full professor on those grounds alone, even though you'd done twice as much work as it took to qualify. Carolyn told him, 'Arthur, you pull that piece of crap on Michael and you'll see me waving from the first train out of Cedar Bend.' "

Now they had Carolyn and Arthur into it. Jellie kept wandering away from the subject, but he understood why. There was a door closing behind them, and she wanted to keep it open all the while she was pulling it shut.

"Jellie, let's let it rest where it is. You know where to find me. Come by if you feel you can. Hell, I just like to be around you, to look at you, to smell your perfume when I get close, which I haven't done nearly enough."

"I don't think so. There's something about being in each other's presence that's just too strong for me—for both of us. I came off the plane clearheaded and ready to tell you exactly how I felt and what I was going to do, now here I am turning into mud pie. I've got to get my life organized again. I'm going to take another class this fall, so

I'll be on campus three days a week. If I feel okay about it, I'll stop by to see you. If I don't, and I probably won't, it's not because I'm not thinking about you. You understand that, don't you?"

"Yes. I understand, Jellie. I don't like it, but I understand. And I'll be thinking about you, too. That's all I ever seem to do anymore."

As they left the Ramada bar, Jellie pulled a small package from her purse and handed it to him. "I forgot to give you this."

He tore open the wrapping. Inside was a belt made of English bridle leather with *Orville* hand-tooled on the back.

Michael took the Shadow out of town and let it go all the way to Des Moines, where he turned around and came back into Cedar Bend through one of those soft August twilights. Going home past the campus, he could hear the marching band practicing, getting ready for the first football game. They were playing some old song from some old movie. Michael Tillman couldn't remember the name of either the song or the movie, because he was thinking about Jellie Braden and wondering how he was going to get through the years ahead without her.

The lights in Bingley Hall flickered on, and the race to December got under way. Jimmy Braden came by Michael's office for new ideas, and the football team was doing well. On those Saturdays when the team was playing at home, the streets were packed with Cadillacs and Lincolns, driven by overweight men who wrote out large checks to the athletic department and whose daughters were in the best sororities.

Michael paced the classroom, tossing a piece of chalk up and down in his right hand. "Consider, for a moment, the nature of systemic problems, the elements of a puzzling issue and the subtle, intricate relationships among those elements. What we must do is learn how to overcome what I long ago began to call the Archimedean Dilemma." He always hesitated at this point and looked out at the class. "Who, by the way, was Archimedes?" They all focused on their notebooks, pretending to be doing something.

He pushed and prodded, and finally a young man (bad complexion, front row) said hesitantly, "Wasn't he some kind of scientist or something?"

Michael gave them a two-minute capsule on the life and times of the Greek mathematician. After that, he picked up the thread of the lecture again. "Archimedes said, 'Give me a lever and a place to stand, and I will move the world.' That's what structural modeling is all about, finding a lever, a place to stand, an angle of entry into complexity." He paused, thinking of Jellie, while the students wrote in their notebooks and wondered if he would ask about Archimedes on the first examination.

During the second week of school he was looking out the window while covering a fine point in Boolean algebra, looking at nothing except the quaver of now turning leaves in the wind of September, and saw her. At first it didn't register, since he was working hard at getting the students to appreciate the intellectual leavings of one George Boole, the nineteenth-century mathematician who took formal logic up about fifty notches. But the long-legged walk and tweed cap finally got his attention—Jellie. He stopped talking, he wasn't sure how long, and watched her wind along a sidewalk, knapsack over her shoulder. Jellie from a distance, always from a distance. When she moved out of sight, he turned back to the class. They were all looking at him in a strange kind of way. His face, maybe, or his body. They saw something, in his eyes or the momentary sag of his shoulders, and they knew they hadn't seen it before. Michael glanced at the wall clock. Five minutes to go. "That'll be all for today," he said. As he scraped up lecture notes from the desk in front, they filed out, some of them giving him sidelong glances and talking to one another. A young woman whispered, "Did you see how he looked? What happened to him all of a sudden?"

Michael hadn't realized how much it showed. Jellie was right in believing they had to stay apart. Aside from protecting themselves from each other, people would start to pick up on how they felt, even if they were merely in the same room together. He'd been looking at advertisements for faculty positions in the *Chronicle*, but at his salary and rank it would be difficult to make a move. Besides, with his mother's health declining, he felt a responsibility to stay in the middle of the country and not be too far from her. Still there might be something somewhere that met his requirements and took him away from the town where Jellie Braden lived.

It's hard to say where all this might have gone if it hadn't been for the ducks. Probably to the same place by a different route. The history of the situation is this: University presidents relish new buildings, so do Boards of Education. Bingley Hall was just fine—old, but with a patina of learning and struggle rubbed into its corridors and heavy in its air. Still, the president decided one of his premier colleges needed a new building. Presidents don't bequeath knowledge or grateful students to the world, they leave behind bricks and mortar. Whether those bricks and mortar are actually necessary is irrelevant. The important thing is to get money and build buildings carrying the names either of heavy donors to the university or members of the administration who served the university loyally, though not necessarily brilliantly. *The Arthur J. Wilcox College of Business and Economics*— you could see the lettering in the dean's rodentlike eyes as he scooted around Bingley Hall with rolled-up blueprints clutched in his sweaty paws. Fat chance.

The money could have been used for faculty salaries or student financial aid, but that's never in the cards. As the president was fond of saying, privately, of course, "It's much easier to get money for buildings than it is for faculty salaries." But, in spite of hard economic times in the state, the board floated a bond issue and ponied up $18 million for a new building. That had occurred the previous winter, and final construction plans were now being drawn.

Arthur posted emerging versions of the plans in the coffee room for everyone to slobber over. Michael was standing there looking at an updated set and noticed the location of the new building had been moved fifty yards from its original site. "They're going to put the sonuvabitch right over the duck pond," he said to no one in particular. The other faculty members present looked at him in a way that said, "So what?"

Michael went to see Arthur and explained to him the rather neat and profound role the pond played in the traditions of the campus. It wasn't much in terms of water area, elliptically shaped and maybe a hundred feet long by fifty feet wide. But it was home for little geezers with orange legs who looked at Michael when he walked by and went "Quack" when he grinned and said hello to them.

It was also a place for moonlight walks and tender thoughts, a place where ten thousand engagement rings had been slipped over shaking fingers through the years, not to mention various other assignations getting a little more carnal late at night. When Michael looked out his office window, he could see the ducks on their pond a block away, and often he had found solace in that when dealing with education gone berserk.

But guys like Arthur J. Wilcox have no appreciation for tradition, it's not tangible enough. Michael talked hard, but it didn't register. Arthur just kept saying, "But, Michael, we need a new building."

"What about the ducks?" Michael was angry. "Where will they go? Are we going to build a new eighteen-million-dollar pond for them, too?"

Arthur didn't understand ducks, either. You could see it on his face. That and the plain wish Michael would just go away and leave him alone with his blueprints.

Michael was pretty sure he wouldn't have raised as much hell about the duck pond as he did if he hadn't been half-crazed with sorting out his feelings in those days, trying to push Jellie far back and out of his mind and failing in that attempt. He worked his way up through the provost, who didn't understand ducks any better than Arthur. Stomping past Clarice's desk on his way out of the provost's office, he turned around, then talked with her for a moment.

Next he made an appointment to see the president. Michael laid out his case: Move the building, keep the duck pond. The prez was smooth. Years of dealing with demented faculty and recalcitrant alumni who stapled their checkbooks shut when they saw him coming had provided him with a sheen and style worthy of the very best (or worst, depending on your point of view) slithering public relations man.

"Professor Tillman, I do understand your concerns. Tradition is important, I agree with you. But in evolving times we must sometimes cast off our old traditions and establish new ones. I like ducks, too. In fact, I'm a member of Ducks Unlimited and go duck hunting every fall."

Michael was wondering if, in addition to professional incompetence and moral degradation, presidential dismemberment was sufficient cause for loss of tenure.

One of the best students Michael ever had went on to law school and stayed in Cedar Bend after graduating. Michael called him. "Gene, what can be done to prevent these clowns from pouring cement over ducks and tradition?"

Gene always had a soft spot for radical causes, so he looked into it. He called back in two days, flat out saying the building couldn't be halted by legal chicanery. Something to do with state law and a Board of Education master plan for masterful buildings and a master race.

"Screw 'em, Gene. I'm going to plant myself

right in the middle of that pond and make 'em drag me out with chains."

"Michael, I'll defend you free of charge if you do it. But you're going to lose. You'll be better off spending your time looking for another home for the ducks."

Knowing bureaucrats hate bad publicity more than anything else, Michael wrote a long article for the university newspaper, making what he thought was a powerful and eloquent plea to save the duck pond. That started a fair amount of debate over the whole affair, which drove Arthur dotty.

Arthur went completely out of his mind when the longhairs from the Student Socialist Brigade made up signs reading "Save the Ducks" and began marching around Bingley Hall in their Birkenstocks. Recruiters from the Fortune 500 who were on campus interviewing savvy students told Arthur they were looking for good corporate citizens, not radicals. He took them over to the faculty club for cocktails and reassured them this was merely one of those periodic outbreaks coming down to us as a result of universities being too lenient in the sixties and it would soon be over. Afterward he took the recruiters to his office, unrolled his blueprints, and showed them all the wonderful space the new building would have for interview rooms. They liked that a lot better.

The university newspaper was flooded for a few days with letters pro and con. One of the bookstores printed up T-shirts with the logo *Ducks, Not Cement* and sold them for twelve dollars each, proving once again capitalism can profit even from the concerns of its enemies. Michael was surprised to see Jellie write a letter to the newspaper in support of his position. It was a nice letter. And he knew it probably caused her trouble at home, since Jimmy had dropped by to talk with him about the issue and seemed utterly amazed, or perhaps bewildered, that Michael could get so worked up over eight or ten ducks.

But nobody except Michael cared very much. The longhairs marched, Arthur fretted, and the earth-moving machinery was carted into position on the back of big, muddy trucks. Gambling on having a mild winter, the contractors would begin digging on the following Monday. Michael was sure the tame ducks wouldn't know how to handle the filling of their pond and contacted the Humane Society. He and the society put a notice in the paper saying anyone who wanted to help in getting the ducks moved should show up early Saturday morning and be prepared to get wet.

Light frost lay upon the grass of autumn when Michael rode the Shadow through early light and parked it by the pond. While he sat on the bike, taking one last look at tradition and little geezers who slap-slapped about on orange legs and flat feet, he noticed someone walking down the road toward the pond. Jellie. Jellie in the morning, Jellie at the duck pond. She wore old jeans and her hiking boots, a heavy sweater and a red stocking cap with *Grownup* printed on the front. Her hair was in a ponytail, and she was smiling as she walked toward him.

"Hello, Michael. I came to help you find the ducks a new home."

He cared for her more at that moment than ever before.

"Jellie . . . thanks for coming. It's going to be something of a mess, I'm afraid. But the little folks need somewhere to go."

She walked over to him, wrapped both her arms around one of his, and leaned against the Shadow, putting her head against his shoulder. The physical contact was unnerving and surprised him, but he thought, Maybe we're going to work it out and be friends, nothing more. He only thought that for a moment. Being merely Jellie's friend and nothing more was impossible for him.

The Humane Society troops pulled in, a professor from the biology department riding along with them. He had cages and a net that could be fired out over the pond with small rockets, which took him about twenty minutes to get set up. Jellie didn't say much, Michael didn't say much, watching the professor and his helpers from the Humane Society, all of whom wore chest-high rubber waders. They strung the rocket net along the shore while the ducks woke up and swam around in circles, alarmed and telling everyone who would listen about how they felt.

Jellie and Michael walked over near the water where the professor was crouched, making adjustments on his apparatus. He straightened up and said, "Ready." Everyone stood back while he threw bread crumbs onto the water. Alarm is one thing, bread crumbs are something else, and the ducks swam toward them, quacking. When the ducks came within range the biologist fired his rockets, which scared hell out of the ducks. But the net arched across the pond, went down past the face of a rising sun and over ten frightened ducks.

The biologist waded into the water, motioning for the Humane Society to follow him. They got around on the pond side of the net, gently pushing the net and ducks toward shore. The professor obviously had done this before. He glanced up at Jellie and Michael. "We'll hand you the ducks. You two can put them in the cages, very carefully, if you please." So saying, he rolled up his sleeves and began reaching under the net, which now formed a small semicircle near the shore. It was all very crisp, easier than Michael had thought it would be. He and Jellie put the ducks in cages, Jellie petting them and talking in a low, sweet voice as she handled the terrified birds.

The operation took less than ten minutes. The biologist rolled up his net while Michael and Jellie carried three cages to the Humane Society truck and put them in the back. A woman in a tan shirt with a *Humane Society of the United States* patch on it said, "We're taking them out to Heron Lake north of town. You know where that is?"

Michael nodded. "I'll follow you on my bike." He looked over at Jellie. "Want to come? There's room in the truck, or you can ride with me."

She turned to the woman from the Humane Society. "We'll meet you out there." At that moment, Michael felt as if some kind of decision beyond transportation had been made.

He kicked the Shadow's starter and helped Jellie climb on behind him. She'd never been on a motorcycle before, so he gave her a twenty-second lecture on where to rest her feet and how to lean with him in the curves. She wrapped her arms around his waist and said, "This is fun, Michael," as he pulled out behind the truck.

The campus was quiet early on a Saturday, air warming rapidly, prodded on by a fat, red sun. The Shadow rolled smoothly down the streets of Cedar Bend and out into the countryside through tunnels of red and yellow leaves. Jellie's arms tightened around Michael. He could feel her body tucked against his lower back and rear. They could be far into Minnesota by evening if he just let the Shadow run on toward wherever the highway went.

They swung into the state park entrance, still

following the Humane Society truck and its little cargo. Through the park and on to Heron Lake, lying cool and flat on a windless morning. The ducks were shown the water and knew what to do with it, waddling out of their cages and paddling around, looking for food. The biologist said, "It'll take them a while to adjust. With all the people at the university handing out grub, they're not used to foraging on their own. But I'll check on them every few days. Eventually they'll get accustomed to life out here. Portions of the lake stay open during winter."

This was the way it was meant to be, Michael was thinking as they rode back into town. Jellie and he, and the Shadow, and bright autumn mornings with the road out in front of them. Instead he was taking her home to James Lee Braden III, who probably had tickets for the football game that afternoon. He glanced at his watch—eight-fifteen—it was going to be a long day and a long life.

Jellie was trying to say something, but Michael couldn't hear her over the wind and sound of the engine. He eased off the Shadow, letting it slow down and coast, and tilted his head back toward her. She put her fingers on the side of his neck, speaking in a soft voice, right into his ear: "Michael, can we go to your apartment?" He turned his head for an instant and looked into the gray eyes. She was half smiling, half not smiling. A strange, warm, loving look.

He nodded and began to shake a little. She laid her cheek against his back and put her hand under his jacket and inside his shirt, moving it slowly back and forth over his chest and stomach. The Shadow took him toward home, as it had taken him there so many times over the years. And it took him and Jellie Braden toward a future he'd long ago decided would never come. When they got off the Shadow at his apartment, smoke from burning leaves was drifting through the neighborhood. In the distance voices were singing the university fight song at a morning pep rally.

He held the door for her and they went inside, into the world of a man who lived alone and stayed mostly to himself. Dishes in the sink, a pair of jeans on the floor, streaks on the windows. Small kitchen, large living room, bedroom off through another door. In a corner of the living room nearest the kitchen was a scarred maple table where he took his meals. The three chairs around the table were each of a different kind and Goodwill rough. Plain, ceramic salt and pepper shakers sat on the table next to a stack of paper napkins.

Near the table and along the wall was his work area. His desk was a nine-foot unfinished door laid across sawhorses. Brick-and-board bookcases flanked the desk, with one long board running over the top of it, holding reference books. In the middle of the desk was a computer, turned on and with words typed across the screen, cursor blinking. The far end of the desk held a stack of audio equipment, tapes in desultory piles on and next to the equipment.

Jellie took off her stocking cap and laid her coat over the back of a chair. As she looked around, it struck her that she knew very little about Michael Tillman. More than that, she'd never been completely alone with him. "I think I need a drink," she said. "Do you have anything with alcohol in it?"

"Beer, wine, and maybe"—he opened a cupboard door and looked inside—"a little whiskey." He took out the whiskey bottle and held it up. It was a third full. Clarice sometimes preferred whiskey when the nights were long and wild and getting wilder.

"About two fingers of the Jack Daniel's over ice with a little water"—Jellie took a deep breath—"should do it."

Michael stood for a moment, holding the whiskey bottle, looking at her. "You okay?"

"Yes." She smiled and brushed loose strands of hair back from her face. "About eighty percent, at least."

"I could take you home if you want."

She shook her head, small silver earrings from her early days in India moving as she did it. "Let's try the Jack Daniel's first."

He owned four glasses. All of them were in the sink, dirty. He washed one and pulled an ice cube tray from the refrigerator.

Jellie walked slowly past his desk, trailing her

finger along the edge of it. Above the desk were notes and two snapshots. One of the pictures was her standing by a stone wall in Ireland. The other was a yellowed, curling, black-and-white shot of a young woman in a long dress and a bearded man in a dark turtleneck sweater, jeans, and sandals. She stared at the second photo and recognized the eyes. "Is that you?"

He looked up from the counter where he was fixing her drink. "Yes. A long time ago in Berkeley." He poured Jack Daniel's and handed the glass to her. "The woman's name was Nadia. She's an implacable feminist now—was starting to become one then, in fact—works for the National Council of Women. We exchange notes at Christmas."

Jellie didn't say anything. She read the words typed on the computer screen: *In this place I hear the quiet rasp of things as they used to be. I come at dawn, I come at nightfall, and all the hours in between. I come to hear the rustle of twilight robes and songs from the time of Gregory. I come because old things live here, things I understand without knowing why.*

"Is this something you're writing?" She sipped on her whiskey and pointed at the screen.

"Yeah, I keep fiddling around, thinking I might have a novel inside me." He set the bottle of beer he was drinking on the counter.

"Do you?"

"Maybe. It's harder than I thought it would be. Writing the academic stuff and essays, you're always bound to reality. So far I'm having trouble dealing with the freedom to make up anything I want to say. It's kind of strange—in fiction you get to tell lies and are applauded for it."

"Justifiable lies," she said. "I suppose that happens sometimes in real life, too."

"If you're a relativist it does. And maybe now and then if it's absolutely necessary to cushion someone from a world gone too harsh and bitter."

In the far corner of the room was an easel folded and leaning against a window. "Do you paint?" Jellie asked.

Michael grinned, shoved his hands in the pockets of his jeans. "I try. I know a guy named Wayne Regenson over in the art department. He and his wife periodically fight like hell. When that happens he drops by for a little male support, which I'm not very good at, but better than nothing, I suppose. In return he's been trying to teach me oil painting. It's coming real slow. Real, *real* slow. In some ways, though, it can be a lot like mathematics—true mathematics—the same feelings in your brain. The elegance of saying much with little, bringing together left-brained technique and right-brained shapes."

"Like the long-range jumpshot, too?"

He thought for a moment. "Yes, that too."

"Is this one of yours?" She was looking at an oil painting, framed and hanging on the wall. It was a group of black, vertical lines sprouting slashes of green and a ribbon of yellow winding away from the viewer, back into the vertical lines. Farther and farther the streak of yellow wound, disappearing then in a splash of red.

"Yes, it's the only one I can bear looking at. Actually I kind of like it."

"So do I. Does it have a title?"

"I call it *Butterfly Gone.*"

Jellie tipped her glass and took a serious drink of Jack Daniel's. She turned and looked at him, then out the window. In the hard, south light of November, he noticed for the first time the early lines of age coming to her face.

"This seems very strange, Michael. All our talks, our resolutions about right and wrong . . . all of that." The university band was marching down the street a block away, playing the fight song, *"We will go undaunted, hear our cry, hear our cry."* Jellie Braden watched the dark curling leaves of late autumn stir and begin to tumble across the grass as a light breeze came in from the west.

Michael always remembered how she had looked that morning in Cedar Bend, staring outside at the things of autumn. Still looking out the window, she'd reached up and taken the elastic band from her ponytail, shaking the thick black hair loose and long. She'd looked over at him then, the gray eyes soft and no longer like an arrow in flight, saying, "I'm a little shaky. It's been a long time since . . . well, a long time."

"When are you expected home?"

"I have the day. Jimmy's attending a reunion of his fraternity on campus. They're all going to the game and out to dinner after that. All that arm punching and male bonding was more than I could think about tolerating. Besides"—she smiled—"there were the ducks."

In midafternoon they heard the roar of the football crowd from the stadium. The sound of it came faintly over tapes of Cleo Laine ballads and sweet obscurities whispered in Tamil by Jellie Braden on an autumn afternoon in the high latitudes.

"If God lives at all, God lives in moments like these," a man had once said to her. And she had said that to Michael Tillman in English, looking up at him, touching his face with her hands, loving him and missing that other man and sometimes confusing the two of them even though she didn't want to on that afternoon.

Michael looked down at the pulse of blood in her throat, at her eyes widening as she arched her breasts and belly toward him, eyes looking first at him and then straight upward as India rolled within her and time went back to the high country of an older land where dark hands had moved over those same breasts and a voice had commanded her, "Wider now, Jellie, wider still, everything, Jellie. Give me all of you, and I'll give you back yourself when we have finished." And in the high country she had screamed aloud in some combination of fear and pleasure. And she had done that once more in a bed in Iowa, then turned the scream into a dwindling, involuntary cry for all the things she had once felt and now felt again with another strange man who lived in his own far places.

Michael had a sense that day she was feeling and doing things not attributable to her life with Jimmy Braden. It was obvious this was a woman who had gone before into sensual frontiers where he was sure Jimmy never ventured. Something about how nakedness did not bother her. Something about how she moved freely and uninhibited beneath him and with him, how she touched him with hands that were practiced and surprising in what they did. Something about the directness of her words when they first lay on the bed, still dressed, and she had pulled back from him, smiling. "I seem to remember it's necessary for me to take off my jeans if this is going to work out in the best possible way."

Later, with post–football–game traffic moving along the streets outside, he fetched beers for them. When he came back into the bedroom Jellie was sitting on her knees, legs under her. She'd grinned at him, hair hanging in disarray above her breasts. He lay down beside her, and she touched his chest. "It was worth the wait," she said quietly. Malachi lay in the doorway, head on his paws, brown eyes turned up toward the bed. Casserole sat on the dresser and licked a paw.

Michael ran his hand slowly along Jellie's

body. "*Now* it seems worth the wait. It didn't seem that way while waiting." He raised up on one elbow. "One of my many quirks is I get crazy hungry after making love. How's a toasted cheese sandwich sound? That's about all I have."

"Make three, and we'll each have one plus another to share." She leaned over and kissed him. "My secret passion is fried potatoes with a little onion mixed in. You got potatoes, motorcycle man, big fresh ones?" She smiled. "Out in the kitchen, I mean."

"I got potatoes, Jellie-Who-Sometimes-Talks-Raunchy-in-the-Afternoon. I also got onions and lotsa beer."

"We're in fat city. You cook the sandwiches, I'll handle potatoes. Deal?"

"Deal. Do we have to get dressed, though? I love seeing you naked."

"God, no. Given what I suspect—what I hope—will go on after we eat, that'd be wasted effort." She bounced off the bed. "On to the naked kitchen for naked lunch, then. Who said that, naked lunch? I should know. William . . ."

"Burroughs. Ol' wild and woolly William S. It's the title of one of his books."

"Get out the bread and show me the potatoes, Captain America. I'm starving, too."

Two weeks later she was gone. She'd had surges of guilt about Jimmy. So had Michael. Jellie cried once, thinking of it. "How can I be so callous and yet not care I'm being callous? I want you so much nothing matters, not guilt or anything like that."

But something had gone wrong in her marriage. It had been there for a long while, and the semester in England had underscored it, brought it into hard, sharp relief. Michael asked if that was merely rationalization to salve over what the two of them were doing.

She shook her head. "I keep thinking of the word *inertia*. Sometimes, I think people stay together because of inertia and not much else. I have the feeling Jimmy and I are riding a tired horse, but we just keep going on because we don't know what else to do. Jimmy wants to be a university administrator, a dean or something, and I can't get very excited about that, about being a good little administrator's wife. I told him I want to finish my master's, go on for a Ph.D., and find a teaching position. He only said it would be difficult for both of us to find jobs we want at the same university. We had a couple of bad arguments about that in England."

Michael let her talk, let her work through all of the complicated things she was feeling. In some ways, Jellie was a traditional woman. In other ways, she was the new and emancipated woman, intent on finding her own way in the world. All of that was difficult enough to sort out by itself, and now he'd entered the situation and cluttered it up even more. Though, when Michael mentioned that, she was kind enough to say he was not part of the clutter. But he was.

Jellie had to go to Syracuse for Thanksgiving. Her parents had come out to Cedar Bend last year, so it was her turn to visit them. Jimmy's folks were coming up from Rhode Island. She and Michael spent the entire afternoon together the day before she left, and he picked up something a little different in her behavior, something that started to haunt him.

"Anything the matter, Jellie?"

She looked at him lovingly. There was no question about how she felt, as far as he could tell. "No, not really." He didn't push it, figuring it would pass.

Michael fiddled around over the long Thanksgiving weekend, counting the hours until Jellie would return. He fixed a tuna sandwich on turkey day and ate it while looking at the Polaroid of Jellie standing by a stone wall in Ireland. The computer keyboard was dusty, and the Shadow needed work, but he couldn't find any motivation to do anything except jog in the mornings and think about her.

On Sunday evening the department head called and asked if Michael could cover Jimmy's econometrics class the next day. Jimmy had been delayed in Syracuse, some kind of personal emergency was all the department head knew. Michael went crazy, paced the floor, pounded the walls, Malachi and Casserole watching him in a kind of wonder.

Monday night and still no word. He got the Markhams' phone number from information and dialed it. Eleanor Markham answered. Jesus, it would have to be Mother Markham. Michael used the pretense he was covering Jimmy's class and wanted some idea of how long he might be away. Shallow, transparent, but then he wasn't thinking very well.

Mrs. Markham was cool, very cool—brittle, in fact—and said Jimmy was on his way back to Cedar Bend. She had known something about Jellie and the motorcycle man a year ago. She knew a great deal more now, Michael had a hunch. She'd said *Jimmy* was on his way back. She hadn't used both their names or a plural pronoun, indicating both of them were returning. Michael was screaming inside and wanted to ask about Jellie, but he had the clear sensation Eleanor Markham had no interest in talking with him about anything.

He hung up and went absolutely wild in his head. The phone rang fifteen minutes later. It was Jimmy. He was back and wanted to come over. Michael said, "Yes, come right away, no problem, come as soon as you want to," obviously overplaying it, but Jimmy didn't have a feeling for that kind of stuff and missed it completely.

He rapped on Michael's door five minutes

later. Michael knew there was serious business afoot, just by looking at him. No tie, rumpled clothing, hair askew. Not the Newport Jimmy Braden Michael had come to know.

"Michael, something terrible has happened, and I don't have anyone to talk to about it. I'm close to falling apart."

The voice inside Michael's head was shouting, "Jimmy Braden, you fey little bastard, what's going on? Where's Jellie?" It was screaming loud enough for Jimmy to hear, but he didn't because he wasn't listening. Jimmy merely sat on a kitchen chair, put his head in his hands, and cried. Michael brought himself down—level, brother—get level, stay level, and ask the right questions.

"Talk to me, Jimmy. What's happened? Does it have something to do with Jellie?"

He sobbed and moved his head up and down in the affirmative. Don't panic, get the information, get to the bottom, omit the extraneous junk and side issues. "Where's Jellie?"

Jimmy looked up, crying hard, and got it out: "She's gone to India."

"What?" Michael nearly shouted. "India? What the hell for? What's going on? Get straight and talk to me, Jimmy. I can't be of any help unless you do that. Why'd she go?"

"I don't know. We didn't have a fight or anything. Saturday morning Jellie just said she had some things to think about and was going to India.

Christ, Michael, I begged her, groveled, said whatever it was could be worked out, but she wouldn't talk about it. She wasn't mean or cold, none of that, just far away from all of us, thinking about something. It was an awful scene, an absolute hell. Her parents were screaming, my parents were screaming, I was stumbling all over the place, and Jellie was packing her suitcase."

"Okay," Michael said. "We don't know *why* she went, but do you know *where* she went? She once mentioned a place called Pondicherry, in the southeast. Is that where she went?"

"I don't know."

Jimmy was sniffling again. Michael scrounged around for a box of tissues, couldn't find any, went in the john and brought out a new roll of toilet paper. Jimmy ripped off a wad and worked on his eyes with it, his voice thick and wet, phlegm in his throat. He blew his nose and said, "I tried to find out where she went, but the airlines won't give out that information on passengers. India's a huge place, so it's hard to say where she is, but, yes, she spent time in Pondicherry when she was there before."

Jimmy didn't drink coffee or beer. Michael poured him a glass of orange juice, lit a cigarette, and went over to the Shadow, straddling it, arms folded. He looked up at the wall and saw the picture of Jellie hanging there, decided it wasn't a good idea for Jimmy to see it displayed so prominently. When Jimmy went back to wiping his eyes, Michael took it down and slid it under some papers on the desk. Jimmy Braden sat bent over, elbows on his knees, at the same kitchen table where Michael had made love with his wife a week ago, scraping the salt and pepper shakers onto the floor as he laid her down. She was laughing then.

"When did she leave, Jimmy? What airline was she taking out of New York?"

"Saturday night. She left Saturday night. She took a flight out of Syracuse to Kennedy. Wouldn't even let me or anyone else go to the airport with her and wouldn't tell me what airline she was taking out of New York."

"Somehow none of this sounds like Jellie," Michael said. Smiling, warm, caring Jellie. It didn't sound like her at all.

"I know it doesn't. That's what makes it so strange, Michael. It seems so unlike her."

Or maybe it isn't, Michael thought. Maybe there are things about Jellie Braden none of us know, or at least that he and Jimmy didn't know.

"Jimmy, I'm going to ask you a question. You can choose whether or not to answer it. I don't have to know, but I've somehow gotten this sense Jellie doesn't like to talk about her India days. Did something happen to her over there?"

Jimmy looked up. "Michael, I can't say anything about that. I'd tell you if I could, but I just can't. I just can't. Please understand."

Michael appreciated him for feeling that way and sticking to it. It would have been easy at a time like this to spill out the whole story, but he didn't. Michael decided Jimmy Braden might be a better man than he'd given him credit for.

"All right, then let me ask this: Do you think whatever happened to her in India had anything to do with her going back there now?"

"I don't know. I can't imagine why, if she's told me the truth about her time in India. Like I said, I can't talk about it, but I guess I *can* say what occurred in India was over a long time ago, or at least I thought it was."

Michael needed time to think, be by himself and start working out the options. Yet he didn't want to let Jimmy go home alone in this condition.

"Jimmy, want me to arrange for someone to take your classes for a while, until you get yourself together again?"

"No, I need to be doing something. I've never been good at just sitting around and thinking, at introspection. I've got to get myself squared away somehow, and maybe getting back to school will help. Jellie just needs time to think, I'm sure."

Michael lowered his opinion of Jimmy by an amount greater than he'd raised it a moment ago. Jesus Christ, he thought, don't put up with this shit, man. Screw the university. Get on the first plane to India and start looking for your wife. Talk to her, try to sort it out. That was not the way of

Jimmy Braden, though. He was going to lie back and take it, and hope.

But Jimmy Braden had never changed the oil in a banker's car when summer was high and the wind from the western lands was hot and made your greasy clothes stick to your body. He'd never stuck his head under the hood of an automobile and listened to the turn of an engine while his father staggered around with a flask in his pocket and yelled at him. And Jimmy Braden had never cut hard to the right and gone into the air with his knee swollen and twelve thousand crazed assholes screaming for and against him.

Jimmy had counted on the momentum of blood and wealth to carry him along. He'd never ridden in steerage, which made him inert when assertiveness was required—if there's no need to climb, then there's no reason to learn how to climb. That was Jimmy's way, and Michael understood it.

But it wasn't Michael's way. And, at that moment, he felt something deep and sad for Jimmy Braden. Inside of Jimmy, someplace, there had to be the old push from our times forty thousand years back, out on the grasslands, when the choice was either to fight for what was yours or have it taken by the malevolence around you. Civilization has its benefits, but it had robbed Jimmy and others like him of the basic instincts.

When things stabilized and Michael was reasonably sure the husband of Jellie Braden could make it through the night, he got him into his Buick and on the road. Jimmy said just talking about getting back to his work made him feel better, that at least he still had his work and maybe they could talk some more tomorrow.

He also blurted out a curious statement, saying he believed how he felt was mostly a matter of pride. Some of the old ways from the grasslands evidently *were* still there, but he couldn't take the next step. Before Jimmy's car turned the corner, Michael was looking in the Yellow Pages for airline telephone numbers.

# Eight

If you want to get to India fast, you deal with Air India. It's the national airline and a good one. Every night at eight-thirty flight 102 lifts off from Kennedy and makes a two-hour stop in London the next day. Afterward it heads nonstop for either Delhi or Bombay, alternating between the two cities, depending on the day.

There are other options, some of them convoluted. Aeroflot can get you to Delhi, but you have to put up with a long layover in Moscow. Before it collapsed, Pan Am went to Delhi twice a week from New York via Frankfurt. Those were the major eastern routes, except for British Air, which Michael had never ridden out to India. The western routes can get even more circuitous—several different airlines and overnight layovers in Bangkok or Kuala Lumpur or Singapore.

After checking his atlas to make sure he knew where Pondicherry was located, Michael called Air India. It was booked solid for the next fourteen nights, with two seats available on December 11 and one on December 13, then solid again until after Christmas. Given the number of expatriates and former citizens out in the world, India has relatively sparse international air service, but the Indians all go home around Christmastime, and things get very tight from Thanksgiving forward.

He rummaged his bookshelves until he found a world airline guide three years out of date. British Airways showed a nonstop from Chicago to London and then a later flight straight out to Madras on the east coast. Pondicherry was about 150 kilometers south of Madras, on the Bay of Bengal. Michael wasn't worried about that leg; if he could make Madras, he could make Pondicherry. All he really was concerned about was getting to the Indian subcontinent. India has the best rail service in the world, in terms of number of trains going here and there. If not a train, then a bus. If not a bus, then a car and driver. If none of the above, he'd walk. It didn't matter. What mattered was Jellie Braden somewhere in the swirling crowds of India. If she wasn't in Pondicherry, he'd be in tough shape. She'd be almost impossible to track down if she decided just to lose herself out there. But, by God, he was going to try.

He called the British Airways 800 number. Yes, said the quite lovely, very British, very female voice at the reservations desk, that flight was still operating, but there were no openings for the next three weeks. Did Mr. Tillman want to be put on a waiting list? Yes. He called Air India again and also had them put him on a waiting list, with the date open. Anytime, he told them. Anytime.

Things to do. His mother first. He called her, and they talked for a long while. He'd never missed spending Christmas with her in the last twenty years but told her he had to go to India right away and didn't know when he'd be back.

Her ears were failing her, but she heard something in the way he spoke, urgency, intensity. "Michael, don't tell me you've finally found a special lady for yourself? I've never heard your voice sound quite like it does now. Is that it?"

"Mom, the answer is maybe. That's all I can say. It's just real important I do this thing—go to India—but I hate to miss Christmas with you, if it comes to that."

"Michael, thank you for caring and for asking. I'm glad we've gotten to be with each other as much as we have over the years. Go to India and find this lady, whoever she is. Then bring her home so I can meet her. I still haven't given up hope on having grandchildren, you know."

"Mom, I promise I'll come out to Custer as soon as I'm back, though I'm not sure when that will be."

"Fly on, Michael. If this is your moment, take it. Stop talking to me and get to India."

The departmental secretary was a first-rate person who knew the systems and ways to get around them. Michael always gave her a bottle of wine at Christmas and sent her flowers at the end of the academic year. She agreed to fill out his final grade sheets and forge his signature on them. She didn't even ask why. He asked her not to say anything, and she said, "Don't worry, you and I understand each other. Wherever you're going in such a hurry and whatever you're going to do when you get there, I'd like to be a fly on the wall." She finished her words with a strange little knowing smile.

Jimmy Braden had come back on Monday night. On Tuesday Michael announced to his classes they were shutting down that day. Since he wouldn't be giving a final examination, he told them everyone got one-half a grade higher than what the scores in his grade book currently showed. To hell with it, once in a while you're entitled to be flaky. Hats flew in the air, and a young woman's voice came from far back in the classroom: "We love you, Professor Tillman. Merry Christmas." He gave one of the MBA students who lived upstairs in his building a hundred bucks to make sure Malachi and Casserole were well cared for.

Travel light. Real light. He'd booked a flight to New York, but no reservations beyond, and he might get hung up anywhere on his way to India. New York, Moscow or London, Cairo or Athens. Anywhere. It might take him a week or more to get to India. Jimmy Braden could sit in Cedar Bend and pray and mope all he wanted. Jimmy had already told his story to at least five other people, so he was getting lots of sympathy.

But Michael was going to India to find Jellie, and he was going now. There was a reason she pulled out, and he had a pretty strong feeling it had something to do with him. Maybe not, but that's how he guessed it. People get lost in India. That's why a lot of them go there. He had to find Jellie before she just drifted off and, for whatever reason, retreated to a mountain commune or ashram in the boondocks where he'd never find her.

Old L.L. Bean knapsack. Three shirts, only one of them clean. Wear the clean one, blue denim. Jeans, one pair on the body and another pair in the bag, and some khakis. Wear bush jacket en route. Navy blue cotton sweater. Shoes? Wear the old field boots, take sandals, too. He could buy clothes in India if he needed them; the *khurtas* and some pajamalike bottoms underneath worked just fine for him. Other essentials, including a good map of the India subcontinent he'd purchased on his last visit, showing railroad and domestic air routes. Small flashlight, old cotton hat with the wide brim.

Damn, no malaria pills. Take the risk. No, have physician call the drugstore, pick them up on the way to the airport, even though he should have started taking them a week ago. Working hard, throwing clothes around the bedroom, folding shirts, rolling up the jeans and khakis with underwear and socks inside the roll, Malachi and Casserole watching. Jam the old pair of sandals in the top, cinch it up. The knapsack bulged. He hefted it—not too bad. Anything else? Small canteen. It can be a long time between drinkable water supplies in India.

The taxi came at eight A.M. on Thursday morning, sixty hours after Jimmy had sat at Michael's kitchen table, bawling his guts out. It was bizarre all right. Jimmy Braden was lurching around Bingley Hall telling people, in so many words, about how poorly Jellie had treated him, running off that way. And Michael was on his way to find her, but Jimmy didn't know that. A stop at the pharmacist's, another at the bank. Three thousand in American Express Cheques, $100 units. Five hundred in cash.

At the local airport, waiting for the commuter jet to Chicago, Michael remembered a detail he hadn't taken care of and called the departmental secretary. After he cleaned up the detail, she said,

"Michael, a cable for you just came in, hand-delivered."

He thought for a moment. This was dicey if it was from Jellie, which he had a feeling it might be. "Betty, read it to me, and I'm swearing you to secrecy ever after concerning the contents. Deal?"

"If I told everything I knew about what happens around here, Bingley Hall would implode in the world's largest cloud of dust. Besides, I have some vague sense of what's going on. I've seen your face change in the last few months. I saw you on your motorcycle out near Heron Lake early one morning not long ago, and I also saw who was riding behind you. But I've never said anything, and I won't. Now, I put that together with the weeping going on in Jimmy Braden's office—all over the building, for that matter—and it doesn't require a mathematical genius like you to make it add up."

"Betty, Betty, Betty . . . you may end up being one of the great loves of my life. Read me the cable."

"Okay, I'm opening the envelope. It says thirteen hundred hours. Let's see, that's . . ."

"That's one in the afternoon, Betty. What's the date?"

"It's today's date. How can that be?"

"Time difference. It was sent about one-thirty A.M. this morning, our time. What's it say?"

"It says, 'M, Please try to understand. There are feelings so strong within me I need space and

139

time to work them out. I'll be in touch sometime, I promise I will. J.' "

The hell with space and time, that's what Michael Tillman thought. Sometimes you let circumstances go their own direction, in the way Jimmy was doing, but sometimes you have to get in the middle of situations and manage them. He had a feeling Jellie was pretty confused, and he wasn't going to let her just wander off in a fog. If he screwed up her life by going to India to look for her, she'd have to live with it, and so would he. But he wasn't about to sit on his duff in Cedar Bend and hope for better days.

"Betty, where did the cable come from, what city?"

"Madras. Did I pronounce it right?"

"No, but that's okay. Everybody in the States gets it wrong. Betty, run the cable through your shredder, please."

"I will. Don't worry. And, Michael? . . ."

"Yes?"

"I'll be back here cheering for you. Go find her."

"Thanks, Betty. Do you prefer necklaces or bracelets?"

"You know that's not necessary. But I'd like a bracelet sometime from some exotic place, if you insist."

"Done. Good-bye, and thanks again. My plane is boarding."

" 'Bye, Michael. Good luck."

\* \* \*

At O'Hare he called Air India and had British Airways check to see if anything had opened up. Nothing. "What if I go down to the gate and see if there's a no-show?" he asked the woman running the British Airways counter.

"You can try." She looked at his ticket. "Your flight for New York leaves before ours departs for London. If you wait for us, you'll miss your New York flight."

"I'll chance it. I'm feeling lucky, somehow."

She shrugged and typed his name into the computer as a standby. "We're in the new United terminal, at the far end. Good luck."

He bought cigarettes and coffee, then went to the United terminal. An hour and fifteen minutes until British Airways 42 would leave for London. The passengers were lined up, long line winding back and along the terminal wall. Baggage . . . he never could understand why people carry so much. Huge suitcases tied with ropes. Christmas presents, bedrolls, tired kids with winter colds and runny noses tugging on their parents' hands, crying.

The line moved slowly. Twenty-five minutes before departure. Then twenty. Only two people left to check in. "Michael Tillman, Mr. Michael Tillman, please come to the British Airways podium."

He was there in four seconds.

"Mr. Tillman, we have a seat for you on the London flight departing in approximately fifteen minutes. However, we are not able to confirm a seat for you on flight 34 to Madras. Do you still want to go with us tonight?"

"Yes. I'll pay for the ticket with my Amex card."

Six hours later he was looking at Ireland down below in first light, and he thought of Jellie standing along a stone wall somewhere down there, having a Polaroid picture taken, which eventually hung on a wall in Iowa. Except the picture was now in the pocket of his bush jacket. If you're going to be a tracer of lost persons, a photo might be useful. He'd thought of that at the last moment and brought the photo with him.

Heathrow was chaotic, as usual. Michael passed up the transit lounge and went out into the main terminal, where he could look in the eyes of ticket agents. No problem. As the agent told him, people often book more than one flight under different names, and several cancellations had come in during the night.

"Do you wish to book a return flight from India, Mr. Tillman?"

He told her to put him down for January 12, a few days before the spring semester started. Indian officials strongly prefer you have a return ticket before a visa is issued. That's a precaution flowing partly from the old hippie days when Western kids went seeking truth and enlightenment and ended up being dope-smoking, social welfare problems for the Indian government.

Michael pulled out his Amex card, got the ticket, and located the tube into London. He told an official he needed a visa to India and was steered in the right direction. Three hours later he was back at Heathrow, through security, and sitting in the transit lounge. Five hours before his flight to Madras.

Time always moved pretty fast for Michael in big airports. He liked to watch people come and go, read a little, nap a little. After going into the restroom and washing his face, he bought a copy of the London *Times*, settled down on a chair, and put his feet on the knapsack. But he couldn't concentrate on the paper and fished the picture of Jellie out of his pocket. He sat there looking at it while the public address system summoned people to planes leaving for distant places. And somewhere out in those great spaces was a woman named Jellie Braden. She was out there, somewhere . . . somewhere.

# Nine

In spite of his smart-lip comment to Jellie one time, Michael Tillman was not jaded. Maybe a little cynical, probably more than he had a right to be, but not jaded. Never had been. That's an advantage coming down from the kind of childhood he spent. You grow up not expecting too much, so when good things happen in your life you're amazed they happened at all. Long-haul travel was that way for Michael. When the pilot came on the intercom and said they were passing over Baghdad, he looked down from his window seat and saw a brown city in the desert forty thousand feet below.

He'd done that before on his first trip to India,

thinking, Baghdad—I never thought I'd be flying over Baghdad. And he reached back like a mule skinner with a whip, pulling the memories forward, seeing himself working on the Shadow in his father's gas station thirty years before. Working on it and looking out at the highway and knowing the Vincent Black Shadow could take him down that road if he learned all there was to know about valves and turning wheels and highways running eastward.

When the plane was two hours out of Madras, Michael took his shaving kit out of the knapsack and went to one of the tiny restrooms. This kind of travel leaves a film on the body and mind, and he'd developed the custom of shaving and cleaning up before landing. Somehow that also cleaned up the mind a little.

The cabin was still dark, most people sleeping or trying to, a few reading lamps on. The flight attendants were talking quietly with one another in the midplane kitchen. He stuck his head in and asked for a cup of tea. They fixed him up, and he went back to his seat, steaming cup in hand, in good shape overall but with the special, taut feeling in his stomach he always got when approaching a distant place, particularly India.

He lifted the window shade and looked out. India coming up below, like a woman sprawled in the sun. Daylight, rugged brown hills, green splotches of jungle. The cabin lights came on, breakfast was announced. He didn't feel like eating much but puttered around with fruit and toast, knowing it might be a while before he ate again.

The plane came down over the jumbled spread of Madras, port city on the Bay of Bengal. Estimated population over four million. India treats such numbers casually, however, since the cities have a constant flow in and out, mostly in, of a wandering people. India is on the move, that's the dominant impression Michael always had. Look anywhere in the countryside or in the cities, and there are people walking, riding bicycles, hanging off roaring buses or leaning out of train windows. Moving . . . moving . . . India.

He walked in from the plane past men holding military rifles. Long line at the desk for those with foreign passports. Michael settled himself. You don't hurry India. India has its own style, its own pace, and high-strung Westerners who demand all tasks be carried out with speed and crisp efficiency don't do very well there. Warm and humid, and Michael was glad to be traveling light. The brown face above a dark green uniform looked at his passport, checked the ninety-day visa, and pounded the stamp.

Customs was no problem since Michael wasn't carrying anything of value except cash and traveler's checks. But he was bringing in more than $1,000 U.S., and a form was required. India loved forms, though Michael had always been skeptical about where these forms eventually found a home. It was hard to believe that a currency official somewhere actually paid attention to the millions of handwritten documents gushing from the pens of travelers: "Hmmm, I see that Michael Tillman from Cedar Bend, USA, brought thirty-five hundred dollars with him on 2 December. We'll need to keep track of him in this country with nearly one billion people and a telephone system that, at best, wobbles along."

Outside the protection of a large Indian airport, no rules applied. Touts, hundreds of them, pushing whatever could be imagined. Maybe a few rupees could be bilked from the tall white guy with the knapsack. Except he looked a little roadwise, no luggage, looked like a hard traveler. It would be better to move on to someone with a little more fat. Thousands of people were milling around, coming and going, many of them simply hanging on for the entertainment value provided by a major airport. The cops kept most of them outside the airport, where they pressed their faces against dusty glass and waited for passengers to exit.

A tourist desk in the lobby was actually open for business, which was a new twist. India was apparently working harder at getting gringos to come and leave some foreign exchange on their way through. On Michael's earlier visits, he had the clear sense nobody cared whether you came or didn't, whether you died in the customs line or went home.

The man at the desk spoke understandable English. Michael said he wanted to go to Pondicherry. The man told him it was a three-hour ride by car if the traffic was heavy and would be happy to arrange a car and driver for Michael. He quoted a price of $30 U.S. That sounded steep for India, and Michael said as much.

"Oooh, but you see, it is a six-hour round trip for the driver, since he must go to Pondicherry and come back empty. So you must pay for both ways."

Michael knew better. He knew the driver would hang around Pondicherry and maybe get a fare back to Madras. How about the guys outside with their cabs?

"Oooh, yes, sir, they will say they will take you for quite a lower price. But, sir, they are not quite reliable and may just take your money on the way, leaving you stranded." Michael knew the man was speaking with some accuracy.

How about buses? Trains? The tourist official rambled on, running his finger up and down grimy, complicated schedules, and Michael started thinking, C'mon, Tillman. For chrissake, what are you doing? You're here in a panic to find Jellie Braden, and you're standing around haggling over a few bucks. For a moment, the spurious masculine pride in cutting the sharp deal, which seemed to lie throbbing in the hormones until called upon, had caused him to lose his way. As it usually did.

The official arranged a car and driver, telling

Michael to wait by the tourist desk. Michael asked the man if he had a guide to Pondicherry, maps, anything at all. The man produced a torn little magazine from under the counter, which he claimed was his only copy (Michael believed him) and started looking through it. A lecture on Pondicherry followed concerning the famous ashram founded there by a mystic-philosopher-poet-patriot named Sri Aurobindo, about hotels and restaurants and the beauty of the seawall.

Was there a city map in the booklet? Yes, there was one, indeed, sir, a very nice map. Michael laid a five-dollar bill on the counter, keeping most of it covered with his hand, and said he'd very much like to take the Pondicherry guide with him. It was Michael's in less than a second, and his driver in a smudged white outfit came up to the counter, smiling.

Outside, the sun was a hammer. Other taxi drivers swung open their doors and said they would take Michael to wherever he was going for half of what the fellow in the smudged white uniform was charging. Michael said thanks, but he'd already booked a car. After that they stopped smiling and were not his friends anymore.

As Michael's car pulled away from the airport, the driver began rubbing his thumb and forefinger together in the universal symbol for legal tender and pointed at his gas gauge, all the while saying, "Petrol." Indian taxi drivers were always running on empty, and he needed an advance. On Michael's last trip, two drivers had run out of gas while he was riding with them.

Impatient, Michael tapped his foot while the tank was being filled. He noticed a fruit stand nearby and bought three bananas and two oranges, which he stuffed into the side pockets of his knapsack. Back in the car he waited for the driver. A ragged man bent down and looked in the window, displaying the grisly stump of an arm severed just above the elbow. Michael gave him five rupees. The man touched his forehead and backed away.

Finally they were rolling through the noise and smoke and dust that was India and would always be India. Michael's nose was still adjusting to the thick odors—smoke from factories and open cooking fires, leaded gas, excrement from humans and animals, all of it mixed together and forming the dense and penetrating smell defining India. He never completely lost that smell. Michael noticed when he watched a travelogue on India back in Cedar Bend, his brain immediately pulled up those old India smells from wherever the memories of smells are stored. No other country had drilled its odors into him in the way India had.

The women. He'd temporarily forgotten how beautiful were the Indian women, even the poorest ones. It was easy to fall in transient love every few seconds in India. A superb gene pool, male and female alike, maybe the best gene pool in the world when it came to physical appearance. Orange saris and green saris, red ones and blue ones, and gold upon their bodies, bracelets on their arms and combs in their hair. The women were lithe and walked just above the earth, so it seemed. Some with gold or silver chains running from nose to ear.

He watched them as the driver constantly honked at goats and cattle and people, weaving through traffic, waved on by cops standing on small pedestals at the busier intersections. Into the countryside on a two-lane, severely bruised black-top. Ashok and Tata trucks with workmen riding on top, their headwraps blowing in the wind. Buses careening around the curves, bullock carts in front of them, an old woman pedaling a wheelchair contraption in the other lane, people walking, herds of goats crossing.

The driver turned up his radio, giving him and Michael the sound of a flute and drummers playing complex rhythms on tablas beneath it. He pounded the horn and made the occult Indian hand signals telling other drivers what his intentions were. India: moving . . . moving . . . tablas and flutes and dust, the road in front looking like a ragtag caravan put together with all the travelers and vehicles from the last five hundred years.

Michael held a banana over the front seat. The driver took it and gave Michael a flash of perfect white teeth, leaned on his horn, and peeled the banana, hot air roaring in through the open windows. They entered a town, and Michael unfolded his map of India. Must be Chengalpattu. They'd be going slightly southwest to Madurantakam and then would make a southeast turn at Tindivanam, where a small blue line ran over to Pondicherry on the Bay of Bengal.

Michael thumbed the five-dollar Pondicherry guide, looking at confusing street maps, reading the town's history. It was a union territory, a city-state much like Washington, D.C. The state of Tamil Nadu on its west, the bay on its east. Settled by French traders in the seventeenth century, returned to India in 1954. Jellie, are you there along the streets of Pondicherry? On the off chance she had ridden with this same driver to Pondicherry, if she had gone to Pondicherry at all, Michael took out her picture and handed it to the driver.

The driver looked at it, turned his head, and grinned, shouting over the wind and flute music, "Pretty lady. You go see her in Pondy?"

Michael worked back down into pidgin English. "Lady ride this car?" He pointed at Jellie in the photo, then at the driver and the interior of the car. Michael said it again: "Pretty lady ride this car?"

It took the driver a second, but he got the meaning and shook his head. "No, no see lady." Michael nodded and put the photo back in his bush jacket.

The guide said Pondicherry had a population of 150,000, but Michael knew that was probably a best guess, far under the true count. Where to start? Like all Indian cities, he figured it would be a maze of little streets and complex buildings tied in with one another via walkways and alleys. Even if she was in Pondy, it was not going to be easy. The ashram attracted people from all over the world who came to study the teachings of Sri Aurobindo and his consort, a French woman known only as "the Mother." Both of them were dead. But, according to the guide, the ashram flourished. A visionary settlement called Auroville, also known as the City of Dawn, supposedly fashioned around the teachings of Aurobindo and the Mother, had been developing for over a decade just outside of Pondicherry. The guide quoted Mother: "Auroville will be a site of material and spiritual researches for a living embodiment of an actual Human Unity."

That sounded like Jellie. Anthropologists, many of them, at least, had a strong inclination toward matters of the spirit, something to do with their trade. If Jellie was running and seeking spiritual guidance, the ashram and Auroville might be a good place to start.

He'd need a place to stay and looked at advertisements in the guide as the driver swerved and honked and signaled.

Ajantha Guest House—An Oasis of Luxury
Hotel Aristo—A Touch of Class, Truly an Aristocratic Experience

Hotel Ram International—It's a Whole New
 World

To the Western eye and ear, Indians had a
penchant for overstatement, not to mention hyper-
bole, and Michael discounted heavily what he read.
Not that he was fussy. He'd stayed many nights in
small Indian hotels where a hole in the floor worked
as a toilet and the shower was cold, if there was a
shower at all. After a few nights, however, he'd
forget there was any other way than cold showers
and a hole in the floor, and it all worked just fine.
A hot shower, in traditional south Indian terms,
would justify the claim "Truly an Aristocratic Experience."

He concentrated on Jellie, thinking hard about
her ways and what he knew of her preferences.
Where would she stay? The Park Guest House was
part of the ashram and had a Spartan attitude toward smoking, liquor, and human weaknesses in
general. Jellie had come to think things over, according to her cable, and the guest house with
its gardens, vegetarian restaurant, and meditative
overtones spoke to that way of life.

Initially Michael thought that finding Jellie,
if she was in Pondicherry, would not be all that
difficult. White skin stood out in most of India.
But it was a much larger town than he'd anticipated, and the guide stated many Westerners came
to bathe in the rarefied spirit of Sri Aurobindo and
the Mother. And, as Michael had already consid-

ered, it was easy to get lost in India if that's what you wanted. India could present a silent, impenetrable face when it chose, leaving you on the outside with no view to the interiors. Jellie was an old India hand, apparently with good connections, and would know how to conceal herself if she made up her mind to do that.

If you were in a hurry, India could be infuriating. The driver decided lunch was in order at Madurantakam. He pulled over and went up to an outdoor food stand. Michael wasn't hungry but drank a cup of tea and ate one of the Snickers he'd bought in Heathrow. People gathered around him at a respectful distance and stared; routine curiosity, nothing more.

The sun was high and hard at noon. He clumped the old cotton hat on his head, fending off the kids who were less circumspect than their elders and wanted something, anything, from him. He bought some more oranges and handed them around, though the kids would have preferred something more wondrous, such as a cheap ballpoint pen from America. Sweat soaked through his shirt, ran down his chest and back. Michael was wiping his face and neck with a red bandanna when the driver signaled it was time to leave.

Forty-five minutes later they made the turn at Tindivanam and headed southeast toward Pondicherry, running along a rough surface in worse shape than the road they'd just left. This was semiarid land, palm trees arching over the road. People were spreading stalks of grain on the pavement, drying the grain, and letting vehicle wheels act as kind of a primitive threshing machine.

Outskirts of Pondicherry. The map fastened in the back of the city guide indicated they were coming in on Jawaharlal Nehru Street, apparently one of the main thoroughfares. Michael decided against staying at the ashram's guest house, mostly because he wasn't sure how Jellie might feel if he suddenly showed up. If she saw him before he saw her, she might retreat with whatever secrets she carried and become impossible to find once she knew he was here looking for her.

The Grand Hotel d'Europe at Number 12 Rue Suffren was in the same general area as most of the ashram's workshops and not far from the guest house. It was run by an old Frenchman, a Monsieur Maigrit, according to the guide. Michael suspected the food would be continental, which suited him fine, since he tended to burn down pretty fast on a straight Indian diet.

Michael motioned for the driver to pull over and showed him the map. The driver had trouble reading it, started talking rapidly, pointing ahead. Michael let him go on, and they halted at a busy street corner where two hundred bicycles waited for a green light. The driver got out with the map and talked to several men standing in front of a tea shop. Arms waved, heads shook, hands pointed.

All of this went on for a minute or two before the driver returned. He said something Michael didn't understand, zigzagging his hand, which Michael took to mean they should work their way through the city and then turn right.

That seemed to fit, based on the map. They plowed up the busy main drag of Pondy and eventually hit a dead end at Rue St. Louis. The driver got out, went through the arms–head–hand language again, and came back to the car. A right turn, then skirting a large park on whose benches sat both Indians and aging French Legionnaires by the looks of their caps. A few blocks farther on another right, then a left. Painted on a building were the words *Rue Suffren*. Number 12 came up a half block later.

Michael knocked on the high wooden gate. An old Indian man in tan shorts and a white head-wrap peeked out. Michael said, "Room?"

The gatekeeper glanced at the car and driver, then back at the tall American with wrinkled clothes and no luggage except a knapsack. Almost reluctantly he swung the gate open and indicated Michael should come into the courtyard. It was an old building, covered with vines and bougainvillea. Maigrit, Michael assumed it was him, came out of a doorway. Michael bowed slightly. "Do you have a room for a tired traveler?"

Maigrit looked at him, said nothing. Michael had arrived without prior reservations, which was probably considered a serious breach of decorum. Michael didn't speak much French, having forgotten most of what he'd learned as part of his Ph.D. language requirement. But he smiled the good midwestern smile that seemed to get him by in most of the world and gave it a try: "*Je voudrais une chambre?*"

Maigrit smiled back, recognizing incompetence but approving of the effort. Yes, a room was available for 150 rupees, about 9 dollars a night. Michael figured with advance reservations and a little haggling he could have knocked it down about a third or maybe half, but he was tired, and the location suited him.

Maigrit informed him the daily afternoon water shutoff was in progress, so a bath was not possible, but the *boy*, who was about seventy-five, would bring a small bucket of water if Monsieur Tillman wanted to wash up. Michael thanked him and said that would be appreciated. And was laundry service available? Shirts could be washed, ironed, and returned in four hours for double the normal price. The regular price was six cents a shirt.

The boy delivered water, took the shirts, and Michael washed his face, then lay down on the bed and thought. Home was forty-six hours behind, though his internal abacus lied and said it was longer, years maybe. A week ago he'd been sitting in his apartment waiting for Jellie to return from

Syracuse. Ten days ago she lay naked on his kitchen table while he rubbed red wine over her breasts. "Jellie, are you somewhere on the other side of these walls, close by, living out what you never want me to know?"

# Ten

Michael awakened a little before six when the old man rapped on his door. He'd slept for nearly four hours and got up feeling hot and stiff and road weary. He opened the door, took the shirts, and gave the man a tip. The old man bowed and left, looking back at Michael over his shoulder.

Michael checked the faucets. The water had come back on, and he was a little surprised when the left tap gave him a warm stream. He ran a small tub, shaved, and got himself presentable with a clean body, clean shirt, and fresh pair of Levi's.

The proprietor was on the veranda, reading a French newspaper. What Michael needed first was flexible transportation, a motorcycle. He'd seen a number of smaller bikes when the driver brought him through town. Yes, a small motorcycle could be rented at a location on Mahatma Gandhi Road. Maigrit had the gatekeeper call a bicycle rickshaw for Michael and spoke in Tamil to the rickshaw man, giving him the address. Maigrit said the ride would cost a quarter, and a dime tip would be about right.

Michael watched the bulging leg muscles of the man pedaling him through the streets of Pondicherry. Unlike some Westerners who had never traveled in these places and frowned on the use of rickshaws as something next to slavery, Michael didn't see it that way. If you asked the rickshaw man how he felt about it, he wouldn't understand the question. It was how he made his living, and he was quite happy to deliver you somewhere for a fee. It was called participating in the local economy. As Michael once told a colleague who disdained such colonialist behavior, "Pay the rickshaw man New York cab fare, maybe it will make you feel more politically correct." Taxi or rickshaw, it was all a matter of muscle power with differences in the degree of it used.

India was, in many ways, an evening country. The heat and dust settled down late in the day, and the streets were crowded. Merchants stayed open late. Time then for long, leisurely dinners and laughter in the cafes, commencing around nightfall. The rickshaw man turned left on Sastry Street, pedaling a straight line toward MG Road. Michael sat there feeling exposed, not wanting Jellie to see him coasting along through the streets of Pondi-cherry.

Christ, he thought, how strange this is. Here I am looking for a woman with whom I've made love, a woman who rolls in pleasure beneath my touch and says over and over again how much she loves me. Yet I'm worried about her seeing me. It's a curious world, Michael Tillman. That's what he said to himself as the rickshaw bumped along through the south India twilight.

The motorcycle rental outfit was located in a little garage next to the Cool Cat Coffee Bar with grease everywhere and parts scattered about. Michael felt at home. Two machines leaned against the door, two more were torn down inside. Michael could have either of the two by the door. He looked them over. They were rough as the roads they traveled and pretty well banged up. The old Kawasaki looked like it might run, and after a few kicks he had it going. The proprietor stood watching him, hands on hips, not smiling. Michael pointed to tools on the workbench.

Ten minutes later he had the chain tightened and the carburetor adjusted. The garage man was grinning. Technical competence always brought respect. Michael paid a fifty-dollar deposit and re-calibrated his mind to driving on the left-hand side of the road, then took the Kawasaki out into evening traffic, running easy until he got the feel of driving in what always seemed the wrong way.

He took the same route back to the hotel as he'd come, picking up two plastic containers of bottled water on the way, and parked the bike in the courtyard. Tonight he'd walk. When the search needed to be expanded or he had to get somewhere in a hurry, the bike would take him there.

Maigrit greeted him and said what a handsome machine Michael had found. Michael took out the picture of Jellie and said he was looking for her.

Maigrit looked at it, then at Michael, and asked, "*Amour?*" Michael smiled and nodded. Maigrit was sorry, but he'd never seen her. "There are many Western women who come here to participate in the ashram. They look for comfort and inner peace, perhaps a new way of life."

The Frenchman no longer operated a restaurant in his hotel, but if Michael wanted continental food, the Alliance Française was not far, just opposite the Park Guest House. It was a club, though membership rules were not tightly enforced. Simply walk through the gate, cross the courtyard, and go up the steps.

Michael thought twice about going there. He wasn't too worried about running into Jellie, because he figured she wanted to sink back into Indian ways and would take her meals at Indian restaurants or, more likely, cook for herself. But word moved fast in these Indian towns, and he had a feeling the Western community would pass the news about a newcomer who wore jeans and sandals and seemed to be looking for someone.

But he was hungry and wasn't ready for Indian cuisine yet, so he walked through quiet streets in the direction the Frenchman had directed him. A few people sat on steps in this section of the city, but most of the houses were behind high walls. Two white men with shaved heads and wearing saffron-colored wraps, bare legs poking out from thigh level down, went by in the opposite direction, paying no attention to Michael.

He turned left on Rue Bazare St. Laurent, missed his right turn on Rue Dumas, and came to Cours Chabrol—Beach Road—running along the seawall. The night breeze was kind, and Michael stood in the shadows at the end of Rue Bazare St. Laurent without crossing over to the seawall. The walkways were crowded with evening strollers. Off to his right, just up the road, was the gated entrance to the Park Guest House, the ashram's hotel.

When two Western women in Indian dress came along the sidewalk, he turned around, heading back up the street he had just come down, feeling odd, as if he were involved in an international espionage operation. Jellie, what have you done to me? I was content, if not supremely happy, before we met, and here I am walking the back streets of India looking for you, and in some small part of me not wanting to find you, fearful of what you might say, of what you might tell me you are going to do with the rest of your life.

A guard stood at the Alliance Française's gate. Michael pointed at his own chest, then pointed inside and said, "Restaurant?"

The guard nodded and motioned him through the gate. There were trees and flowers in the courtyard. Off to one side was a cement platform where an Indian woman was dancing to the rhythm of a drummer sitting cross-legged in the shadows behind her.

No one else was in the courtyard, but he could hear an accordion playing a French song in the building ahead of him. Michael watched the dancer for a moment. She was oblivious of him, stopping after a moment and speaking to the drummer, who then started off again in a slightly different rhythm.

The first floor of the place had a unisex bathroom and a black-and-white photography exhibition hanging on its gray walls. Music and laughter came from the floor above, and he went up the stairs into the restaurant. Half of it was covered, the rest was open to the night. Waiters were moving rapidly around in white uniforms, and a young Indian in dark slacks and purple shirt came toward Michael, speaking in French. Michael smiled and said, "Dinner, please?"

"Just one, monsieur?" His English was very good.

Michael nodded.

"Do you prefer indoors or outside?"

"Outside, please."

The maître d' seated Michael at a small table off in a corner. Michael's entrance caused a few curious heads to turn, but the laughter and eating and drinking quickly resumed. He ordered beer and a chicken brochette from the open-flame barbecue built into the wall across the room from where he was seated. Stars were out, the scent of jasmine came on the night wind, and he sat there alone, staring at his hands.

The food was excellent, served with rice and French bread. And chocolate cake with good strong coffee afterward. He was starting to feel somewhat whole again. On his way out, an older man had taken over the maître d' role. When Michael walked over to him, the man smiled warmly.

"Did you enjoy your dinner?"

Michael told him it was very good, then showed him the picture of Jellie. The maître d' looked at it, then at Michael, repeated those two moves, and stopped smiling.

"Have you seen her?" Michael asked.

The maître d' stared at him and didn't answer.

"I'm looking for her; it's very important I find her."

The man lit a cigarette, looked at the picture again, then handed it back to Michael. "Long time ago, maybe."

"How long? A week? How long?"

"Long time. Ten, fifteen years. It's hard to say; the woman I'm thinking of was much younger. Excuse me, I have work to do."

Michael took a deep breath and wondered. The man had looked at him and the photo, friendliness turning to curt dismissal afterward, almost as if the maître d' recognized Jellie's picture and wanted to be done with Michael as soon as possible. Michael walked back to his hotel through dark, quiet streets, still wondering.

For two days he wandered Pondicherry with no organized search strategy. On the third day he took the bike out to Auroville, but it was spread out over miles, little settlements and houses scattered about. If she was there, he'd never find her. In early evenings he sat on the seawall near the ashram guest house and watched traffic coming for the evening meal. He tried talking with the austere woman guarding the front desk of the guest house, but that was useless. People came there to get away and be left alone. When Michael showed her the photo of Jellie, the woman shook her head and went back to her ledgers.

He was getting nowhere and asked Maigrit for directions to the college he'd read about in the guide. Maigrit ran his finger along the street map, showing Michael the location and how to get there. Michael wheeled the Kawasaki out of the hotel courtyard, kicked the starter, and rolled north through the city.

The college was in a shabby section of Pondicherry. Cruising around the small campus, Michael saw a weathered sign reading "Department of Management." Time to flash the credentials. He introduced himself to a secretary, telling her who he was and where he was from. This was a situation where titles would help. Indians loved credentials and respected professors only a little less than credentials. She went down a hallway into an office, coming back in less than a minute, followed by a short, round, Indian man in his fifties. He wore glasses and a necktie reaching about halfway down his chest.

Friendly smile. "Ah, Dr. Tillman, how good of you to call on us."

He wanted to know all about Michael's academic life. Michael ran the list of degrees and experience, impatient to get on with the reason he'd come. But India observed its courtesies with a fair amount of pomp, and he was bound to reciprocate. Before long they were joined by two economists, with tea served by the secretary shortly after. One of the professors excused himself, saying he would return momentarily. When he did, a copy of *The Atlantic* was in his hand. It was opened to Michael's article on tax incentives. He pointed to the article, then at Michael. "And did you write this, Dr. Tillman?" Michael nodded. The professor smiled then, big smile. "Quite a brilliant piece of work. Very nice indeed."

Credibility had been established, Michael was on his home ground, and these were bright, decent people he was dealing with. He told them about searching for Jellie, leaving out the background details, saying only it was extremely important he locate her. They didn't recognize her photo, but when Michael mentioned Jellie's interest in anthropology, the department head called to his secretary and spoke to her out in the hall.

"I have requested my secretary summon one of the anthropology professors to talk with you. There are many projects in anthropology going on in Pondicherry. The French especially have strong interests in those areas, having established an institute some years ago with which our college cooperates."

In ten minutes a woman appeared in the office doorway. She was fortyish and wore a pink sari. The department head stood, introducing her as Dr. Dhavale, professor of anthropology. The photo of Jellie, which was becoming a little shopworn after being held by a hundred hands in the last few days, was lying on the desk. Immediately the anthropology professor picked it up, glanced at it, then looked at Michael.

His heartbeat went up twenty points. "Is there any chance you know the woman in the picture?"

The professor's face was cautious. "You say your name is Tillman? Michael Tillman?"

"Yes."

"From a place called Cedar Bend?"

His pulse jumped another ten points. "Yes."

"May Dr. Tillman and I have words in private, please?" She was addressing the department head.

"Oh, yes, of course, Dr. Dhavale. Dr. Tillman, could we impose upon you to give a lecture or two while you are in town? I know our students and faculty would very much appreciate it."

They'd been helpful. Saying no was a problem, a matter of both courtesy and gratitude. "Dr. Ramani, I will be happy to do that sometime. First, however, I must not delay in finding Mrs. Braden. When I have done that, may I contact you and set up the lectures if I am going to be in Pondicherry?"

"Yes, yes, certainly. We understand, though we are disappointed you must hurry off. Please let us know when you can lecture for us, and we will set up a very nice afternoon with a reception afterwards."

Michael said he'd do that and followed Dr. Dhavale out of the building across a courtyard into another building, where her tiny office was located. For the first time in seventy-two hours he did not feel tired.

She sat across her desk from him, black eyes bold and cool, sizing him up. "Jellie Markham and I became friends years ago, during the time she was here for her thesis work." She used Jellie's maiden name and the French pronunciation with the soft

j—JahLAY—for her first name. "We have corres-
ponded with each other through the years and have
remained close."

Michael said nothing but began to understand
how dumb he'd been for the last three days, using
Jellie's married name and the American pronunciation of her Christian name. Even if someone had
known her, they wouldn't have recognized the
names he was giving them if she'd assumed the
French version when she lived in Pondicherry. And
that would make sense, given the heavy French
atmosphere permeating the city.

"Dr. Dhavale, I'm forty-three. It took a lot of
years for me to be able to feel about someone the
way I feel about Jellie. I care for her, I need to find
her, I need your help to do it."

The anthropologist studied him as if she were
deciding on a final course grade. "I do not wish to
violate her confidence, so I'm not sure of how
much to say, Dr. Tillman. But I know Jellie has
strong feelings for you. She has lived a complicated
life, more complicated than you can imagine. But
those details are for her to tell you when she
chooses. She sent a letter to you, giving you my
name and address in case you wanted to contact
her. But I don't think she anticipated you would
show up on my doorstep. Did you receive her
letter?"

"No. I must have left before it arrived in Cedar
Bend. I found you quite by accident."

"This is very difficult for me, Dr. Tillman, please understand that. I want to help you, but I do not wish to upset Jellie and ruin our friendship by saying what I shouldn't. I know she felt bad about not saying a proper good-bye to you." Chitra Dhavale looked out the only window in her office, dusty window, then turned back to Michael. "She left several days ago for Thekkady. Do you know of it?"

"No."

"It is a village quite near a beautiful place called Lake Periyar. Jellie told me you spent time in south India, so I thought you might have heard of it. She is staying with people named Sudhana who live in the countryside near Thekkady."

"May I ask what she is doing there? Do you know?"

"Yes, I know, but that is part of what is not my place to tell you, and I am afraid I have already violated her confidence by saying what I have said."

"What is the best way to Thekkady? The best route?"

"You could go back to Madras and fly to Cochin or Madurai, taking a car after that. Perhaps a better, though more tiring way is to take the early afternoon train out of Pondicherry. It is a meter-gauge railway, so you ride it just down to Villupuram Junction, which is approximately forty kilometers from here. From there you take the

*Trivandrum Mail* southward and get off in Madurai. After that you can either take a bus or hire a car and driver to take you on to Thekkady. It is an arduous trip, Dr. Tillman, but it is probably the quickest route. Your other alternative, flying out of Madras, may be frustrating. You might arrive there and not be able to find a seat on a flight for several days."

She looked at her watch. "It's a little before twelve. If you hurry, Dr. Tillman, you can catch the one o'clock train to Villupuram. I have a feeling you are anxious to be on your way, am I not correct?" She gave him a warm, Indian-woman smile. "If you find Jellie Markham, please tell her of my distress over this and ask her to forgive me if I have done wrong by telling you where she is."

"I will. Thank you, Dr. Dhavale."

As he went out her office door, Chitra Dhavale said, "Dr. Tillman?" He turned, paused.

"Jellie may be using the name Velayudum instead of Braden or Markham. Don't ask me why. Just accept what I have told you. And I should add this: If you find her, things may seem somewhat strange and perhaps quite disappointing, or at least unsettling to you. As I said before, Jellie has lived a complicated life."

So it was the *Trivandrum Mail* south to Madurai and a car westward after that.

# Eleven

hekkady lies on the border between the states of Tamil Nadu and Kerala, in the high country of southwest India. On the edge of town is a gate across the road, a red bar that reminded Michael of the old Checkpoint Charlie in Berlin. The driver halted and went into a small office near the road. Any moment Michael expected to hear Richard Burton's voice speaking the words from a John Le Carré novel, something about a man coming in from the East tonight.

All hell broke loose in the office. The driver showed his papers, but apparently crossing from one state to another in this area was pretty much the same as going from one country to the next.

From what Michael could make out, the Kerala authorities refused to honor the much trumpeted, all-India driver's license.

Michael got out, leaned against the car. More words that turned into shouting and what sounded like threats. He pointed to the bar, lifted his knapsack, and asked with sign language if he could cross. It was more complicated than he'd thought, requiring a twenty-dollar bill in the hand of the border official to get him through after paying off the driver. Baksheesh, it's called, and it was everywhere and always had been.

Cool mountain air and thin yellow sunlight, quiet village in midafternoon, dusty road. Michael walked down it, his boots leaving deep footprints. "Hey, boss, you go lake?" The young Indian man was standing by a jeep.

Michael looked at a name scribbled in his pocket notebook, then walked over to the jeep man and said, "Maybe. Find people called Sudhana, first."

"No, boss, we go lake only." He whacked the side of the jeep. "Two hundred rupees for ride. Pretty place there."

It might be pretty, but that wasn't where Michael was going. He held up three one-hundred-rupee bank notes. "Find house of Sudhana, first. Then two hundred more if I want to go to the lake." It turned out maybe the jeep didn't have to go to the lake after all.

The young man was in no hurry and started talking to several others hanging around. They looked at Michael and laughed. The young bastards were always brave in groups. They knew he had cash, big cash to them. Stuck in his belt, under his wrinkled bush jacket, was a short-bladed hunting knife he carried in these parts of the world. He could feel the handle pressing into his back.

A few years ago he'd held the knife against the throat of a taxi driver late one night in Mysore, north of here, when things were getting rough and a crowd of young smart-asses was encouraging the driver to dump him and a female companion out of the cab. When the Mysore driver felt the blade against his skin he let out the clutch as if he were having a muscle spasm, knocking two of the smart boys on their rears.

An older man came out of a store, shouting. From what Michael could tell, the man owned the jeep and was ordering a general shaping up and getting on with business. There was chatter in multiple dialects, the name *Sudhana* mentioned several times. The older man sketched on a piece of cardboard and handed it to the younger one, who had called Michael "boss." He walked over to the jeep, grinning, patting the jump seat, and motioning with his head for Michael to climb in. The young one and another bundle of insolence about the same age got in the front seats.

They bounced off down the dirt road and

turned south onto a different road running high above the eastern side of a fast mountain stream. More turns, winding around a low mountain, then left up a smaller road. The driver slammed to a stop in front of a house with tin patches on the sides and roof. "Sudhana, there—" He pointed. "Cigarettes?"

Michael gave them each an American cigarette, which was something of a luxury in these parts. Both lit up immediately, and Michael walked on unsteady legs toward the house. The old doubts? Was this the place? Was he doing the right thing? Jellie, don't turn me away, don't do that. Whatever is going on, let me be part of it.

The forehead and eyes of a crone appeared over a windowsill, then disappeared immediately when she saw the good-size white man walking toward her. "Sudhana?" Michael called out. Nothing. "Jellie? Jellie, it's Michael." Still nothing. Then slowly the door opened a crack, and the old woman looked out. She spoke rapidly in words he didn't understand. "Jellie . . . JahLAY. Jellie . . . JahLAY." He said her name over and over again, then added the surname he had been told she might be using, and the words were strange on his tongue. "Jellie *Velayudum*. JahLAY *Velayudum*."

The woman shook her head, spoke rapidly in a croaking voice, and pointed in a direction that looked as if it were inside the house. Christ, had something happened or what? Was Jellie lying in there?

The driver swaggered over to where Michael was trying to climb the wall between cultures. "Cigarette, boss? I know what old woman is saying." More baksheesh. You get a little tired of it after a while. It's not the money or the smokes, it's the bloody damned arrogance, the use of leverage.

Michael gave him half a pack of Merits. "She say woman called JahLAY Velayudum is at old hunting lodge in the middle of the lake, place called Lake Palace Hotel. You want go there?"

Michael nodded, and the driver flipped his head toward the jeep. They went down around the mountain and got on the road along the river again. Seven minutes later the jeep came over a rise, and Lake Periyar looked blue and calm in the distance.

The jeep driver dropped Michael off at the Aranya Nivas Hotel, a hundred yards from the lakeshore. He asked for more cigarettes, and Michael told him to stuff it. Michael Tillman was tired of smart young bastards, whatever country they came from, and said as much. He'd been too passive, too intent on finding Jellie, putting up with too much nonsense. The driver retreated in the face of Michael's anger, shrugged his shoulders, and backed his jeep out of the hotel driveway.

Michael went inside, grubby and tired. The woman at the desk was perfectly done, turquoise sari and a face that would launch a thousand Porsches back in the States. She was polite and efficient, and he was ready for some of that. He asked about the Lake Palace Hotel. She told him it was an old maharajah's hunting lodge with only six guest rooms and that reservations were handled here at the Aranya Nivas. While she flipped through a reservations book, Michael stared at a photograph on the wall behind her. It was slightly faded, but still a beautiful shot of a tiger coming out of tall grass on a foggy morning and carried the signature *Robert Kincaid*.

The clerk said there were rooms available for the next four nights. After that it was completely booked for a week. Three continental meals each day were included in the price.

The big question. He asked it: "I'm supposed to meet a woman at the Lake Palace. I wonder if she has checked in yet. Her first name is Jellie . . . JahLAY. I believe she is registered under the name Velayudum, though she might be using Markham or Braden." It all sounded rather suspicious, vaguely clandestine, but he had decided to cover all the bases.

"Three of the rooms are currently occupied out there." She looked up at him. "And you say you are to meet someone?"

"Yes. My arrival date, however, was uncertain."

"I have a Velayudum listed here. There are two people registered under that name."

Michael staggered inside himself. All the months, all the miles, the dreams. Forty-three, and he was standing there looking stupid while Jellie was registered under an Indian name and sharing the room with someone, most likely a man named Velayudum from somewhere back in her India days. Jellie—all the things I don't know about you.

Michael would always remember how alone he felt at that moment, incredibly alone and lonely and discarded. It must have shown, because the woman asked, "Sir, would you still like a room at the Lake Palace?"

He could go back to Madurai, fly to Madras, and change his homeward flight. Then he thought, This is foolish male vanity you're suffering, Tillman. You're not thinking clearly, afraid of what you might find in the middle of the lake. You're not going anywhere except out to that hotel and hit the end of this at full speed, if that's what it comes to.

"Put me down for one night, please. The hotel is on an island, is that correct?"

"Yes, we call it an island. There is a narrow strip of swamp connecting it to the mainland. It's approximately a twenty-minute boat ride from the jetty."

"What boat, what jetty?"

"Go out the front door, turn right, and walk down the path. You'll see a small building with a sign reading 'Periyar Wildlife Sanctuary.' Purchase your boat ticket there. The ticket agent will direct you to the proper boat. The island is in one of India's largest tiger preserves, and since you will be staying there you must also purchase an entrance permit to the preserve. If you want to take a safari into the jungle, you can make arrangements for a guide at the same time you purchase your boat ticket. Without a guide, you will not be allowed to leave the hotel grounds, since there are large animals about and it is much too dangerous."

As Michael turned to leave he asked, "Was the photograph behind you taken here?"

"Yes, on the island where the Lake Palace is located. I'm told the photographer who took it came here often some years ago and always stayed at the Lake Palace."

Down the path to the sanctuary office. Hundreds of Indian tourists milling around on the jetty below and several old excursion boats rocking in the water. Michael handed the room voucher to a wildlife officer at the office. He issued a boat ticket, saying Michael should show his hotel voucher to the pilot of the *Miss Lake Periyar*. The pilot would then drop him off at the hotel.

It was a mess. Travel was never easy in India, and this was something altogether different. There were three excursion boats, two of them in the process of loading, one already packed with Indian tourists. Two hundred future boat passengers, porters, and assorted hangers-on were packed on the jetty. The loaded boat had *Miss Lake Periyar* painted on its starboard side.

He fought his way through the crowd, got on

the boat, and showed one of the hands the hotel voucher. The man seemed disinterested but nodded and indicated with a toss of his head that Michael should find a seat. The dominant feeling permeating all travel in India was one of ambiguity, and Michael had serious doubts as to whether the pilot would be notified he was to be dropped at the hotel.

The boat was constructed with two levels, a glassed-in first level and an open upper deck. There were no seats left, but there was shouting and laughter and calls to those left on the jetty, the sum of which was pandemonium. Children ran up and down the steps between the first and second levels, people got off the boat to talk to those left behind, then got back on again.

The boathand Michael had talked to was making a reasonable attempt at crowd control but was failing miserably, overwhelmed by the crush. How, Michael wondered, could any animals be spotted along the shore, if that indeed was the main thrust of the boat tour. The boat would sound like pharaoh's army coming over the water toward them.

The boathand got tough when the engine turned over. He ordered people to sit down and stay seated. Michael checked again, but every seat on the boat was filled, so he hunkered down on the steps leading to the upper deck with a young boy sitting on the step just below his feet. The boy twisted his neck and looked at him while Michael stared out over the water.

The boat moved away from the jetty and chugged slowly down the huge, narrow lake, a reservoir stretching for miles behind the Periyar Dam, constructed by the British in 1895. A narration came from small loudspeakers mounted at various places on the boat, sometimes in English, sometimes in one of the Indian languages, telling the passengers they might see various animals ranging from leopards to tigers to elephants to wild pigs. Michael figured if they saw any animals at all, they'd be flopped down in laughter at the strange mammals packed onto an old green contraption that should've sunk twenty years ago.

Late afternoon now, sun dropping. Michael's boat and the two eventually following were the last sight-seeing runs of the day. Heavy jungle along the shore except for fifty feet or so of bare dirt running down to the water in some places. Michael stood up for a moment and could see a high hill with trees, looking as though it sat hard and straight in the boat's course.

Ten minutes later the boathand shook Michael's knee and said, "Lake Palace." Michael was tight, so tight his breath was coming in short little intakes and exhales, as if he were finishing a long sprint, which he was. Across the sunlit water of India on a December afternoon Michael Tillman went, fearful, terribly so, of what he was going to find ahead of him.

A wooden jetty stuck out fifteen feet from the island's shore, and he could see wide stone steps behind the jetty leading up into heavy forest. A long red tile roof was visible through breaks in the foliage. On the jetty was an Indian boy of about fifteen. The desk clerk at the Aranya Nivas had radioed the lodge to say a guest was on the *Miss Lake Periyar*.

The pilot expertly swung the boat broadside to the jetty's end, and Michael jumped off. The boy pointed at the knapsack on Michael's shoulder, and Michael gave it to him. They began the long climb up the stone steps to the lodge, which sat a hundred and fifty feet above them. Halfway up Michael touched the boy's shoulder, signaling he wanted to stop for a moment.

He sat on a wooden bench beside the steps, put his head in his hands, and thought, imagining what he might see at the top of the steps and thinking about how he would handle whatever was there. The boy stood patiently, looking off into the jungle.

After a minute or two, Michael got up and they continued. At the top of the stairs he followed the boy over a red dirt area where the jungle had been cut back around the entire circumference of the lodge. Off to Michael's right an Indian couple sat on the veranda in front of their room. They were drinking tea but paused to watch the new arrival come across the dirt and onto the veranda south of them. The manager appeared with a room key, looked Michael over, and said dinner would be served at seven, adding informal dress was appropriate. He asked if he could get Michael something to drink. Michael ordered two Kingfisher beers and followed the boy along the veranda.

The room was spacious with a double bed and a bath area in a separate room to the rear, furniture of slightly battered white wicker. Two large windows with heavy wooden shutters that were closed faced the veranda, and an overhead fan turned slowly. A smaller window in the bath area also had the same heavy shutters. The boy put Michael's knapsack on one of the beds and scurried around, turning on lights. Michael tipped him, and he was gone, closing the door behind him.

Michael looked at his watch. Three hours before dinner. He showered and dressed in a clean khaki shirt and jeans, traded his boots for sandals, drinking Kingfisher and preparing himself for what was to come. He was ready, if there was any real way to be ready for what he was sure he'd discover. No excuse to lounge around in the room, so he walked outside on the cement veranda, which was empty of people along the entire run of the lodge.

A trench, about five feet deep and three feet wide, circled the lodge out beyond the open dirt area where the jungle began. Michael was pretty sure the trench was designed to hold at bay unreliable things snarling along on short legs or crawling on scaled bellies, tongues flickering.

The Indian couple he'd seen earlier were standing near their room at the far end of the lodge.
They were on the crest of a hill dropping off to
the lake and were looking through binoculars at
something across the water on the opposite shore.
They called the boy over and asked him a question.
"Wild pigs," he said.

Purple-blue flowers curled from the roof. Far
down the lake Michael heard a sound. It took him
a moment to recognize it: elephant. In the distance
he could hear the low beating of an excursion boat's
engine. He sat there on the south end of a veranda
in south India, lit a cigarette, and started on his
second beer, feeling like a warrior about to enter
battle.

Behind him and north along the veranda he
heard a door open and the sound of voices, one of
them Jellie's, he thought. Adrenaline hit Michael
Tillman's arteries in a surge faster and stronger
than anything he'd experienced in his basketball
days or, for that matter, ever before in any circum-
stance. The warrior had come to fight for his
woman, his body was preparing itself.

Now was the moment. *Now*—do it, Tillman.
Do it and get it over with, settle your affairs, here
in the jungle. Where else have men ever settled
their affairs? He turned and saw a young Indian
woman, fifteen or sixteen years, come out of an
open doorway. Her black shining hair was in a
long braid, and she had on a sari of a deep orange

color, bracelets on her arms and around one ankle, silver toe rings, and straw-colored sandals.

Jellie Markham/Braden/Velayudum, or whoever she was on that day, came out of the same doorway and looked across the stretch of open dirt toward the jungle. "It's a beautiful evening, Jaya," Michael heard her say.

The young woman answered her, "Yes, it is. This is the loveliest place I've ever seen. The mountain air is so clean and cool after the lowland heat. I've always looked forward to our time here."

Jellie looked down the veranda, gray eyes taking in the scenery, casually glancing at a man sitting by himself at a table. The young woman started to speak but saw Jellie's face and followed her eyes. They both stared for a moment, then the young woman looked again at Jellie's face, but Jellie never took her eyes off Michael Tillman. He waited for a man named Velayudum to come out of the doorway and put his arm around Jellie, but no one came.

Jellie was frozen where she stood. Michael looked back at her. She wore the traditional Indian woman's outfit called a *salwar kameese*—long tunic and loose, flowing bottoms gathering themselves just above her white sandals, all of it done in the palest of lavenders. She had a red scarf draped around her neck with the ends of it hanging over her shoulders and down her back. And, like the young woman, she wore an ankle bracelet and toe rings. Her hair shone in the half-light on the veranda, and hung straight and long, parted off to one side, just as she wore it back in Cedar Bend, sometimes tucking it up under a tweed cap.

Cedar Bend? Where in the hell was that? Did it exist anymore, or had it ever existed? Maybe . . . maybe somewhere in another time, somewhere back down along the crinkled chain of living and loving and working, it had once existed. Back in the same, forgotten, and ancient world as Custer, South Dakota, where a boy worked late in the night shooting baskets and repairing an old English motorcycle that would take him over the roads of his life, eventually with a woman named Jellie riding behind him.

Jellie took the girl's hand and came toward him. He stood up, saying nothing, watching her eyes, which never left his. She let go of the girl's hand, put her arms around his waist, and laid her head against his chest. He touched her hair. She lifted her face and kissed him.

She turned to the girl. "Jaya, this is Michael Tillman, the man I've been telling you about." Her eyes on Michael's face again, steady eyes. "Michael, this is my daughter, Jaya Velayudum."

# Twelve

Dhiren Velayudum: revolutionary, member of a radical separatist group that fought everyone and everything connected with the central Indian government. And Jellie Markham, young and idealistic back in the middle sixties, young and idealistic and off to India to write her thesis. Movie stuff: Tamil warrior-poet meets young American woman with her own dreams of how things ought to be. At bottom, Dhiren Velayudum was a terrorist, and Jellie became his lover and confidante. Though it didn't seem like terrorism in their nights of loving and days filled with quixotic visions of a great revolutionary flow that could not be halted. She married

Dhiren in a traditional Indian ceremony. The shrieking death-dance of her parents when they found out could be heard all the way from Syracuse.

Things went bad for the radicals, and there were wild months of running with Dhiren, hiding in villages and cities. Then came an afternoon road winding high into the Western Ghats, the same road Michael would travel one day years later. The car in which Dhiren and Jellie were riding moved slowly around hairpin curves.

Suddenly Dhiren was pushing Jellie, shouting for her to get out of the car and hide. She got out, carrying Jaya, and crouched behind a jumble of deadfall. Dhiren pitched from the other side of the car and ran for the trees on the opposite side of the road, nine-millimeter, Russian-made pistol in his hand. The sound of automatic weapons. Bullets spitting into the dust like an animal with a hundred claws tracking him and closing fast, then crawling up and across his body. Dhiren spinning, stumbling into the forest.

That night at the Lake Palace Hotel, Jellie and Michael sat on the veranda for two hours after Jaya went to bed. She told the story, all of it, leaving out nothing. How she felt about Dhiren, her memories of him. How she carried her baby along the night roads of south India after Dhiren had been shot, walking all night into Thekkady, where there were sympathizers with the radicals' cause. How the India government punished her by refusing to issue an exit visa for Jaya so Jellie could take her to the States.

She told him how Leonard Markham had come for her, all the way to Delhi, and the words he'd said: "Let's go home, Jellie. We'll find a way to get your baby to America." She looked off into the night. "It's amazing what parents can forgive."

Jellie told him how she fought for years to get Jaya a visa and failed, her father helping her and pounding on authorities from Washington, D.C., to New Delhi. But India put on its silent, impenetrable face, and nothing happened.

Jellie sat with her knees pulled up, her arms wrapped around them while she talked. "Chitra kept track of things on the Indian side and wrote to say it was still not possible to get the necessary papers for Jaya. I tried to come back, but the Indian government denied me an entrance visa.

"Can you imagine the agony, Michael? Three years it went on that way. I kept applying for a visa, and then for no reason I've ever been able to figure out, they issued me one. I simply became unimportant to them after a while, I guess.

"I could have given up my U.S. citizenship and perhaps become an Indian citizen, but I wasn't ready to do that, and I'm not sure India would have accepted me. I still believed I could get Jaya out of the country. I even thought about smuggling her out, but everyone I talked to said it was too risky, that I could end up in an Indian prison for years and leave Jaya without any mother at all.''

Michael nodded, his face serious. When something important was being said, when attention was called for, Michael Tillman was a world-class listener. And he was listening now to what Jellie Braden was saying. He narrowed his eyes, then rubbed them with his palms, trying to settle himself as he started to understand things he hadn't anticipated. It began to sink in, hard: he'd underestimated Jellie. She wasn't simply a bright, goodlooking woman married to one of his colleagues. Instead, she had lived another life alien to anything he could have imagined. She was far more an adult than he had realized, far more sophisticated in a worldly fashion than he would ever be. She was talking about a different Jellie, who had lived before, one he would not be able to comprehend or experience, no matter how much she told him, how much he thought about it. Jesus, automatic weapons and mountain roads, a man who had given her a child in a swirl of flight and idealistic revolutionary doctrine. She had laughed and cried with this man, and loved him wildly and freely and carried her baby as she ran with him. He felt a strange combination of sadness for her and envy for Dhiren Velayudum, who had touched places in her that he, Michael Tillman, could never touch. What a goddamned stupid joke, he thought, his wrong and undue assumptions about himself and Jellie and how he presumed Jellie saw him—for the last year he had been measuring Michael Tillman against Jimmy Braden, not against a man with the power and spirit of Dhiren Velayudum, a man who had lived for just the right amount of time and died at just the right moment to create a larger-than-life image in the far back memories of Jellie Braden. It was an image that would never have any equal, for it had never been lessened by the slog of ordinary, daily existence. Michael let out a long breath, while Jellie caught hers and continued.

"All of this time Jaya was becoming a young Indian girl. I finally decided maybe it was best she be raised in Indian ways. I didn't seem to have any other choice. The decision was made: Jaya would continue to live with the Sudhanas until she was old enough for boarding school, and I would visit her as often as I could.

"I sent money to the Sudhanas, tormenting myself all these years that I was not here to see my little girl growing up. Yet I don't know if it could have worked out any better. Jaya is a fine young woman. But I did visit every year, and we always came out here to the Lake Palace for a while. So at least she got to know her real mother pretty well, though we have become more like sisters than mother and daughter. I've always saved most of my salary from whatever job I've had over the years, and that money went to India, to the Sudhanas and to Jaya. She entered boarding school when she was six and has been there since.

"When I met Jimmy Braden and married him, all I said was I'd been involved with an Indian man who had died and I still had a lot of friends over here who needed financial help. The lie rested in what I didn't say. I told him I would be coming alone to visit every year. Jimmy, I think, would have agreed to anything, just to get me to marry him—I know that sounds terrible, but it's true— so he said it was not a problem. He's never complained once about my visits to India, and he's never asked any questions about what it is I do when I'm over here. As I've said before, Jimmy has his good qualities."

Michael got up and walked behind her, put his arms around her, and kissed her hair. Jellie Braden looked off into the night. Something large and moving fast crashed through the jungle fifty yards back of the lodge.

Jellie stood and looked up at him, put her hands on his face. "Michael, Dhiren was a lot like you, in some ways, but I don't want you to think you're some kind of latter-day surrogate for him. That's not true at all, and you must believe me when I say it."

He smiled and said, "I believe you, Jellie," though he wasn't quite as sure about it as he sounded.

"I came to India this time because I needed to

think and to talk with Jaya about us. I wanted to make sure of how I felt and for her to understand. When you found me this evening I was already turning for home, Michael. I was turning for home, toward you."

In his room he laid her down and kissed her in all the places she liked to be kissed. Later there was heavy scratching at the door and the sense of great bulk moving around outside. Michael sat up. "What the hell is that? Sounds like a bear."

"I think that's what it is. I heard it last night."

"There used to be a lot of them in the Black Hills. They go on like that. I have some fruit in my knapsack, and the bear can probably smell it. He'll go away after a bit."

The bear left and was replaced by the tickety-tick of fast little feet running over roof tiles. Michael and Jellie lay in the darkness together. "Sounds like India on the move again," he whispered to her.

Jellie went back to her room an hour before dawn. Michael lay awake, thinking about all they had talked about. Twenty minutes in front of first light he dressed and went outside into heavy, dripping fog wrapped around the lodge and turning open spaces into closed ones, turning the jungle into vague, threatening shapes in gray camouflage. Across the lake, which was only about a hundred yards wide where the island divided it, a monkey called, sounding far and lonesome. The classic jungle sound from old Tarzan movies. Elephants again, closer now. The monkey let go once more and was joined by a few others, along with intermittent calls from awakening birds.

His small flashlight took him through the fog and down the stone steps to the water. Why he was doing this he wasn't certain. Something to do with loving Jellie and knowing where he stood with her, a little early morning celebration of his own, some time to rearrange how he saw her in light of what she'd told him about her early years in India. He sat on a jetty post where he could look out to the opposite side of the lake and down the shoreline to his right. He sat there and waited, listening for sounds beyond the lapping of small waves. First light came up, translucent through the fog.

He was staring off into space, thinking about Jellie and Jaya asleep in the lodge above him, not looking at anything in particular. The fog swayed in an early breeze and began turning into a yellowish mist as the sun poked its way through a gap in the eastern hills.

The tiger saw Michael before Michael saw him. The cat was thirty yards down the shore, drops of water coming off its muzzle as it lifted its head after drinking. It didn't move, just kept that big head pointing in Michael's direction, its body still perpendicular to the water. Long red tongue came out and flicked away the droplets on its white chin.

The plan? What plan? Stupid, Tillman, real dumb, Michael was thinking. The lodge was a forty-second sprint up a flight of steep, rough steps, or longer via a jungle route, and a Bengal in full stride could cover a hundred yards in four seconds. If the tiger wanted him, Michael could do nothing. Running would be pointless. And pathetic.

Somehow, though, Michael wasn't worried. He never quite understood why when he thought back on it. He just wasn't. In fact, all the time he was thinking how serious wildlife watchers would give up their butterfly nets for life if they could have this experience. Talk about a *Saw-It!* merit badge, talk about counting coup. A lot of folks were out there practicing a kind of visual banditry and grunted sourly when the stagecoach didn't stop. It had stopped here, in the fog, at dawn.

Michael began to take pleasure in just staring back at the tiger, in the simple purity of contemplating its existence, in knowing not everything wild and strong had been snuffed out by condos and shopping malls. There was something good and exhilarating about that, about knowing that creatures who crawled toward trenches or went bump against your shutters in the darkness or stared at you from a misty shoreline in south India were out there, and they cared nothing for your passing joys and sorrows, and they were free to return to the jungle when they chose.

The tiger lowered its head, lapped at the water, looked at Michael again, then shambled down the shore in the opposite direction. At fifty yards it turned to look at Michael once more, looked at him for a long time. At a hundred yards the big cat angled off into the jungle. The sun ran up its flag hard and bright, and the fog lifted.

"Good morning, Michael."

It was Jellie, and Jaya, carrying cups of hot tea for themselves and a big cup of coffee for the tiger expert who was busy sewing a merit badge on his sleeve: *Saw It!* Michael said nothing about the tiger, thinking they might feel sorry about having missed it and thereby spoiling a first-class sunrise for them. When he told them later they were both sorry and glad—sorry they'd missed it, glad they weren't there.

"Michael"—her gray eyes were full of good, loving signals as they looked at him—"we didn't talk about travel plans. Jaya and I are booked here for another three nights, can you stay?"

Stay? He'd have slugged it out with the Bengal for the privilege. "Jellie, I'm free until mid-January. My return flight is January twelfth. What's your program, as they say in India?" Jaya smiled.

"Well . . ." Jellie was a little hesitant. He sensed it was money.

"Let me suggest something. You're looking

at a guy who lives in a cheap apartment, drives a thirty-year-old motorcycle and a fifteen-year-old Dodge Dart, and makes a passable salary. If the two of you feel like it, let's travel, go where we want to go. Take the canal boats through the Kerala estuaries, lay around up on the Goa coast for a while, ride the steamer up to Bombay and stay in the Taj Hotel. My treat and no holds barred."

"That will cost a lot of money." She bent over and kissed him good morning.

He whispered, "We can work it out on the kitchen table back in Cedar Bend."

She rolled her eyes. "My new profession now becomes clear." Then Jellie laughed, and Jaya laughed, too, though she seemed a little unsure of why she was laughing. But Michael thought he knew—she was laughing because her mother was laughing, because her mother was happy and loved a man and wasn't afraid to let her see it. She'd figure it out after a while.

And they did that, traveled. Stayed on at the Lake Palace for three more nights, then went off to Kerala to see the famous Chinese fishing nets and stayed in the Malabar Hotel, where they swam in the pool and had late suppers served on white linen by the bay. They hit Goa and lounged on the beach, took the steamer to Bombay and checked into the Taj Hotel for five days. Flew up to Jaipur to see the Pink City and took a camel safari into the Rajasthani desert.

On January 5 they put Jaya on a plane for Cochin and school, which left Jellie and Michael a week to themselves. They spent it in Pondicherry, staying with Innkeeper Maigrit ("Ah, monsieur, you found her, I see. May I politely say she was worth the search") and taking their evening meals in the small restaurants of Pondicherry. They went far up the beach one afternoon and made love in the sand, then swam naked in the warm Bay of Bengal and made love again in the water. And Michael lectured at the college, paying his debt to Dr. Ramani.

Jellie was moved by the fact Michael had booked his return flight for the twelfth of January, that he'd been prepared to spend over seven weeks looking for her. He said, and meant it, "If I hadn't found you by the sixth, I was going to call home and tell them to find a substitute for the spring semester. I was—Jellie, I truly mean this—fully prepared to go on with my knapsack until I found you, no matter how long it might have taken."

On January 12 they rode British Airways toward Heathrow, reading, laughing, holding hands. Then serious at times, preparing themselves for laying all of this in front of Jimmy.

Between London and Chicago, somewhere over the Greenland ice pack, Jellie leaned her head against Michael's shoulder. He looked at the gray eyes, noticed something pensive in them.

"What is it, Jellie?"

"I was just thinking. People once called Dhiren 'the Tiger of Morning.' "

She went to sleep then, resting against him. He gently fished a notebook out of his pocket and wrote, "The Tiger of Morning lives forever."

# Thirteen

James Lee Braden III was a middle-grade rationalist. What could not be explained in terms of empirical evidence did not exist. Except for God, who received immunity from rational inspection and was dealt with on Sundays at the First Presbyterian Church. Turn of the key, click of a door lock, and Jimmy looked up from the autobiography of John Maynard Keynes he was reading. His wife walked in with Michael Tillman behind her.

This time Jimmy didn't cry. And he wasn't all that surprised. Parallel events—Jellie gone, Michael pulling out a few days later. Teeter-totters in the park, a faculty wife who had seen Jellie and

Michael leaving the Ramada together, speculation in the offices. Matters passed over originally but recalled later on when the time was right—data, incomplete and soft, but data nonetheless. Induction and tentative conclusion: Maybe Jellie Braden and Michael Tillman were more than friends.

January evening 1982, conclusion no longer tentative. Jimmy said he understood how Jellie and Michael would be attracted to each other. His primary concern was, in his words, "how we all carry on from here." He seemed almost relieved, more worried about style than substance.

Jellie was less rational and quite a lot less stylish than her husband at that moment. She'd been married to Jimmy Braden for eleven years, that counted for something. She got herself worked up pretty good, telling Jimmy how sorry she was, how it was not right to behave as she had. Jimmy eventually said, "Our decision to marry was probably a good one at the time, but people change. There's no point living with choices made by people who were different eleven years ago than they are now."

Jellie gathered herself and her things and moved in with Michael. They painted his old apartment and gradually converted it into something both of them could tolerate. The Shadow stayed in the living room. That was not open for debate or compromise. Jellie did suggest a dropcloth to protect the nice oak flooring from greasy tools. Michael smiled and said it was a large concession but agreed.

He rolled back into teaching, dog-paddling his way through the wash of sideways looks and gossip that ultimately became a minor part of the university saga. Jellie retrieved her maiden name, finished her M.A., and was accepted in the anthropology Ph.D. program. And Jimmy? He went away. Arthur Wilcox found him an associate deanship at a private school in the Northeast, near Jimmy's parents. All were pleased.

Well, not everyone. Eleanor Markham was appalled and forever would view Michael as a social misfit and home wrecker. She was especially appalled at his travel habits and happened to be looking out the window of her Syracuse home one afternoon when the Black Shadow rolled up her driveway. The Shadow was no longer an amusing abstraction sitting in some lunatic professor's living room. It was real now, and her forty-four-year-old daughter was riding behind the lunatic. Probably it was Jellie's leather jacket, boots, and mirrored sunglasses that got her. It'd been a long life, and she'd hoped for something better.

Michael and Jellie's father escaped to the trout streams. Leonard Markham never said harsh words about anybody, and he mentioned Jimmy only once in Michael's presence. He was laying out a Royal Coachman fly after several elegant backcasts.

The Coachman landed soft as you please below a big rock where the water eddied. He puffed on his pipe, twitched the fly, and said, "Jim Braden was afraid of water. Can you imagine that, Michael?" Michael didn't say anything. Leonard twitched the fly again. A brookie rolled beside it but thought better of the enterprise and left the fly alone, in the way Leonard Markham left the subject of Jimmy Braden and never came back to it.

Jellie and Michael traveled to India once a year. In 1984 they brought Jaya back to meet her grandparents. Afterward the three of them visited Michael's mother, who was confined to a nursing home in Rapid City. She was old and pretty wobbly, but sentient most of the time. Ruth Tillman took Jaya's hand and held it for a long time, smiling. It was the best Michael could do in the way of a grandchild, and in some strange way Ruth Tillman found it enough.

So it went. Not undiluted peace and tranquillity, but workable part of the time, most of the time. Michael Tillman was a loner, something of a recluse, always had been, always would be. He would go away from Jellie, sometimes on the Shadow, sometimes only in his mind. And she resented that.

"People aren't motorcycles, Michael. You can't just take the chain off and hang it over a chair until you get around to it."

He grinned at her. "You're right. You're always right about that stuff. Women know things men don't when it comes to the gender interface. . . . Jesus, how's that for psychobabble . . . gender interface. Next thing you know I'll become a 'gender reconciliation facilitator.' Saw that in a magazine the other day. There are hot new job opportunities out there I never dreamed of."

She rolled her eyes, crossed her arms. "I don't think you're the least bit interested in facilitating gender reconciliation, here or anywhere else."

"You're right again, mostly, wrong about here. I'm a good ol' boy from the bad ol' days in certain respects. Nadia Koslowski made some inroads in taming the Y chromosome, but she left before the work was finished. You've continued where Nadia left off and already discovered I'm only marginally educable in that area. I'm interested in peaceful coexistence, but I'm also interested in my work and fishing and riding around on shadows, two-wheeled ones and otherwise. My attention shifts, I wobble like Mercury's orbit. I'll try to do better, really I will. But I probably won't improve a whole lot. And I'm not altogether sure you really want me to change all that much. You might end up with a limp, obsequious piece of crap you don't care for."

"Michael, sometimes I think I should pour plastic over you and preserve you just the way you are in these moments. We could prop you up in the Smithsonian and hang a sign around your neck that says *Homo past-hopeus*, let future and more enlightened generations stare at you. Carolyn was right when she said you're incorrigible."

He held up his hands in a position of surrender. "Hell, I'm guilty as charged. I've discovered it's easier to plead guilty to everything. Less argument that way. And even though I don't share your faith in the wisdom of future generations, I kind of like the Smithsonian idea. But make sure I'm sitting on the Shadow with a fly rod in my hand. And make sure you remember Dhiren and how happy you were with him, and how unhappy you were with Jimmy Braden. You once told me Jimmy was so conciliatory and ambivalent it damn near drove you crazy. You're a strong woman in a lot of ways, Jellie Markham, but you like your men a little wild and untamed. I will, however—and being completely aware of my failings and general unworthiness—extend my offer of marriage once again, as I do almost weekly."

She scuffed her tennis shoe on the floor and looked down at it. In some ways he was right. She'd never quite sorted it out, the tradeoffs. The men she truly cared for made her happy in some ways, unhappy in others. Still looking at her shoe, she said, "As I've mentioned before, being married twice is enough. Three times seems a bit much somehow." She cooled down and smiled at him. "Thanks for the proposal, however. I always appreciate it when you ask. Maybe sometime I'll surprise you and say 'yes.' "

"The offer remains open. How about two fingers' worth of Jack Daniel's, a bath, and then the kind of reconciliation we seem to do best. Cut and paste, make peace and make love."

"We need groceries. You always get hungry afterwards."

He pulled on his leather jacket, grinning. "So do you. In atonement for my many sins I'll go to the store. Got a list?"

"No, do you?"

"No. I'll buy beer, potatoes, and whatever else I think of on the way."

An hour later they were sitting in the small tub together, hot water deep and soapy. She put her feet on his shoulders, he ran his hands along her thighs and told her for the thousandth time she had the greatest breasts in the universe. She looked at him over the rim of her glass and started laughing.

"What's the matter? Your breasts are serious business."

"Nothing. I was just thinking about plastic and the Smithsonian again. Think I'll do it when you're gone and defenseless."

"Okay by me. You can prop Arthur Wilcox up beside me, label him *Homo go-squatis, Driven Bonkers by Homo past-hopeus*. Put some blueprints in his hand." He leaned back in the tub. "Let me change the subject. Remember that nice area in the Black Hills called White Bear Canyon I showed you once?"

"Yes."

"After you finish your degree, let's move out there. I'll quit teaching, get my retirement annuity under way, and do a little writing. There's a small college called Spearfish State nearby. Maybe you could get a teaching job there if it suits you."

"It's a possible; I'll think about it later." She put her legs around him and slid up on his lap, arms around his neck. "Right now I'm getting a lot more interested in moving to the bedroom." She leaned her head back and shook it. "UUhhh, men! You're all nuttier'n hell."

Michael kissed her long and sweet, on her mouth, on both her breasts, and ran his tongue along her throat. "Not all of us are nutty . . . only the ones you like."

Jellie received her doctorate in 1987. Michael was allowed to attend the ceremony in full academic regalia, though his robe and soft, six-pointed cap, which had lain unused for years, needed two runs at the dry cleaners before they were presentable. When she walked across the stage and was handed her diploma, he damn near fainted with pride, knowing how much it meant to her. Michael threw a small party for her at the apartment and had a bottle of champagne all to himself, grinning while he sat on the Shadow and watched her gray eyes as people congratulated her.

Jellie Markham had become whole, professionally, at least.

Later that evening when the guests had stumbled back to wherever guests go when they leave, she came out of the bathroom with her academic gown and mortarboard on. Michael was still sitting on the Shadow, barefoot in T-shirt and jeans, a bottle of champagne balanced on the gas tank. He said, "*Dr*. Markham, I presume."

She grinned that old salacious grin of hers, the one she put on when it was time for serious matters of the flesh, then parted the robe and showed him she was wearing nothing beneath it. "Dr. Markham is now ready for her graduation present, if Dr. Tillman is prepared." He was indeed, and the evening concluded in splendid fashion with Michael straddling the Shadow and Jellie straddling Michael, Miles on the tape deck. Jellie chewed on his ear and whispered "Vroom, vroom," while she moved slowly up and down with quiet, blissful intensity on the motorcycle man.

Michael's mother died in 1988. A realtor called eight months later and said he had a buyer for the little house in Custer. Classes started in a week, but Michael cranked up the Shadow and headed out.

It all went smoothly, and he brought the Shadow back toward Cedar Bend, starting with the Black Hills and staying on secondary highways for the entire distance. He ran into heavy rains a little east of the Missouri River, but he was short of time and pushing hard, his yellow slicker flapping in the wind. Night caught him at the Iowa border.

He looked down at his old friend, patting the gas tank. The engine was bolted directly to the frame, and he could feel the vibrations at the level of his cells. "Let's open things up a bit, big guy, see what you're made of here on your thirty-seventh birthday." The Shadow responded and ran like a black cat over the wet pavement, its headlights sweeping across woodlands on the curves.

It happened in the hills east of Sioux City. The semi slid around a blind curve, drifting into the other lane. Michael's visor was a little fogged, and his night vision wasn't what it used to be. He blinked, then squinted hard. The truck was moving fast in the hands of a sleepy driver hammering eighty thousand pounds of vehicle and its load of tractor parts toward Omaha. The driver came to full alert as the truck skidded, fought to control his rig, and saw the yellow slicker fluttering a hundred feet straight ahead of where his hood ornament pointed.

Michael was blinded by the lights, truck closing and no way to lay the Shadow down and slide. He thought of Jellie and tigers. For some reason he thought of Jellie and tigers in that instant, then took the Shadow off the road and into the trees at seventy miles an hour. A yellow blur rocketing 30 feet into the forest . . . 100 feet . . . 200 feet . . . steering and braking and running the maze in a wild flash of tigers and Jellie and the way she looked at him in those times, holding her breath, eyes wide and her breasts and belly coming up to meet the tiger and him, Michael Tillman, and he smiled, and for a moment, just a wild and fleeting moment that became vanishingly small, he believed he was going to make it. Until the yellow blur became a butterfly gone.

In those stretches when he was conscious, Michael could hear the hum of life-support systems to which he was fastened. Sort of a faint and steady background noise. Sometimes a certain machine kicked in and the noise would get louder, which he didn't like but which he couldn't do anything about.

He was pretty well beat up. The doctors laid it out straight and hard: cracked pelvis, two broken arms, compound fracture of one leg, internal injuries. He thought he was dying, so did the doctors, and he tried to come to grips with that fact, hanging on until Jellie could get there, hanging on to see her again. He concentrated on Jellie's face, formed it up cool and clean in his mind, got her to smile for him, and he was still around in the morning.

Outside his room at the desk guarding the intensive care unit, he vaguely heard a panicked voice. "Where's Michael Tillman, please, I'm his wife." His wife—he'd never thought of Jellie that way.

She bent over him: "Oh, Michael . . . Michael. I came as fast as I could. Michael, get better, and I'll take care of you forever. Don't worry, it'll all be fine."

"Jellie, touch my face." His throat was wrapped around a tube, and he couldn't talk above a whisper, a hoarse one, but she heard him and stroked his cheek. He felt tears, big tears, coming out of both eyes, his eyes. It wasn't self-pity . . . well, maybe it was. He didn't know, didn't matter. He was feeling the touch of her hand on his face, thinking about how much he loved her and that they'd never make their old, sweet laughing love again, and that he'd never take her out to Heron Lake on the back of the Shadow again, and that they'd never sit on the veranda of the Lake Palace Hotel again, looking for tigers he knew were out there because he saw one once on a foggy morning when the world was beginning to turn his way.

Jellie was crying but trying to hide it from him. He floated in and out of consciousness for days, but finally the old body decided to give him another chance. He blinked open his eyes on a rainy Tuesday. She was sitting near his bed and looked up at him, smiling. "Welcome back, Michael."

In a few weeks Michael was on his feet, with Jellie's help, looking like a clumsy snowman, in his casts. He was not a patient patient; his mind called for action while his body wanted rest. After the casts were off, Jellie would come home from the university, where she was working as a temporary instructor, and find him attempting push-ups or sitting bent over his desk chair, trying to make the muscles in his arms learn to type again.

"For God's sake, Michael, I'm doing all I can do to get you better, and you're not helping. I have classes and shopping and you, and that's a full load. You have to cooperate a little, take things slow as the doctor said. And don't look at me in that little boy cranky way of yours; I'm too busy for nonsense."

"I feel inadequate, that's all. Sloppy, too, lying around here drawing disability pay."

"Think of it as if you were practicing the jumpshot, Michael. Invest now, get the benefits later."

"Too logical, nurse Jellie, too logical."

"You're the logician, Michael, except when it comes to yourself."

"That puts me in the great mainstream, right? Only time I've ever been there, and I don't like the feel of it."

"Well, you can like it or not like it. I'm going to the library. I have six hours of preparation to do for the survey course."

She put on her coat and stomped out. Two hours later she called him from a pay phone in the library. "You okay?"

"Yep. The little boy is no longer cranky and will attempt to remain as such. Sorry for the hassle. Christ, I did this to myself, and now I'm externalizing the results of my own stupidity on to you."

"Michael, I love you, really I do. But it's not easy sometimes. You understand that, don't you?"

"Yep again. Do you really have six hours of class preparation?"

"No. I was just escaping from the Walnut Street rehab ward for a while. I think I'll come home and fix us something to eat."

"Wrong. I'll rustle up some soup or its equivalent, have it bubbling when you get here."

Eventually, Michael's ability to type came back, ideas started to form, and the computer screen glowed blue in the evenings. After three months he could walk outside by himself and started jogging slowly a few weeks afterward. There was laughter again, and there was loving.

But living with Michael's intensity was not easy. Jellie had known it before the accident, and that intensity came back even stronger as he recovered. It was constant, unrelenting, a never-ending push toward frontiers of the mind and spirit, frontiers he redefined as he approached them, causing them to recede so the chase could go on. Michael chased frontiers and Jellie helped him chase the things he lost because his mind was always somewhere else, never paying attention to where he put car keys or checks or his latest draft of an article.

"Michael, you don't 'look' well. You riffle

around through a stack of something or shove things here and there on top of the refrigerator and think you've really searched. After that, you yell, 'Jellie, have you seen . . . ?' "

"I use the lost horse method for finding things." He was eating an apple and had just finished complaining that he couldn't find last month's paycheck, which he was taking to the bank as soon as he located his car keys and found his gloves.

"What's the lost horse method?"

He was holding the apple between his teeth and scrounging around on top of the refrigerator, talking through the apple at the same time. He sounded as if he had a severe speech defect. "If you lose a horse, go where you saw him last and start there."

"What if you took the horse somewhere, to start with, and forgot where he was before you took him somewhere else? Your system wouldn't work, would it?"

"All my methods are flawed." He grinned, flipping the half eaten apple over his shoulder from behind his back and catching it with his other hand. "Help me find the goddamn check, Jellie, so I can then look for my goddamned keys after which I'll search for my goddamned gloves. Please, Jellie. You're looking at a disabled searcher. All men have the disability; it's another one of those many flaws in the Y chromosome."

Jellie continued working as a temporary instructor at the university and enjoyed the teaching. Michael became more and more unhappy with the constraints of an academic bureaucracy that operated, as he saw it, for its own benefit, for its own survival and nothing else. Jellie could ignore that, and took delight instead in her students and her own research. This was new territory for her; Michael was more than two decades into it.

In 1990, after talking it over, they moved to White Bear Canyon. Jellie had misgivings about the move, about surrendering her own professional life to follow the drift of Michael's ways. But he had been unhappy at the university, and there was the possibility of a teaching position for her at Spearfish State. Life in the canyon was quiet and pleasant, but Jellie was restless. Though Michael worked alone and enjoyed it, Jellie needed an organization, a place where she could teach and do conventional research in her field.

A year later Jellie went to India alone. The birth of Jaya's second child was a complicated delivery, and she needed help afterward. Jellie stayed on longer than she'd intended. Two months, three months. India starting pulling on her again, Elsa Markham's genes turning her in directions that pointed a long way from White Bear Canyon and the problems of living close with a difficult man. A French architect from Auroville invited her out to dinner. He was handsome, worldly. She went with him once to the Alliance Française but declined the next time he asked. It didn't seem fair to Michael. The architect continued to call her. He sent flowers, left notes tacked to her door.

Michael knew nothing about the Frenchman, but he was worried. He called and asked, "When are you coming back?" His voice was pensive.

"I don't know," she said in a flat, noncommittal way.

"There's a job for you at Spearfish State beginning next fall. They called two days ago."

"I don't know right now. That's all I can say."

Spearfish State versus the excitement of a cosmopolitan life in Pondicherry. Dinners at the Alliance Française, a handsome Frenchman who was smooth and attentive, who seemed to understand and appreciate the feelings of women. She went out with him again. He wanted to take her to Paris and show her around. It was simple, uncomplicated, living this way. No problems. And she was near Jaya and the grandchildren, which enabled her to do penance for the mother she never had been. The university in Pondicherry offered her a part-time job, and she almost went to bed with the Frenchman on a night when the sweet smell of jasmine rode on slow winds from the Bay of Bengal, but she pulled back at the last minute. She was falling into something different, another life that seemed far off now. The next time she wouldn't pull back.

Michael called again. His voice was cooler
than she remembered. He'd lived alone before, he
could do it again, she knew that. He'd come to
India after her once; he wouldn't do it a second
time. When they said good-bye, his voice changed,
got a little soft and sad.

"I miss you, Jellie/JahLAY."

And she cried then for reasons she didn't understand.

In the white sun of an India morning, the seawall at Pondicherry curved into the distance and
looked like something from Mediterranean lands.
Come evening, the locals strolled there while the
streets and buildings of the city breathed out the
heat of the day just past. After talking with Michael, Jellie walked to the seawall and sat there for
a long time. A slice of yellow moon hung thirty
degrees up, off in the general direction of Burma.

Back home she went to a mirror and looked
at herself. Fifty-one. The Frenchman said she
looked no more than forty. Men still turned to
watch her when she passed, and that was good,
she supposed. She brushed her long black hair,
straightened her scarf, and returned to the mirror.
She whispered, "Jellie Markham . . . Jellie . . . the
song is almost finished. Just what the hell are you
doing here when the only man you truly care for
is half a world away?"

Two days later she walked slowly along a

winding road in the high country near Thekkady. Dhiren seemed far back. Twenty-five years had passed since that day of blood and fear in the dust now covering her feet. The afternoon breeze lifted her hair while she sat quietly on a log and remembered her warrior-poet, remembered him and the way he touched her, remembered him running for the trees. That evening she visited an old woman named Sudhana. They ate simple food and talked of other times.

Chitra Dhavale rode with Jellie to the airport in Madras. "I'll miss you, Jellie, but I am glad you are going back. It's the right thing."

"What a strange, messy life it's been, Chitra. Irresponsible, too." Jellie had tears in her eyes. They were standing near the gate to Jellie's plane.

Chitra put her arms around her and said, "Yes . . . strange and messy . . . and irresponsible in some ways, I suppose. All of that . . . and quite wonderful also when you think about it, depending on who's doing the measuring and by what standards. But you at least know what it's like to come into high plumage and catch the southern winds. Most of us don't and never will. It's a lucky person who can have a single great love in her life. You've had two. One when you were a girl, and the other when you became a woman."

Jellie smiled then. "And one was a warrior-poet and the other is a motorcycle man. God help us all." They laughed together while she dried her tears, and forty minutes later Air India lifted off. Chitra Dhavale watched morning light flash from the 747's wings as it turned toward South Dakota.

Jellie had not told Michael she was returning and rode the airport limo by herself from Rapid City through the Black Hills. On the front porch of the cabin in White Bear Canyon was a disassembled motorcycle, the Shadow II. Michael had found it six months before at a convention of motorcycle enthusiasts and was rebuilding it. It would never take the place of the old Shadow destroyed in the accident, he knew that. The original was a symbol of his youth, and when it was gone, some boyish part of him went with it. He mourned both the losses.

The cabin was empty. But she could smell traces of pipe smoke. Her father's suitcase was in the spare bedroom. Michael had said Leonard Markham was planning on visiting him to fish the trout. Packages of fly line lay on the kitchen table along with lures, a bottle of Jack Daniel's, and Michael's beat-up cap with its *Real Men Don't Bond* logo. She'd given the cap to him as a birthday present just after his accident. When she'd handed him the sack containing the cap, she'd said, "This is in no way capitulation to the good ol' boy in you. Understand that. I just thought you'd like it."

She stood quietly, looking around. It felt a little strange, but also familiar in good ways. Casserole lay on Michael's desk, old but doing fine apparently. Jellie walked over and petted her. The cat stretched and yawned. Out back, Malachi was barking at something.

Michael's first novel, *Traveling with Pythagoras*, lay on the desk. He'd written it from the viewpoint of Pythagoras' mother, who, legend had it, accompanied her mystic son on his journeys through Egypt and Babylonia. It had done pretty well for a first novel, thirty thousand copies. She picked it up and read the inscription on the title page: "For Leonard Markham, who gave me a woman to love." Beside it lay Michael's second book, a nonfiction work dealing with philosophical issues in applied mathematics, *The Algebras of Illusion.*

Underneath the books was a manuscript. She stared at the cover page—*The Tiger of Morning*—then laid the books on top of it again. She knew Michael carried a low, burning, and unspoken sense that he could never replace Dhiren. Maybe this was his way of getting it out of his system. Jellie figured he'd tell her about the manuscript when he was ready.

She opened the back screen door and looked out through the trees toward the trout stream fifty yards away. Her father was bent down along the shore, fussing with his tackle. Michael, wearing sunglasses, and the sleeves of his blue denim shirt rolled to the elbow, was wading deep water that surged around him, cigar clenched in his teeth, favoring the leg he'd injured in the motorcycle accident. He was fifty-three, and the leg was going to give him trouble the rest of his life. She held her breath for an instant when he stumbled and nearly fell, but he caught himself on a boulder in mid-stream.

He straightened up and began his backcasts. Jellie Markham leaned against the door frame and watched him, remembering what Chitra had said about high plumage and southern winds, about warrior-poets and motorcycle men. And she smiled, shook her head, and began laughing softly to herself. "God help us all." She changed out of her India clothing and walked down toward the stream in an old sweater, jeans, and hiking boots. Malachi saw her and came running, bouncing and barking. Leonard Markham heard the dog and looked up, put his hand high above his head, and waved to her. Behind him, water sprayed jewellike off Michael Tillman's fly line as he reached back in the last sunlight of a blue, mountain evening.

# *Acknowledgments*

Thanks to the usual suspects—Georgia Ann, Rachael, Carol, Shirley, Gary and Kathe, Susan, J.R., Linda, Mike, Bill, and Pam—who are kind enough to read various drafts of what I write and offer comment. And thanks also to Maureen Egen and the rest of the folks at Warner Books for their patience with a wandering man. The standard disclaimer is in effect: my work is better because of these people, the weaknesses are mine. And, of course, thanks to the Aaron Priest Literary Agency and all the readers out there who make this curious, reclusive life of words and imagination possible.

**RJW**
*Cedar Falls, Iowa*
*January 28, 1993*